PRAISE FOR MARIO ACEVEDO'S FELIX GOMEZ AND
X-RATED BLOODSUCKERS

"Part hard-boiled private eye [novel], part soft-core erotica, and part pure humor."
Statesman Journal (OR)

"Hard-boiled action mixes with soft-core titillation. . . . Zippy banter and witty repartee. . . . Acevedo has a natural flare for the hard-boiled idiom, and readers who enjoyed Felix's first adventure will find this follow-up equally entertaining."
Publishers Weekly

"Deliciously unique. A smooth combination of Anne Rice and Michael Connelly, with a generous portion of Dave Barry. Loaded with thrills, sex, violence, and laughs."
J.A. Konrath, author of *Bloody Mary*

"My built-in garlic factor usually puts me off vampire books, but Mario Acevedo has come up with such a fascinating character—Iraq war veteran Felix Gomez, who is a private detective as well as a vampire— that I was won over."
Chicago Tribune

"Vampire P.I. Felix Gomez is irresistibly entertaining."
Rick Riordan, Edgar® Award-winning author of *Mission Road*

"[Acevedo] manages to update vampire lore in clever and imaginative ways."
El Paso Times

By Mario Acevedo

The Adventures of Felix Gomez

THE NYMPHOS OF ROCKY FLATS
X-RATED BLOODSUCKERS

And forthcoming in trade paperback

THE UNDEAD KAMA SUTRA

X-RATED BLOOD SUCKERS

Mario Acevedo

An Imprint of HarperCollins*Publishers*

This book is a work of fiction. References to real people, events, establishments, organizations, or locales are intended only to provide a sense of authenticity, and are used fictitiously. All other characters, and all incidents and dialogue, are drawn from the author's imagination and are not to be construed as real.

EOS
An Imprint of HarperCollins*Publishers*
10 East 53rd Street
New York, New York 10022-5299

Copyright © 2007 by Mario Acevedo
Cover art by William Staehle
Excerpt from *The Undead Kama Sutra* copyright © 2008 by Mario Acevedo
ISBN-13: 978-0-7394-9362-5

Printed in the U.S.A.

To the memory of Jad Duwaik

ACKNOWLEDGMENTS

SPECIAL THANKS to the wonderful people at Harper-Collins and especially my publisher, Rene Alegria, my editor, Diana Gill, her assistant, Will Hinton, and my publicist, Michelle Dominguez. There's no mention big enough for PMA Literary and Film Management, Inc. and my agent, Scott Hoffman, now at Folio Literary Management, LLC. I'm grateful for the support given to me by booksellers across the country. Writing about corpses involved special research, and thanks to Lt. Ed Winter at the Department of Coroner, County of Los Angeles, for giving me the short tour. The burdens of my travels were eased by the many people who welcomed me into their homes: Rebecca Hulem, Bob Hadaya, Joni Mulder, David Lacy, and Joe Flynn. To Erika Paterson for her advice, friendship, and the occasional dance lessons. I got a lot of wonderful props from those rabble-rousers at La Bloga: Manuel Ramos, Dan Olivas, Rudy G., Michael Sedano, and Gina Ruiz. A big smile for that special vampire writer, Marta Acosta, who contacted me out of the blue and dragged me into her blogosphere. My critique group who kept after me until I got things right: Hcidi Kuhn, Jeanne Stein, Sandy Meckstroth, Margie and Tom Lawson, Jeff Shelby, Jim Cole, Kevin Tracy, and Sue Viders. To *mi gente* at El Centro Su Teatro: Tony Garcia, Tanya Mote, and Mica for pushing the Chicano vampire bandwagon. I still look for inspiration from my friends in the Rocky Mountain Fiction Writers and my fellow scribes at the Lighthouse Writers Workshop: Andrea Dupree, Mike Henry, William Henderson, Shari Caudron, Eric Olson, and Amanda Rea. Then there is that malicious bunch in the Mystery Writers of America: Gwen Shuster-Haynes, R.T. Lawton, Chris Goff, and Bonnie Ramthum (who gave me a bottle of vampire wine). Zooming in at low orbit is the creative and hard-charging bunch of the DogmataDenver team: Russ Wright, Tadd Moskal, David Menard, Jennifer Mosquera, Eric Matelski, and Amy, his smarty-pants wife. Finally, to my sister Sylvia and her partner Janet, my brother Armando, my sons Alex and Emil, my aunt Angelica, and my uncle Sam and tia Alma.

CHAPTER
1

IT'S ABOUT MURDER," said Katz Meow.

Murder? I had trouble accepting the premise from such pillowy and succulent red lips.

I gave Katz the vampire once-over. A quick study of her eyes, the portals to a human's consciousness. Mascara clumped her eyelashes, making them seem like ragged penumbras around the shiny blue marbles of her irises. Her high-boned cheeks were round and perfect.

My gaze dropped to her neck, and I studied the hollows between the tendons of her throat, marking the choicest spot to sink my fangs and tap her jugular.

Should I fang her, there could be one of three outcomes.

If I only sucked her blood, I could modulate which of the enzymes in my saliva flowed back through the punctures. These enzymes deepened vampire hypnosis and could induce permanent amnesia, and make her swoon with orgasmic pleasure or writhe in searing pain.

If I sucked too much blood, I would kill her.

Or should our blood commingle after the fanging—especially through an open-mouth kiss as was done to me years ago—then she'd be damned to walk the earth as a vampire.

The low collar of her dress arced like a smile across her voluptuous cleavage. My eyes went back to hers, lingering for an instant in fleeting lust.

Morning sunlight illuminated my office.

Sunblock and makeup covered my translucent complexion. Katz didn't know I was a vampire. Humans couldn't know. They must never know. Superstition and skepticism protect us, the undead. The moment humans discovered we exist, they would hunt us down. Those vampires the humans didn't exterminate would be imprisoned and dissected. I had to be careful what cases I accepted as an undead private detective.

Katz fidgeted in the leather chair facing my desk, as if she sensed my wariness.

"Whose murder?" I asked.

Katz wrung her hands, the manicured white-tipped fingernails crisscrossing. "My friend Roxy Bronze."

"Never heard of her."

Katz reached into the large Gucci handbag—real or knockoff—resting by her ankle. Gold bracelets jangled from her wrist as she offered me a plastic DVD case.

The cover of the DVD showed Katz and a statuesque brunette, holding each other by the waist. Both wore matching black bikini bottoms and bolero vests, and stood on clear plastic stiletto slut pumps. They had wanton grins as lurid as what the DVD title blared in fluorescent green letters: SUPER-VIXEN SKANK FEST, VOLUME EIGHT. Printed across their respective muscular thighs were their names: KATZ MEOW and ROXY BRONZE.

Katz brushed a tangle of blond hair from her forehead and looked away. She tapped one of her wooden-soled clogs against the oak floor.

The reverse side of the DVD case was a collage of Ms. Meow and Ms. Bronze in what looked like a high-impact version of the Kama Sutra as they played together, with other women and sex toys, and an assortment of men with amazingly large penises.

I flipped the DVD over and examined the cover again. My gaze traced across Roxy Bronze's face. The narrow bridge of her nose, the pronounced dimples in her cheeks, a chin tapering to a neat point—this last detail emphasized the elongated outline of her face. Her smile curved up in a pronounced U, exposing a neat row of porcelain white teeth.

Roxy looked familiar. But from where? Maybe I had seen her picture somewhere else.

I handed the DVD to Katz.

Katz took the case and dropped it into her bag.

My mind held the images of Katz and Roxy screwing like farm animals. "You're a . . ."

She finished the sentence for me. "An erotic film actress."

Fancy way of saying she nuzzled crotches for a living. When receiving new clients, I was tempted to read their auras, since they betrayed much about what humans think. Auras were more expressive than facial gestures. But special contacts covered my eyes, hiding the *tapetum lucidum*—the mirrorlike retinas vampires share with other nocturnal predators—so I was out of luck. The contacts allowed me to appear human, though at the cost of diminishing my night vision and losing my ability to read auras and hypnotize prey at will.

"You live in L.A.?" I asked. We were in my Denver office, a long way from California.

"Yes, the Valley."

"What valley?"

Katz smirked. "San Fernando."

Of course. The San Fernando Valley was to porn what Maine was to lobster fishing. "Katz Meow is your stage name, I take it."

"It is."

"And your real name?"

"Katz Meow is my real name."

"Where were you born? A pet store?"

She sighed and said, "My real name is Wilma Pettigrew. I'm originally from Shelbyville, Indiana."

I didn't blame her for changing names. Katz Meow conjured silk lingerie and Porsches. Wilma Pettigrew, gingham aprons and Buicks. "Ms. Pettigrew, where did—"

"Please, Felix," she interrupted, "Mr. Gomez, I mean, don't call me Ms. Pettigrew. I hate that name." Her voice took on a flat, nasal quality, as if the mention of Wilma Pettigrew took her from Southern California and back to her midwestern neighborhood. "I'm Katz. Katz Meow. Ms. Meow. But never Wilma Pettigrew."

I acknowledged her request with a nod. "Very well . . . Ms. Meow, where did this murder take place?"

"L.A.," she said. "Hollywood, to be specific."

"And you've come to Denver. You couldn't find someone out there willing to take the case?"

Katz held her gaze on me.

"Or that you trusted?"

"It's both," she replied.

"What about the police? There had to be an investigation."

"There were cops and paperwork, a real dog and pony show. They said it was probably a holdup gone bad, claiming Roxy was at the wrong place at the wrong time. But I know their story was a sham."

"What makes you sure?"

Katz's voice sharpened. "Roxy had enemies. Powerful enemies."

What kind of enemies could a porn star have? A jealous lover? Drug dealer? A mobster pimp? Any one of these was an easy mark for the police or a young district attorney eager to add a scalp to their trophy belt. Perhaps the problem was that Katz couldn't let go of the tragedy.

Katz kept quiet. Her radiance faded and she looked like a plucked flower starting to wilt.

I perused my notes scrawled on the desk blotter calendar. This month I had the usual: cheating spouses, embezzlement, insurance and workers' comp frauds. Every assignment was in the bag. I needed time alone with the offending parties to zap them with vampire hypnosis and pry out the necessary info. With that knowledge I'd slap together incriminating evidence. Cases closed. Checks in the mail.

Now Katz comes with her tales of a murder conspiracy. I thought of the porn business as attracting the addle-brained. A bunch of neurotics who accumulated problems the same way a dog's hairy ass collected burrs. Maybe Katz needed counseling, rather than my services.

"Ms. Meow, this is the way I see it. You've lost a close friend under random and tragic circumstances. Perhaps, instead of me, you should seek another kind of professional help . . ."

Katz jerked upright. "What are you getting at? That I need therapy? Well, I don't." Her complexion had been peaches and cream; now it was red as sunburn. She lifted an envelope from her handbag. "What I need is for you to find out who murdered Roxy and why." The tone in her voice became tough like gristle.

I took the envelope.

What did this involve? Murder. Pornography. And all the twisted threads that bound them. Suppose Katz had a legitimate case? "If I agree to help, I'd have to go to California. This investigation would be expensive."

Katz's eyes narrowed, as if my comment insulted her.

I opened the envelope. Inside was a cashier's check for $100,000. I felt my eyebrows rise.

"I see you made this out to me. How were you so sure that I'd take the case?"

"I knew you had to."

She replied with such naïve confidence that I stifled a

laugh. A hundred thousand bones was a lot of money but not enough to buy me. I waved the check. "Is this *your* money?"

"Every penny."

Katz had come a long way to ask for help, and I needed a moment as I considered her case. I swiveled my chair around and looked out the window.

A pickup truck pulled up to the burrito stand across the street. My office was at the corner of Tennyson and Forty-fourth in northwest Denver, on the second floor above the entrance to the Oriental Theater. The neon sign of the theater, a gigantic phallus with letters spelling ORIENTAL down its length, was fixed outside my window. At night, the sign swamped my office with a fiery orange glow.

This murder case was an opportunity far beyond snagging cheating spouses or insurance chiselers. I ticked over my reservations. Travel to California. Unfamiliar territory. Dealing with humans I didn't know. The money was tempting, but I didn't need it. I didn't want the challenge—I had nothing to prove to anyone. I couldn't think of a reason to take the case.

I swiveled back and faced Katz. "Why me?"

"You won't believe this, but it's true." Katz glanced over one shoulder to the closed door of my office. She leaned over the edge of my desk, and her eyes filled with sincerity. "It's because Roxy's murder involves vampires."

CHAPTER
2

HER WORDS SMACKED ME with the force of a pool cue in a bar fight. How would a human like her know about vampires?

Within my belly, my *kundalini noir*—that black serpent of energy that animates the undead—thrashed in alarm. My fingertips buzzed to signal danger.

Katz Meow couldn't be allowed to live with this knowledge. I would hypnotize her to glean what she knew about vampires. Then I would kill her. I had no other choice.

I dropped my hands behind the desk to hide my extending talons. My growing fangs nudged against the inside of my lip.

"You look like you're coming unglued." Katz gave a short, nervous laugh. "I'm not crazy."

I let my fangs retract. "Then you don't believe in vampires?"

"Should I?"

"Why did you bring them up?"

"Because someone told me Roxy's murder is connected to a deal between people and vampires."

What kind of a deal? My *kundalini noir* writhed in distress. "Someone who?"

"A friend."

"Give me a name."

Katz crossed her arms. "I came here thinking I was going nuts for even pretending to believe in vampires. I mention the word, and you go ballistic."

She was right. I had lost my cool. My talons withdrew and I placed my hands on the desk. "You mention murder. Next you bring up vampires. I was about to throw you out."

"But you haven't," Katz replied.

"Then talk."

"Rebecca Dwelling," she said.

"Pardon?"

"That's my friend who told me about vampires."

"Why would Rebecca Dwelling think she's run into vampires?" I scribbled the name on my blotter.

"She works at a club where she claims vampires mingle with people," Katz said. "It's a secret place like an SM dungeon. Visitors offer gifts and their blood to vampires. Sounds sick, I know. The people hope that if the vampires find them worthy, they'll be transformed into vampires as a reward."

My senses went back into full alert. What Katz described were chalices, humans who willingly gave themselves to vampires in the perverse hope of becoming vampires themselves. Chalices were the only humans allowed to live with knowledge of the undead, a secret they only dared reveal under the penalty of a swift and gruesome death. Their vampire masters had the responsibility of enforcing this pact, and their failure to do so demanded an immediate execution of both chalice and vampire. Had the secrets of the supernatural world been compromised?

"Do you believe this?" I asked.

"Rebecca does."

"And you don't?"

"Believe in vampires?" Katz chuckled. "Give me a break, Felix. I quit believing in the supernatural, fairy tales, Bible stories, all that crap, after my Sunday school teacher molested me."

"Sorry to hear that."

"That I don't believe?"

"No, the other part. About your Sunday school teacher."

Katz shrugged. "It happened and I moved on. What concerns me are the people who murdered Roxy."

"Would these be the powerful enemies you mentioned?"

"Read for yourself." Katz produced a thick bundle of papers from her handbag. She laid the papers on my desk.

I took the bundle and removed the rubber band. The papers were copies of newspaper clippings and printouts from numerous Web sites. SMUT LADY WINS BATTLE AGAINST PORN COMPANY. QUEEN OF RAUNCH TESTIFIES AGAINST DEVELOPERS. PORN STAR FOUND DEAD IN ALLEY.

"Give me a rundown of these powerful enemies."

"Cragnow Vissoom is the president of the video company Roxy was contracted to."

"What was his problem with her?"

"Roxy had bought out her contract and wanted to start her own company. Cragnow was afraid she'd take his best people."

"Such as you?"

"Me and other girls."

"So?"

Katz rolled her eyes. "It would make Cragnow look like a real chump. What kind of a boss can't control his talent, especially in the skin trade? Plus Roxy made him rich. Before she hired on, Gomorrah Video was small potatoes. Thanks to her, Cragnow became number one in triple X sales and rentals."

People had been murdered for less. That was one suspect.

"And the rest of the enemies?"

"Project Eleven."

"Excuse me?"

"Project Eleven," she repeated. "That's the name of the effort to redevelop the area around the city of Pacoima." Katz raised an eyebrow. "Ever heard of Pacoima?"

Unfortunately. I had spent my childhood bouncing from southern New Mexico to Pacoima as my parents fought, made up, and fought some more. I lived for months at a time with my aunt and mother, until my dad came around and we pretended to be a family again. I had felt tiny and brittle. Nothing seemed mine. Not my emotions, thanks to my parents. And not the few belongings I had, thanks to the neighborhood thieves and drug dealers.

Yeah, I knew Pacoima.

I looked back at Katz. "I know where it is. But I don't know beans about Project Eleven."

"It was a huge public works boondoggle that Roxy worked to defeat."

Roxy.

Pacoima.

Now I remembered where I had seen Roxy before. "Let me see that DVD again."

Katz leaned away in surprise.

"Come on," I insisted.

She gave me the DVD. I studied Roxy's face, especially her dimpled cheeks and the radiance of her eyes.

During one of my stays in Pacoima, I had buried my troubles in an atlas and become my elementary school's champion in the geography bee. After winning the all-city contest, I was invited to get my award at the public library downtown. At the time I was as dark as a coffee bean and wore tight, high-water pants because my good trousers had been stolen off the clothesline. All the other kids were well-off and white. They and their parents arrived in fancy cars while I hitched a ride with my teacher in her old Datsun. Everybody gave me fake, polite smiles, as if to tolerate my presence. When I got handed my trophy—a desk globe from *National Geographic*—I felt like a trained monkey getting a prize for being especially clever.

A guy from the newspaper took pictures of the rich kids and their parents. Some high school girls herded the students from a Glendale elementary together for a group shot. One of those pretty girls saw me alone with my globe. She invited me over and stood beside me in front of the group. She gave me the only genuine smile I got from anyone that afternoon.

After all these years, that girl had a name.

Roxy Bronze.

Now someone wanted me to find her killer.

How did that young woman with her privileged life and beautiful personality wind up doing porn? And then get murdered?

I returned the DVD to Katz.

"What was that about?" she asked.

"I might want to buy a copy. Where were we?"

Katz tapped the papers she had given me. "Look into these people. Councilwoman Petale Venin. She hated Roxy for undermining Project Eleven. And there's developer Lucky Rosario. He liked to hang around Cragnow and score with the actresses."

"That include Roxy?"

"If he had the chance, but that never happened. If Lucky was ever alone with Roxy he would've strangled her."

I wrote Lucky Rosario on my blotter and underlined it. "Why?"

"Roxy helped the local community fight Project Eleven. She not only humiliated Venin and Rosario, but the attention also forced the city council to withdraw the plan. Cost both Venin and Rosario a fortune."

Interesting cast of villains. "How do vampires tie in?"

"That's the connection between Cragnow, Venin, and Rosario."

"What? That they're vampires?"

"They might be."

"Might be?" I asked.

Her tone made it seem as though being a vampire was a casual diversion. She had no idea of the burden we carried because of the sorrow from the loss of our souls. I had lost mine during my service as a sergeant in the Iraq war. I was overcome with grief after mistakenly slaughtering an innocent family when an ancient Iraqi vampire—an *ekimmu*—lured me close and turned me into one of the undead. I never thanked him for it—the smelly bastard.

"Look, I feel stupid mentioning it, but I have to," said Katz. "That's what Rebecca Dwelling told me."

"Where is Rebecca?"

Sweat beaded on Katz's temples. "Back in Los Angeles."

I thumbed the papers. Discounting the vampire angle, there was enough evidence and motive to persuade even the most skeptical of cops that Cragnow, Venin, and Rosario had something to gain by Roxy's murder. Obviously the police knew and didn't act. Katz had good reason to be paranoid.

One big question remained.

"Katz, why me?"

"Rebecca said Coyote passed your name along."

My fingers tingled again. I didn't know a Coyote in Los Angeles or anywhere else. "Who's Coyote?"

Katz wiped the sweat collecting on her brow. "Someone she met at the club."

"He's a vampire?"

"Go ask Rebecca." Katz pulled a small amber bottle of pills from her purse. She glanced at the watercooler. "Could I have a drink?"

I got up and approached the cooler. Now to find the truth. With my back to Katz, I removed my contacts and put them into their plastic case. I turned about and offered her a paper cup filled with water. She reached for it and looked up to my face to say thanks.

Our gazes locked. Her pupils dilated. Her red aura blazed like I had hooked her up to an electrical socket. Her jaw relaxed, and those delicious lips parted. The amber bottle fell from her hand and rattled onto the floor. Her aura swirled like glowing syrup.

I set the cup on my desk. I picked up the bottle—prescription Xanax—and placed it next to the cup.

Taking both of her hands, I kneaded the tender webs of flesh between her thumbs and index fingers to deepen my hypnotic control. I couldn't risk fanging her. If she found marks on her neck, however faint, that would certainly confirm what she suspected about the existence of vampires.

I massaged her hands. "Katz. Ms. Meow, close your eyes."

With her eyes closed, she appeared angelic, a creature far removed from the licentious wench on the DVD.

Hypnosis dulled a human's mind, and I had to prod Katz's consciousness for every answer. What she couldn't do was lie. I questioned her for ten minutes and asked her to repeat every detail concerning Roxy.

My fingers trembling, I struggled to replace my contacts. I ordered Katz to wake up.

Katz's bosom heaved. Her eyelids fluttered. She gripped the armrests with a start.

"Are you okay?" I asked, feigning concern.

She blinked, tapping her chest as she took deep breaths. "I feel light-headed."

"You passed out for a second," I said, presenting the cup of water. "Happens. It's the altitude."

Katz read her gold wristwatch. "A second? Feels more like minutes." She opened the bottle and shook out two pills. "So there's no misunderstanding: Felix, you are taking this case?"

"I am. Give me time to clean up business on my end."

"A few days, no longer." Katz downed the pills and chased them with a gulp of water.

Her breathing relaxed. The Xanax hadn't yet taken effect, but the ritual of downing them soothed her.

She picked up one of my business cards from the plastic holder and wrote on the back of the card. "My plane leaves this afternoon. Here's my number. Call when you get to L.A."

Katz collected her handbag and fluffed her tresses. I walked her to the door and wished her a safe trip.

I returned to my desk and studied the papers Katz had left for me. My thoughts turned black with worry. This case was a tangle of murder, revenge, big money, and vampires. And the worst part? My hypnosis of Katz Meow confirmed that it was all true.

CHAPTER
3

I SAT AT MY DESK for several minutes after Katz Meow left. An anxious spasm tore through me. My fingers clutched at the desk blotter.

I forced my hands flat on the desktop and stared at the wall to settle my nerves. A forgotten woman returned from my past and the memory of her tapped a well of shame from my childhood. Shame so toxic that even as a vampire I wanted to pull away from myself. The woman had remained unknown except for the bit of kindness she had shown me. Now I knew who she was, and I had to find her killer.

And the murder involved vampires colluding with humans.

Impossible.

Crazy.

Even if true, why would vampires risk catastrophe?

I tried to imagine every scenario where vampires and humans could mutually benefit from such collusion. How? We were enemies. Predator and prey.

Did the Araneum know about this collaboration? The Araneum—which is Latin for *spiderweb*—is the secret global network of vampires and should be made aware of this alleged vampire–human collusion. To protect the community of vampires, the Araneum had its feelers everywhere. And like the web tended by a spider, one suspicious tug on a strand would summon the Araneum to investigate, and if need be, strike.

But what if they didn't know? To quiet my fears, I had to ask. My previous contact with the Araneum had been through my vampire mentor, who was now dead, having been killed by vampire hunters shortly after I arrived in Denver. I called Carmen, the head of the local *nidus*—vampire nest. I could trust her. Her voice mail picked up and said she was in Florida, "working on her tan."

Very funny, Carmen.

I couldn't share this suspicion of collaboration between the undead and living with any other vampire until I knew what was at risk. So I had to contact the Araneum on my own. I logged on to an antiquarian booksellers Web site, The Sagging Bookshelf, and requested a first-edition copy of the 1940s classic *Dental Care and Sexual Hygiene for Post-Adolescent Women*. I added that a buyer from Los Angeles had inquired about the book.

Ordering this title from this bookstore was a coded signal to the Araneum alerting them of compromising contact with humans by the Los Angeles *nidus*. Centuries ago, vampires had ruled with impunity over their terror-stricken fiefdoms. Now humans with their technology had the means to hunt, capture, and exterminate the undead. Our best defense was to remain hidden within the skepticism that flowered over myth and fantasy. Humans wouldn't fight what they didn't believe existed.

After I had sent the message my nerves should've calmed, but they didn't. Instead my thoughts invented gruesome plots where even the inner cells of the Araneum had been compromised. For an instant, in my mind's eye, the sky was crowded with helicopters catching vampires in the daggers of spotlights and tearing their bodies apart with rockets and cannon. The survivors were doused with gasoline and set afire. Bulldozers plowed the burning and squirming survivors into pits. I had seen the barbarity of war, in the time before I was made a vampire. Humans had committed these atrocities against one another; why would I think the undead could fare better?

My *kundalini noir* slithered within my belly like a snake trying to escape a trap.

I brewed herb tea mixed with Saint-John's-wort and goat's blood. To work off my nervousness, I paced my office, walking across the floor, up the eastern wall, across the ceiling, and down the other wall, pausing at my desk to sip tea. I walked this circuit until the teapot was empty.

I went downstairs to see what was in the mailbox. Checks had arrived from recent clients, assignments involving philandering spouses and an insurance chiseler. In one case I had given a client and her lawyer a digital video of her husband churning the water in a hot tub with his blond personal trainer. Of course, the husband in the other case got a similar video of his wife giving her boss highway head.

The man accused of insurance fraud told me under hypnosis where he had cached the "property stolen from him" and in what other states he committed identical scams.

After returning to my desk, I endorsed the checks and went through my files. I took a coffee break to enjoy shade-grown Mexican java mixed with type B-negative. I watched the blood drip from a Tupperware cup into the coffee. This was blood I had saved from a victim.

When I first became a vampire, human blood reminded me of my contribution to the misery and tragedy in this world. As a human I had murdered innocent people; blame it on the fog of war, but that was no excuse. I had taken aim and fired. And for a long time, I refused to drink human blood until I nearly died from weakness—and nearly let others be killed because of it.

Since then I've accepted my place in the cosmic game. I didn't invent the rules. God made me need the blood of my human prey. Like any predator I have to hunt and sometimes kill, and if I'm to survive I'd better be good at it.

Something rapped on my window. Since I was on the second floor, the noise startled me and I spilled coffee on my desk blotter.

A crow peeked in from the outside windowsill. The bird was a sleek inky shape in the glare of the bright sunlight. Its eyes, twin onyx beads, beckoned impatiently. The crow rapped its beak on the wooden frame of the screen.

I looked at the bird and pulled open the sash. The sunbeam warmed my hands and face, my skin protected by Dermablend and high SPF sunscreen.

The bird rapped the window again. Did it want to come inside?

This was an old building, and layers of paint kept the window screen firmly in place. I dug at the edge with a letter opener. I pried loose one corner of the frame and pushed it open, trying not to crack the wood.

The crow squeezed into the gap and twisted its glossy black body until it emerged onto the inside sill.

The crow flew into the shaded coolness of my office and landed on my desk. An ornate metal capsule the size of my little finger was fastened to its right leg.

Was this my contact from the Araneum? A crow? Of course—what should I expect? An ostrich? Or a penguin on roller skates?

I read my watch. I had sent the email three hours ago. The Araneum responded already?

I had imagined the Araneum as somewhere in Europe, a sheltered enclave as secretive and forbidding as the Vatican. Had the crow flown all that way in three hours? Or, more plausibly, the Araneum had agents here in Denver.

I expected the crow to talk. Instead it kept mute and preened its wing feathers.

I cupped the silky, warm body. Its heart thrummed against my palm. The crow weighed less than a small chicken. It held still while I undid the metal clasp holding the capsule in place.

Its leg free, the crow squirmed from my grasp and hopped back to the desk. It strutted back and forth, claws scratching the paper of my blotter. The crow stopped beside my coffee cup and dunked its beak inside. It tilted its head back and suddenly hacked.

"Thanks a lot." Crow spit now flavored my coffee. "You can finish the rest."

The crow resumed walking across my desk.

"Behave yourself," I said. "Crap on my desk and I'll bake you in a pie."

The crow swiveled its head to fix one glassy eye upon me and snorted.

The capsule was filigreed with delicate loops of gold and platinum. Tiny rubies lined what appeared to be a cap. I twisted the cap, and it unscrewed. The funky odor of stale meat leaked out. A slip of paper was curled inside, which I dug out with my fingertip.

The paper was a rolled sheet of speckled parchment that looked like onionskin and unfolded to the size of a postcard. Someone with exquisite calligraphy had written:

Our esteemed Felix Gomez,

For several months, we have suspected that vampires in the Los Angeles area have compromised the great secret. For what purpose, we don't know. Our inquiries have gone unanswered. Araneum agents sent to investigate have disappeared.

We ask you to infiltrate the Los Angeles nidus *and question their leader, Cragnow Vissoom.*

The name snagged my attention and I stopped reading. Cragnow Vissoom. The porn king. Katz Meow's boss. One suspect behind Roxy Bronze's murder. And the leader of the Los Angeles *nidus*.

I finished the message.

> *Direct action against family and outsiders is authorized. Report when completed.*
> *Araneum*

Direct action against family and outsiders? Rarely did the Araneum allow preemptive deadly force against family—vampires. And outsiders—humans.

I reread the message, wondering how much had been left out of the text.

The great secret was of course the existence of the supernatural.

We ask you. Ask? The Araneum asking had the same weight as a commandment—with an implied "or else." The Araneum apparently didn't appreciate Cragnow's lack of cooperation. For him, I was the "or else."

To infiltrate? My investigation into the murder of Roxy Bronze would be a convenient cover. But were her death, the disappearance of the Araneum's agents, and vampire–human collusion related?

The crow yanked the paper from my hand. I swatted after it. The bird flew toward the window, into the dazzling column of sunlight. The crow sat on the sill, holding the parchment in its beak.

As I reached forward, the parchment smoldered. I flinched. The crow dropped the parchment as it burst into a puff of gray smoke. A stench of burnt flesh swirled through the room. The smoke alarm above the front door went off.

The only thing that would combust in contact with sunlight like that was . . . vampire skin. The smell confirmed my suspicion. A clever if macabre way to destroy the message. What part of the body did the patch come from? And from whom? And why? A rogue vampire convicted by the Araneum?

The crow returned to my desk and rolled the message capsule with its beak.

The wail of the smoke alarm grated on my ears. The bird could wait. I walked up the wall to silence the noise. The crow squawked and clicked its beak against the capsule, annoyed that I ignored it.

The alarm quiet, I returned to my desk. The crow rubbed one leg against the capsule. I opened the clasp and slid it over the crow's leg. The bird shook its leg, as if testing the security of the attachment. Then it jumped to the window-sill, tapped its beak against the window, and squawked. I pried open the window screen and the crow shimmied out. The capsule rasped against the frame.

Without glancing back, the crow leapt into the air and soared over the roofs and trees. Its morose caw echoed across the neighborhood.

I lowered the sash and locked it. I slumped in my desk chair and thought about the chasm of murder and conspiracy I was about to fling myself into.

Alone.

But not powerless.

I opened the upper desk drawer. I was going into a situation greatly outnumbered. Better that I even the odds with human technology. I pulled out a Colt .380 automatic and racked the slide. A silver-tipped cartridge glittered momentarily before being rammed into the chamber.

I had a plane to catch.

CHAPTER
4

AFTER ARRIVING AT LAX, I rented a sedan and headed to my hotel in Culver City. I checked in and picked up a box marked TRAINING MATERIALS. Since 9/11, to avoid the scrutiny of traveling commercial air with a weapon, I had express-shipped my pistol from Denver.

Returning to my car, I opened the box and dug through the bubble wrap to retrieve a Ziploc bag. In it were my Colt automatic, holster, twenty-one silver bullets divided evenly among three magazines, and the remaining twenty-nine bullets that came in a box of fifty. Plenty of ammo for every conceivable scenario. If I needed more firepower, I'd steal a machine gun.

My cell phone remained quiet. Why hadn't I heard from Katz Meow? I'd called last night and left a message that I'd be here soon. She'd replied with voice mail that she expected me. My last call had been when I arrived at the airport, and still nothing from her.

Katz didn't seem the type to ignore me, especially since the trip was on her dime. Perhaps she had misplaced her phone. Or maybe there were other reasons, more sinister reasons, which were the real purpose for my investigation.

I kept an Internet hacker on retainer. I didn't know if this person was female or male, only that once a month I sent five hundred bucks to a private mailbox in Kalamazoo, Michigan. In return I had a keyhole into almost every database wired to the information grid. Some months I needed squat, so the money was a colossal drag on my overhead. Other times, what I got was worth every dollar.

Courtesy of my hacker, I carried a sheaf of background info on the principals in this case, including phone numbers, home and work addresses, photographs, and other documents.

Roxy Bronze emerged from the past as if she were a corpse washing up on a beach. She was born Freya Krieger in nearby Burbank. Her father was a marketing executive and her mother a Realtor, which provided Freya with a comfortable middle-class upbringing. A high school honor student and track star, she turned down an athletic scholarship and Olympic tryouts to pursue premed studies at the University of Southern California. She graduated magna cum laude. After that, Freya attended the Johns Hopkins School of Medicine. She returned to L.A. to intern as a cardiac specialist with La Brea Mercy Hospital. She became the victim of an operating room scandal, which destroyed her medical career. Freya Krieger had climbed to impressive heights, only to tumble off and become Roxy Bronze.

Roxy's obituary mentioned she had been cremated. That meant no more clues from her remains.

I had two mailing addresses to Katz Meow, one c/o Gomorrah Video, the other a private mailbox. Wilma Pettigrew rented a place in Encino, close to the private mailbox address. I'd start there.

One more thing. I knew from experience to keep plenty of money handy in case it wasn't wise to use plastic or visit an

ATM. Cash withdrawals left a trail. I took eight thousand dollars in hundreds and tucked it into the lining of my overnight bag. I also carried a backup credit card under an alias. These precautions should keep my whereabouts hidden for a while.

Seen from the freeway, the sprawl of the San Fernando Valley stretched in relentless monotony. A line of homes clung to the surrounding hills like the ring around a bathtub.

The place in Encino was a two-story townhome on a narrow, winding street. I parked in the fire lane and got out. Enameled planters with pink and white impatiens flanked the entrance to her home. A sticky note was on the aluminum screen door. The note was written in loopy cursive letters.

Katz.
Where you been??? Call!!!
Cindi

The *i*'s in *Cindi* were dotted with tiny hearts.

Who was Cindi? A friend, no doubt. Obviously she couldn't find Katz either.

I rang the doorbell. No one answered. The front door was locked. No evidence that anyone had forced it open. I looked under the doormat for a key. Nothing. I checked in the planters and along the trim above the door. Again, nothing.

I went to the alley and counted houses until I found Katz's. Her back door faced a row of detached garages. I tugged on the handle of the garage I presumed would've been hers. Locked.

As I put on a pair of thin leather gloves, I looked about to see that no one watched. I twisted the garage door handle until metal snapped. I gave the handle another pull, and the garage door slid up.

I half expected to find Katz's corpse rotting inside. Instead, the garage yawned empty. Oil stained the concrete floor. A bicycle with a broken chain and flat tires leaned against one wall. Cardboard boxes sat in lopsided stacks on the far side. I checked the boxes and found only women's clothing.

I shut the garage door and climbed the back stoop of Katz's house. The door and windows were locked. Curtains prevented me from peeking inside. But the windows on the second floor were open.

The backs of the other townhouses faced the alley. I examined the rows of windows, concerned that I might be watched, and saw nothing to trouble me.

I scaled the wall by climbing along the gutters. I pulled back on the screen of the closest window and slipped into Katz's bedroom.

For a woman whose occupation would've earned her a dishonorable mention in both the Old and New Testaments, the bedroom was decorated in pedestrian tastes: simple pine furniture, striped linen, pictures of birds and flowers on the walls. No leather harnesses, whips, or boxes of dildos.

I checked the rest of the house. Nothing remarkable in the kitchen or bathrooms.

I found a filing cabinet in the spare bedroom closet. Katz kept receipts, bills, bank statements, contracts, even personal letters in meticulous order. Must have been the lingering midwesterner inside of her. None of the documents provided anything useful.

What I didn't find were the usual carry-it-with-you possessions. A ring with car and house keys. Purse or wallet. Cell phone.

Nada.

It seemed Katz had walked out expecting to come back, except that she hadn't.

I went out the window the same way I'd come in. Until Katz called me, if she ever did, I'd work on the list of murder suspects, starting with her boss and the leader of the Los Angeles *nidus,* Cragnow Vissoom.

CHAPTER
5

FROM KATZ'S HOUSE IT was a quick drive west to Canoga Park, home to Cragnow's porn studio. Gomorrah Video was off Sherman Way where I turned right at a corner with a Tio Taco and a store with the sign ETHICAL PHARMACY. I passed a print shop and a plastics distributor and circled a two-story complex in white stucco.

A tall metal fence surrounded a parking lot. I entered through an open gate. At the far end of the lot, a cargo truck was backed against a loading dock. The other cars in the lot included two Sebring convertibles, an Audi, and a Hummer.

After parking the sedan, I took off my sunglasses to remove my contact lenses. Red auras surrounded the few humans down the street. I put my sunglasses on and clipped the holster and pistol into the back of my trousers.

The entrance to Gomorrah Video was a nondescript glass door flanked by windows facing the sidewalk. Mylar film covered the glass on the inside.

The door buzzed as I entered. A chest-high counter divided the reception area. An interior door opened to the right. A video camera watched from above that door.

A lanky brunette, almost as tall as my five ten, stood behind the counter. She kept her attention on papers she shuffled on the countertop. A cropped Miss Kitty T-shirt stretched over small breasts round as tangerines. Tribal tattoos curled around the biceps of her toned arms.

Vampire? I slipped my sunglasses a bit, enough to glimpse a red aura. Human.

"You're late. The audition was at two," she said, not bothering to look up. She pushed a form across the counter toward me. "Hope you brought two types of IDs like you were told."

I adjusted my sunglasses and cleared my throat.

"This ain't a babysitting service," she said. "You wanna work, then buy a goddamn watch and use it." She lifted her head. Her gaze dropped from my face to my crotch. Her forehead creased in puzzlement. *"You're* here for an—"

"Audition?" I replied. "No. Apparently I don't have enough of a middle leg."

She gathered the papers into a pile. "Then why are you here?"

I could zap her and walk in, but the camera would record me. Considering that at least one human had been murdered, not to mention the disappearance of vampire agents from the Araneum, I'd better be careful about drawing attention. I couldn't smash through the city like a wrecking ball and expect to sift for clues in the debris.

"I'm here to see Cragnow Vissoom."

"You got an appointment?" She tucked one strand of hair behind an ear studded with rings.

"Tell Cragnow that Felix Gomez needs to see him. Mention that it's family."

"Family," she repeated in a shocked whisper. She pulled her arms back and stepped away. Her blue eyes signaled alarm.

Unless she was a chalice, why did she cringe at the word *family,* code for *vampire*? If she was a chalice, she should be better trained than to exhibit such public telltale behavior.

She fumbled under the countertop, brought a telephone receiver to her ear, and pressed buttons. "Andy, it's Rachel. Someone's here to see Crag." A pause. "Felix Gomez. Family."

Rachel glanced at me, then to the floor. "I'm sure he is." She hung up. "Crag . . . Mr. Vissoom will see you. It'll be a minute."

My fingers tingled with caution. I backed against the wall. The pistol pressed into my lower spine. The entrance and front windows were to my left, the interior door to my right. In case of an ambush I'd spring to the ceiling, tear through the acoustical tile, and bash my way out the roof.

The interior door opened. Two young men entered, both shaved bald. One was Caucasian and the other Afro-American. They wore sunglasses, T-shirts, black leather vests, and jeans. Their vests were unfastened and bulged unnaturally, barely disguising the shoulder holsters tucked underneath.

I peeked over my sunglasses to catch auras simmering with suspicion. Orange auras. Vampires.

Thick muscles roped across their torsos and arms. Intricate tattoos covered the arms and neck of the white vampire like a puzzle of geometric bruises. His companion's dark skin appeared waxy despite the makeup. He was obviously a recent vampire. Squat and short, in matching outfits, they looked like they were auditioning to be Ninja Turtles.

They waited at the threshold of the door and stared from behind their sunglasses in practiced macho postures.

"We gonna sniff each other's butts or what?" I asked.

The black vampire tipped his head down the hall. "This way."

"You first," I replied.

Tattooed white vampire beckoned with his hand. "Humor us, tough guy."

We proceeded over a polished floor, past several doors and a shipping bay. Stacks of DVD boxes and computer components lined shelves inside the bay.

The hall led to stairs we climbed to the second floor. Posters of porn actresses spanned the adjacent walls. One door along the hall was open, revealing a bed and klieg lights. An antiseptic smell pervaded the air, evidence of the mopping up of love puddles accumulated in a day's work.

The hall ended at a set of wooden double doors. Fixed to one door was a brass name tag engraved with CRAGNOW VISSOOM, PRESIDENT.

The black vampire knocked once and opened the door without hesitating. "Go on in."

The room was decorated in the current retro vogue. The low ceiling emphasized the horizontal design of the furnishings. At the immediate right stood a liquor cabinet and bar in Danish modern. On the left, soft light illuminated a large aquarium.

A slender man got up from a leather executive chair set against a desk, also in Danish modern. An abstract mural covered the wall behind him.

He stood at an impressive height—at least six foot two. "I'm Cragnow Vissoom." Trendy wire-rim glasses sat on an aquiline nose. His eyes lacked a wolfish sheen, meaning contacts dulled his *tapetum lucidum*. "Felix Gomez?"

"I am." I took off my sunglasses.

Cragnow's aura surrounded him like the corona of a glowing chunk of coal. The aura shone steadily, revealing either a calm disposition or that he was very good at hiding his emotions.

My vampire escorts motioned me forward.

Cragnow smiled as I crossed the room. Wrinkles furrowed his cheeks and around his eyes. Graying temples offset a mane of thick hair. In human years, he looked to be in his midfifties.

When I drew close, Cragnow pointed to a red suede love seat. He gestured past me. "Give us a few minutes." The escorts withdrew and closed the door.

I remained standing until Cragnow sat. Coasters, napkins, and a basket of bagels rested on the kidney-shaped coffee table between us.

In his pressed plaid shirt and khaki chinos, Cragnow looked like an accountant on casual Fridays instead of a porn mogul. "Felix, what brings you to my corner of sunny California?"

I wondered if the previous agents from the Araneum had been so warmly received. And then as warmly exterminated.

"Katz Meow," I said.

Cragnow's aura brightened. He straightened, then stood. "You know where she is?"

I hadn't expected this reaction. "I was hoping you could tell me."

"You a boyfriend?"

"No. An interested party."

"Interested party," Cragnow mumbled to himself. He walked to the bar. "She missed the morning photo shoot for the cover of her latest video, *Seven Brides for Seven Gangbangs*. Certain to be a classic."

"A must for the connoisseur, I'm sure," I replied.

"It's not like her to be absentminded." Cragnow opened a small refrigerator tucked inside the bar. He pulled out a chilled 450-milliliter bag of human blood. "Care for a pick-me-up? Type A-positive?"

The offer caused my thirst to rise. I had long been "cured" of my aversion to human blood and would enjoy a taste of flesh nectar. Yet I wasn't convinced of the sincerity of his hospitality. So I didn't answer.

Cragnow snipped one corner of the bag with scissors and squeezed the thick, red contents into a blender. He added ice and a can of espresso drink. After mixing the brew into a frothy blend, Cragnow filled two highball glasses with the frappé. He touched the cap on a bottle of Finlandia vodka. "A little extra zing?"

"No thanks."

"Take the starch out of your jockstrap, Felix. You're among family." He measured two shots into one glass and stirred it with a swizzle stick.

Cragnow wrapped napkins around each glass and handed the virgin drink to me. *"Salud."*

I brought the frappé close to my lips and hesitated. The

aroma of coffee enhanced the meaty notes of the chilled blood, but I couldn't bring myself to taste it.

Cragnow sighed. "Oh come on. I invite you to my office, and you act like I'm trying to kill you." He offered his glass. "Let's trade. Careful, mine's got booze, so it might crinkle your shorts."

I waved him off and sipped from my glass. At the first indication of distress, I'd draw my pistol and blast him. The icy blood rolled over my tongue, and the delicious rush refreshed me to my bones.

Cragnow nudged the basket of bagels toward me. "Try one. You won't find any as good west of the Hudson River."

I chose a whole wheat bagel and paused. Why the eagerness to have me eat?

"You are a suspicious bastard." Cragnow snatched the bagel from me and bit. He held the bagel, showing the ragged crescent of his teeth marks. "Satisfied?"

"It's my nature. My apologies." I sorted through the bagels. A business card from the Blue Star Bakery and Delicatessen rested on the bottom of the basket. A scrawl along the margin of the card read:

To Crag. Thanks for everything.
Morty

There were no Mortys on my list of suspects. There was now. I focused my attention back to Cragnow and studied his aura. "So where's Katz?"

Cragnow sipped his drink and licked the froth from his lips. "I don't know."

Not a ripple of emotion disturbed his aura. His reaction remained too steady, the supernatural version of a liar's straight face.

"Enlighten me, Felix. What's your interest in Katz?"

"I'm a private detective. She hired me."

"Hired you for what? To play hide-and-seek in Los Angeles?"

"She wants me to find who killed Roxy Bronze."

Cragnow cupped the glass in both hands. "Roxy Bronze." He leaned back into his chair. "Even dead she torments me."

"I didn't know she tormented you at all."

"We had our differences." Cragnow took a sip. "What's the reason you've come to see me?"

"Katz provided a list of people . . . and vampires who may want to share what they know about Roxy's death."

"Ask the police. It was their investigation."

"I'll get to them."

"What's in it for you?" Cragnow asked.

I placed my drink on the coffee table. "It's my job."

"How much did Katz pay you?"

"That's privileged information."

Cragnow put his glass on the edge of his desk. He stared at the ceiling. "Let's wave a magic wand and pretend that Katz Meow gave you, say a ballpark figure, somewhere around"— he rocked forward and glared—"a hundred thousand dollars."

Exactly the retainer she had offered me. "Okay, so Katz can't tinkle, much less make a bank withdrawal, without you knowing about it. What are you getting at?"

"Let me wave that magic wand again, and suppose I give you two hundred thousand to drop the case and go home."

"And Katz?"

"Should you run into her, refund the money. You'll still be ahead two hundred thou. And if you never run into her, you'll have three hundred." Cragnow's aura sparkled with self-assured confidence. "Pretty sweet deal."

I picked up a napkin and wiped my lips. "Let me tell you something about myself, Cragnow. I have a habit of finishing what I start."

He nodded and smiled. "You're a vampire who confuses ego with principle. And you think I should admire you for it." The tips of his fangs protruded past his upper lip.

Cragnow's smile deepened into a leer. The smooth sheath of his aura formed into points like the claws of a poisonous centipede.

CHAPTER
6

CRAGNOW'S AURA BRISTLED with malevolence. It was a good show, and I should've been impressed. But I could overpower Cragnow, dig my talons into his throat, and squeeze until he told me what I wanted to know. How far would I get before his goons rescued him? Certainly the other vampire agents had tried to muscle information . . . and failed. To get answers I'd need guile, not brute force.

Cragnow headed the Los Angeles *nidus,* one of the largest in the world, his own barony of the undead. However, that power had demands I would use against him. Chief among his obligations as *nidus* leader was keeping the community hidden from the blunt-toothed humans.

"Tell me about your chalice," I said.

The points of Cragnow's aura recoiled in suspicion.

Good, I'd knocked him off balance.

His smile vanished. "Who do you mean?"

I motioned in the direction of the front desk. "Rachel. The receptionist."

"She's not a chalice."

"Oh?" I arched my eyebrows. "Then explain her reaction when I mentioned that I was family. How could a human, other than a chalice, know about that?"

The points of Cragnow's aura withdrew into the glowing sheath surrounding him. His fangs receded behind his upper lip. He pushed back into his chair. The surface of his aura became prickly.

He clasped the edge of his eyeglasses. He hesitated at removing them. I knew he regretted not taking them and his contacts off sooner, leaving me with the advantage of reading his aura while he couldn't see mine. He'd done so out of arrogance, and to remove them now would be an admission that I threatened him.

Cragnow lowered his hand and smiled. The skin around his eyes wrinkled. "That's a question only a vampire from the Araneum would ask."

"If you're implying that I'm here on behalf of the Araneum, I'm not," I lied. "My question was one any vampire would ask. Aren't you the head of the local *nidus*?"

"That's no *family* secret."

"Then it's your job to enforce the protocol that protects us."

Cragnow's aura softened into an even, inscrutable facade. He paused and drank from his vodka blood frappé.

I asked again, "What about Rachel?"

Cragnow tightened his expression. "Let me worry about her." He stood and walked toward the bar. He held his glass up. "Care for a refill?"

"I'm fine."

Cragnow kept his back to me as he refreshed his drink. "I've changed my mind, Felix. Since you're not going to drop the case, I'll tell you what you can do for me." He turned about. "Go ahead and find out who killed Roxy Bronze."

Lucky for me that Cragnow wore contacts, otherwise my

aura blazing in surprise could've blinded him. I paused to regroup my thoughts.

"Okay, Cragnow, let me be honest. You were my number one suspect."

"Why? Because I was Roxy's former boss?"

"You and she had disagreements."

"Many. But that doesn't mean I killed her."

"She bought out her contract with you and was going to start her own video and distribution line." I gestured to the walls. "She made Gomorrah Video. How much did her loss affect you?"

"Let's set the record straight." Cragnow's aura bristled with a fuzz of annoyance. "*I* made Roxy. *She* didn't make me. There are many more where she came from. I've got beauty queens, suburban moms, eighteen-year-old cheerleaders fresh off the bus from Kansas, eager to pump spoog for Gomorrah. Roxy was past thirty, a goddamn hag in this business."

"So her leaving didn't bother you."

"Hell yes. But you're talking as if that never happened anywhere else. In Hollywood, the legit movie business, mind you, backstabbing is more common than a handshake." Cragnow picked a newspaper from the magazine crib beside the bar. He tossed the newspaper on the coffee table. "Here's the *Wall Street Journal.* I dare you to open that and not find one article about business partners screwing each other's balls deep."

"I don't understand your problems with Roxy," I said, wanting to bait Cragnow into revealing more. "Should've zapped her with hypnosis to keep her in line."

Cragnow replied, "You surprise me, Felix. I thought you'd have more experience with humans than that. Posthypnotic control is not reliable outside of the trance, especially for someone with a strong personality."

"Like Roxy?" I asked.

"*Especially* her."

"Did Roxy know you are a vampire?"

Cragnow's aura tightened.

"It's a simple question. Answer yes or no."

Cragnow's eyes narrowed. "No."

"Was she aware of vampires?"

"I'm positive she wasn't," Cragnow said.

"To be clear about this, you didn't murder Roxy?"

"No." Cragnow closed his eyes and pinched the bridge of his nose. "And to answer the next question, I don't know who killed her either."

These denials meant little. I lied about being here for the Araneum, and Cragnow could lie about his involvement in Roxy's murder.

"A minute ago you offered me two hundred thousand to drop the case," I said. "Now you want to know who killed her. Why?"

"Not out of sympathy, that's for sure. Roxy got what she deserved. But talking to you made me realize there's a lot more to this." Cragnow rested an elbow on the edge of the bar. "When Roxy died, I thought that was the end of that headache. Now Katz Meow is missing." He looked at me. His aura churned with swirls that betrayed worry. "Maybe I'm next."

"Meaning whoever killed Roxy could be after you?"

"I have to consider that." Cragnow poured more vodka into his frappé. He jammed in a swizzle stick and swirled it. Pink froth spilled out. He ran a finger around the rim of the glass to wipe the foam and then licked his finger clean.

"Don't get me wrong, Felix, I'm not on your side." He returned to his chair, a drunken wobble disturbing his gait. He eased into the leather seat. "It's that your visit has turned on a little lamp in my head. Maybe I've been too complacent about my plans . . ."

"What plans?"

Cragnow's aura tightened to the smoothness of glass. An equally tight grin curved his lips. "My plans for Gomorrah Video, what else?"

That's what I needed to find out.

"Since you're being straight with me"—his grin widened and the fangs showed—"at least as straight as I'm being with you, do this. Find out who killed Roxy Bronze. It'll be a favor."

"A favor to the leader of the L.A. *nidus*? What an honor. What do I get in return? A merit badge?"

The grin faded. "Don't push it. You're working for Katz Meow, not me."

Cragnow was feeding me rope, and it wasn't a lifeline.

I asked, "Would you know someone named Coyote?"

Cragnow answered with a nod and said, "Haven't seen him since I fumigated my house."

"What's that mean?"

"I'm sure you'll find out." Cragnow fumbled for the corner of his desk and pressed a button. Staring at me, he sipped from his drink.

The room grew quiet until the loudest sound was the gurgling of the aquarium. The door swung open. The black vampire bodyguard motioned me out. His vest was folded back to expose the big pistol holstered against his chest.

I replaced my sunglasses, gave Cragnow a salute, and followed the bodyguard down the hall and to the reception area. Rachel wasn't there. The bodyguard held the front door open and watched until I got into my car and drove off.

Traffic on the Ventura Freeway crawled along like a sleepy river. A great mass of inhabitants swelled within the San Fernando Valley, and I was but one speck among the millions. I felt the pressure of countless anonymous eyes smothering me. I wished I was back in Denver, safe and in control.

I whipped off my sunglasses and scanned cars and buildings, looking for the telltale blossom of an orange vampire glow against the sea of red auras. I realized my mistake in assuming that the danger came only from vampires. With the threat of vampire–human collusion, any one of these humans could be after me.

Again I raked my gaze across the confusion of auras,

searching for a glow—orange or red—luminescent with malice against me. Icy fear pumped through my limbs. I was like a swimmer convinced that a shark lurked unseen in the surrounding waters.

A stream of self-absorbed humans swirled past. There was nothing around me except hurried indifference.

Thirst parched my throat. I took the exit into Sherman Oaks and stopped in the parking lot of a strip mall lined with boutiques. I pawed through the box my pistol had been shipped in. Under a layer of bubble wrap rested a large Ziploc bag with six 450-milliliter bags of human blood. I removed one, chiding myself for not storing the blood properly. But the plastic bladderlike bag felt cool, so the blood inside should still be safe.

I fanged one end of the bag and sucked the delicious meaty fluid. An invigorating energy flowed through me, quenching the ache of dread like salve on a burn. I relaxed against the driver's seat, rolling up the bag of blood as if it were a tube of toothpaste, and squeezed the last liquid morsels over my tongue. Satisfied, I stuffed the empty bag into the well of the center console.

Guilt crept into me. Guilt for showing weakness because I had lapsed into paranoia.

In previous assignments—against Chinese drug lords, Transylvanian vampire-hunters, and even assassins from our own government—I had never been scared like I was a moment ago. Why now?

Other vampires, that's why. I glanced left and right for orange auras. Certainly by now, Cragnow had warned his undead minions about me.

Why had he let me slip away? Was I bait to draw out his enemies? How concerned was he about Roxy Bronze's murder, provided he wasn't one of the killers?

Resting a hand on the remaining pile of blood bags, I thought about nourishment, another of my worries. All the usual sources—butcher shops, blood banks, chalice parlors— would be watched and my visits reported to Cragnow. The classifieds on the HollowFang.com—a newsletter for the undead disguised as a fanzine for vampire wannabes—wouldn't list anything safe. I could forage for human necks but shuddered at the idea of prowling the streets, even ritzy Rodeo Drive, with the verminous lust of a junkie.

The dashboard clock said it was midafternoon. Time to quit fretting and get back to work. Besides, I had enough blood for two days.

Next on my list of suspects was Lucius "Lucky" Rosario, the real estate developer whose plans for big profits at the public trough were thwarted by Roxy. I pulled out a photo of Rosario clipped from the newspaper, and a map to his office.

Was Rosario human or undead? Unfortunately, there was no registry of vampires available that I could query. Was he involved with vampire–human collusion or was he only a party in Roxy's death? Or neither?

I got back onto the freeway and headed east into downtown L.A. Rosario's company, Lucky Developments, was in a gigantic high-rise near Fourth and Hope. I turned into the entrance for the basement garage and pulled close to the attendant's booth.

He leaned out of his booth. "No public parking, sir."

I raised my sunglasses, zapped him, and instructed him to raise the entry bar.

Along the edge of the map I had written Rosario's license plate number. Inside the basement garage, I passed a black Porsche Cayenne SUV bearing his plates. At least his car was here.

Lucky Developments was on the seventeenth floor. I kept my sunglasses on while I rode the elevator.

A blond receptionist sat behind a desk in the company foyer, her gaze fixed on a monitor. Conversations buzzed from fabric-walled cubicles stretching down the hall to the left.

"I'd like to see Lucky Rosario," I said.

The receptionist folded her arms. "*Mister* Rosario's not here. Give me your name and number and what this is about, and I'm sure he'll call you."

I removed my sunglasses and hit her with a good blast of vampire hypnosis. "Here's my appointment."

The receptionist's red aura pulsed like the flash from a strobe light. Her eyes jerked wide, looking like green pellets floating in circles of milk. Both arms dangled toward the carpet. Her mouth gaped, and a drop of spit gathered on her painted lower lip.

I glanced down the hall to make sure we wouldn't be bothered. "Where's Rosario?"

The receptionist worked her mouth. The spit slid to her chin. "Lucky," she whispered, "Lucky's in his office. The door behind me."

"Good girl. Now close your eyes." I placed the receptionist's arms across the keyboard and leaned her forehead against the computer screen. "Have a nice nap."

Her jaw fell open, and she began to snore. I approached the door, turned the knob, and entered.

A portly man in a white shirt and stylish tie sat behind an immense wooden desk, his back to the panorama of Los Angeles filling a picture window. A red aura surrounded him. Good, a human.

I locked the door behind me. This interrogation wouldn't take long.

His shirt creased into the folds of his fat torso. Fleshy jowls widened the bottom half of his face and tapered to an angular forehead topped by a short haircut.

The cuffs of his shirt were folded back, exposing thick, hairy wrists. His hands held the grip of a disassembled pistol. The rest of the gun and bullets lay across a rag on the desktop. Why the gun?

Narrow-set eyes flicked toward me from either side of a bladelike nose. The web of broken capillaries on each flabby cheek flushed into red splotches. "Who the hell . . ."

We locked gazes. His face matched the photo. Smiling, I pointed a finger and gave Rosario my best vampire hypno-stare. "Bang. Bang."

CHAPTER
7

ROSARIO'S AURA FLARED, then settled into a turbulent neon mass swirling around his bulk. His gaze clung to mine. His eyes dilated into wide, black dots surrounded by the thin rims of his brown irises. The pistol grip assembly fell from his hands and clunked against the desktop.

I circled the desk, swiveled his chair toward me, and grasped his beefy hands. Massaging the flesh between his thumbs and forefingers, I deepened the trance. His aura settled into a soft glowing texture like phosphorescent chenille.

Dark concentric wrinkles filled his eye sockets, appearing as if they had once been bruised and never completely healed. I focused into the black wells of his eyes that led into his subconscious mind.

"Lucky," I said, "did you kill Roxy Bronze?"

Streaks indicating worry snaked through his aura.

"Lucky, answer me."

He drew a breath and kept quiet.

I stared deeper into his eyes. "Did you kill Roxy Bronze?"

He inhaled and his reply came out as a sigh. "No."

Strike one. Okay, he hadn't murdered her.

"Relax and listen to me." I kept massaging his hands. "Do you know who killed Roxy Bronze?"

More streaks pulsed through his aura.

Under hypnosis, some humans gushed like faucets. They yakked so much I wanted to send them a bill for therapy. And for some, like Rosario, questioning them was like dredging through mud.

I kept repeating my question and Rosario got around to giving me another "No."

Strike two. Still nothing on the killer. "Lucky, have you met a vampire?"

Again, the answer took a long minute to arrive. "No."

Strike three. Rosario knew nothing of vampire–human collusion. I dropped my head and exhaled in frustration.

Vampire hypnosis wasn't getting me any traction. In this situation, fanging him wasn't worth the trouble, especially if I had to put my mouth against the wattles of that fat neck. Better that I quit wasting time and try my luck gleaning information from the office surroundings and then his conscious mind.

I released his hands. They plopped into his lap.

"Close your eyes."

I turned Rosario's chair against the desk and set his forearms on the desktop. He wore a fancy gold wedding ring. Around his left wrist he had a gold watch with diamonds on the crown, a band of thick links, and the U.S. Marine Corps insignia enameled on the watch face. On his right hand he had a pinkie ring with a ruby, no doubt a poseur memento of imagined goombah roots.

One wall was decorated with permits and certificates as well as his undergraduate degree in accounting from UCLA. The southern wall had business plaques and photos of Rosario with celebrities and politicians. There were none of him with Roxy or Cragnow. A cabinet of cherrywood spanned the northern wall. The shelves held awards and various photos of Rosario with a nice-looking, young brunette and two children, both preadolescent girls. Above a middle shelf hung a portrait of a stern-faced and much slimmer version of Rosario in a Marine Corps uniform before a U.S. flag.

Lucius "Lucky" Rosario: accomplished business leader; family man; military veteran; amigo to the famous. A real civic peach. Nothing in the room alluded to graft or cavorting with porn stars.

I pulled out my contacts case and put the contacts on. I opened the office door a crack and stood, as if I'd just crossed the threshold.

"Okay, Lucky, wake up."

Rosario's breath quickened. He blinked. His head reeled back, as if he had suddenly lost his balance. His arms jerked across the desktop, scattering the pieces of his disassembled gun. A couple of cartridges rolled off the desk and thumped against the carpet.

Rosario sat upright and shook his head, the slabs of his swarthy jowls quivering. His gaze swung dizzily across the desk and then onto me. His bushy eyebrows arched in astonishment.

Rosario wouldn't remember anything from the instant before I zapped him.

He stared at me, to the door, then back to me. "How'd you get in here?"

"Your receptionist let me in." I closed the door and approached the leather chair in front of his desk. "Mind if I take a seat?"

He looked past me again, his face darkening with annoyance. He rose from his chair. "Who the hell are you?"

"My name is Felix Gomez. I'm here to talk about Roxy Bronze."

"Felix who?" He halted midway up from his chair. The

capillaries on his cheeks turned crimson. His eyebrows tightened low on his brow. "Why are you asking about Roxy?"

"I'm an acquaintance of Katz's."

"Katz Meow?" Rosario's glare mellowed. He eased back into his chair. "What kind of an aquaintance?"

"A professional one." I took Rosario's softening attitude as an invitation to sit. What about her had this tranquilizing affect on him? "Katz hired me to find out who killed Roxy Bronze."

Rosario lifted his chin, and his walruslike eyes appraised me. "Hired? As in what?"

"A private investigator," I replied. "Katz told me you could help. As a favor to her."

Rosario paused. His gaze darted from me to his desk, as if deciding what to do. "For Katz, huh? What do you want?"

"She told me Roxy had plenty of enemies."

"A few." Rosario collected pieces of the military issue .45.

"What's with the pistol?" I asked.

"Why? You some kinda gun-control liberal?"

"Not hardly."

"Then it's none of your business."

"Fair enough," I said. "So tell me about Roxy Bronze."

"Her? There was a line of folks that wanted Roxy out of the way."

"Out of what way?"

"Come on, Felix, don't play dumb ass." Rosario fit pieces of the gun together. "You've done your homework. If you haven't, then you aren't worth shit as a PI."

Rosario worked the slide onto the pistol grip assembly. He fit the slide pin into its hole in the receiver but had the pin backward. He struggled to make the pin align correctly. He bit his lower lip and squinted. Sweat dotted his forehead and nose. I debated helping him but decided against it.

Rosario's hand tightened on the grip of the gun, the whiteness of his knuckles a gauge of his frustration. The pin fell out. He grabbed the pin and forced it in.

A smile of self-congratulation creased his pulpy cheeks. He wiped his brow and looked at me as if expecting an applause.

"Katz told me you financed porn movies," I said. "With whom?"

"You're asking me like you don't know. Cragnow Vissoom, of course," he replied.

How strong a tie did Rosario and Cragnow have? "You friends with him?"

"He's got money; he doesn't need friends."

"Did you have the hots for Roxy?"

Rosario pushed the recoil plug over the spring under the barrel of the pistol. The plug popped free and ricocheted off his forehead. He blinked in surprise. His free hand chased the plug rolling on his desk. "You ever meet Ms. Bronze?"

"Never heard of her until after she was dead."

"Choice piece of tail, that one. If Helen of Troy had half the snatch on her that Roxy did, then the Trojan War would've been worth the slaughter." Carefully, he replaced the plug.

"What about Project Eleven?"

Rosario's gaze cut to me.

I would've liked to read his aura. But if I didn't hypnotize him again, he'd remember my eyes and that I wasn't human.

"I understand her involvement against Project Eleven cost you money."

"Cost me my goddamn ass. I lost out on my share of three hundred million."

"Over or under the table?"

Rosario's lips curled in scorn. "What's it to you?"

"Maybe it had to do with Roxy's interest in Project Eleven."

"You'd have to ask her, but you can't, can you?" he replied. "Roxy had another side to her besides being primo trim. She fancied herself a crusader. She joined up with that meddlesome bitch, Veronica Torres, and the two of them undermined Project Eleven."

Veronica Torres was the activist who spearheaded the neighborhood attacks against Project Eleven, claiming it was nothing but a piggy bank for the well connected.

"And this crusading is what got Roxy killed?"

"Wouldn't know 'cause I had nothing to do with it."

"You don't buy that she was the victim of a robbery gone bad?"

Rosario hesitated. He lay the pistol down. His nostrils widened and contracted like bellows as his gaze flitted about the room. He set his elbows on the desk and folded his hands together in front of his chin. His eyes swiveled back to me and he gave a subdued, "No."

"Why?" I asked.

Rosario cocked a thumb toward the picture window behind him. "I didn't get this view being an idiot." The bluster returned to his voice. "The police report was the biggest piece of fiction since the president's last State of the Union address."

"Why?"

"You mean why did I vote for the Ivy League bastard?"

"No," I replied, "'the biggest piece of fiction' part."

Rosario said, "Rumors."

"What kind?"

"The cops lost the investigation files. Blamed it on a computer glitch. What's been reported is based on conjecture. Bullshit guesswork, in other words."

"What about the original reports? Evidence? The bullet, for example?"

"You'll have to ask the police," Rosario replied.

"Who exactly?" I asked.

"Deputy Chief Julius Paxton of the LAPD. Good luck talking to him."

"Are you and Paxton good chums?"

"Good enough," Rosario said. "I'm a generous contributor to the police benevolent fund."

I tucked Paxton's name into my memory.

Rosario added, "Didn't help speculation that Roxy's death was convenient for a lot of people."

"You included?"

"I got some satisfaction reading that she got whacked." Rosario panned a quizzical look across his desk, then to the floor. He struggled to lean to one side to retrieve the two bullets that had fallen.

"Then why are you talking to me? I mention Katz Meow's name and you unfold like a dinner napkin. Why?"

"Because I'm getting the willies." Rosario collected all the bullets into his hand and began feeding them into the pistol magazine. "Someone's going through a lot of trouble hiding the truth about Roxy's murder."

"That's got you worried?"

"Of course, Sherlock. I don't know who killed Roxy. Or the reason. Now you come with the kind of questions I've been asking myself and I realize that I'm not nuts for sleeping with a forty-five under my pillow."

First Cragnow. Now Rosario. What could make these two crap their pants?

Rosario inserted the magazine into the butt of the pistol. He had a loaded gun in his hand, but I wasn't worried. Rosario hadn't assembled the pistol correctly, and the only way he could hurt me was to throw it.

"What's your impression of Cragnow?" I asked.

"You've met him?"

"Briefly."

"Watch him when he gets shit-faced, which is often," Rosario said. "He starts ranting about taking over Southern California. Not in a business way. But about lifting humanity to a new partnership with the unseen realm. About the next step in social evolution. His crazy talk, not mine."

My fingertips tingled and my legs tensed. Though he

didn't realize it, Rosario referred to Cragnow's alleged plan for vampire–human collusion.

"Then why do business with him?"

"You kidding? Ain't you got a dick between your legs? The pussy at Gomorrah is like free bonbons."

"When was the last time you saw Katz?"

"Two weeks ago." Rosario wiped the pistol with the rag. "Maybe three."

"How close were you?"

"You mean, did we screw? Once. I doubt she'll ever forget me." Rosario racked back the slide of the .45. The barrel jutted out like a small metal penis.

"Then you haven't seen her lately?"

Rosario raised an eyebrow. "Sounds like *you* haven't either. Is she missing? And you're wondering why I'm looking over my shoulder." He propped his right elbow on the desk and pointed the pistol straight up. "You packing heat?"

It was none of his business that I was. "No."

"Then start." Rosario released a catch. The slide snapped forward, then tumbled loose and clattered against the desk.

"What did you do in the marines?" I deadpanned. "Force Recon?"

"I was a stenographer." Rosario tugged at his necktie. Wet spots blossomed from his armpits. He wrapped the pistol and the slide in the rag, which he dumped into a desk drawer. "Give me your card, Felix."

I gave him a business card, curious about his desire to cooperate. "We talk again, what do you get out of it?"

"Peace of mind."

Good idea. At least I could handle a gun.

Rosario palmed a cell phone. "If that's all, I've got business waiting."

I thought about zapping him again and decided against it. Rosario didn't act as if he had lied. Plus he had shared a lot, and I had to sort through that information first. I rose from the chair and left. His receptionist sat at her place and rubbed her neck. She gave me a perplexed "Where did you come from?" look as I went past.

Down in the garage, I started my car and drove out into the sunlit pavement. I didn't have a single answer to show for my work so far. As of now, conspiracy outfoxed vampire prowess.

I pulled onto the street when my door locks clicked. The front passenger door jerked open. A scruffy, slender man jumped in, moving too quickly for any human.

Vampire.

My *kundalini noir* buzzed like the tail of a rattler. I turned toward him, fangs and talons extended.

He raised a scrawny hand in a gesture of appeasement. *"Calmate ese,* relax."

I grabbed the front of his worn denim jacket and pushed him against the seat. "Who are you?"

He made no effort to resist and tipped a stained ball cap back from his face. A wispy mustache and soul patch above his chin accented his brown, leathery skin.

"Felix, I'm the one who sent for you." He offered his hand. "I'm Coyote."

CHAPTER
8

COYOTE. The one Katz Meow mentioned when she had come by my office in Denver. The one who had summoned me.

Coyote held up his empty hands, his thin wrists extending through the frayed cuffs of the threadbare denim jacket. He smelled like he'd been sleeping in an onion shed. "Well? Aren't you going to ask me questions?" He tapped his temple. "Or are you a mind reader, *ese*?"

I let go of his jacket and eased the sedan against the curb. I removed my sunglasses and contacts. Coyote's aura surrounded him like a calm orange penumbra.

"How'd you unlock the doors?"

"I've been around." His eyes reflected a lupine shine. He spoke with a thick Chicano barrio accent. "Gave me time to learn some tricks."

Since Coyote pronounced his name as if it were in Spanish, I did the same.

"Coyote, how do you know me?"

"I've heard about you, Felix Gomez." He drawled my name. "Vampire detective. Military veteran. Killer." Grinning, Coyote narrowed his eyes. "The only one *chingon* enough to handle this."

Chingon, that meant I was a bad mo-fo. "You said I could handle this. Which is?"

Coyote swept a hand across the urban landscape and the dark shadows cast by rows of old buildings with rusty fire escapes. "This. *Los Angeles.*"

"Meaning?"

"First we go, *vato.*" Coyote flicked his hand to the front, motioning that we move back into traffic. His fingernails were greasy like a backyard mechanic's.

"No. Answer my questions, then we go."

"Vamos a comer." He rubbed his belly and smacked his lips. "If you're not hungry, then you can watch me. We'll talk then." His fangs extended, meaning a blood meal.

Coyote directed me south on San Pedro through the Jewelry District, which despite the name was a shabby place populated with cheap stores whose signs alternated between Spanish and Chinese.

"You've seen him, no?" Tentacles snaked from Coyote's aura.

"Who?"

"Cragnow." The end of each of the tentacles on Coyote's aura sprouted spikes. The spikes curled onto themselves like fingers making fists. "He's a scary dude."

"I gathered that."

"Be careful. You're not the first to have come here."

"Are you talking about the agents from the Araneum?"

"Símon. They didn't last long." Coyote extended a thumb and pressed it against his sternum. He then drew a finger across his throat. Meaning, they were impaled and decapitated. His aura tentacles stiffened and trembled.

"How many agents?" I asked. "When?"

Coyote shrugged. His aura tentacles formed question marks. "*Quien sabe.* Four. Maybe five since last year."

"How do you make your aura do that?" I asked.

"You like, huh? It takes practice."

"I'm sure. Why did you send for me? Are *you* from the Araneum?"

Coyote laughed, a guffawing that turned into a series of howls. His dirty sneakers beat against the floor as his aura pulsed in tempo to his hearty convulsions. He stopped laughing and wiped his eyes. "That's a good one, *vato.*"

"I didn't realize I was a comedian. What's the joke?"

"The Araneum won't have anything to do with me. We don't see *ojo a ojo.*" Coyote used his fingers to spread his eyelids. "They think I'm crazy."

We drove under the concrete tangle of the freeway exchange.

"Really?" I nudged him away and wondered if the Araneum was right. "Why did you send for me?"

"Because Cragnow is messing with catastrophe. He and humans have made a pact."

Vampire–human collusion. The real reason for my mission. My *kundalini noir* buzzed with anticipation for the fight before me. "Describe this pact."

"There are humans close to Cragnow. Humans who are not chalices. He doesn't bother to hide his true nature from them, and they don't fear him."

I remembered Rachel, the receptionist at Gomorrah Video. She knew about family, meaning us vampires.

Rosario's conversation came back to me.

. . . taking over Southern California . . . lifting humanity to a new partnership with the unseen realm . . . the next step in social evolution . . .

My *kundalini noir* coiled tightly, as if to protect itself against a chill.

"Felix. What's up, bro?" Coyote's gaze traced around me as he read the state of my aura.

"Coyote, why do you care what Cragnow does? Has he wronged you? Is this about vengeance?"

"I want to get back at Cragnow, I'll put a dead catfish inside the hood of his Hummer." Coyote's aura made undulating stink lines. He held his nose and waved away an imagined odor.

"Then explain your motive."

"Because, *vato,* I've seen what humans can do. We can't underestimate their viciousness and ingenuity. Cragnow may think he controls them—I don't know what bargain he's made—but it is a marriage with doom."

"Sounds like you're speaking from experience."

"Too much experience." The points of Coyote's aura trembled like reeds before a wind. His expression melted into a somber mask. "Our best defense is not supernatural powers but remaining unseen. Cragnow has compromised that. Our hope, my hope, is that you and I can stop the damage. *Porque, sí no*"—because, if not—"we vampires are destined for extinction."

"Is this your quest?" I asked. "Are you Don Quixote?"

"If I am, then you're my Sancho Panza, and you're too skinny to be him."

"You summoned me through . . ."—I had to think of her name—"Katz's friend. Rebecca Dwelling. Human."

"That was the best way," Coyote replied. "Rebecca knows about vampires. She's a chalice. I told her that you could help Katz."

"How do you know Rebecca?"

"Wait and I'll show you, *vato.*"

"As a chalice Rebecca is forbidden from revealing her awareness about the undead," I said. "If the *nidus* leader won't enforce that, the Araneum will."

"The local *nidus* no longer fears the Araneum."

"I've figured that out. So, did Cragnow kill Roxy Bronze?"

Coyote shrugged. His aura dimmed. "That's a big question, no? Answer that and you'll start to solve everything."

The twin mysteries of my trip—the conspiracy behind Roxy's death and vampire–human collusion—remained parallel yet far apart.

"Why didn't you contact me directly, Coyote?"

"Because I needed to slap you in the face to get your attention. Would you have listened to a *loco* vampire like me? Or to a beautiful woman describing the great secret?" Coyote wagged a finger. "I know you like the ladies, Felix."

"And the L.A. *nidus*?" I asked. "Don't any of them care about what's happening?"

Coyote glanced to the outside mirror. "If you know about Cragnow's plan, you're either with him or you're ash."

"Why aren't you ash?"

"To the L.A. *nidus* I'm as invisible as a bum on a street corner. They don't see me because they don't want to. Sometimes being crazy and looking down-and-out is the best way to hide."

"Maybe you're not so crazy, Coyote."

He clicked his tongue. "Maybe not, Felix."

"How many vampires in the *nidus*?"

"It's not like I've taken roll." He straightened and raised a hand like a schoolboy. "Coyote. Present." He settled back. "I'd guess maybe a couple thousand. Hard to say. Many are just passing through."

A huge *nidus,* regardless. "How many work for Cragnow?"

"Maybe three hundred. More than enough to be dangerous. And they're all over, with the police, the government."

I needed an ally in this wilderness, and Coyote's frankness made him the best candidate. I offered a handshake. "So we're partners. You got a last name, or is it just Coyote?"

His hand was bony, like a paw. After releasing my grip, he closed his eyes and began to howl.

"Okay wiseass," I asked, "how do you spell that?"

Coyote barked for several seconds. He gave a smile of

yellowed teeth. "Don't quote me. I could've been speaking Doberman."

"What's your last name in people talk?"

"Malinche," he said.

"As in the Malinche?"

"La Malinche," he corrected. "My mother."

"Doña Marina?"

"You know of another one?"

La Malinche. The Aztec maiden who served as translator and concubine for Cortès. The woman lauded by the Spaniards for her help in conquering Mexico. And reviled by many Mexicans as a traitorous whore. Yet others found her a compromised woman who had kept history from getting worse.

"She's your mother? Then you must be five hundred years old."

"Like I said, I've been around."

"So your father was the devil himself, Hernando Cortès?"

"Chale"—no way. Coyote recoiled from me. "Rather than settle down with her, after all she had done for him, Cortès kicked my mother out of his house, *porque* he already had a wife . . . imagine that? Cortès was not only a rapist, looter, and murderer; he cheated on his woman. *Que vergüenza.*"

"A real shame," I agreed.

"Before my mother was married off to Cortès's lackey, Don Juan Xamarillo, she had another boy."

Coyote let silence fill the void between us until I understood.

"You?"

"Símon."

"And your father was?"

"One of Cortès's soldiers." Coyote raised his hand in a mock toast. *"L'chaim."*

I had to think about his reply for a moment. Was he

Jewish? Some of the Conquistadors had been Jewish. "You want me to believe that you are the son of a Jewish Conquistador?"

"I'm not asking you to believe anything. I'm only asking that you listen."

"*Your* father?" I asked. "A Jew?"

"*Sí.* Many became Conquistadors to escape the Inquisition. Many still hide out of custom, pretending to be good Catholics in public. For some reason they call themselves *marranos,* though I don't understand why Jews would want to be known as pigs."

Coyote snorted like a hog, the nostrils of his thin nose twitching.

"When did you become vampire?"

"That was a long time ago, *hermano.*" Coyote cupped his crotch. "About the time hairs sprouted around my *chile.* I sought a vampire to escape the torment of being the bastard son of a *gauchupin.*" A Spaniard.

Coyote sighed in a way that made me pity him. Half a millennium had not been enough time to dilute his grief.

"There were legends of a jaguar man living in the jungle. He preyed on the lost and drank their blood. There was no one more lost than me, so I looked for him."

"Obviously you found him," I said.

"I wish I hadn't, *carnal.* There are agonies worse than dying." Coyote's talons and fangs shot out and his aura burned like a bonfire. He was vampire, the tormented drinker of blood, doomed to prowl the earth forever.

"I understand," I said.

"Consider, *ese.*" Coyote's aura settled. His talons and teeth retracted. "When my mother was big and pregnant with me, before she was hitched to that *buey* Don Xamarillo, Cortez figured that Xamarillo had sampled her wares, while Xamarillo thought that Cortès had left her with a souvenir. These murderers were each too much the gentlemen to question the other's integrity. Had they known she bore the bastard son of a heathen Jew, they would have burned her alive.

My mother could not keep me, the evidence of her sin. At my birth, she switched me with a stillborn baby. I was given away and raised by the poorest of the defeated *indios*. Even among them I was a pariah, an omen of what the future held for Mexico."

"And your father?"

"He died of plague. Some said it was divine justice for turning La Malinche into his little knish." Coyote smiled, the pallor of sorrow evaporating. "I also heard that my father died masturbating. His final words at orgasm were *viva Mexico*."

Coyote blinked uncomfortably. Driving under the intense California sun made my eyes water and burn as well. I replaced my sunglasses. Coyote fished a pair of shades from the breast pocket of his jacket. A paper clip held the left temple to the lens frame.

Coyote motioned abruptly as we neared a traffic light. "Here. To the left."

We headed east for several blocks along Vernon Avenue. I explained my investigation as it had progressed so far. Katz Meow and the Araneum had brought me to L.A. Now Katz was missing. And my two prime suspects—porn king Cragnow Vissoom and corrupt developer Lucky Rosario—were each looking over their respective shoulders and had asked me for help.

Coyote listened and nodded. When I was done he said, "*Sí. Mucha caca.*"

I knew that. A big help he was.

Coyote directed me into the parking lot of a bowling alley, a cinder block building bearing the name Majestic Lanes in faded plastic letters along the front. Trash littered the bottom of the walls and front sidewalk. Liquor bottles sparkled among the weeds. Cars crowded the spaces closest to the building. There was a muffler shop and beauty salon across the street.

I found a spot between a Jaguar and a Bentley, cars that looked as out of place here as would a pair of albino elephants. "Pretty fancy wheels for this dump. What's here?"

"Dinner," Coyote replied. "And a concert for the damned."

"Who's the damned?"

"We are," he replied.

CHAPTER
9

I FOLLOWED COYOTE toward the entrance of the Majestic Lanes. "We're eating at a bowling alley?"

"I am," he replied. "Don't know about you. But we're here not just for *refín*. I want you to meet Rebecca Dwelling."

Katz said Rebecca worked at a secret place where humans intermingled with vampires, no doubt a chalice parlor. Talking to Rebecca could clear away some of the smoke in this investigation, as she might know what happened to Katz.

I examined the broken neon and cracked plastic on the facade. "Good disguise. This is the last place I'd think to look for a chalice parlor."

"¿Vato, estas loco?" Dude, are you crazy? Coyote chuckled. "This ain't no ordinary parlor."

We stepped into the shadow of the front awning. Coyote gripped the door handle when he stopped abruptly. "Smell that?"

I caught only warm asphalt, gasoline, and dirty bowling shoes. "What is it?"

"Un lobo."

A wolf in Los Angeles meant that a transformed vampire was close by. Vampires didn't transform into wolves unless they expected getting, or making, serious trouble.

I closed my eyes and sniffed again. There it was, that faint musky odor.

I checked left and right. If a wolf came for trouble, I'd give it to him. "Why would a vampire risk running through L.A. as a wolf? And in the daytime?"

"Maybe he wasn't running through the city," Coyote answered. He put a finger to his lips and whispered, "Maybe he turned into a wolf to sit and listen."

It was as a wolf that a vampire's senses were at their most keen. Transforming into a wolf was common practice when stalking special prey.

Who was his prey?

Me? If so, he was in for a surprise.

Coyote? I looked at my scruffy and wily partner. Good luck catching him.

Then who?

Rebecca.

"Where's the wolf?" I asked.

"Don't know. The scent is cold."

"Let's go find Rebecca." Grasping Coyote's arm, I hustled him through the entrance and toward the rumbling of bowling balls and the crashing of pins.

Most of the lanes were occupied. I peeked over my sunglasses. Everyone had a red aura. If this was a chalice parlor, where were the vampires?

Coyote led me across the carpeted aisle on the upper level, looking down on the lanes. He turned the corner and approached a gray metal door marked EMPLOYEES ONLY.

He opened the door and we entered a dark corridor sloping to the left, parallel to the lanes and filled with the racket of machinery, bowling balls, and pins.

Coyote removed his sunglasses and so did I. A red bulb illuminated the corridor. An oily, mechanical odor from the pin machines grew more intense the farther we walked down the incline.

At the back of the hall, Coyote stopped before a metal cabinet. Dents and graffiti covered the front. Coyote opened the double doors of the cabinet and ducked inside. The back of the cabinet swung away. Coyote stepped down, as if descending stairs.

I followed him, taking care to shut the cabinet doors behind me.

We were on a metal landing. Stairs led to another door beneath the Majestic Lanes. The door had a placard for a Cold War Civil Defense shelter. We climbed down. The muted crashing of the bowling machinery rumbled through the concrete wall. Coyote knocked on the door.

A view port at face level opened. A pair of shiny vampire eyes peeked out. I expected Coyote to say, "José sent me."

But he said nothing and the door swung open. Our orange auras must have been our pass in.

Jazz music flooded out, a raunchy blare of saxophones against the energetic accompaniment of a keyboard, guitar, and drums. The aroma of fresh human blood sent my nostrils tingling and my mouth watering. No trace of a wolf.

A vampire bouncer waved us through. He was huge and his muscles were overinflated; most likely he was a steroid juicer before he was converted to the undead.

Laughter and playful snarls swirled around us. Orange and red auras filled the room. The psychic glows flashed gaiety and lust. The ambience was a combination Juarez cantina and Chicago speakeasy. A sign on the wall read: NO UNDEAD CONVERSIONS ON THE PREMISES. NO SEX ON THE TABLES. NO DANCING ON THE CEILING.

Below that, someone had scrawled with a black marker: AND TIP, YOU CHEAP BASTARDS.

Vampires crowded the bar to my right. A naked female chalice lay facedown across the top. Blood seeped from puncture wounds lacing her shoulders, buttocks, and the back of her thighs. The vampires around her sipped cocktails and chatted, stopping occasionally to lap and nibble on the chalice, as if she were a plate of hors d'oeuvres.

More vampires sat at the tables lining a terraced auditorium, which faced a stage. I guessed that the place, with its low black ceiling, could hold a hundred patrons.

Six musicians—humans—played on stage, three women sax players, the rest men. They wore either scarves or leather collars to cover bite marks and advertise their status as chalices. Sequined jackets sparkled under the colored spotlights. The women swayed on bare legs in tempo to the music. Their costumes were just the jackets, plus black bikini briefs and shoes. The women looked delectable, but the men, in loafers and with hairy bellies sagging over their briefs— well, that was a taste others preferred.

Coyote pointed to the woman at the far right of the combo, the short one with a gymnast's body, stocky and muscular. "That's Rebecca."

She had a round, pretty face that placed her anywhere from sixteen to the midtwenties. Her cheeks puffed and her ponytail wobbled as she wailed on the sax.

"Why not get us drinks and nachos," Coyote said, "while we wait for Rebecca to finish this set."

I stopped a passing chalice waitress. She was dressed—or to be more precise—barely dressed with costume beads looped over her naked shoulders and perky breasts. Metallic glitter freckled her face and torso. A studded red leather collar encircled her delicate neck. She wore tap pants, mule pumps tied with ribbons around her ankles and calves, and a silly pillbox hat resting at a slant over her brown hair.

We ordered the day's special—a fanged martini: the house vodka, vermouth, and type O-positive.

The waitress smiled and turned about. The bottom curves of her firm butt winked from under her tiny pants.

Coyote motioned toward an empty table that offered a

clear view to the stage. "Over there, where we can keep an eye on Rebecca."

The band started a fast and raucous rockabilly tune. Vampires whooped and crowded the floor. They shuffled and kicked and flung their chalice dance partners. Some of the vampires leapt and clung to the ceiling, dancing upside down, their feet knocking pieces of acoustical tile to the floor. Now I understood the rule about no dancing on the ceiling.

This was the concert for the damned? Lucky us.

What about this joint? Every other chalice parlor I'd been to before had the languid mood of an opium den. This place had a happy hour, dancing—a cold breeze tickled the back of my neck—and air-conditioning. How could so many vampires and chalices congregate without the local human populace finding out?

Our waitress arrived with drinks and the plate of nachos, which was drizzled with melted cheese, diced jalapeños, and— from the aroma—goat's blood. She had twenties and hundreds heaped on her tray.

Who raked in all this money? I could smell the graft. Certainly this parlor—make that saloon—pointed to the vampire–human collusion I'd been sent here to investigate.

Coyote flipped through a jukebox-type device on the table. Instead of songs, each tab on the device listed a chalice on the menu with a photo and description.

F 9. Jason—a thirty-year-old Asian male from Newport Beach. Type B-negative. Very lean. Smoker. Hearty metallic taste with pepper and menthol notes.

"Naw. *Muy flaco*." Coyote raised his voice. The music was very loud. "Too skinny. Plus it took me a hundred years to kick my nicotine habit. I fang him and boom, I'm back to those goddamned Marlboros."

He kept flipping and stopped on G 34. Darlene—a forty-six-year-old from Willowbrook. Type A-positive.

"*Bien gordita*. I like them chunky." Coyote touched the order button. "She okay for you?"

In her picture, Darlene looked plump, happy, and most delicious, as juicy as a marbled steak.

"Sure," I answered. "But don't order until after we've met with Rebecca."

"*Bueno.*" Coyote pulled his finger off the order button. "You can cover the check, no? I'll owe you until payday."

"I didn't know you had a job."

"I don't. But with the economy turning around, I'm optimistic. I've got résumés all over town, *ese.*" Coyote tugged at my elbow and leaned close. "I've even applied as a pilot with Pan American." He winked.

"Pan Am went under years ago," I said. "Don't expect them to call."

"I'm not," Coyote said, laughing, "because I don't have a phone."

The band played harder and faster. The dancers hurried their frenetic pace to match the rhythm. The finale had the subtlety of a bottle truck smashing into a fireworks stand.

The band members, their bodies glistening with sweat, bowed to rowdy applause. The curtain closed before them. The house lights brightened. Vampires and chalices returned to their chairs.

I sipped my martini, munched nachos, and surveyed the surrounding vampires as I looked for an aura that betrayed danger.

Coyote scooped blood with a nacho chip and crunched on it. "*¿Nada, verdad?*" Nothing, right? "Maybe the wolf presence has nothing to do with us or Rebecca."

"You believe that?" When on a trail leading from murder, there was no such thing as a coincidence.

A door to the left of the stage opened. The band filed out. Coyote and I remained seated, finishing our drinks as we waited for Rebecca to appear.

A minute passed and still no Rebecca. My *kundalini noir* sounded the alarm.

I folded a twenty under my martini glass, got up from the

table, and approached the band members milling around the door. Coyote followed.

"Where's Rebecca Dwelling?" I asked.

The keyboard player replied, "In the dressing room."

Coyote and I went through the door and behind the stage. Towels damp with sweat lay strewn on chairs and the floor. A chalice tidied up the place.

"You seen Rebecca?" I asked.

He pointed to a door at the far end. "She and a customer left that way."

"Vampire?"

"What other customers do we have?"

Smart-ass.

Coyote and I hurried past him. The other vampire had beaten us to Rebecca. Why hadn't I anticipated this? I should have told Coyote to stay behind in case the vampire and Rebecca came out another way.

The door opened to a hall that led past the storage rooms, the kitchen, and finally to the bar. And the way out. Damn.

Coyote and I went up the maze we'd come through and back to the bowling alley. I put on my sunglasses. Better not get careless and give myself away to unsuspecting humans.

We walked through the bowling alley. I looked over the top of my sunglasses. No suspicious auras.

Outside, heat waves shimmered over the empty cars in the parking lot. The intense California sun warmed me uncomfortably, and I retreated back into the shadow of the front awning.

The situation felt wrong. I walked around the bowling alley to the back.

A pair of pink human feet jutted over the rim of the Dumpster, toes up.

My *kundalini noir* twisted in distress. I didn't need to think too hard about whose feet they belonged to. I crept close—Coyote watching my back—and grasped the top of the metal Dumpster. I levitated and looked inside, hoping that I was mistaken.

The woman wore olive green capri pants and a yellow top. Her head rested against a pizza box, as if it were a pillow. A scarf in a flame motif covered her neck. Her eyes stared blankly at the sky. One blue flip-flop sat where it had been flung atop a plastic garbage bag. The other flip-flop had fallen into a big empty can of tomato sauce. A battered saxophone case was jammed into one corner of the Dumpster.

I touched her left leg. It was still warm.

I took off my sunglasses. The body emitted no aura. Rebecca Dwelling was dead.

CHAPTER
10

COYOTE WALKED TO THE DUMPSTER. He levitated to stand on the rim by Rebecca's feet and stared at her. He turned his ball cap backward, bent forward, and grasped her ankles. *"Watcha."* Look.

He lifted her body. A dozen flies took to the air and buzzed around us. "There are no wounds. No blood."

Coyote shook the body. Her ponytail and hands brushed across the garbage. "See how her head wobbles? Whoever attacked Rebecca twisted her neck like a bottle cap."

Even though she was dead, the way she dangled looked humiliating. "Do you have to do that?"

"Why?" Coyote answered. "If she starts complaining, that would be a good thing, no?"

Coyote let go of her ankles. Rebecca's head settled into a pile of juice cartons. Her legs doubled over so that she rested butt up in a perverse yogalike posture. Flies landed on the insoles of her feet. I wanted the toes to twitch, but of course, they didn't.

Rebecca's neck had been broken. I reached down and lifted her hand. I didn't see any hair, skin, or blood under the fingernails. There were no marks of a struggle on her or the surrounding ground. Which meant she was attacked with such surprise she didn't have a chance to defend herself.

She hadn't been dragged out here. Inside the Majestic Lanes, there had been no commotion. Rebecca must have known and trusted her vampire attacker.

My gaze returned to Rebecca's trim body and the still rosy skin. What a pity. Had I been more alert and less careless, I could've prevented her death. Here she was in her youthful prime, cut down to feed maggots.

Rebecca had been casually tossed into the Dumpster, which meant her killer wasn't worried about the police finding a corpse behind the Majestic Lanes. Maybe this happened often. After all, we were in L.A.

We were alone, but I figured not for long. To reassure myself, I touched the Colt pistol hidden under my shirt. "It's best that we leave." I didn't want to risk gunplay, not until I learned more.

Coyote turned his cap around. "I'm still hungry. Those nachos weren't much."

"After seeing Rebecca like that, you wanna eat?"

"*Vato,* no matter what happens, the world keeps spinning and your appetite returns."

I couldn't argue. We headed back to my car.

Coyote recommended a dive in Watts. Since I was the only one with money, I paid for the meal. We ate outside under a tattered picnic umbrella. Coyote had five beef and red chile tamales to my two. We smothered the tamales with blood from a bag I had stashed in my car.

I sipped a Carta Blanca.

Why was Rebecca killed? And why now? I assumed it was to keep her from talking to me.

The next question: what did she know?

I asked Coyote, "Why did you tell Rebecca about me?"

Coyote pushed a hunk of tamale through the blood on his plate. "Because, *carnal,* she was friends with Katz Meow. I knew Katz was looking for someone to solve Roxy's murder."

"How did you know that?"

"*Vato,* I listen to *chisme,* rumors. Roxy's death was suspiciously convenient for a lot of rich people."

"Like Cragnow?"

"Especially *ese culo vampiro.*" That vampire asshole.

"Did you know Roxy?"

"We never met."

"How did you know about Rebecca being friends with Katz?" I asked.

"I followed Katz around. She and Rebecca hung out together. I eavesdropped on them."

"They didn't notice?"

"No, but I was right there in plain sight." Coyote extended his index fingers, as if they were antennae sprouting from his forehead. "*Como una mosca.*" Like a fly.

"Katz needed help," he continued. "I recognized Rebecca from the Majestic Lanes. That's where I told her how Katz could find her champion."

"Champion? Me?"

Coyote licked a dollop of blood clinging, like sauce, to his mustache. He grinned. "*Símon.* Who else?"

"Rebecca was murdered just before I had a chance to question her. Who knew I was here? Katz. Cragnow and his goons. Lucky Rosario." The next name was difficult for me to say but I had to. "You, Coyote."

His eyes turned toward mine. He lapped blood from his fingertips and waited a moment before answering.

"*Hermano,* I knew you'd get around to that question. I should be offended but I'm not. You at least have the *cojones* to ask me to my face."

"What do you care about Roxy?"

"Maybe I don't. What's another dead human among the billions already here? But what I know is that Cragnow and his buddies who run this *nidus* are setting us vampires up for a disaster. This deal with humans, whatever it is, is a countdown to catastrophe."

"Why doesn't Cragnow see it that way?"

"Because he's blinded by arrogance and his thirst for power. *Vato,* I can't stop him alone."

Coyote took a swig from his beer and belched. "Felix, do you trust me or not?"

"I have to."

"Good, because I'm still hungry and I need to borrow something for a burrito."

I gave him a five. "Make it to go and keep the change." I heaped my bottle, plate, and napkins together and shoved them into an overflowing trash can. "There are others we need to question. Like Councilwoman Venin and Roxy Bronze's ex."

Coyote held up his plate and licked it clean. "Who'd be easier to get to?"

"Let's try the ex. Fred Daniels."

From Watts we took the Long Beach Freeway north toward Rosemead. I followed the directions from MapQuest on my wireless laptop. Coyote peeled back the aluminum foil of his burrito and ate.

I told him what I'd learned about Roxy from my research before leaving Denver. She had been married to Fred Daniels, who introduced her to the porn business. Together they were to be the first couple of smut. Daniels took the screen name of Peter Pipe.

A year later, Peter Pipe and Roxy Bronze quit billing themselves as a couple. Except for gay porn, the business was all about women, unless the guy had a prodigious pipe, which Daniels didn't. He worked as her manager and, like his on-camera "acting," failed at that. Daniels occupied himself with booze, cocaine, and the easy pickings around porn sets. Roxy was Daniels's meal ticket until she jettisoned him after a nasty divorce.

I found the address and parked against the curb.

"Que bonito chante," Coyote said. What nice digs.

The house was a fine example of midcentury Atomic Ranch: a big picture window, long horizontal lines, and plenty of ochre-colored brick. The garage doors were closed.

I removed my sunglasses and sat in the car for a moment. I studied the well-kept neighborhood and scanned for suspicious auras. Coyote and I then got out. The lawn smelled freshly watered.

The front door was tucked into an outdoor foyer paved with flagstone. A decal to an alarm company decorated the glass bricks around the main entrance.

I looked through the window in the door and saw the alarm on the opposite wall. It read: SET.

"Let's go around back," I said.

Coyote brushed past me. *"Pa'que?"* What for?

He touched the door handle. The alarm flashed DISABLED, and the dead bolt snapped. He pushed the door open.

Coyote gave a broad, ragged-toothed smile. "I can do more than look handsome."

Ugly, tricky bastard.

The air inside was cool and moist. A welcome relief after the rush-hour drive under the sun's punishing glare.

Lounge music drifted from the stereo receiver on a buffet table. I couldn't detect the presence of anyone in the house.

Coyote walked across the front room to check the hall. I went into the kitchen.

A glass pitcher with iced lemonade and a half-empty bottle of white rum rested on the counter. The sliding glass doors at the back of the kitchen opened to a fenced yard with a swimming pool.

I stepped around the counter and paused at the threshold to replace my sunglasses to temper the harsh sunlight. A terrazzo walkway surrounded the pool. The only sound was the gurgle of the pool filter.

Beyond the pool was a strip of lawn bordered by rose-bushes and boxwood shrubs. White plastic chairs sat on the grass.

I was sure the house was Daniels's divorce settlement. Probably the only smart move in his life was that he married an ambitious porn star and mooched off her for all he could get.

Where was Daniels? The way my case was going, I wouldn't be surprised to find his drowned corpse lying on the bottom of the pool. I walked to the water's edge, expecting to find his bloated and dead face.

"Don't you move."

I turned to the left.

There was a stainless steel outdoor bar at the corner of the yard, under the shade of two magnolia trees.

Fred Daniels rose from behind the bar and aimed a Beretta pistol.

CHAPTER
11

DON'T DO ANYTHING STUPID," I said evenly.
    Daniels looked like he did in his photos. Late twenties. Blue eyes empty of deep thought. An impossibly smooth forehead, probably from overdoing Botox.

He was shorter than me. Very tan. His brown hair was gelled into spikes with blond highlights. A cream-colored linen shirt sagged over his lean torso. In his pictures he flashed a smile; here he threatened with a scowl and a 9mm pistol.

The muzzle of the Beretta and the gold links of his tennis bracelet trembled. With his left hand, Daniels picked up a glass tumbler from the bar. I smelled the lemonade and rum.

Keeping his gaze fixed on me—a gold piercing cinched over his eyebrow—he brought the tumbler to his lips and gulped nervously. Lemonade dripped down his chin and to his shirt. He set the tumbler down, and the ice tinkled. He wiped his chin and rubbed his fingers against his shirt. The trembling of his hand eased and the black malevolent hole of the gun barrel held steady on me.

I calculated my options.

Daniels stood about thirty feet away. Too far to zap with hypnosis even after I removed my sunglasses. I could try and rush him, but that would risk getting shot. Or I could draw my pistol and start blasting. But I needed to ask questions. Better that I let him drink until Dutch courage turned into a drunken stupor.

Daniels kept the muzzle trained on my chest. "How'd you get in without tripping the alarm?"

"I opened the door. If that's a problem, talk to your security company."

"Unless I shoot you as a trespasser. Then it'd be *your* problem."

Cheeky dipshit had better mind his manners.

In my short stay so far in L.A., pistols seemed as ubiquitous as sunglasses. "You always keep a gun handy?"

"Cragnow warned me."

That double-dealing undead son of a bitch. He wanted my help and then alerted Daniels to meet me with a pistol at the ready. What was Cragnow's agenda? What didn't he want me to know?

"Warned you about what?" I took a step toward Daniels.

"Don't come closer. Cragnow said to tell you that he gave me special bullets. I don't know what's so special about them, but he said you'd know what he meant."

Damn right I did. Silver bullets. Probably painted to look like regular steel-jacketed slugs. I could take several hits to my body with conventional bullets; one silver bullet in the right place would leave me flopping on the terrazzo like a speared fish.

The afternoon sun reflected off the pool and into Daniels's face. The gold hoops of his earrings glittered. He squinted, and his free hand groped for the Ray-Bans lying on the bar. Daniels put the sunglasses on. Now if I wanted to hypnotize him, I'd have to get close enough to knock off his shades.

He hadn't shot me yet, and the way he held the pistol signaled that he wasn't comfortable with violence.

"What now, Lone Ranger?" I asked. "You going to use those *special* bullets?"

Daniels relaxed. "Look man, I just want to be left alone."

"I got no problem with that." I kept my arms loose and gestured with my hands, palms up. "How about we just talk about your ex."

"What for?" The edge in his voice returned. He steadied the pistol. "The police know everything. You could wallpaper the city with what's been printed about me and Roxy. There ain't nothing more to say."

"I'm not convinced of that," I replied. "Every time I mention Roxy's name, people act like roaches about to scatter."

"Why don't you scatter?"

I couldn't wait to hurt this douche bag. Fist, then fangs. Where was Coyote? I could use him to distract Daniels.

"You know where I could find Katz Meow?"

"Ask Cragnow. She worked for him."

A cell phone resting on the bar chimed.

"Step back," Daniels said.

I didn't.

The pistol went off. The bullet ricocheted between my legs. Daniels seemed as astonished as I was.

The phone kept chiming.

Daniels's surprised expression turned into a sneer. "Hey, that wasn't hard." His grip tightened on the Beretta. "Now get back."

Luckily, the last shot was low. The next one might hit my belly, or worse. I took a step back.

His eyes remained fixed on me and he picked up the phone. "Yeah I know exactly where he's at." Daniels smirked. "Right in front of me."

He folded the cell phone and his shoulders relaxed. "Cragnow's men are on the way." His smirk deepened. "Maybe *they* can help you find Katz."

Why did mention of Cragnow's goons sound like bad news?

Coyote stumbled out of the kitchen. Daniels swung the pistol toward him.

"Don't shoot," I yelled.

Coyote spit an ice cube and tipped the empty pitcher of lemonade over his upturned face. *"Estoy bien pedo."* I'm really shit-faced.

Daniels stabbed the Beretta toward me, then to Coyote, and at me again. "Don't move."

Coyote lurched to the edge of the pool, teetered, and dropped the pitcher into the water.

"What the hell you doing?" shouted Daniels. "Get against the wall, the both of you."

"Good idea," Coyote mumbled. He staggered close to the wall and unzipped his jeans over a row of potted flowers. "All that lemonade has gotta come out. Might as well make it now, bro."

"Not on my plants," Daniels whined. He stepped from behind the bar. "Get back from them, you drunken wetback bastard."

I lunged forward. Daniels jerked his gun toward me and popped a round that zinged past my ear.

"¡Al la Madre!" Holy Mother! Coyote jumped from the wall. A stream of fire shot from his crotch onto a big chrysanthemum. *"¡Auxilio! ¡Auxilio! Llamen los bombaderos."* Help! Help! Call the fire department.

Flames rolled against the stucco wall and turned into black smoke that curled back on us.

Daniels started shooting again. The bullets peppered the air. One of those bullets was bound to hit Coyote or me.

I grabbed Coyote by his collar and yanked him into the kitchen.

Bullets cracked against the sliding glass door.

A wall of fire erupted across the kitchen threshold behind us.

I ran out the front door and dragged Coyote along. His feet slammed against the furniture. Fire dribbled from his open fly. We got into my car. Smoke mushroomed over the roof of Daniels's home like it had been hit by artillery.

Once the engine kicked over, I stomped on the accelerator. My tires screeched like banshees with hemorrhoids. Coyote fumbled with his zipper.

My *kundalini noir* settled enough for me to finally speak. "How'd you do that?"

"*Fácil, vato.*" Easy, dude. "I had to pee really bad."

"I mean pissing fire."

Coyote sucked air through his teeth and appeared contrite. "My fault. I keep forgetting that I shouldn't drink rum." He cupped his balls. "Next time I might end up with *huevos flambé*."

"Stay away if you decide to fart," I said. "That would be another Hiroshima. Anyway, thanks for saving me."

"Don't mention it, *carnal.*"

I headed south on the freeway.

Fred Daniels was the weasel I expected him to be. Trouble was, he acted like a cornered weasel—holding a gun loaded with silver bullets. At least he was alive. For now. Which meant I could get to him later.

And Cragnow? He was hiding something. Why else would he ask me to help him, then turn around and warn Daniels? And he gave him the deadly bullets, meaning that if all went to shit during my visit, the chances were good that I'd be the one full of holes.

"If all my leads are going to be so much trouble," I thought aloud, "this is going to be a long investigation."

"Felix, *no te preocupes,*" Coyote said. Don't worry.

"Are you talking in a general sense or is there something else?" I replied.

He shrugged.

"Don't play games, Coyote."

He grasped the door handle. "Too bad, *vato,* because that's all I know."

Coyote pushed the door open. Traffic was heavy and moved at a steady clip of forty-five miles an hour. He tumbled out. The door slammed shut and the lock snapped closed.

Astonished by his departure, I tapped my brakes and looked into the mirror, but as a vampire, Coyote wouldn't show. I craned my neck, expecting to see him dodging cars that swerved and were panic-stopped.

Nothing. Just lines of automobiles rolling in long, impatient columns.

Coyote was gone. Quick as a blink.

Don't worry, Coyote had said. What did he mean? Would I see him again?

The car behind me blared its horn. I resumed speed and headed for my hotel and a much needed rest. Thinking that I might have trouble finding a coffin to sleep in, I had brought inversion boots and planned to relax hanging upside down in a closet.

Back in my room, the red light on the telephone flashed. I retrieved the message.

"Felix Gomez, my name is Veronica Torres."

Roxy's partner in their campaign that undermined Project Eleven. A sworn enemy of Lucky Rosario and councilwoman Petale Venin, among others.

How did Veronica know I was here?

She spoke crisply, with an intriguing lilt to her Chicana barrio accent. Puerto Rican? Central American? "I got a text message asking me to call you . . ."

Message from whom? Coyote?

". . . something to do with Roxy Bronze. If you can, let's meet tomorrow morning. Here's my number . . ."

When I called Veronica back, I asked if she knew who had left the text message. She didn't and told me caller ID said the number was unknown.

I asked if she knew anyone named Coyote. She didn't

know that either. Finally I asked, "Don't you think it's strange you got an anonymous message to call me?"

She replied, "There's a lot of things about Roxy's death that are strange. An anonymous message to call you is the least of them."

We made an appointment to meet at 9 A.M. at the Barrios Unidos center in Pacoima.

I rigged a chin-up bar inside the closet. After I undressed and put on my pajamas, I latched the inversion boots around my shins and hooked the boots over the chin-up bar. Vampires can defy gravity but only through conscious effort. If I planted my feet against the ceiling and dozed off, gravity would pull me down.

I put my cell phone and the loaded Colt pistol on the floor within arm's reach. As I hung there, waiting for sleep, I worked the investigation over in my head.

Until now, I had thought of only three motives for Roxy's murder: revenge for thwarting Project Eleven; interfering with Cragnow's scheme of vampire–human collusion; and leaving Gomorrah Video.

Perhaps I overlooked an equally compelling and sinister motive. Who else would profit from her death? I stuck on the word *profit*.

Profit as in money.

My hacker told me Roxy Bronze had a million-dollar insurance policy that paid out to two parties. Half of the million dollars went to Barrios Unidos. The other half went to the Open Hand in Reseda, a nonprofit medical clinic for porn actors and other sex workers.

Could someone at either of these places have put the bullet in Roxy's skull?

The idea was almost too fantastic to contemplate. Nonprofits were always scrambling for money. Murdering someone for the insurance payout was a dangerous scheme as a fund-raiser. Then again, it was half a million dollars.

CHAPTER
12

THE NEXT MORNING I arrived in Pacoima—a blue-collar Latino community on the north side of the San Fernando Valley. Small homes stood beside subsidized housing projects. People who tended gardens and cleaned toilets for the rich had to live somewhere.

Even with supernatural mojo, I still felt queasy coming here. Since I had left many years ago, vowing never to return, I had graduated from college, gone to war, become a vampire, and settled in Denver. And here I was, back in Pacoima anyway.

Terrific.

Once I got off the freeway, I drove north a few blocks. Surprisingly, Pacoima looked a lot better than I remembered. I counted only one boarded-up storefront and no abandoned cars. Small shops lined the boulevard: nail salons, taco stands, auto parts. I turned right at the corner with a convenience store and gas pumps that used to be a vacant lot.

Barrios Unidos occupied a cinder block building whose original tenant was a Pentecostal church. Beige paint blotches covered graffiti on the walls and the base of the steeple. Weeds and trash collected along a chain-link fence. I parked at the end of a row of a half-dozen cars in the gravel lot.

I entered through double doors that had steel mesh over the windows. A threadbare carpet covered the floor, which creaked when I walked in. From behind the closed door of an adjoining room, children sang a folk tune in Spanish. An easel held a calendar listing the center's events for the month: kindergarten, literacy programs, prenatal clinics, Friday open-mike poetry, and a workshop for novice writers.

The front hall doubled as an art gallery. The exhibition was a series of modern interpretations of the Virgin of Guadalupe. The Virgin as seamstress. The Virgin wearing boxing gloves. The Virgin working the drive-thru window at McDonald's.

At the end of the hall stood a table heaped with dried flowers and small mementos. On the wall above the table was a portrait of the Virgin, but the face of this Virgin belonged to Roxy Bronze.

To the left hung a framed front page of the *Los Angeles Times* dated from seven months ago. The headline read, PROJECT ELEVEN IS A GONER. Below the headline, there was a photo of a victorious crowd waving banners on the steps of L.A. City Hall and giving the thumbs-up.

A door to the right of the table opened into an office. There was one desk when I walked in and two more along the far wall. A pair of young women sat at these desks, their backs to me as they chatted on phones and tapped on keyboards.

A woman stood by the first desk, a battered piece of furniture that looked donated from a thrift store. A paper taped to the desk had the words OPERATIONAL MANAGER marked through and replaced with, *La Reña de Todo.* The Queen of Everything.

Her head was tipped to one side, and she raked a brush

through her wavy brown locks. The air around her smelled of apricot shampoo.

"I'm looking for Veronica Torres," I said.

The woman waved the brush. "That's me."

I introduced myself. Veronica was taller than I expected. We were almost eye to eye. I glanced to see if she wore heels. Nope. Sandals.

She looked to be in her midthirties. A very well preserved midthirties. A trim form in blue capris and a matching sleeveless blouse. High cheekbones and smooth skin a nice mestiza hue of *café con leche*. Her alert mahogany brown eyes complemented the inviting curve of her smile with its glamour magazine gloss. And she had a taut, succulent neck. The gums around my incisors began to itch.

She asked if I had problems finding the center. Considering that I was here to discuss the murder of her friend, Veronica's tone seemed unusually casual and loose.

Boxes filled with papers lay about haphazardly, making the place look like a recycling bin instead of an office.

Veronica pointed her brush to a chair beside the desk. I removed a carton of markers from the chair and sat.

She resumed brushing her hair and looked at me through the corner of one eye, a reaction that made me suspect a patch of pale skin was showing through my makeup.

I touched my cheek. "It's a skin condition. My souvenir from the Iraq war. Nothing to worry about."

Veronica nodded. She dropped the brush into an open gym bag between her desk and a swivel chair.

I heard the quick steps of a child approach. A toddler rushed into the office. A plump woman in a Guatemalan peasant dress hustled in, apologizing, and took the little rug rat with her.

Veronica waved good-bye and settled into the swivel chair. The open laptop on her desk said she had fifty-six new emails.

"When we talked earlier, you said you were an investigator. But you didn't say what kind." She closed the laptop. "You don't seem like a cop."

"I'm a private investigator. Katz Meow hired me." I waited for Veronica to respond to the name.

She turned her head and broke eye contact. Her jaw hardened and her breathing slowed. At times like this I wished my contacts were out so I could read auras and determine how genuine these reactions were. But I couldn't risk revealing myself, not here with these ankle biters running loose and getting in the way.

After a moment she brought those big brown eyes back to me. "Felix, whoever murdered Roxy needs to be punished."

"I'm here to make that happen. First, any idea where I could find Katz?"

"No." Veronica shook her head. "We weren't friends. I only met her once."

The phone rang. A young woman at the opposite side of the office answered and called out, "Veronica, line one."

"Take a message," Veronica replied in Spanish. "Tell them I'm busy with an appointment." She spoke with a rapid-fire Central America staccato that made her English seem like a drawl.

"Where are you from?" I asked.

"Panama," she replied.

"That's a long way from L.A. What drew you here?"

"*Chicanismo* is a state of mind. The barrio called and I answered."

The diploma on the wall was her master's in nonprofit management from George Mason University. I could imagine Veronica at any major foundation as the resident Latina hotshot. Instead of a nice salary with fat perks, Veronica slogged through the trenches on behalf of this community for what she could make managing a Burger King.

Veronica didn't see Pacoima the same way I did. For me, it was a dump to escape as soon as I could. For her, this was a place where she could fight injustice and bring hope.

I gestured toward the art exhibit in the hall. "Roxy must have made quite an impression on the people here."

"She was one of the most charismatic women I've ever met." Sadness tarnished Veronica's features. I preferred to see her smile.

"You're a community activist. Roxy was a porn star. What brought you together?"

"One day, she walked in to offer both her time and money to help stop Project Eleven."

"And that meant what to you?"

"Are you kidding?" Veronica replied. "This is not some black-tie nonprofit like save the sea otters or whatever. We're always short of volunteers and funds. Project Eleven was going to stomp through Pacoima like Godzilla. Roxy was our patron saint."

A porn star saint? "In what way?"

"In a huge way. Her money paid for advertising. Mailers. Legal help. Pro bono only goes so far. Plus we could bus residents to council meetings. Stopping Project Eleven was a drain on our time. Roxy's generous support let us hire extra staff."

"But at first," I asked, "a wealthy porn star arrives here, checkbook in hand, didn't that seem suspicious?"

"Hell yeah, it was suspicious. This is Pacoima. Shit like that never happens. Our fight against Project Eleven was going to be a public relations battle. This smelled like a setup. I get help from a porn star and I'd be handing our enemies ammunition."

"What did you tell Roxy?" I asked.

Veronica folded her hands on the desk. Her fingernails were short and painted bright red, just like her toenails. She had silver rings on her index fingers and a matching band on her left thumb.

"I told Roxy it wasn't my place to judge. She was upfront about how she made her money. I'm no prude, but I didn't like it. That business is all about the exploitation of women. Roxy's success was the exception."

"What changed your mind?"

"I never changed my mind about pornography. But I came to respect and admire Roxy."

"Seems she would've been the worst kind of magnet for slander and a big distraction from the campaign."

"She was. Those Project Eleven bastards were ruthless vampires."

The word shocked me. "Vampires?"

Veronica snapped her teeth in a playful gesture. "Absolutely. They were a gang of bloodsuckers. We tried our best to drive a stake through their evil hearts."

"You're joking."

She settled against the back of her chair. "You're taking me literally, aren't you?"

I forced a sheepish smile. "Of course not. It was just an unusual choice of words."

Veronica reached across the desk and grasped my wrist. The touch of her silver rings burned my skin but I didn't flinch. The pain curled my toes. I clenched my other hand to endure the agony.

"You should've seen your face," she said. "It was like you really believed in vampires."

I wanted to yelp in distress and could barely hold my smile. "Silly me."

Veronica pulled her hand back. The relief was exhilarating. I dropped my wrist from her view to hide the scorch marks.

Veronica wrinkled her nose. With a puzzled expression, she looked around the office. "Do you smell that?"

"Smell what?" My seared flesh, what else?

"Chicharones."

Great, I've always wanted to remind a woman of pork rinds.

Veronica showed me a photo of Roxy and her standing together, smiling like sisters.

"They attacked Roxy again and again but it always backfired. Like when Councilman Krutz, the pious windbag *cabrón,* thumped the Bible about protecting *his* community's values. According to him, taking money from that *puta* was a bribe from the devil."

Veronica's cheeks dimpled and a smile warmed her words. "Roxy worked her connections in the adult trade, then brought a cute young male escort to a Project Eleven meeting. The kid winked at Krutz, who toppled over with a heart attack and was wheeled out on a gurney. You didn't need a script to know what that was all about."

"With you and Roxy spending so much time together," I said, "that must have created rumors of you two being . . . lesbians."

Veronica crossed her legs. "For the record, Felix, I've never munched a rug in my life."

So what if she had? Veronica could nosh on me while I munched her rug. In the time I'd been here, it was a heroic effort on my part not to stare and drool at the choicest parts of her body.

But I hadn't come here to make Veronica or sink my fangs into her tempting neck. As noble as Veronica appeared to be, the chance to score a half-million dollars could twist anyone's principles. Maybe the idea of killing Roxy for insurance money wasn't so far-fetched.

"Barrios Unidos was a beneficiary of Roxy's life insurance. Five hundred thousand dollars." I studied Veronica's expression. "What happened to the money?"

"The money was nothing compared to losing Roxy." Veronica paused and bit her lower lip. She closed her eyes, opened them, and said, "It's in the center's trust account."

"Meaning you haven't spent it?"

"We draw from the interest. To pay operating expenses. Get new projects started." She motioned to the clutter around us. "It's obvious that fixing up this place hasn't been a priority."

So far it seemed that Veronica's involvement with Roxy's murder was about as plausible as me getting a halo. Still, I needed to verify it through hypnosis. "What did Roxy do as a volunteer?"

"She was great at digging out facts about Project Eleven."

"Such as?"

"Conflicts of interest. 'Independent' consultants not disclosing that they worked for the developers. Contracts let out ahead of time. Silent partners who were not so silent. Off-the-record meetings between elected officials and lobbyists."

"Sounds like business as usual for a city project. What was so different about this?"

"The blatant audacity. It began when Lucky Rosario's people showed up and threatened my staff with trespass. This center was scheduled for demolition, even though Barrios Unidos owns the building. That's how I learned about Project Eleven."

"There was no public comment?" I asked.

"Only the pretense. The Project Eleven committee intended to sneak this three-hundred-million-dollar stinker past us." Veronica went to the window and raised the blinds. "See this neighborhood? It was to be bulldozed for a corporate office park and hotel. That library"—she pointed to a green building with a curved roof—"was only recently built. Still, the city was going to tear it down because it was in the way of progress."

"I was told Project Eleven would bring jobs."

"Oh yeah. Replace family-owned businesses with dead-end service work. Project Eleven was a scam, a huge bag of stinking pork. Know what made it worse? The project was to be paid for by a special tax levied against us, the community. In other words, we were to pay Project Eleven to screw us."

Veronica returned to her desk and rummaged through the gym bag. She brought out a pair of high-heel pumps. "But this Project Eleven Godzilla made one mistake."

"What was that?"

Veronica pointed the shoes' long, slender heels at me.

"They never thought we'd come after them with stilettos. You know, woman-power. Roxy and me."

I reflected on the surroundings: the dilapidated furnishings, the cracked plaster, the mountains of boxes, and wondered about Roxy's true motives. Why had she come to Barrios Unidos to join their battle against Project Eleven?

"What was Roxy getting out of this?"

"*¿Quien sabe?*" Who knows? Veronica put the high heels back into her gym bag. She sat again, propped one elbow on the desk, and circled her fingers through her hair. "Roxy had her demons."

"What demons?"

"I don't know. For all the time we spent together, she kept a lot to herself. But Roxy had something to prove. To whom? *No se.*" Veronica shrugged.

"There are two players I don't see involved in this," I said. "Cragnow Vissoom. Roxy's former boss at Gomorrah Video. If anyone had it in for her, it would've been him. What about Councilwoman Venin? She was the force behind Project Eleven. But I don't see a connection between Cragnow and Project Eleven." Or between Project Eleven and vampire–human collusion. "There are a lot of missing pieces to this puzzle."

"Maybe the next step," Veronica said, "will be to find out what demons brought Roxy Bronze to the barrio."

CHAPTER 13

VERONICA SAID, "We need privacy."
    We certainly did.

She scooped her cell phone from atop her desk and slipped the phone into the small cargo pocket of her capris. "Let's go outside."

That wasn't the privacy I had in mind, to be honest. I was hoping for a room with a locked door. And a bed.

I followed her out to a side hall, through a cluttered but clean kitchen, and to a door between a refrigerator and the pantry. Veronica turned around and pushed against the latching bar of the door with her round and attractive rump.

We stepped onto a concrete slab surrounded by scruffy grass and picnic tables. Veronica led me to a concrete bench beneath a carob tree.

The hot California sun pressed through the thin spots in my makeup and sunscreen. The shade under the tree was a refreshing shelter.

With her attention away from me, I removed my contacts and put them in their plastic case. Veronica's red aura glowed like the filament of an electric bulb.

Veronica sat and dug a packet of Nicorette gum from her pocket. She popped a tablet into her mouth and turned to face me.

Our eyes locked. Her aura pulsed in surprise. Her eyebrows arced and her pupils opened like twin camera apertures. I caught her at midchew, and the ball of gum sat between the teeth in her open mouth. The look was unbecoming, so I flicked the wad away and closed her jaw.

I sat beside her and grasped her hands to massage the webs of flesh between her thumbs and index fingers. I stared into the concentric brown and black circles of her irises and pupils. Now to get the obvious questions out of the way.

"Veronica, did you kill Roxy Bronze?"

She took one slow breath. Then another. "No."

That answer was comforting. I had plans for Veronica other than seeing her cuffed and taken to jail.

"Veronica, do you know who killed Roxy?"

Another breath and another comforting "No."

"What about vampires?"

Another no.

At least I knew enough to cross her off my list of suspects.

Veronica remained still, her mind pliant as clay. Her smooth and elegant neck beckoned. My fangs protruded.

The lot behind Barrios Unidos faced the back fences of neighborhood homes and their cluttered yards. Other than a few cars passing on the side streets, we were alone.

This was going to be easy. If I embraced her, we'd look like we were necking. Really necking.

I brushed the hair back from her collar to bare her neck. The top two buttons of her blouse were open, revealing a nice crease between her breasts. A lacy, powder blue brassiere cupped her full bosom. I fought the temptation to undo the rest of the buttons and slip a hand into her blouse.

Okay, so it was creepy of me to hypnotize a woman and think about copping a feel. But I'm a vampire, not a Boy Scout. I bite people on the neck and suck their blood. Occasionally I even kill them. Compared to that, putting my hand under Veronica's blouse would be like swiping a pen from work.

Besides, sex with a vampire was an extraordinary thrill. At least, that's what I told myself.

Desire pumped into my crotch. Feeding on her wouldn't be enough. But out here in the open? No, the rest would wait for later. I held Veronica by the shoulders and brought my fangs to her neck.

She was a fountain of appetizing aromas. The sweet shampoo, lilac soap, her morning coffee, peppermint from the gum, and an underlying scent of pheromones. The anticipation of tasting her skin and blood made my mouth water.

The sudden and loud caw of a crow grabbed me by the ears.

I pulled away from Veronica and wiped the drool from my lips. A crow stared from the rain gutter along the eave of the Barrios Unidos roof. The bird cawed again, louder this time. I didn't know if it was the same crow that delivered my orders from the Araneum back in Denver. Even if it wasn't, I got the message.

We're watching you, Felix. Get your ass back to work.

My fangs retracted. The warm swelling in my crotch ebbed with frustration. I smoothed Veronica's hair over her collar.

The crow sidestepped along the rain gutter, its claws ticking against the metal. Its beady eyes gave me the harsh glare of a zealous chaperone.

I closed Veronica's eyes and massaged between her thumbs and fingers again. Her aura dimmed as she relaxed. I commanded her to awake.

In the moment that I waited for Veronica to come to, I put my contacts back in and thought about what clues I hoped to find here.

Veronica opened her eyes. "What was I saying?" She touched her forehead in an absentminded gesture. "I lost my train of thought."

"We were going to talk about Roxy Bronze and her demons."

Veronica nodded. Her face took on a dark hue. She reached for a pod of carob seeds on the ground and picked at it. As Veronica shared what she knew about Roxy, the crow lifted from the rain gutter and flew off, the feathered bastard.

Veronica repeated what I had already learned on my own. When she was done, Veronica kept quiet until the gloss from the tears in her eyes faded.

She dropped the carob pod. "Know what 'Freya' means?"

"It's the Norse goddess of love and beauty," I replied.

"An appropriate name." Veronica blotted her eyes and wiped her fingertips across one thigh.

I was a vampire, supposedly cold and hard like iron. But the sincerity of Veronica's affection for Roxy warmed me. I wanted to share that affection, and suddenly I felt myself wanting to know Veronica as man to woman, not vampire to prey.

She asked, "Do you know what happened to Dr. Freya Krieger?"

"Roxy . . . Freya was accused of negligence in the death of a patient and had her license suspended by the state medical board," I said.

"That was the official version. A guy I dated . . ."

Dated? Past tense I hoped.

". . . a lawyer . . ."

Sleep with the dogs, why don't you?

". . . told me of cocktail gossip among the attorneys. Roxy had been railroaded by the medical board to protect the head surgeon and staff at La Brea."

"I read about the investigation in the *L.A. Times*," I said. "There was also a long feature in one of the weeklies."

"The controversy was that there were three different versions of what happened." The quickening tempo of Veronica's words matched the rising emotion in her voice. "The first was that the patient died of complications. It was supposed to be a routine bypass. It didn't help that he was a smoker. And two hundred pounds overweight. Despite 'heroic measures' by the team, he died on the operating table."

"That's the first version," I said. "The second concerned Roxy's trouble with the hospital's report of the patient's death."

"That's right," Veronica said. "She confronted the staff and the head surgeon, Dr. Mordecai Niphe. Then she filed a complaint with the state board."

"Roxy took on the head surgeon?" I asked. "As an intern? What made her do that?"

"Duty, if you knew Roxy. She said Dr. Niphe was negligent. He ignored the anesthetist's warnings. The patient suffered pulmonary arrest and died needlessly. Roxy accused the hospital of fabricating records. You know, to protect the surgeon and themselves."

"And the inquiry turned against her?"

"Yes. Suddenly every doctor who had ever known Roxy came forward with the same testimony. That she was arrogant. That she was brash. Reckless with protocol. Incompetent. These were the same people who had praised her before." Veronica's voice cracked. "Now they said you couldn't trust Roxy with a Q-tip, let alone a scalpel. La Brea changed its story, too. They admitted to 'therapeutic misadventures.'"

"What's that?"

"Medical-speak for 'the doctor killed the patient.'"

"Why would they say that?"

"To protect Roxy, if you can believe that. The hospital settled with the patient's family to get the mess over with."

"And Roxy?"

"They wanted to make an example out of her for betraying Dr. Niphe." Veronica reached into her pocket and pulled out the cell phone. "You should talk to someone who was there. Roxy's lawyer. I'll text you his number."

"The way she was crucified by her colleagues, this lawyer doesn't seem to have been that good."

"Actually, he's one of the best. Medical malpractice and fighting the state board is his specialty. But even his legal juju wasn't enough." Veronica scrolled through the address book of the cell phone and tapped some keys. "The fight bankrupted her. Dr. Freya Krieger was ruined forever. If she appealed, then what? Who would hire her? Where would she work? After the board suspended her license, she disappeared. Then she resurfaced as Roxy Bronze."

"What's this lawyer's name?"

"Andrew Tonic."

"As in gin and tonic?"

"More like vodka and tonic."

"How do you have his number? Is he the lawyer you dated?"

"Oh no." Veronica laughed, which sounded pleasant. "The men I date must have a soul."

Definite speed bump.

"And he's married," Veronica continued. "I hit Tonic up for a pledge to Barrios Unidos. Tried to pull a sentimental string about Roxy. What a waste of time. Try and imagine a sentimental lawyer."

"What did Tonic tell you about Roxy?"

"Nada," Roxy said. "The records were sealed. Tonic had nothing to gain by telling me anything."

"Why should I talk to him?"

"Because, Felix"—Veronica gave me a sly wink—"I have a suspicion that you can get Tonic to say more than he should."

How much did Veronica know about me? "Why would you say that?"

Veronica's brow wrinkled and she pulled away. "If you're not a hotshot detective, then what are you doing here?"

"Obviously not impressing you."

Veronica smiled. "I'll hit the reset button. You get another chance."

"Thanks. Where was Roxy's family in all this?" I asked.
"L.A. was her hometown."

"For that, *tenia un candado en la boca.*" She had a pad-lock on her mouth. "She didn't open. I wouldn't pry. What I learned about Roxy's past I found on my own. She acted as if Dr. Freya Krieger had never existed."

"Does seem strange," I said. "On the one hand, she buries her past, then throws herself as a porn star into the public eye of her home community. Every one of them would have recognized Roxy Bronze as Freya Krieger. Maybe those were the demons that brought her to Barrios Unidos. To let the world know that she's resurrected herself and to say, look, I'm still here and raising hell."

"Perhaps. Roxy always went forward at maximum speed, *como una nave.*" Like a ship.

"Still, that's quite a fall. From surgeon to porn star. Such a life-changing experience can disturb you." Take my word for it. I'd gone from soldier to vampire in one snafu-filled night.

"We never talked about it. Being a porn star allowed Roxy to get rich. She saw how the truth was perverted to destroy her. So her reputation didn't matter."

No doubt. Fame as the champion mouth of circle-sucks meant you had long since given up any notion of being elected Miss America.

"Felix, I'm glad you're here. It's time someone asked questions about what happened to Roxy. The police never did." Veronica stood. "I hope I was able to help you."

"I still don't see a connection linking the medical com-munity, Project Eleven, and Roxy. Whatever harm the staff at La Brea wanted to inflict upon her, seems they'd done a good job. No reason to follow that up with murder."

Veronica brushed dust and carob leaves from the back of her capris. I would've helped but I was afraid that damn crow would return. She started for the door into Barrios Unidos.

Veronica led me through the building and to the entrance,

a polite way of sending me off without saying so. She laid her hand on my shoulder, an act I couldn't decide was friendly or forward.

"Call me," she said. "I want to hear what Andrew Tonic says."

"Over coffee, then."

"No. Over dinner." She pushed away, waved, and turned around.

Provided that nosy crow left me alone, I was going to get lucky. And I didn't even need vampire powers.

My next stop would be La Brea Mercy Hospital. I'd see if I could unseal those records.

I drove south on Van Nuys Boulevard and stopped to get waved through a construction zone near the westbound on-ramp for the Golden State Freeway. A homeless bum on the median solicited donations by shaking a Styrofoam cup.

My fingertips tingled. A warning? Of what? A slight tremor started up my legs. Earthquake?

The tingle in my fingers became a buzz of alarm. At the edge of my left peripheral vision, I saw it. A dump truck charged out of a parking lot, crossed the·street, and flattened a line of orange traffic cones. The immense truck rumbled toward me like an avalanche of steel.

CHAPTER
14

IN THAT INSTANT before the dump truck turned my
sedan into a heap of crumpled steel and plastic, I undid my
safety belt, opened the door, and bolted clear. Even vampires panic, and how fast I had moved surprised even me.
Hell, a mongoose would've been impressed.

The cops arrived. A patrol woman asked, "Sure you're
okay?"

My *kundalini noir* settled. "I'm doing better than my
car."

Firefighters aimed a hose to wash the fluids leaking from
under what was left of my rental sedan. Fragments of shattered glass glittered in the puddles.

The dump truck had struck the left rear door and crunched
over the roof. My driver's seat was wadded inside the pile of
mangled steel and under the huge tires of this enormous
truck.

Four other patrol cars and two motorcycles had arrived.

The cops shepherded traffic past the accident scene and through the construction bottleneck.

The homeless bum staggered from the median toward us. His eyes were wide circles of astonishment on his unwashed, bearded face. He pointed at me with his Styrofoam cup. "I saw that. You . . . you moved faster than a goddamn bullet."

The female cop looked at him, then at me.

I said, "A regular bullet perhaps but not a goddamn bullet."

The bum stumbled close. He carried a stink like sour milk. He squinted. "Ask him how he done that?" The bum paused for a moment to steady himself. "One second he's in the car, then poof, I seen him standing right there."

The cop waved him back. "I'll get to you in a second, sir." She faced me and shook her head. "Isn't even noon yet and he's beyond shit-faced. Gonna be a long day."

The cop finished taking my statement while her partner interviewed a number of bystanders. No one could verify where the runaway truck had come from. The truck had barreled out of the parking lot, and my vehicle was the only one hit. It had obviously come for me.

The truck had no plate or company markings. The construction crew didn't own it. The female cop guessed the truck was stolen. "Miracle you survived."

Some miracle all right. A stolen truck with no one in the cab just happened to hit *only* my car.

A black Ford Crown Victoria—all it needed was a banner on the roof that said UNMARKED POLICE CAR—drove over the curb and parked on the sidewalk close to the wreckage. A dark-skinned man got out of the passenger's side. His complexion looked like umber paint right out of the tube. His nappy black Chia Pet head had a reflection highlight at the front of his receding hairline. He wore a shiny gray shirt with the cuffs rolled back, a fashionable tie, and wraparound sunglasses. He slipped an ID tag out of his shirt pocket and let the tag dangle on a cloth neckband. The sun glistened off the police badge clipped to his belt next to a compact pistol.

He brought the vampire equivalent of B.O., a faint cadaverous odor he disguised with Aramis cologne. I read his ID. Julius Paxton. Deputy Chief, Foothills Division. LAPD.

And certainly the beneficiary of Lucky Rosario's largess. Add to that, as a vampire and a ranking officer in the LAPD, most certainly Cragnow Vissoom's head goon.

I didn't need to remove my contacts and sunglasses to study Paxton's aura. He didn't stop by to ask about my health or my opinion of Los Angeles traffic. His frown told me enough. He expected to find me smashed into pulp, and instead I stood here, still definitely upright and undead.

Paxton introduced himself to the patrol cop and told her he'd like a word with me, alone. We stepped away.

"Paxton, I'm honored," I said. "Since when does a honcho like yourself pull traffic duty?"

Paxton's stern face broke into a smile so deep it looked like a chrome radiator grill. "Felix Gomez."

We had never met before, so hearing my name was like an electric jolt.

He knew my name. He knew I was here. He certainly knew my business. Cragnow Vissoom must have told him. I pointed to the wreck under the dump truck. "You seem disappointed that my carcass is not tangled in that mess."

His teeth looked impossibly shiny, as if he buffed instead of brushed them. "Lucky you. Maybe fate's telling you to buy a lottery ticket."

Back at Paxton's car the driver got out and stood behind the open door, as if prepared to reach inside and grab something—perhaps a riot gun loaded with silver buckshot.

If Paxton still wanted me dead, he could've signaled his driver to start shooting. Judging by his stance, the driver was human and I'd beat him to the draw. The other cops were busy with traffic, so he was the only available shooter. I was next to Paxton and wild bursts of fire would get him, too. Plus a shoot-out beside the freeway was something Paxton wouldn't risk. I felt safe for now.

"You got something you want to share with me, Paxton?"

I couldn't see his aura but I could feel it, like the heat from a stalled engine. Paxton was sizing me up, to see what kind of an opponent and threat I was.

"Who sent you?" I asked. "Cragnow?"

Paxton's smile went flat. "Mr. Vissoom doesn't control—"

"*Mister*? I expected *His Highness* from you."

That smile with those blade-shiny teeth returned. His expression said: Keep it up, smart-ass, and see where it gets you.

"Since you're here, Paxton, maybe you can help."

His smile dimmed again and he raised an eyebrow.

"Any idea where I could find Katz Meow?"

His eyebrow took a long time to drop. "Who?"

Liar. "A friend of Roxy Bronze's."

"Felix, I don't expect you to do my job, so don't expect me to do yours. Aren't you a PI? Find her yourself."

Paxton started to walk away. He stopped and looked back at me. "In case you don't get it, don't think for a second that any of this"—he meant the accident, his arrival, and his knowledge of me—"was a coincidence."

"You don't need to spell it out," I told him.

"Really? 'Cuz I did figure you to be that stupid." Paxton returned to his Crown Vic.

Stupid or not, I was harder to kill than he thought. Paxton, as a deputy chief, had a lot of authority and with that, plenty of visibility. He couldn't be brash in his attempts to finish me and blow his cover.

Paxton drove off as two wreckers arrived. The bigger one pulled the dump truck off the rental. The other wrecker winched the remains of the sedan onto its bed. I signed a release and wondered how much time I was going to waste trying to sort this out with my insurance company.

I walked up the block and retreated under the shadow of an awning outside a dry cleaner. I could go back to Barrios Unidos. But what kind of impression would that make? I was supposed to be the white knight, and within minutes of leaving Veronica, I all but crawl back, after barely escaping an attempt to crush me like an egg.

I called a cab for a ride back to my hotel. As I waited, I reviewed the in-box of my cell phone and opened the text message from Veronica. It was the number she had forwarded for Andrew Tonic, Roxy's lawyer.

I called him. A woman receptionist answered. When I told her I wanted to speak to Tonic about Roxy, she caught herself in midbreath and immediately switched me over.

I expected his voice mail and was surprised when a man's voice came over the phone.

"Andrew Tonic speaking," he chirped.

I introduced myself as a private investigator looking into the death of Roxy Bronze. "I understand you were her attorney at the hearing before the state medical board."

"I was, but I can't answer any questions about that."

"Of course not," I replied. "Wouldn't dream of asking. I was only hoping that you and I could meet to talk about Roxy in general terms."

"General terms?"

"Her background. Your impressions of her."

"I can tell you that right now. Roxy Bronze—Freya Krieger—was one of the sweetest, most conscientious people I'd ever met. Another Joan of Arc, which in this town meant she had plenty of enemies ready to burn her at the stake. What happened to Roxy was a travesty. It was no hearing but an administrative gang rape." Tonic paused, as if regretting what he had just said. "That was a *general* term, okay? Don't quote me on it."

"On what?"

He laughed. "What do you need from me?"

"I'm putting together a list of people who might have had a reason to kill her."

"That would be a long list," he said.

"That's okay. I got a new pen and lots of paper."

Tonic sighed.

"Something bothering you?" I asked.

"Yeah. It's a disgrace what happened to her."

"Then why haven't *you* looked into this?"

"Can I ask you a question, Mr. Gomez?"

"Go ahead."

"Is this a hobby for you?"

"No. It's my job."

"Exactly. If I'm going to defend the moral high ground, I do it for a client and at my hourly rate."

"So you won't talk about Roxy?" I asked.

"I never said that. We agreed that I'd discuss Roxy in general terms. There are plenty of people I wouldn't mind seeing squirm over this."

"People on that long list?"

"Let's not get ahead of ourselves, Mr. Gomez. You want to talk, I'm free . . . let me check. Next Tuesday? You know Trixie's Bistro on Wilshire?"

"I can find it."

"Let's say lunch. Noon. A patio table. If you get there first, do me a favor and order a vodka and tonic. Make sure it's Belvedere and Schweppes. Anything else and you're better off letting a skunk piss into the glass."

"Got it. Trixie's. Next Tuesday. Lunch. No skunk."

We hung up. A cab arrived and I took a long, expensive ride back to my hotel in Culver City.

I spent the rest of the day on the phone talking to the insurance and the rental car companies. I argued with some kid, who despite assurances that he was from Ohio, his accent made me suspect he was sitting inside a cubicle in Cennai, India. Too bad we were on the phone; otherwise, I would've put the vampire whammy on him.

"By this evening," the kid kept repeating, "you should have a replacement automobile."

Evening came and went and still no replacement. The hassle with bureaucracy left me more drained than the recent attempt to kill me. I put on my inversion boots and hung inside the closet for the night. Sleep came slowly as I wondered: Julius Paxton had found me before; would he strike again at the hotel?

In the stillness of the dawn, I detected a faint movement. Light appeared as a red glow through my eyelids.

The closet door was open.

I reached for my pistol when a rubber-soled shoe pressed upon my hand. I opened my eyes and stared at a familiar dirty sneaker. Looking up, I saw Coyote's wrinkled face.

"Te canto las mañanitas, huevón," he said. I'm singing you good morning, lazy-ass.

"How'd you get in?"

He clucked his tongue, as if the question was too stupid to answer. *"Ya levantate."* Get up. *"Ponte la lisa y los calcos."* Pachuco slang for put on your shirt and shoes. "We got some investigating to do, *vato.*"

CHAPTER

15

COYOTE HELPED HIMSELF to one of the bags of human blood that I had in an ice bucket on the dresser. He warmed the bag in the microwave by the vanity sink. After punching holes in the bag with his fangs, Coyote slurped the blood. He turned his cap backward, slouched on my bed, and watched TV while I shaved and did my morning business. Vampires aren't supposed to use the bathroom. True . . . on an all-blood diet. But if the tacos come in, they have to come out.

I combed my hair and applied Dermablend and sunblock–makeup to cover my undead pallor. I poured from the tiny coffeemaker into a tall glass. I warmed the other bag of blood and stirred it into the coffee. As I drank my breakfast, I told Coyote about yesterday's ambush with the dump truck. He barely seemed to listen. He kept his attention on a morning news program featuring a local cat show. A fat tabby stared at the camera.

"A splash of olive oil. A little oregano," Coyote said, licking his lips, "and you got some good fajitas."

I snatched the remote from the nightstand and clicked off the TV. "They tried to kill me," I repeated.

Coyote replied with an irritated look. "*Vato,* you say that like it's a surprise. You think Cragnow and his *diablos* sang the other agents to sleep?" He leaned forward and touched the power button on the TV. The fat tabby's hairy face returned.

Coyote squeezed the last drops of blood out of the bag and onto his tongue. He crinkled the empty bag like it was the wrapper from a candy bar. Coyote tossed the bag toward the trash can by the TV. The bag bounced off the wall and rolled to the floor by my feet.

"Goddamn it, Coyote." I picked the bag up and jammed it into a corner of my open Pullman. "Why don't you just write on the walls 'vampires were here'?"

I clicked the TV off again. "You said we've got some investigating to do. What's the plan?"

Turning his cap around, Coyote stood and then grasped my pistol from where it rested on the dresser. He tossed the gun, still in its holster, to me.

I snagged it with one hand. "You expect trouble?"

"No, *pendejo.*" No, dumb ass. "I'm expecting a parade down South Central."

Stupid question on my part. Of course we should expect trouble. "Where are we going?"

"You tell me," he said. "It's your investigation."

"Yesterday, before I got hit by the truck, I was on my way to the La Brea Mercy Hospital in Glendale."

Coyote stared for a long moment. He wrinkled his nose, as if sniffing for something. I couldn't guess what he was thinking about. Probably to see what else he could mooch from me.

At last, Coyote responded. "Why that hospital?"

I told him about Dr. Mordecai Niphe and Freya Krieger, a.k.a. Roxy Bronze.

When I was done, Coyote bobbed his head in agreement. "Then that's the plan. First, pack your shit, *ese*."

"Why?"

"Because there's a new way to spell *pendejo*. F-E-L-I-X. *Vato,* how long will it be before Cragnow finds where you are? What are you waiting for, a second dump truck to climb over your back?"

"And go where?"

"Another hotel. Or with me."

"You have a home? What is it, a park bench?"

Coyote gave an indignant snort. "Felix, it's a palace." He shoved his hand down the front of his trousers and scratched.

I couldn't see myself rooming with him, even in a crypt. But Coyote was right. He had snuck in here and surprised me. I didn't think any other vampire could, but I'd be foolish to risk it. I filled out the express checkout card on the table and collected my belongings.

Coyote walked to the vanity sink and took all the little soaps and bottles of toiletries, which he stuffed into the pockets of his denim jacket. There was an extra roll of tissue under the sink and he took that, too.

We went down the stairs and out a side door instead of through the lobby.

"How are we getting about?" I asked. "I still don't have a car."

"We don't need no car, *vato*. Instead we got a magic carpet ride. Think of Santa's sleigh, only better."

A sleigh? Knowing Coyote, he probably meant a burro pulling a melon wagon.

I followed Coyote around the back of the hotel to an old Ford pickup. Blotches of gray putty and primer covered the faded green paint like a mange. Rust outlined the bottom of the truck and the fender wells. A good breeze seemed enough to rip the body right off the frame.

"This is a magic carpet ride?" I looked for the burro hitch.

"*Vato,* you can always walk."

I wrestled the passenger's door open. A tattered serape was fitted over the bench seat. I tipped the seat forward and crammed my bags into the space.

Coyote climbed into the driver's side and squeezed behind a steering wheel that seemed as large as a manhole cover.

Boards had been nailed—not screwed—to the floor panels to support my feet over a big rusted hole.

Coyote put the column shift lever into neutral. He reached under the instrument panel and pinched the dangling wires together.

"Ready," he said. "Blast off." He twisted the screwdriver stuck into the ignition lock. The engine groaned. Coyote pumped the gas pedal. "Come on, you *puta*." You whore.

The engine spurted and rattled but wouldn't start. After a moment of referring to the truck as every possible variation of whore or bitch, Coyote released the screwdriver and pulled his foot off the gas. He slumped forward and rested his forehead against the steering wheel.

I asked, "Do you want me to push?"

"Por favor."

I pushed the truck out of the parking spot. How much better was this jalopy than walking? Coyote aimed it away from the other cars. Grasping the edge of the tailgate, I gave the old Ford a hearty vampire shove. The truck zoomed forward, belched, and slowed when Coyote tried to start the engine, then lurched forward again. Success. With a wave of his hand he beckoned me to catch him. I sprinted, jumped onto the running board, and plopped inside.

Coyote turned the big steering wheel like he was at the helm of a tugboat. We chugged out of the parking lot, made it onto the Santa Monica Freeway heading east, then went north on Interstate 110 and Highway 2.

Surprisingly, the old Ford held together, and we rolled into Glendale. Map in hand, I told Coyote how to get to the La Brea Mercy Hospital.

We passed through a tunnel of stately trees lining the

street in an older, upscale neighborhood. The hospital was at the next block. We circled for an empty parking spot and eventually found one that seemed as far from the building as the planet Pluto.

We got out and hiked to the hospital. An ambulance sat in front of the entrance to the emergency room. We stopped at a sign that had an arrow pointing right: PUBLIC ENTRANCE. And an arrow pointing to the left: MEDICAL STAFF AND EMPLOYEES.

I started to the left.

Coyote pivoted to the right. *"Dame un momento."* Give me a minute.

"Where you going?"

Coyote waved me off. "I'll catch up."

What kind of mischief was he going to cause? This is why I preferred to work alone.

The sidewalk turned the corner and led to an entrance on the north side of the building. I had come to see Dr. Mordecai Niphe and ask—no, interrogate—him about Roxy Bronze.

A couple of women in blue scrubs approached from the employee parking lot and climbed up the steps to the staff entrance. As they approached the door, they held ID badges up for a security guard to inspect. At this time of day the hospital would be busy. Sneaking in and prowling about was going to be tricky.

Coyote appeared around the corner behind me. He held a pair of dark sport coats and two plastic name tags.

"Welcome to La Brea Mercy Hospital, Dr. Dilip Gupta." He handed one of the sport coats and name tags to me. "They're waiting for us inside."

CHAPTER
16

EACH NAME TAG HAD the logo of the SoCal Cosmetic Surgery Association, the name of a doctor, and today's date. I put on the larger of the sport coats; the other was a navy blue blazer. "Where are the owners?"

Coyote put his hands together beside his cheek and tilted his head to indicate *night-night*.

Even with a blazer, in his tattered ball cap, jeans, and sneakers, Coyote didn't project the image of any physician I'd trust. But this was L.A. Maybe he looked like the typical Hollywood quack pill pusher.

The security guard glanced at the name tags clipped to the lapels of our coats. He nodded and motioned down the hall.

The guard hadn't examined our name tags or he would've noticed that Coyote didn't look like a Dr. Annabelle Cunningham.

We passed hospital staff in scrubs. I searched for Mordecai Niphe, listening for his name and letting my gaze flit across the ID badges. I had no idea what he looked like, as I couldn't find his picture on the Internet or anywhere else.

Coyote and I stopped in the hall at a table scattered with the leftovers of a continental breakfast. A poster for the So-Cal Cosmetic Surgery Conference rested on an easel beside the table. A sign on the double doors said: QUIET. MEETING IN PROGRESS. CELL PHONES AND PAGERS OFF.

I didn't know if Dr. Niphe was in there but I had to look. Carefully, I opened one of the doors. The room was three-quarters full with around a hundred people, doctors, I presumed, sitting and facing a stage. Large, flat-screen video monitors flanked the audience.

A tall, handsome man in a lab coat stood on the stage, next to a gynecologist's examination table with chrome foot stirrups. The business end of the table was turned toward the room. Music played, a cheesy corporate tune that I had heard before at a pitch for timeshare condos.

A breathless infotainment voice on the soundtrack introduced the man in the lab coat as *the* cosmetic surgeon to the stars and the presenter for today's lecture on new developments in aesthetic cosmetic enhancements and opportunities for revenue growth. Unfortunately he wasn't who I was looking for, Dr. Niphe.

I was about to turn away when a statuesque blonde, wearing nothing but a white robe and high-heeled pumps, stepped onto the stage. She paused beside the examination table.

The surgeon welcomed her. She smiled, disrobed, and removed her shoes. Completely nonchalant, she sat on the table, lifted her legs, placed her feet into the stirrups, and scooted her naked butt to the edge of the table. Every eye in the room was pulled to her vulva. The men in the audience leaned forward. The women crossed their arms and legs and sat rigid.

Coyote worked his way around me and pushed his head under my arm to gape. *"Vato,"* he whispered, "I don't know whether to take notes or play with myself."

"Take notes."

A tiny camera on a telescoping boom rose in front of the stage. While the doctor fit on latex gloves, he recited the lecture bullets superimposed over a giant image of the woman's open crotch filling the monitor screens. In the morning presentation he would cover the newest trends in cosmetic surgery: vaginal tightening and labial aesthetic reconstruction.

A couple of female doctors sat close to us. One leaned to her colleague. "Geez, men are always bragging about the size of their dicks. So why is a loose pussy the woman's problem?"

Her friend replied, "And since when are labia ugly? Obviously the doc up there hasn't taken a good look at his own scrotum."

I doubted Dr. Niphe was here. As the head surgeon of the hospital, Niphe had more important matters than this peep show. Unless he suddenly jumped up and said, "Here I am," Coyote and I had to go find him.

I pushed Coyote back and closed the door. We went down the hall away from the hospital entrance. This wing of the hospital was conference rooms or records storage. At the hub of the building complex, a sign by the elevators said: SURGICAL STAFF, 3RD FLOOR.

No mention of Dr. Niphe, but there was a good chance he'd be there.

A security guard greeted us when we got off on the third floor. He gave a polite yet wary smile. "May I help you?"

Coyote stepped close and scratched his armpit. "Where is H.R.? I'm looking for a job, *ese*."

While Coyote distracted the guard, I removed my contacts.

"Actually," I said, "I need to find Dr. Mordecai Niphe."

The guard's gaze swiveled to lock with mine. His eyes opened and his aura sizzled like a sparkler.

Coyote found a storage room. I pushed the guard inside and joined him.

I kept my focus deep into the guard's pupils. "Where is Dr. Niphe's office?"

"Room three-forty-six."

"Is Niphe here today?"

"Yes."

"Where can I find him?"

"I . . . I . . . don't know."

An interrogation using vampire hypnosis can cause distress if the victim can't find an answer. Okay. I had enough info to start. To further confuse the guard when he came to, I unbuckled his belt and dropped his pants. Who would he complain to when he found himself like that?

I closed the door and joined Coyote in the hall.

The chattering of men's voices echoed toward us.

I fumbled to get my contacts out of my pocket. I didn't have time. I put on my sunglasses.

A group of seven men in green scrubs approached the elevators. They wore hair covers. A couple carried clipboards. They mobbed around us and conversed jovially. The cloth necklaces holding ID badges were tucked into the front of their scrubs. Was one of them Dr. Niphe?

An elevator pinged. The doors opened.

They crowded into the elevator. Just as the doors closed, one of them said, "So, Morty, you still got money on the Cardinals?"

A short man, with a rosy complexion and a thick shadow already on his cheeks and chin, flashed a smile in response. The skin crinkled at the corners of his eyes. His slate blue eyes beamed confidence through the lenses of circular wire-rim glasses. He stood in the center of the group, obviously the man in charge.

Morty.

Where had I seen that name? In the moment that I paused to reflect on where I'd seen that name, the doors started to close. My mind raced back to my visit to Cragnow's office. He had offered bagels, and in the bottom of the basket was a card with the inscription:

To Crag. Thanks for everything.
Morty

Short for Mordecai?

Dr. Mordecai Niphe. The head surgeon. Roxy Bronze's former boss and the man who had destroyed her medical career. Why was Dr. Mordecai Niphe thanking porn king Cragnow?

This Morty? Damn good odds.

I raised my sunglasses to zap Niphe and the others, but none made eye contact. Their red auras simmered like a bed of warm, inviting coals. I should've yelled to get their attention. But I hesitated, and my hands slapped the doors after they had shut.

The elevator climbed to the fourth floor and halted.

My *kundalini noir* writhed in frustration. I clenched my fists to maintain composure. I looked in vain for the stairs. Mordecai Niphe had been standing right beside me and I didn't get him.

CHAPTER
17

THE ELEVATOR STARTED AGAIN, rose to the fifth floor, and stopped.

I rubbed my forehead to settle my thoughts. If my goal was to kill Dr. Niphe and damn the consequences, I could pull the doors open, climb up the elevator shaft, break through the bottom of the elevator, and rip the doctor to pieces. But I needed to get information from him and get it as inconspicuously as possible.

One positive discovery; I had gotten a good look at Mordecai Niphe and his aura, which was as unique and recognizable as his face. I told Coyote about finding Mordecai's name—as Morty—in Cragnow's office. What business did Mordecai and Cragnow have together?

Coyote nodded in understanding. *"Sí, es mucha mas caca."* Yes, it's a lot more shit. "So what now, Felix?"

"Niphe was dressed like he was going to surgery. Even if we locate the doc, getting to him will be difficult." I started following the room numbers. "Let's see what we can find out about him in his office."

Room number 340 was the receptionist's foyer. Niphe's office was somewhere behind her.

I hypnotized the receptionist while Coyote stood guard. All the offices were empty. I found Dr. Niphe's. A printout next to a laptop computer on his desk listed today's schedule. He was in surgery until noon. Then a luncheon with the hospital's board of directors. Followed by a group consultation. More meetings. Dr. Niphe was a busy man. I wouldn't have the opportunity to get him alone here in the hospital, not today.

Dr. Niphe's desk was locked. I touched the keyboard on the laptop and got prompted for a password.

Coyote signaled with a loud cough, and I hustled out of the doctor's office. Coyote motioned that someone was coming down the hall toward us. I could've asked the receptionist for Niphe's home address but as it was, I barely had time to wake her.

Coyote and I left the foyer and passed a group of men and women in scrubs approaching from the direction of the elevators. Dr. Niphe wasn't among them.

"Niphe has to leave, no?" Coyote asked.

"Eventually," I replied. "We'll stake out the parking lot and get him there."

We went outside to the staff parking lot. The asphalt was packed with SUVs and expensive cars.

Coyote tilted his cap back and squinted. "Which is his, dude?"

"Easy," I replied. I walked to the closest parking spot to the entrance. A sign posted to the sidewalk said: RESERVED FOR THE HEAD SURGEON. VIOLATORS WILL BE TOWED IMMEDIATELY.

The car parked in the spot was a long, sleek, black BMW coupe. It looked like a torpedo with wheels.

I cupped my hands and peered into a side window. A red light for the alarm blinked. On the front passenger's seat rested a yarmulke and a brochure with a Star of David and titled with what seemed like a Hebrew fellowship of some kind. Niphe didn't sound Jewish, but Mordecai did. Maybe his last name had been Anglicized or his family had converted.

Coyote rubbed his fingertips. *"Ese,* I could break in and poke around. I'll bet there's something useful in the glove box."

I stood away from the car. There were black globes on the hospital building corners. Inside the globes were security cameras. "Better not chance it."

A stand of tall, mature trees shaded the northwest corner of the hospital grounds. Up in the branches we'd have a good view of the staff entrance and the parking lot. Even though Niphe's schedule said that he wouldn't leave for hours, he might have a change in plans, and we'd have to follow him.

I scouted for the best vantage and selected an especially lush maple. We ditched the coats and name tags into a trash can. I placed my fingers and toes against the bark and ascended the trunk with the ease of a gecko.

Coyote simply walked up.

I settled on a thick, well-shaded branch. It was still morning and yet I was hot and hungry. Coyote found a branch in the shadows, lay on his back, pulled his cap down over his face, and began to snore.

The stakeout. The least glamorous and yet often the most valuable activity in investigations. To endure the agonizing boredom and forestall restlessness, I slowed my metabolism into near rigor mortis until I was nothing more than a pair of eyeballs fixed on the area around Dr. Niphe's car.

The sun arced overhead and began its gradual descent over the San Fernando Valley. People came and went. A praying mantis climbed over my face and perched on my nose, where it snagged little bugs trying to fly up my nostrils.

At last the cool veil of night fell upon us. The praying mantis went wherever insects go to sleep. I sped up my metabolism, flexed my cramped joints, and blinked to moisten my eyes. Nine o'clock approached. Still no Dr. Niphe.

I heard slurping from behind. Coyote sat on the fork of two branches and sucked on the neck of what looked like a large headless rat.

"What are you doing?" I asked.

Coyote wiped blood from his mouth. *"Es una zarigüeya."* It's an opossum. "Want some?"

"No thanks."

"It's fresh."

"Not anymore, it's not."

I called Katz Meow on my cell. Still nothing but her voice mail. I feared this was all I would ever get from her now.

At a quarter to midnight, Dr. Niphe and a group of other people came out of the hospital. Their glowing red auras bobbed in the darkness. They clustered around his car. A security guard watched from the hospital entrance.

"Coyote, it's time."

My initial plan was to intercept the doctor here and zap him. But with all those people around, I'd have to stalk him and pounce somewhere else. That meant following him. In what?

All we had was Coyote's wreck on wheels.

Keeping in the shadows, Coyote and I shimmied down the tree and snuck back to his truck. The straight six in the old Ford did a good job of wheezing and groaning but little else.

Cursing my luck, I pushed the truck away from its parking spot. When Coyote had the front end pointed north, I held on to the tailgate, ran, and pushed.

Up ahead, Dr. Niphe started his BMW. With a cell phone pressed to his face, he backed up and maneuvered toward the exit. His aura burned hot as a flare. He obviously still had a lot of business on his mind.

Coyote's truck acted as if it never wanted to get going. "C'mon, you pile of junk," I said. "If you don't start, I'm going to turn you into a box of nails."

Whether or not the old Ford understood my threat, I don't know, but the engine did crank over. I dashed beside the cab and jumped in. I held back the urge to punch Coyote for putting me through this hassle.

He kept his attention on the truck, as if driving this heap was as difficult and delicate as piloting a nuclear submarine.

Niphe drove his BMW like he intended to flog every horse under the hood. He rolled through stop signs and barreled down the streets. Good luck keeping up with him.

"What's the itch in his pants?" I asked.

Coyote doubled-clutched and winced when he mashed the gears. He had a bad case of opossum breath. *"Algo vergonzoso."* Something scandalous. *"Tiene que ser por dinero o una vieja."* Has to be for money or a woman.

Niphe aimed his BMW onto the Glendale Freeway and headed north. Once on the freeway, Niphe zipped around traffic like he was in a fighter jet. In Coyote's beater we'd lose him for sure.

Fortunately, Los Angeles traffic rescued us. The freeway slowed to a near stop. We joined the other cars bunching around Niphe. Everyone's aura brightened in agitation, Niphe's more than anyone else's.

Traffic crawled forward and separated. We followed the doctor when he merged into the lanes going west on the 210 toward Pasadena.

Something under our truck rattled loose and clanged onto the road. Coyote tipped his head out the window to see what had fallen off. "I hope you're wearing comfortable shoes, *vato.*"

Niphe exited and headed uphill on Lincoln Avenue. We followed him through northern Pasadena and then Altadena. The trees and rooftops of the neighborhood were silhouetted by a white glow coming from uphill.

Niphe turned east on Loma Linda Drive, which ran parallel to the steep foothills of the Angeles National Forest.

The glow came from light reflected off a huge white obelisk fixed atop an octagonal plinth. The plinth sat on a truncated pyramid that straddled the intersection of long four-story buildings set at right angles. The predominant architectural theme was acres of glass and chrome siding. Under the glare of dozens of spotlights the building complex looked like a gigantic piece of costume jewelry.

Coyote let his pickup coast to a halt.

His lupine *tapetum lucidum* reflected a surreal glow. He whispered, *"Me voy a pegar ciego."* I'm going to go blind. He rubbed his eyes and blinked as if in disbelief, then put on his sunglasses.

"Whatever you do," I said, "don't stop the engine."

Too late. The six-banger coughed and sputtered. Coyote pumped the gas and slid the choke, but all went quiet. Both Coyote and I hung our heads and sighed.

Niphe's BMW turned off Loma Linda and onto the wide driveway flanked by a simple Christian cross about ten feet tall. Standing next to the cross was a granite marker the size of a garage door. Engraved on the marker was: WELCOME TO THE HOME OF THE JOURNEY WITH GOD™ MINISTRIES. REVEREND DALE JOURNEY, PASTOR.

I'd seen snippets of Reverend Journey on his television show in between the channels presenting bass fishing and how to get rich selling distressed real estate. Journey bagged souls for Christ and evidently made a handsome living off his finder's fee.

The driveway led to two terraced parking lots, both of which were gloomy and empty. Niphe paused at the west end. The dim light of a cell phone outlined his face. Who was he talking to? And why was he waiting here?

The growing smell of deceit and conspiracy was enough to drive the needle on my internal stink-o-meter into the red.

We had a megachurch that looked liked it was designed for the fat Elvis. Then there was Dr. Mordecai Niphe, chief inquisitor and author of Freya Krieger's demise. As far as I could tell, the medical community considered Niphe an upstanding doctor. So why was he—a Jew—driving like a demon in the middle of the night to one of the largest Evangelical ministries in the country? How did that fit into his palling around with the porn mogul Cragnow Vissoom? Did Niphe know Cragnow was a vampire?

Under hypnosis, what would Niphe reveal? From where I sat in Coyote's truck, the distance to Niphe was about two lengths of a football field. His aura looked fuzzy from the tendrils of anxiety and wariness that writhed about him. Other than the cross and granite marker, there was no cover between the doctor and me. Moving even at vampire speed I doubted that I could cross the openness and surprise him.

Coyote took off his sunglasses and pulled his arms out of his denim jacket.

"What gives?" I asked.

Coyote began unbuttoning his shirt. "He'd be expecting a man."

"So you're going to transform into a . . ."

"They don't call me Coyote for nothing."

A coyote would be a surprise but not unusual here along the foothills.

"Good," I said. "Distract him enough for me to get close."

"*Vato,* if he gets out of his car, you'd better bring a shot for rabies."

Niphe closed his cell phone. His aura's undulating tendrils calmed. The BMW coupe continued up the driveway, past the upper tier of the parking lot, and disappeared behind the main building.

Now my stink-o-meter was at full tilt.

Who had Niphe come to see? Maybe they had something to do with the death of Roxy Bronze and vampire–human collusion, or maybe they didn't. There was one way to find out.

I would ask.

Politely.

With my talons around their necks.

CHAPTER
18

COYOTE AND I STEPPED OUT of the truck and trotted toward the church.

Halfway across the lower parking lot, Coyote stopped. He began walking backward toward his truck. *"Vato . . ."*

A searchlight from uphill bore upon us. The light hurt my eyes and I brought my hand up to shield them.

A voice yelled through a megaphone. "This is private property. You are trespassing."

Two red auras moved behind the glare of the spotlight. At our far right, two more red auras sat in a vehicle with the lights dimmed. The vehicle rolled down the driveway on the eastern side of the parking lot. Yellow lights suddenly flashed and rotated on top of both vehicles.

Security guards. Armed perhaps. But no matter, subduing them wasn't worth the risk of blowing our cover.

The second vehicle hit us with another spotlight. Scissored between the two intersecting shafts of light, Coyote and I skulked back to his truck. To add to the humiliation, his Ford wouldn't start and I had to push.

A guard taunted us through his megaphone. "Next time get a truck with a motor, you stupid bastards."

Asshole.

When we rounded the turn and headed down the slope on Lake Avenue, the spotlights went off.

For all my street smarts and vampire cunning, we were driving down the road to nowhere. "What the hell is with this goddamn investigation?"

Coyote shifted gears and the truck lurched forward. "*Simon*. It's confusing."

"More than confusing. What do you think is going on?"

Coyote's expression became uncharacteristically serious. He tipped his ball cap back. A wispy tuft of hair curled free. "Don't put me on the spot, *ese*. I'm not much in the 'think' department."

"Let's start at the beginning. Interrupt when you have something to add," I said. "Freya Krieger rats on Dr. Mordecai Niphe for botching an operation and killing the patient. Niphe gets his revenge by destroying Freya's medical career."

"And she comes back as Roxy Bronze, the porn star working for that *pinchi* Cragnow Vissoom," Coyote said. "I'm with you."

"Then for reasons I still don't fathom . . ."

"Fathom?" asked Coyote.

"It means 'understand,' " I explained. "Roxy teams with Veronica Torres at Barrio Unidos to stop Project Eleven— the plan to redevelop Pacoima. Which they do."

"And that pissed off a lot of rich people because they lost money," Coyote said.

"One of those people is Lucky Rosario, who it turns out has been siphoning . . ." I waited for Coyote to interrupt again.

"I understand *siphoning*," he said. "That's how I get gas for my ride."

"Rosario funds Cragnow's movies and in return gets to play with some porn tail. Now it turns out that Dr. Mordecai Niphe is sending thank-you gifts to Cragnow."

"Let's not forget the dump truck treatment, *ese*."

"I haven't."

"*¿Porque?*" asked Coyote. Why?

"Don't know," I said. "Does it have to do with money? Sex? Or something else? If that's not confusing enough, now we've got Dr. Niphe sneaking off to meet with the Reverend Dale Journey."

Coyote slowed at a traffic light and gunned the engine to keep it from stalling. "You sure, *vato?*"

"What do you mean?"

"Dr. Niphe only went to Journey's church." The light turned green and Coyote let the truck jerk forward. "We're not sure who he went to see."

"True. But I'll bet that Niphe wouldn't have been invited unless Dale Journey knew about it. Notice that the security guards didn't show up until we got there."

Coyote frowned. "*Vato,* that's too much shit for me to think about. And you still haven't gotten to why Katz Meow is missing or why someone killed Rebecca Dwelling."

Or mentioned a lot of other people I knew wanted Roxy dead.

"Don't forget the real reason you're here, *raza* . . ."

I hadn't been called *raza* in a while. Short for *La Raza*—the race—meaning us mestizos.

". . . to find out what this has to do with vampires and humans."

Whatever had been going on in L.A. was serious enough to alarm even the Araneum. They expected me to infiltrate the suspected vampire–human collusion and bring the offending bloodsuckers to undead justice. Trouble was, I hadn't done much so far except practice push-starting Coyote's wreck of a pickup.

Discussing the investigation with Coyote should have helped. Instead, reviewing the details of the case and coming up with zip made me feel like one big dumb ass.

Coyote grasped my shoulder. "You okay, Felix?"

I brushed his hand off. My aura should've told him how pissed I was. Plus I hadn't eaten anything since morning, so I was cranky with hunger.

Working in the daytime, no matter how much we vampires tried to adjust to the cycle, left us with perpetual jetlag. After a few days of having the sun leach psychic energy from our bodies, we needed a nice blood meal and a good nap in a coffin to refresh us and smooth the kinks out of our attitudes.

"Relax, *ese,*" Coyote said. "We'll go to my place, get something to eat, and take a snooze." He circled a finger next to his temple. *"Mientras"*—meanwhile—"you get those gears turning in your head and see what we have to do next."

I had plenty of gears to turn; problem was, I couldn't get any two of them to mesh.

One traffic light from the freeway on-ramp, a red Ferrari rumbled beside us. The young man at the wheel looked up at Coyote's truck and sneered. He gestured to someone beside him, and a woman's face appeared in the driver's window, laughing no doubt at the heap Coyote and I were in.

Bad timing on the part of these two yuppies. I was pissed at the world and hungry. Might as well get these two birds with one stone, or rather one stare.

I turned my face to them and flashed my fangs.

CHAPTER
19

THE TWO YUPPIES in the Ferrari responded with slack-jawed, blank-faced stares. In their red auras they looked as if they had been dipped in sweet-and-sour sauce.

"Coyote," I said, "time for dinner."

He smiled with anticipation.

"Just me. You've already snacked. Follow me and wait until I'm done." As I was about to get out, I clutched Coyote's thin, sinewy arm. "And for God's sake, if this truck stalls, I'm not pushing it again. I'll make you carry me piggyback to your house."

"*Vato,* I got a bad hip and—"

"Try me." I let go of his arm and got out of the truck.

I told the driver of the Ferrari to unlock his door. I swung the door up and pushed him over the center console to jam him on top of his stylish female companion.

I settled into the driver's seat, snapped the door closed, and reflected on how low the rumbling Ferrari sat against the road. I examined the controls and instruments. Detecting a whiff of cocaine, I searched about and found a vial of the white powder in the console.

Naughty yuppies.

Grasping the steering wheel, I released the clutch and eased the gas pedal. The rear tires spun out, and the car swerved through the intersection. Regaining control, I veered into an alley, scraping the bottom of the Ferrari, and halted next to a brick wall and a Dumpster.

Since the guy was on top, I fanged him first. He was bulky and firm—obviously a muscle head—and his blood luxuriously tasty. Male blood had the full-bodied richness of testosterone. I detected notes of gin, dry vermouth, anabolic steroids, and cocaine.

To get to the woman, I had to reach over them and fumble for the release catch to fold the passenger's seat down. I wrestled with their bodies, as if rearranging sacks of potatoes. When I finally had her on top of the pile, I stretched her neck back and feasted like an undead king. Little Miss Nordstrom also enjoyed the nose candy.

I relaxed against the driver's seat and burped. The traces of booze and dope gave me a nice buzz, and suddenly the world and my problems appeared much more tolerable.

I had lapped plenty of saliva into the fang punctures to accelerate the healing, so by morning, when these two yuppie coke heads came to, there would be nothing but faint yellow bruises on their necks. To give them something else to think about, I got the vial of cocaine and dusted their rumpled forms with the white powder. If finding themselves disheveled and tangled like this wasn't enough to get them both into a 12-step, then they were beyond my magnanimous help.

Coyote's truck rattled beside the curb outside the alley. I got in and slouched on the bench seat.

Coyote narrowed his eyes. *"¿Somos amigos, no?"* We are friends, no? "You should've shared."

"You can share this." I gave him the bird and motioned to get going.

The old Ford sputtered onto the freeway. The jostling of the truck and the dreamy haze from dinner made me sleepy. I remembered the woman's trim body under mine. I could've had my way with her. The longing for the heat of female skin turned my thoughts away from the yuppie woman and toward Veronica.

Her ripe body was more delectable by comparison. An affair with Veronica could seriously complicate my investigation.

A worthwhile risk.

We arrived at a confusion of concrete and asphalt where the Santa Monica, Golden State, Santa Ana, and Pomona Freeways tangled together. We exited and clattered down Whittier Boulevard through a neighborhood marked with signs in Spanish. Young people clustered under streetlamps or in the doorways of the *tienditas*—small, corner markets. Spray-can graffiti murals declared the area as Atzlan.

"Where are we?" I asked. "East L.A.?"

"Technically we're in Boyle Heights."

A homeless man pushed a shopping cart heaped with his junk possessions.

"More upscale, *vato.*"

We turned on Euclid and after a few blocks headed onto a short street that dipped into a wash. Coyote halted at the top of the incline.

He pointed. At the bottom on the right, past the other ramshackle houses, was a sagging chain-link fence along the cracked sidewalk. Behind the fence and next to a ravine was a small home cobbled together from discarded materials.

"Your palace?"

"*Símon, ese.* The queen of England once asked to stay, but I had to turn her away. We're not zoned for royalty."

Coyote shut the engine.

"Why are we stopping up here?" I asked.

Coyote pointed down the hill. "You wanna push again?" He meant letting the truck coast to start.

"What if it stalls out and we're stuck at the bottom?"

"Then we push uphill, *pendejo*."

We dismounted. The one streetlamp was broken but no matter, with my vampire vision I had no problem seeing through the darkness. Shoes dangled from the power lines.

I grabbed my bags and followed Coyote over the sidewalk and through an opening in the fence. The yard was dirt, rock, trash, and weeds. Piles of dog crap here and there. Frayed corrugated fiberglass sheets were tacked against the wall of his house. Roof joists jutted unevenly from under the eaves. We could've been in any Third World slum.

A large dog's skull rested on a metal stake like a warning.

"What's that about?" I asked.

"Some *culo* up the street was hassling me about parking in front of his house. One day he sicced his rottweiler after me." Coyote patted his belly. "I ate the best tamales for a month."

A dim yellow light shone through a curtained window by what I guessed was the front door. I smelled frijoles simmering in boar's blood. A short roof extended over the door and a slab of concrete to make a small porch. Coyote stepped up to the porch and peeled back a sheet of fiberglass siding. He reached through and opened the door from the inside. The door swung open, and the dim light washed over Coyote. The aroma of blood and frijoles got stronger.

I followed Coyote into a kitchen. A blackened stockpot, the source of the aroma, sat on a battered gas stove. An illuminated happy face lamp rested on the windowsill. Bags of pinto beans and rice lay against the wall along with a pile of rat traps.

I dropped my bags on a table covered with faded red-and-white-checkered contact paper. One of the table legs was splinted with a crooked two-by-four.

"Maybe you recognize my home from last month's *Architectural Digest*," Coyote said. He hooked a loop of coat hanger wire over the knob to secure the front door. A threadbare woman's knit sweater hung from a nearby nail.

"You have a woman?" I asked.

"Had," replied Coyote.

"Chalice? Vampire?" I couldn't imagine a woman of any kind stepping foot in this squalor.

"More than a chalice," Coyote said. The lines on his face deepened. *"Era mi vieja."* She was my old lady.

"She lived here?"

"We had a different place."

Good for her. "Your *vieja's* name?"

"Heather."

The idea of a woman named Heather shacking up with Coyote was so ridiculous I wanted to laugh out loud. Any girfriend of his would've been a hag. Heather was the name of a coed, rosy-faced and plump as a strawberry. "Where is Heather?"

Coyote's aura tightened in sadness around him like orange shrink-wrap. "She went to the place all humans go when they get old and die, *ese*."

"What was Heather—"

Coyote cut me off. "You'll sleep downstairs." This conversation was over. He pointed to the short, narrow door on the wall adjacent to a stove.

"You have a basement?"

"I told you I lived in a palace." Coyote unfolded a towel covering a stack of flour tortillas on the counter by the stove. He turned one of the stove handles with a set of pliers and let the gas hiss.

"Where are you sleeping?" I asked.

Coyote motioned at a tattered curtain hanging over the threshold to another room. "In there."

He struck a match and tossed it into one of the burners. A fireball whooshed and settled into a blue ring of flame. Coyote set a tortilla over the lit burner.

When the tortilla began to smolder, Coyote picked it up and bounced it in his hand to let it cool. Folding the tortilla, he spooned from the stockpot to make a burrito. He offered it to me. "Unlike you, I'll share."

"No thanks, I'm full."

"No kidding, *buey*." Ball-less asshole. Coyote chewed the burrito. Some frijoles dribbled down his shirt and onto the floor. He bent over to pick them up. He brought them to his mouth and stopped. Coyote glanced back to the sweater, sighed, and tossed the beans into the sink. Maybe one of Heather's rules had been "No eating off the floor," and this act of cleanliness was his homage to her.

Coyote pulled the small door open and stooped to enter. "Bring your shit, *ese*."

The creaking, wooden stairs—made of fence posts, plywood signs, and lumber scraps—led to a basement with a low ceiling. A string dangled from a ceiling bulb, but there was no point in turning it on. The dirt floor was swept smooth. Cabinets and a workbench cluttered with tools stood along one wall. A big sturdy table sat in the middle of the room. A gray metal coffin rested on the table.

"Heather?" I asked.

"*Chale*. What am I, a ghoul? That's your bed, *ese*."

In that case, tired as I was, this coffin looked more inviting than a Posturepedic mattress.

Coyote plodded up the stairs. "I'll see you *mañana*." He closed the door.

I put my bags on the workbench and climbed on the table to inspect the coffin. Knowing Coyote, I expected mice and roaches to spring out when I opened the lid. But it was empty, smelling as it should, like stale vampire. No crumbs anywhere from midnight snacking. The satin lining was dry and free of stains. Nothing worse than sharing a coffin with a bed wetter.

I changed into pajamas, folded my street clothes on the table, and stepped into the coffin. I wiggled my hips to settle into the lining, laid back, and stretched my legs and arms. I yawned and reached to close the lid. I let sleep overtake me until a rustling and the squeaking of wood awoke me.

What was that? I wondered how long I had been asleep. I opened the lid only enough to grope for my watch. Even though I had night vision, I liked pressing the stem of the Timex and watching the face glow. Time was 6:40 P.M. Saturday. I had been out awhile.

Pushing the lid open, I felt refreshed and invigorated enough to arise vampire style, keeping my body rigid and rotating upward on my heels. But I had forgotten about the low ceiling and thumped my head. Dust sifted over me.

Massaging my forehead, I climbed out of the coffin and sloughed off the dust. The floor above groaned as someone, I assumed Coyote, moved about the kitchen. I sniffed the odor of rodent blood. Breakfast? I hoped not.

During my sleep, the details of the investigation had circled my head like orbiting moons, distant, yet exerting their pull. As I got dressed, I realized who might provide information that I needed.

Veronica Torres. There was one question I had forgotten to ask her.

I got my cell phone. Reception in the basement was lousy. I climbed the stairs, and when I got a good signal, dialed her number. Voice mail picked up. I said hello and added, "Veronica, did Roxy Bronze leave any files that the police missed? If so, call."

Call regardless, we need to get together.

I entered the kitchen and was overwhelmed by the smell of animal flesh and spicy peppers.

Coyote stood beside the table, scooping bloody lumps out of a bucket and cramming them into a meat grinder. "Buenos *tardes, flojo.*" Good afternoon, lazybones. "I'm making rat chorizo. Know what my secret ingredient is?"

Industrial waste? I shrugged. *"El amor?"*

"Love? You're a funny guy, *ese.*" Coyote laughed. "No, the secret to good rat chorizo is to leave the tails on." He plucked a tail from the bucket and slurped it like a strand of spaghetti.

I wondered if the cuisine had killed Heather, not old age. Looking to the nail by the door, I saw that the sweater was gone.

A percolator with hot coffee sat on a front burner. Coyote kept bags of human blood in his refrigerator. I heated one in the microwave. I filled a tall cup with coffee and blood. After toasting a couple of tortillas, I tore them and dipped the pieces into my drink, doing my best to ignore the stink of Coyote's sausage making.

While he busied himself with rat chorizo, I filled a basin with warm water to wash and shave.

My cell phone buzzed. I had a text message from Veronica. She didn't waste words. Her reply was: YES

I texted her back: WHEN CAN I GET THE FILES?

A minute later she answered.

NOW

CHAPTER
20

VERONICA TEXTED ME her address in Hollywood. By the time Coyote dropped me off at her place, it was already after nine. Since Veronica had asked me to visit on a Saturday evening, and remembering she had said earlier we'd get together for dinner, I inferred that her offer included breakfast as well. Being the optimist that I am, I brought along my overnight bag and condoms.

Her home was in a two-story four-plex in pastel green stucco. Lush grapevines, thick as quilts, draped the walls. Small balconies with wrought iron railings jutted from the upper levels. The fragrance of jasmine shrubs and orange trees wafted through the night air like incense.

I scoped the area with my contacts out to check one last time for suspicious auras. The coast clear, I put my contacts back in and climbed the short concrete steps.

Veronica's address was curiously 518¼. I entered a tiled

breezeway and stepped around small palms and ficus plants growing in terra-cotta pots. Newspapers wrapped in plastic bags and junk mail were piled in one corner.

Her apartment was to the left at the top of the stairs. I rapped on a scuffed and tarnished wooden door. Veronica peeked through the small window at eye level. The dead bolt clicked and the door opened. An aroma of apricot-scented shampoo escaped.

Veronica wore white shorts and a loose short-sleeve blouse with a jungle print and stood barefoot on the oak floor. She had the burnished, muscular legs of a dancer.

With a nod, she beckoned me in. Expecting a hearty embrace and a lusty kiss, I was surprised when she kept a cool distance when she led me inside.

The floor creaked as we walked under a Moorish arch separating the front room from a dining area. I set my bag on a dinette table. There wasn't much furniture. Some mismatched chairs and a couple of end tables with flowering planters on top. The corners and walls were crooked from where the building had settled over the years.

Veronica's mood puzzled me. She didn't act nervous, the way someone would if anticipating trouble. Not that I suspected her, since my vampire sixth sense detected no threat. Just to make sure, I examined the room again. Nothing out of the ordinary.

So why the frosty act? Maybe Veronica had heard bad news. Maybe she didn't feel well. Or maybe she was being fickle in the way women can be and resented my intrusion into her life. In any case, I'd peruse Roxy's files and leave. Good thing condoms have an expiration date.

Veronica waved that I follow her into the kitchen. She pointed to a document box sitting on the counter by the refrigerator.

Her expression stiffened, her face a protective mask. "Felix," she said without prompting, *"lo siento."* I'm sorry.

"For what?" I replied. We both spoke in Spanish.

"I *was* eager to see you. To invite you into my home,"

Veronica explained. "But when I put the box there for you, it hit me what your visit was really about."

"You mean Roxy's murder?"

Veronica stared at the floor and nodded. She gathered stray hair behind one ear. It was a gesture that betrayed her struggle to maintain composure. "After Roxy was killed and I knew no one was serious about investigating her murder, I promised myself that she would get justice."

Veronica looked out the kitchen window. I wanted to remove my contacts so I could witness the animated display of her aura expressing her inner turmoil. I expected to see her lower lip quiver and the shine of tears in her eyes.

Instead, her jaw hardened, and that was it. This was the limit of sadness she would allow herself to show. My attention in this case had been so centered on Roxy Bronze that I had forgotten she was Veronica's lieutenant in the campaign to stop Project Eleven. Veronica picked the fight with the Los Angeles City Council and its millionaire patrons not only out of principle but also to win. She was no one's wallflower. Veronica jumped into the fray like a tough, seasoned paratrooper.

Roxy had provided money, and the sexy, scandalous angle the media craved, but it was Veronica's nerve and drive that marshaled the community and turned the city council on its heels.

"I haven't thought about those files since I brought them here." Veronica said this in a monotone, as if testifying under oath. "Despite my best intentions, my duties at Barrios Unidos, my family obligations . . ."

"I understand," I replied. "Life gets in the way. A murder investigation isn't a hobby, especially this one. That's why people hire me."

Veronica gave a smile of thanks. She stood beside me, close enough that she brushed my arm. I could feel the heat of her skin.

I removed the box's lid. Thick hanging folders were braced from the sides. "How long have you had this?"

"Since a couple of weeks before Roxy was killed."

Several months, then. "This could be considered withholding evidence from a murder investigation," I said.

Veronica shook her head. "I'm not withholding anything."

"What do you mean?"

"After her death—her murder rather—the cops raided Barrios Unidos to look for *evidence,*" Veronica replied. "All they said was 'Show us Roxy's desk.' They emptied the drawers. They took everything: personal photos, pens, even a box of paper clips." In the excitement of telling me the story, Veronica returned to her quickstep Spanish. "I was surprised the detectives didn't scrape the gum stuck under her chair."

"What about Roxy's computer?" I asked.

"They confiscated that. And we had to give them permission to go to our Internet service provider and dig through our emails. The assholes deleted half of our archives just to be pricks." Veronica turned away and rubbed her forehead, as if the memory hurt.

"How did you end up with the box?"

"After we stopped Project Eleven and got done celebrating," Veronica said, "Roxy and I decided to consolidate the files, which at the time were scattered all over the office. We'd see what to keep or toss out. I took the box, thinking I would go through it when I got the chance. But I never did."

"Where was the box when the police searched Barrios Unidos?"

"In the trunk of my car. Had they asked, I would've given it to them." Veronica shared a look troubled by anxiety. "Roxy was dead. A lot of rich people were happy about that. The cops were only there to purge anything that could further embarrass the politicos behind Project Eleven."

I ran my thumb along the thick stacks of papers inside the hanging folders. "It'll take a while to go through this. Good thing I brought my toothbrush and jammies."

"Your jammies?" The anguish in her eyes gave way to a twinkle. She gave a sardonic laugh. "Okay, you want to stay up all night and play detective, that's your business. You are the professional. But first we get dinner. I'm starving. There's a place down the street that stays open late. We'll talk about something else besides this." She pointed to the box.

Veronica put on sequined flip-flops. We went out and stood in line at a restaurant decorated with bamboo awnings and tiki torches. She chewed a tablet of Nicorette gum and clasped my hand. Her silver rings singed me and I repositioned her hand so that her forearm rested on mine.

I had to skip the first table the maître d' offered, as she wanted to sit us with my back against a mirror. How long would it have taken Veronica to notice in the reflection that she dined alone?

I settled for a corner booth. No mirrors. One candle.

Veronica asked for margaritas. We split an order of swordfish with mango chutney and potato cakes. I tried my best to match her appetite, but without a drenching of blood, even a gourmet offering like this tasted as bland as cold, unsalted oatmeal.

Veronica kept with the margaritas while we chatted about life, her family, and movies. I didn't mention it, but my thoughts kept rolling back to what might be in Roxy's files.

Veronica stopped midway through her third drink and pushed the glass away. "I surrender. Coffee?"

We had the house blend, which sans blood, tasted like muddy water. Veronica nibbled on cheesecake.

On the way back to her place, I kept her on my left side so when we walked arm in arm, her silver wouldn't touch my bare skin. Climbing the stairs to her apartment, she slipped and I caught her.

Veronica clung to the banister. "Give me a minute. My stomach is sorting through this love-hate relationship I have with tequila."

Closing her eyes for a moment, she took a deep breath and exhaled. I helped her trudge up the stairs. We paused at her door while she dug keys from her shorts pocket.

She fumbled with the dead bolt. "Felix, are you enjoying yourself?"

"Of course. Why?"

"You picked at your food. I practically swam in my margaritas. You barely sipped yours. Now you hold me like I could give you cooties."

"Maybe it's me who has cooties."

Veronica slurred a laugh. "You don't have cooties." She pecked my cheek. "See. No cooties. Was that so complicated?"

Being an undead bloodsucker makes everything complicated.

With my hand steadying her shoulder, she guided me into the apartment and her bedroom. Veronica plunked face first onto the mattress. Her feet dangled off the edge of the bed and her flip-flops dropped to the floor.

Veronica's right hand came up and pointed to the hall. "Felix, be my hero," she mumbled, "and bring some water."

I went to the bathroom and filled a glass. When I returned to the bedroom, Veronica had turned onto one side and gathered a pillow under her head. The little screen of an iPod on the nightstand gave an inert glow.

I set the glass beside the iPod, took off my shoes, and lay next to Veronica to spoon. Her firm rump pressed along my pelvis. I pushed one hand under the pillow and laid the other on her hip.

The music playing was a woman crooning about frustrated love. She must've cribbed my notes.

Up close, Veronica was a cascade of smells: sweat, tequila, mango chutney, shampoo, aloe vera lotion, and her delicious pheromones. This beautiful, healthy—albeit pickled to a hundred proof—creature that I rested against was a reservoir of savory blood and sexual release.

I could zap Veronica and enjoy the ride. What would prevent me?

A junkie going cold turkey and finding a syringe loaded with smack, a pyromaniac with matches, gasoline, and an empty house, their temptations were trivial whims compared to the roiling hunger that stoked my desire.

CHAPTER
21

*N*O. I WOULDN'T TAKE advantage of Veronica. God had taken away my soul, but I remained with a free will. I am vampire, not an animal that surrenders to every impulse.

I'd reciprocate Veronica's affection, nothing more. Let her decide, sober and willing, how this relationship would progress.

I held Veronica tight and waited for temptation to pass. My *kundalini noir* finally relaxed and my fangs shrank back under my lip.

Veronica snored faintly and I waited for the songs on the iPod to end.

I stayed with her until 3 A.M., then got up and removed my contacts. Veronica lay swaddled in her red aura, undulating with dreamy thoughts. I walked to the front room. The floor creaked, and I levitated to pad about noiselessly.

Her heart thumped a beaconing tempo.

My fangs pushed out from my gums.

The valves in her veins ticked like stopwatches, counting the seconds before my attack.

My *kundalini noir* coiled as it prepared me to strike and feed.

Something rustled outside the window. A small red aura betrayed an opossum munching grapes.

"Better scat," I whispered, "before Coyote finds you."

The opossum's beady eyes stared from under a crown of grape leaves as it continued eating.

I dug through my overnight bag for blood I brought from Coyote's. I microwaved one package of type B-positive.

While sipping blood through a drinking straw, I opened the box with Roxy's file and removed the first folder. I sat in a chair with the folder on my lap and unfastened a binder clip.

This file contained photocopies of the agendas and minutes from city council meetings. Someone had scrawled along the margins and between the paragraphs. Words were underlined with bold strokes, as if the pen had been slashed across the paper like a blade.

I recognized names from the Los Angeles political scene. Lucky Rosario. Councilwoman Petale Venin. I kept tripping over her name in this investigation. She was the quarterback behind the effort to get Project Eleven on the ballot. I assumed she had plenty of dirt under her fingernails—what politician didn't?—but I couldn't imagine someone in her public position risking murder.

Nowhere in the papers did I see mention of Cragnow Vissoom, Dr. Mordecai Niphe, or Reverend Journey.

I flipped through the stack. It would take a month to go through these documents. I'd get a clearer picture of the battle over Project Eleven, but would anyone have said something to incriminate him- or herself with violent crime? Or even more improbably, vampire–human collusion?

I leafed through the next folder, a collection of grainy black-and-white copies of photographs.

The first photo that caught my interest was of Lucky Rosario standing beside a washed-up Hollywood celebrity. The actor had done a series about a bounty hunter in Miami until low ratings and a drug habit did him in.

Where had I seen these pictures before?

On the wall of Rosario's office.

How did Roxy get these copies? When I first saw the original pictures at Rosario's they didn't mean much. What had I
missed? What was the significance to my investigation?

Something like this next picture.

Three men stood before a restaurant table.

The man on the left was the shortest. Wearing a pin-
striped shirt and fashionable tie, with keen eyes peering
through wire-rims, and a thick mat of kinky hair, was Dr.
Mordecai Niphe. In the middle of the group, a white shirt
rumpled under the armpits, collar and tie digging into a fat
neck, grinned Lucky Rosario. Lucky's arm draped over
Niphe's shoulder like they were best buds.

Standing to the right was a tall, older man in a suit. He
had gray, almost whitish, well-groomed hair. I didn't need a
caption to know who he was.

Reverend Dale Journey.

He projected the arrogant bearing of an elderly senator or
a retired air force general. Yet his smile appeared too tight.
Nervous. The gap between Journey and Rosario told me that
Journey didn't want to be seen in this company.

Journey and Niphe together, with Rosario in the middle.
What linked them? Who lurked unseen in the background?
Cragnow Vissoom?

The time was 5:30 A.M. Sunrise would come soon. I
needed to hide from the deadly rays of first light. Sunblock
wasn't enough to protect me.

The photos were promising, but first I had to protect myself
from the sun. I clipped the file together and set it back in the
box.

The front room faced east. I closed the drapes tight and
retreated to a room at the back of Veronica's apartment, the
west side. I felt like a spider slinking down its hole.

What made the sunrise so dangerous? I didn't know. Perhaps a vampire's psychic defenses weakened over the night
and the splash of sunlight breaking across the eastern hori-

zon was too intense to endure. Or was there a special property of sunlight when it penetrated the atmosphere at a low oblique angle? Let another vampire, some undead egghead, solve that mystery.

I closed the door of the back room and shut the curtains to block any stray reflected sunbeams.

The room was Veronica's home office. A laptop computer sat on a small desk. Assorted notes to call Mom, pick up laundry, dangled from thumbtacks stuck to a corkboard on the wall. Binders stuffed with papers lay stacked on an ironing board.

One paper lay half out of the binder, and I slipped it out. It was a letter from the dean of the Graduate School at Brown University offering a tenured position teaching public affairs and public policy. I opened the binder. The next paper was a letter of introduction from the marketing department of Toyota of America. Buried in the binder were unopened envelopes from Princeton, a lobbying firm in Washington, D.C., and Univision. This was a basket of brass rings, and yet Veronica ignored them to stay where she felt needed most—in the ramshackle surroundings of Barrios Unidos.

What I had run away from, Veronica embraced as her calling.

But I had left years ago. As a boy. Human. Now I returned as vampire on a mission of vengeance.

I waited in a cheap office chair next to the desk. Slowly the curtain turned into an illuminated rectangle as sunrise began. The minutes passed, and the rectangle got brighter and brighter.

A quarter past seven. The window was as bright as it would get. The worst of the deadly rays had abated and the threat passed.

I left the back room to fetch my overnight bag. Veronica remained silent in her room, evidently fast asleep. The kitchen and dining area were lit with sunshine flooding past the curtains. Though I was safe, I felt a tinge of fear, like standing close to a river of hot lava.

I went into the bathroom and covered with makeup–sunblock as much skin as I expected to show. I sat in the kitchen, my wet hair slicked back, my fangs squeaky clean and minty fresh. I wore a T-shirt and shorts, and propped my bare feet on the cool tiles along the edge of the counter. My contacts were in, to keep from scrambling for them once Veronica got up.

After brewing coffee, I mixed half of another bag of blood into my cup of java. The rest of the blood I dumped into a bowl and sopped it up with a warmed cranberry scone.

The third folder from the box rested on my lap. The folder contained a jumble of loose papers, printouts of emails, and Web blogs.

I found a small greeting card. A soft-focus photo of a coffee setting decorated the cover. Tucked inside the card was a restaurant credit card receipt made to Freya Krieger. Time of purchase: 1:12 P.M. The date? Three weeks before the death of Roxy Bronze.

The note in the card was neatly penned in blue:

Sis, Great to see you.
Lara

Who was Lara? *Sis?*

Did Roxy Bronze—Freya Krieger—have a sister named Lara?

They had gotten together for lunch, and because of the card, I gathered the two didn't see each other often. Was Lara visiting, or did she live in L.A.? If the latter case, why the card? Was there an estrangement between the two?

Veronica stirred in the bedroom.

I put the file aside. With the last piece of scone I blotted the remaining globs of blood. I poured plain java into a cup to let it cool, then swished the coffee in my mouth to have the proper breakfast breath. As I washed the dishes and cleared away all evidence of my blood meal, the door to the bathroom closed.

When Veronica came into the kitchen I was arranging the files in the box. She cinched the belt of a white terry cloth robe. Strands of wet hair curled beside her freshly scrubbed face. Even though she smelled of bayberry soap, her eyes still carried the wilted look of overdoing it the night before.

With her hands thrust into the pockets of the robe, Veronica leaned against the doorway from the hall into the kitchen. "Thanks for being a gentleman."

Me? A gentleman? Give me a chance to change that opinion. I filled a cup with coffee. "Cream? Sugar?"

She took the cup in both hands. "Black is fine." Eyes closed, she slurped several times. Every swallow brought more life to her expression. A finger uncurled from the cup and pointed to the box. "Any progress?"

"Some. There's a lot of info. I'll have to take the files to study them."

Veronica rested her hip against the edge of the sink counter. Her brown eyes, shiny as gemstones, stared over the rim of her coffee cup. "What a hot Latina babe I turned out to be."

"Not to worry. My interests are strictly professional." I'm a practiced liar.

An amused smile played across her lips. She glanced to the wall clock by the refrigerator. "I've got brunch with the girls from Barrios Unidos. Wanna come with?"

The girls from Barrios Unidos? Plus Veronica. Could make for an interesting, if tangled, way to pass an otherwise boring Sunday.

"Thanks"—I tapped the box containing the files—"but I should get started."

Veronica looked at the box, then to the clock, and finally to me. She put her cup in the sink. That amused smile returned. "Yes, it's time you got started." She undid her belt and let the robe slip to the floor. "Let's make up for last night."

Naked, Veronica was spectacular.

CHAPTER 22

VERONICA AND I RUSHED down the stairs from her apartment, her flip-flops smacking as we ran through the breezeway to the parking spaces in the back.

"Ay Dios," Veronica said. "I hate this. I'm the one getting after the girls at Barrios Unidos to watch the clock. Now look at me."

She ran to the driver's side of a Nissan sedan and aimed a key remote. The door locks clicked. I opened the rear door on the passenger's side and put the box with Roxy's files and my overnight bag on the seat. I sat up front next to Veronica.

She jammed the key into the ignition and started the car. With one hand on the gearshift she whispered to herself, "Wild Oats. Coffee. Bakery. Fruit."

It was half past ten. Her brunch was at eleven. No way she'd make it.

I, on the other hand, congratulated myself. Veronica surprised me with her expectations for a morning quickie in the kitchen, followed by an encore on the dinette table. The challenge had been to keep Veronica hypnotized enough to remember some but not all of what happened. I wanted her to recall that sex with me was very good, great, outstanding, the best ever, but not that I was a vampire.

When I removed my clothes she would've noticed the pale, translucent skin not covered by makeup. To use hypnosis, my contacts had to go. I had no choice but to use my vampire powers, not to seduce her, but to keep my secrets safe.

I gave her the occasional stare and a measured application of fangs to keep her in a modulated state between conscious and completely whacked out. Her silver jewelry needed to come off to keep from burning my skin when she stroked and clutched in passion.

Vampire hypnosis or not, Veronica showed remarkable initiative when demonstrating her many carnal skills.

She flicked down the sun visor and examined her neck in the vanity mirror. "The hickies you left are barely notice-able, *gracias a Dios.*" She wiped at the corner of her mouth to tidy a smear of lip gloss. She spread her fingers. "Don't remember taking off my rings. How do you do it, Felix? One minute I'm with you. The next I'm fogged over. You're not slipping me something? Roofies?"

"All you're getting is Felix Gomez." And Trojans.

"Besides that, I mean." She put the Nissan into reverse and backed into the street.

I told Veronica that a friend had dropped me off at her place and I needed a ride to the closest car rental. The place was on Beverly Boulevard not far from her apartment and on the way to her morning shopping.

Veronica stopped in the rental lot. We kissed good-bye. She drove off in typical L.A. fashion, foot flat on the gas and a cell phone pressed against one ear.

I slung my overnight bag over one shoulder and carried the box of files into the rental office.

An older woman—blue hair, skinny legs with varicose veins, high-water pants covered with an upchuck of colors—stood against the counter. The woman glared at the tense young man in a baggy dress shirt whose attention was directed at a computer monitor. The little wiry dog in the woman's arms saw me, growled, and started a yapping fit.

The surveillance camera on the wall peered through two mirrors, each at a different angle, so that this single camera could cover a wide area. A thrifty arrangement and one that worked in my favor. I could be captured on video but not if my image was reflected through a mirror.

The rental clerk raised his head and scowled. "In a minute, sir."

The elderly crone wrinkled her face in distain, as if I were a booger with legs.

These two needed an attitude adjustment. "If you please," I said and removed my contacts.

Their auras gave nice bursts of crimson. They stared zombielike. The dog kept yapping.

With the clerk hypnotized, I ordered him to look up my account, override any holds, and issue a luxury car at subcompact rates. Add maximum insurance coverage at no extra cost so I could've rolled my rental off the Santa Monica pier and not owed this company a dime.

I left the clerk and the old woman comatose and naked on a table in the break room. Glazed donuts covered their naughty parts. The pooch swung from the overhead fan, his harness and leash tied to one of the blades.

The rental, a blue Chrysler 500M, was the kind of fancy, overly macho car a Klingon would've appreciated. I locked the box with Roxy's files in the trunk. What new clues waited for me?

New clues about Venin and Niphe.

But first I needed to do something I should've done earlier in my investigation. Visit the spot where Roxy Bronze had been killed.

I drove north to the corner of Hollywood Boulevard and Cahuenga and passed the alley where she had been found. I circled the neighborhood. LAPD Hollywood Station and the city hall annex were four blocks south. What a convenient walk for the detectives "investigating" Roxy's murder.

I parked near the corner of Selma and Cahuenga, next to a café and close to the alley. Wooden scaffolds shaded the sidewalk on the opposite side of the street. Posters covered the plywood sidings. Scruffy men mingled in the shadows, smoking cigarettes and sharing drinks from a bag.

This being Sunday midmorning, other than the customers in the café and the bums, there weren't many people out.

I walked up the street toward Hollywood Boulevard. I passed a couple of shops that sold either porn or really bad art—I couldn't tell through the dingy windows. There was a take-out barbecue joint and at the corner, a twenty-four-hour newsstand. Except for the newsstand and café, everything was closed.

Considering its glamorous reputation, Hollywood Boulevard seemed disappointingly low rent. Grime caked the shuttered storefronts. A dead pigeon rested near an empty tallboy of malt liquor. Trash on the sidewalk sullied the marble stars and brass plaques of the Hollywood Walk of Fame.

I returned to the alley and stopped at the entrance. A multistory office building stood to the right, the northern side. A two-story, gray brick building was on the left, the southern side. Posters for musical acts were pasted to the gray walls.

I walked into the alley, between tall metal gates secured in the open position. The alley turned left and made an L to the south. The asphalt in the immediate area seemed remarkably clean, as if steam blasted. Any traces of Roxy's death had long been obliterated. A roll-on Dumpster stood against the wall at the corner of the L. What little I had learned about the crime scene was that Roxy was found dead beside this Dumpster at a little after one in the morning.

I knelt and touched the spot where Roxy must have fallen dead. I closed my eyes and, in my memory, saw her face again, not the leer from the porno DVD but that warm, empathetic, and gracious smile of a high school girl.

I caressed the rough surface of the asphalt and imagined picking up faint sparks of Roxy's long-evaporated aura. I felt nothing of course; still, there was much of the supernatural world that I didn't know.

Standing again, I wiped the dirt from my hand.

The police report—a breezy, sanitized summary my hacker had found—said that a "small-caliber bullet" entered Roxy's torso at a horizontal angle. But where in her torso? There was no mention of gunpowder residue nor an estimated range from the shooter to Roxy. The police insisted the homicide was a random act, which meant the shot was remarkably lucky—or unlucky, from Roxy's point of view.

According to the report, the murder went like this: Pow. Roxy dropped dead. Happened faster than the snap of my fingers.

One small-caliber bullet dropped her? A .22? A .25? Pistol, according to the newspapers. One small bullet to the torso, and a strong, healthy woman like Roxy just collapsed and died? The one bullet could kill her, of course. Usually the victims bled to death, sometimes within seconds.

There wasn't anything random about the shot. Roxy was gunned down at close range. Meaning she had been comfortable enough with the shooter to let him—or her—get close, especially at that time of night.

There was a lot more to Roxy's murder than the remarkable ballistics of one little bullet. How convenient that the police had lost evidence. Too bad she had been cremated; otherwise, I'd get her corpse exhumed and autopsied again.

The entrance from Selma had battered metal gates, secured open with rusted padlocks. Weeds with yellow blossoms grew between cracks in the asphalt.

A scuzzy area, yes. But dangerous? Maybe at night, this area would be different.

On the drive to Coyote's home, I mulled over the images of the murder scene. They flashed like slides across my brain, and I imagined Roxy's corpse sprawled on the asphalt in the alley with a chalk outline around her body. The trip to Hollywood confirmed the obvious, that I didn't yet have the whole story about her murder.

I got off the freeway. Surprisingly, my Chrysler wasn't the

fanciest set of wheels in the neighborhood. The homies were back in their cribs this Sunday morning. Scores of big customized SUVs and pickups made this part of Boyle Heights look like the impound lot of the Drug Enforcement Agency.

I carried my overnight bag and the box with Roxy's files toward Coyote's home. He sat in the shade under a blue tarp stretched from his porch and tied to a pair of crooked aluminum poles. He tossed golfball-size pellets from a greasy paper bag to the snapping jaws of three scrawny dogs.

Coyote blinked his bloodshot eyes. Even for a vampire, despite his makeup and leather skin, he looked pale.

I asked how he was doing.

"Not so good, *vato*." He shifted in the lawn chair. "It's that rat chorizo. Maybe there's a reason you leave the tails out." Coyote reached into the bag and lobbed a hunk of the malodorous sausage. "What's in the box, *ese*?"

"Homework."

"How was Veronica?"

"Healthy."

Coyote nodded and went back to feeding the dogs.

Inside the house I set my laptop computer on the kitchen table. I sent an email to my hacker and asked for anything regarding Lara Krieger, possibly the sister of Roxy Bronze.

I reviewed the files. I set aside the photo of Niphe, Rosario, and Journey standing together. Finding information that linked them was my immediate task, though if I wanted to dredge through notes and numbers like this, I would've been an accountant. I sorted the documents, cross-checking information, taking the occasional break for a coffee-and-blood pick-me-up. What I really wanted was a Manhattan and another shot of leg . . . Veronica's.

The last folder held large manila envelopes. I opened one and pulled out a cheap spiral notebook. Scotch tape held photocopies of news clippings to the pages. Judging by the dates, this information went back more than ten years, long before Project Eleven.

One photo from the *Los Angeles Times* showed a much

slimmer Rosario and a woman in her midthirties, dark hair, oversize glasses, passing one another in a vestibule within the city hall building. The caption identified her as Councilwoman Petale Venin. The accompanying story described the controversy surrounding the rezoning along Loma Alta Drive in Altadena and the use of eminent domain to displace the residents for commercial development.

But what stood there now was Dale Journey's church. What happened to the commercial development?

I read through the clippings in the notebook and learned that the development trust pushing for eminent domain had gone bankrupt. After the homes had been demolished, the vacant land, with its magnificent views of the San Gabriel Valley, lay fallow.

Then what? How did Journey get the land for his ministry? The files didn't mention what happened next.

Had Roxy found something that led to her murder?

Lots of clues. And lots more questions. But nothing definite about her murder, and zilch concerning vampire–human collusion.

My brain felt like I'd been scraping it against a cheese grater. The clock read 10:14 P.M. Time to set the files aside and take another look at the alley where Roxy was gunned down. I closed the box.

I got my .380 automatic, checked that it was loaded, and holstered the pistol to the back of my trousers.

Coyote sat on the edge of his porch. He sipped a concoction with the aroma of *yerba buena*—mint tea—with lamb's blood, a traditional Mexican vampire's remedy for an upset stomach. He put the cup down. "The next time I mention rat chorizo, please kick me in the ass."

"Can I practice?"

Coyote grabbed his crotch. "On this, *cabron*."

"You up for a ride? Providing you're not going to puke."

"Don't worry." He tilted his face toward me. His eyeballs looked their normal jaundiced yellow. "Where we going?"

"Hollywood."

CHAPTER
23

ONCE INSIDE THE CHRYSLER, Coyote found the controls and moved his seat all the way back and up. He propped his dirty sneakers through the window. As we drove out of Boyle Heights, Coyote bobbed his head in rhythm to a reggae beat tuned on the satellite radio.

"*Vato,* know what would make this ride *bien suave*? Some ganja."

"Fresh out."

Coyote opened his jacket and produced a metal hip flask. "Then mescal will do." He took a swig and belched. He wiped the neck of the flask and offered it to me.

The flask reeked of rat chorizo, which smothered any thirst I might have had. "Thanks, but I don't drink rat and drive."

Coyote shrugged. He upended the flask, and the drink gurgled into his mouth. Suddenly coughing, he folded over and hung his head out the window.

Was this another reaction to the rat chorizo? I pulled against the curb.

Coyote sat straight, panting, and wiped drool from his face. "I forgot about the *pinchi* worm. Damn near choked me."

"Serves you right for drinking that shit."

Coyote capped the flask and inserted it back into an inner jacket pocket. "It keeps the hair on my balls. You ought to try some."

"Too bad it doesn't do anything for your mustache."

I pulled away from the curb. I described our destination, the alley where Roxy had been found dead. My plan was to get a sense of the place at night.

"You mean a stakeout?" Coyote sat rigid, rolled his shoulders back, and thrust his chin out. He swiveled his head robotically to the left and right.

"Sort of," I replied. "If we get lucky, something important will turn up."

We arrived at Hollywood and Cahuenga at 11 P.M. The corner was as alive and crowded as it had been dormant and lonely earlier that afternoon. Cars lined the streets, and I had to park two blocks away.

Customers stood shoulder to shoulder inside the café. People on the sidewalk followed barbecue smoke and queued at the window of the take-out up the street. Men and women milled around open doors of the tiny nightclubs, guarded by bouncers perched on tall stools.

A van was parked in the alley beside the gray building. Men toted amplifiers and guitars from the van to the rear entrance.

Coyote and I walked west on Selma and entered the alley from the south. Both of us checked to make sure no one noticed, then trotted up the wall and onto the roof.

Levitating so we'd move silently over the rooftop, Coyote and I made our way to where we could observe the spot where Roxy Bronze was slain. The flat roof vibrated from music inside the building. This perspective from above rendered us all but invisible. No one bothered to look up.

I removed my contacts and knelt with my elbows on the short wall surrounding the roof. Coyote kept me company, both of us as quiet and absorbed as a couple of anglers watching a pond.

Midnight came. The crowds ebbed and formed again. Some people laughed. Others argued. A few teetered on drunken legs and puked. Pretty lively for a Sunday night.

A Jaguar convertible drove up Cahuenga. The orange aura of the driver announced he was a vampire. I followed his progress along the street. Coyote nudged me and also watched the visitor.

The vampire's large head sat on the broad shoulders of a thick frame. He had sandy hair in a medium-length cut. He slowed and panned the knots of people before continuing to Hollywood Boulevard.

Who, or what, was he looking for?

I whispered, "Coyote, recognize him?"

Coyote shook his head. "Nah."

SUVs with spinner wheels paraded past, disgorging or picking up women in clothes as tight as tamale wrappers.

An orange aura surrounded one of the women. Vampire.

I studied her aura and those of her human companions. The vampire's aura teemed with bright spots and bumps. She advertised the anticipation of feeding on necks later. The humans seemed clueless about her appetite for them. So they weren't chalices. And she behaved like a vampire out on the prowl. She was your new best girlfriend, inviting oodles of trust and gossip, yet biding her time for the chance to clamp sharp fangs on your throat. Typical undead predatory behavior.

"Know her?" I asked Coyote.

"Wish I did, *ese*."

"Seems the type that could twist you in knots."

"Like rat chorizo? *Vato,* I survived that, I could survive her."

The women chatted with the bouncer at the entrance to the nightclub and went inside.

A half hour later, the vampire in the Jaguar convertible returned. He paused by the alley entrance. A human female lay in the narrow backseat. Her tranquil red aura said she was either asleep or passed out. Drunk? Drugged? Under vampire hypnosis?

What was he doing? Trolling for another catch?

To watch him more closely I got careless and poked my head too high above the edge of the building. A human wouldn't have noticed, or a vampire wearing contacts, but my orange aura announced my presence like a Day-Glo banner.

The vampire snapped his gaze upward, his *tapetum lucidum* reflecting the surrounding neon. His eyes locked on mine. A glow of exhilaration brushed through his aura, as if he'd found a prize. At that instant I knew he was looking for me.

Unfolding a cell phone and accelerating toward Hollywood Boulevard, he tossed one final glance back, as if to confirm what he had seen.

"Who's he calling?" I asked. "How did he know to look here?"

Coyote ducked low and his gaze flitted about like a real coyote searching for an escape route. "Feels like a trap, *ese.*"

The Jaguar turned left on Hollywood Boulevard and headed west.

"Trap or no trap, I'll bet that vampire can answer some questions." My *kundalini noir* flexed for combat. Talons and fangs extended. I patted the outline of my .380 pistol. "Traffic's heavy, so we can box him in." I motioned to the right. "You follow and come from behind."

Coyote moved to the edge of the wall. "And you, Felix?"

"If this is a trap, it means trouble. Isn't that what we came for?"

CHAPTER
24

NO TIME TO WASTE if I wanted to catch the vampire. If I moved diagonally across the block, I'd intercept his Jaguar convertible at the intersection of Hollywood and Wilcox.

I took a running leap and sailed across the alley to the roof of the opposite building. I bounded from rooftop to rooftop and levitated to the sidewalk on Wilcox.

I rounded the corner at a sprint and pushed a couple of pedestrians out of my way. The Jaguar cruised in the oncoming lane of Hollywood Boulevard. I sprang from the sidewalk and headed right for the convertible.

The driver's aura erupted in surprise, then blazed with anger. He veered out of traffic and gunned the engine. The glare of his headlights dazzled me.

I wasn't going to step aside and let him get away. I leapt for the driver. The bumper and grille slid under my legs. My talons scratched across the hood and I smashed into the windshield.

The driver's aura burned incandescent with fury. His Jaguar raced across traffic. Horns blared and tires screeched in a chaotic blur. The Jaguar bounced over the curb and I slapped against the hood but held firm to the wipers. We crashed through the steel barricade locked over a storefront.

Broken metal shutters tore at my back, shredding my clothes. Glass showered the air. Hot steam from the radiator sprayed my ankles and feet. A snarl of pain broke from my throat.

The Jaguar burst through a rack of women's lingerie and slammed to a halt. Two cash registers catapulted past my head and ricocheted off the windshield, smashing the glass.

Dazed, I lay still on the hood. The back of my legs ached where the metal shutters had smacked them. My hands tingled from holding on to the wipers during the crash. Both of my feet were wet from the Jaguar's coolant.

Lacy garments fluttered around us like dizzy birds. Remnants of a splintered counter littered the carpet. Overhead banks of illuminated fluorescent lamps hummed, the only noise in the room. Lights at this time of the morning? Inside a shuttered building?

The quiet and my questions didn't last long.

Naked young women jounced around the room in panic, screeching as if splashing through acid. One dangled in a love swing suspended from the ceiling, wiggling like a snared rabbit. The women stumbled over spilled racks of clothing. Two men with camcorders tripped across electric cables and klieg lights.

They were filming a porn movie? Now? I didn't know the skin business had a graveyard shift.

The girl in the backseat of the Jaguar sat up, her head covered by swirls of tangled hair. As her gaze swiveled across the room, she brushed bits of glass from her shoulders. With no expression of surprise, she slithered out of the backseat and over the side of the car.

The driver used his talons to tear away the air bag draping his face. Looking about, he seemed as confused as I was.

But only for an instant.

Fangs bared, he lunged at me through the broken windshield, his talons splayed like the tines of pitchforks.

I locked my fingers into his and used his momentum to withdraw over the front of the Jaguar. Bracing my knees against the bumper, I gave a mighty pull and yanked him fully through the windshield.

I squeezed his fingers and hands and cracked bone. When he screamed I gave him a head butt to his face. I let go his fingers to grab his hair and brandish my pistol. He flailed uselessly while I hammered his face with the butt of the gun. Vampire blood spritzed against my fingers.

I beat the vampire and kept beating him out of my frustration with this case. Every strike to his head accompanied a question. *What's going on? What do you know? What can't I see?*

Sparks of pain flashed through the vampire's aura, marking the tempo of my blows. The sparks faded, and the vampire's arms fell limp.

I didn't want to kill him, not yet. When he first saw me on the roof, he called someone to report he'd found me. Why? I brought my face close to his. "Who are you working for? Who did you call?"

His eyes rolled to the left and right and fixed upon me. His aura smoothed for a moment and became tranquil, as if he were grateful for the recess from pain. A flame of bright orange exploded through his aura. He growled, spittle dripping from his long teeth.

"Let me repeat the lesson." I smashed his face into the hood of the Jaguar like I was working a stapler. His fangs left two crooked rows of punctures and red slobber in the dented metal.

"Again. Who are you working for?" I screwed the muzzle of the pistol into his temple. "Answer me, you stupid bastard, before I ventilate your brain."

He gurgled through the pink froth around his swollen lips. "Cragnow."

The name I wanted to hear. "Why?"

"You . . . you . . ." The vampire gasped and choked.

"Me what?"

Something pounded on the roof. The lights went out. Panels of acoustical tiles, insulation, and chunks of plaster tumbled to the floor from the ceiling.

The women, who were already screaming at air-raid siren volume, let out a wave of even more deafening shrieks. Their red auras boiled with terror.

I let go of the vampire's hair. His face thumped the hood. I aimed my automatic at the ceiling. More tiles fell and exposed a black hole. An orange aura appeared in the void.

Coyote.

He floated to the floor, yelling, *"La jura."* The cops. "They're not wasting time getting here. *Vamonos.*"

I surveyed the damage. The front of the store was demolished. Bystanders peeked through the tangle of twisted metal shutters and their gazes probed the darkness. Several thousands of dollars in lingerie lay about, now useless rags. A totaled Jaguar. One thoroughly battered bloodsucker. I brushed the dust of his dried blood from my fingers.

A public spectacle of vampire-to-vampire combat was a huge no-no. But the problem was Cragnow Vissoom's. As the leader of the local *nidus,* his duty was to keep vampire activity hidden from humans. This was his mess to tidy.

"Give me a minute," I shouted to Coyote. I made for the vampire's pockets to search for his wallet and cell phone.

A police car skidded to a halt outside the entrance to the store, throwing a frenetic kaleidoscope of red and blue lights.

Coyote jumped and glided up through the hole.

I had to forget about the vampire. If I lingered another second, the cops would be on me.

Limping from the Jaguar, I stashed my pistol in its holster, took a couple of painful steps to build momentum, and hopped upward to follow Coyote. We scrambled across the roof and to the street, where we stayed in the shadows, moving like phantoms back to my car. I smelled of radiator antifreeze. My trousers and shirt hung in tatters.

Dozens of police cars circled the block behind us, their flashing lights making the streets look like a pinball arcade. Spotlights fixed on the shiny, anxious faces of people streaming from the nightclubs. A helicopter whirled overhead, and the shaft of a searchlight stabbed the rooftops where we had just been.

The speed with which so many cops responded astonished me. As Cragnow's hired gun, Deputy Chief Julius Paxton must have prepared his buddies in Hollywood Station to muster such a force. Some of these cops had to be undead. Meaning they'd use vampire vision to search for auras. The gloom of night wouldn't protect Coyote, or me.

CHAPTER
25

W E SNUCK TO MY CAR. I took Santa Monica Boulevard east to the Hollywood Freeway and straight to Coyote's home. I checked the mirrors for police. Nada.

My back muscles throbbed from the lacerations. The frustration that overwhelmed me earlier returned and my mind spiraled into a whorl of confusion. The red taillights around me fused into a crimson smear. My thoughts tumbled around the other vampire, as if he and I were locked inside a barrel careening down a hill. What part did this vampire play in Cragnow's plan? Was he a mere lookout, a guard . . . or an assassin? How much did he know?

I recoiled, startled by the rank odor of rat chorizo and stale mescal. Coyote chugged from his flask.

The stench yanked me back to the present like a whiff of ammonia. The taillights of the car in front of me snapped into sharp focus.

Coyote lowered the flask and munched on something.

"You had another worm in there?" I asked, wondering what he chewed.

He shrugged. "Worm, cockroach, don't know."

Coyote's aura pulsed with anxiety. He hunched forward and screwed and unscrewed the metal cap of the flask.

"What did that vampire tell you, *ese*?"

"Not much." I remembered my hand rebounding from the vampire's face. My lips curled into a grin. "He said he worked for Cragnow."

"Surprised?"

I paused. *No.* "Relieved, actually. Means I'm getting close to my answers. He got on the phone too quickly after he saw me. Like it was part of a plan. That confirms what I've suspected."

"What?"

"Cragnow was behind Roxy's murder."

Coyote twisted the cap onto the flask and shoved it back into his jacket. "Don't get ahead of yourself, Felix. It only means Cragnow expected you to visit the alley." Lights from oncoming traffic cast moving shadows across Coyote's withered face.

"You're quick to defend him," I said.

"*Chale.* I dream to see you do to Cragnow what you did to his *matón*." His thug. "Think about it, *ese*. Did that vampire tell you anything about Roxy?"

"I didn't have the chance to ask. But the trail from Roxy's murder leads to Cragnow."

"Don't be too sure."

"I *am* sure," I replied. "Why else would he plant a lookout on the alley?"

"To catch you, *ese*. Why are you here in Los Angeles?"

Seemed an obvious question. "To find out who killed Roxy Bronze. And investigate vampire–human collusion, which seems as rampant here as chicken pox in a kindergarten."

Coyote reeled his fingers, as if to draw out my response. "Why does Cragnow want to stop you?"

Another obvious question. "To keep me from finding out who killed Roxy."

Coyote shook his head in rebuttal. "Let's suppose, *vato,* that Cragnow had nothing to do with her death. In that case, why would he care if you solved her murder or not?"

"Explain this. I ask about Roxy and for my troubles I almost get turned into asphalt pâté. Then this goon tonight tried to play bumper tag with his Jag."

"Cragnow fears you," Coyote said. "Why?"

"Because I'm a threat to his vampire–human enterprise."

"Which is not the same as Roxy's murder, is it?" Coyote grinned expectantly, as if waiting for a dim bulb to light in my brain.

"What about Rebecca Dwelling?" I asked. "Why was she knocked off if not to protect Cragnow? And Katz Meow is still missing. Tell me that's not a coincidence. What's the connection?"

Coyote stroked his mustache and massaged his chin. "Good questions." He touched the button on his armrest and retracted the window. Cool air blasted in and cleansed the interior of rat chorizo and mescal stink. Coyote extended his legs to prop his feet out the window. "You're the professional. You tell me."

Tell him what? That the investigation had so far been a knot of clues in a maze of blind corners?

Back at his "palace," and hungry as always, Coyote poured himself a bowl of pork in *chile rojo,* the *rojo* coming from type A-positive stirred into the sauce.

I washed and changed clothes. Four aspirins and a bourbon straight up dulled the sting from my wounds. I'd be fine by morning.

Email waited from my Internet hacker. He—or she—was still working on retrieving Katz Meow's telephone records.

And I got confirmation that Roxy Bronze—Freya Krieger—had a sister. Lara Krieger, now Lara Phillips, her married name, though recently divorced. The hacker included Lara's address and a telephone number.

A clue or yet another wrinkle to smooth over?

Tuesday I would have lunch with Roxy's attorney, Andrew Tonic. He wanted to talk, and I felt certain that he would help me find the link between Roxy's murder and Cragnow.

And I needed a chat with Lara Phillips. Nothing in the case pointed to Lara about vampire–human collusion or her sister's murder. A quick visit, a little vampire hypnosis, and that would be the end of my interest with Lara Phillips.

Simple.

CHAPTER
26

THE NEXT MORNING, a Monday, I drove to Glendale and got on La Crescenta Avenue. I endured the bumper-to-bumper crawl by listening to an extended mix of African world beat music on the radio and sipping from my to-go cup—Costa Rican blend with goat's blood.

My task was straightforward. A talk with Lara Phillips.

Coyote stayed home to fix his truck. I "loaned" him money for a new starter. I didn't anticipate anything dangerous with Lara, so there was no need for Coyote to watch my back. In case of trouble, I had my vampire wits and a Colt .380 automatic.

My cell phone buzzed, the caller ID announcing Veronica's number. I answered.

"Hey, lover boy," Veronica said, her tone playful. "Catch you at a bad time? Just wanted to say I'm still sore from yesterday morning."

"Sore? In what way?" I asked, worried that I might have been too aggressive.

"A very good way." Veronica gave a smoky laugh. "Any chance we could get together this evening for dinner or whatever?"

The "whatever" part clinched the offer. "Maybe," I teased.

She laughed again. "Maybe? Never figured you to be coy."

"I was thinking about you," I replied. "Wouldn't want you to get too sore."

"Ha. When that happens, I'll tell you."

"Six, then? Pick you up at your place?"

"See you there. Ciao." She hung up.

Now I had two women on my agenda. Lara and Veronica.

I followed La Crescenta Avenue. Considering Lara's almost inconsequential mention—her name was but a note among the reams of papers in Roxy's files—I didn't expect to spend much time interrogating her, as previously mentioned. A quick dazzle with the eyes, a few questions, some answers, and I'd disappear, like a vapor.

Still, she was Roxy's sister. I wasn't as thorough a detective as I thought, considering that I stumbled upon this discovery. My inquiry into Roxy's past told me both her parents died years ago. I hadn't bothered to find out if Roxy had siblings. Or rather, sibling. Lara.

A gap opened in the wall of trees along La Crescenta. I took a left to cross over a large concrete viaduct that separated the neighborhood from the rest of Verdugo City like a moat. The street meandered through nicely tended homes terraced on a hill facing northeast.

Lara Phillips's house was near the top, a cream-colored ranch home with a single-car garage and the ubiquitous red tile roof. A moss-dappled, stone retaining wall held a narrow lawn at hip-height above the front sidewalk.

A small Ford Focus sat in the driveway. Large decals advertising EXPERT MAIDS decorated the car doors.

I parked the big Chrysler in the shade of tall evergreens marking the property line with her neighbor. I removed my contacts and checked the area. For a Monday morning, the neighborhood appeared as it should. Quiet.

I could go to the front door but I preferred to sneak in through the back for greater surprise. I wanted to get in and get out and not leave any impression that I'd been here. Once out of the car, I stayed close to the evergreen trees, my black clothing blending into the shadows.

Peeking over a wooden fence, I saw green umbrellas and patio furniture on the deck. Tall boxwood hedges and honeysuckle along the backyard fence hid me from the neighbors. I hopped the fence and levitated onto the grass as silent as a moth.

I crept across the deck to the rear entrance of the house. The glass door was open. Conversation drifted through the screen door.

A woman spoke, using a peasant's lyrical Spanish from southern Mexico. Unless Lara Phillips had been raised in Chiapas, I doubted this was her. The woman asked about the next house to clean, so I presumed she was a maid.

I listened for someone else. Nothing. Maybe Lara was in a bedroom. Sliding the screen door open, I scooted into the kitchen, which smelled of Comet cleanser.

The maid, a chubby dark woman in a white T-shirt with matching green sweatpants and apron carrying the EXPERT MAIDS logo, stood on the carpet next to a dining room table.

We were alone.

She wound an electric cord around the handle of a vacuum cleaner and talked into a cell phone cradled between her shoulder and jaw. The maid folded the cell phone and dropped it into an apron pocket. She grasped the vacuum cleaner and looked up.

Our gazes met.

I didn't give her time to even look surprised. I zapped her with a high-voltage stare, enough to keep her under for a couple of minutes. She stood frozen next to the vacuum cleaner, surrounded by a swirling red aura.

"*¿Carmela?*" The female voice came from the hall. "*¿Acabaste?*" Are you finished? She spoke with a pronounced *gringa* accent. Was this Lara?

I darted around the kitchen counter and paused at the threshold to the hall.

Someone with a brisk and light feminine stride padded on the carpet.

I jumped out, my vampire glare at full power.

My gaze stopped the young woman in her tracks. With short blond hair, a wide Slavic face, and plump hips, she didn't look anything like Roxy Bronze. Unless Lara liked to wear an EXPERT MAIDS apron for fun, this wasn't her.

I asked, "Where's Lara Phillips?"

The woman's aura bubbled with anxiety. She gurgled openmouthed, as if the words spun midway between her brain and throat.

I tapped her head like it was a TV with a loose connection.

"Not here," she said.

"Then where?"

Again with the gurgling. I tapped her head.

"Not here," she said.

This could take all morning. The first maid might know.

I left the woman there, returned to the dining room, and asked the other maid. "Where is Lara?"

"The-señora-Mrs.-Phillips-is-at-her-lessons-which-she-goes-to—"

Her Spanish came at me like water from a fire hydrant. I pinched her lips shut. "What lessons?"

The maid mumbled.

I let go of her lips.

". . . like-I-was-telling-you-three-times-a-week—"

I pinched again. Sometimes vampire hypnosis was a pain in the ass. The blonde couldn't get one word out without me thonking her head, and the maid jabbered like she was trying for a world speed record.

I started into the maid's eyes to strengthen my control. "Don't say a word." Carefully, I released her lips and she kept quiet.

I didn't see anything in the dining room that could help me. I went to the kitchen, which was outfitted with every culinary gadget and notion, as if Lara had binged at Williams-Sonoma. I'd never seen designer dish detergent before. A wall calendar had names and telephone numbers scribbled over it, but nothing gave a clue where Lara was today. Colorful magnets held coupons and recipes to the refrigerator door. A wipe board listed grocery items, but nothing said: If you're looking for me on Monday morning I'm at . . .

In the living room I sorted through a wire basket on a console table containing unopened mail: bills and junk. So far I hadn't found anything out of the ordinary, and that was the problem. I sat on the edge of an armchair to decide what to do next.

What kind of lessons would a divorced single mom be taking? Yoga? Gourmet cooking? Or did the maid mean school classes like college? Maybe this was a dead end. Was I wasting my time or should I come back?

Copies of *Journey with God* magazine sat on the coffee table. The subscription label carried Lara's name. Lara attended Reverend Dale Journey's church? The same church I'd seen Dr. Niphe sneak to?

My stink-o-meter activated again but I couldn't make a connection between Lara, Niphe, and Journey.

I flipped through one issue. The centerfold listed the monthly calendar for the church campus activities. Circled in red ink was a Gospel aerobics class for women only, Jumping for Jesus, offered 9 A.M. Monday, Wednesday, and Thursday.

Was she taking these classes? Could she be there now?

I approached the maid and asked, "Is Lara at Journey's church?"

"*Sí*-at-*la-iglesia*-she-teaches-I-should-exercise-too-but-with-work-who-can-find-the-time-I-am-getting-fat-maybe-I-will-start—"

I clamped my fingers on the maid's lips to contemplate this news in silence. Lara Phillips—formerly Lara Krieger, sister to Freya Krieger, a.k.a. Roxy Bronze—taught exercise classes at Journey's church?

Niphe and Journey. Add Lara to the equation.

Did Lara have something to do with her sister's murder? The implication was so crazy that even I, cynical private detective Felix Gomez, had problems wrapping my thoughts around the idea. If she had, why? How?

"Carmela," the blonde whispered from the hall. Her vampire hypnosis had worn off.

I rolled up the magazine and shoved it into my trouser pocket. I had learned enough here. Time to find Lara Phillips and listen to what she had to say.

CHAPTER
27

O N THE WAY TO ALTADENA, I wondered about this latest tangle. Roxy Bronze's sister, Lara Phillips, taught exercise classes at Journey's church. Was she also a parishioner? Did she have anything to do with Reverend Journey? Or with Dr. Niphe? Their names moved like mathematical variables.

A plus B plus C equals what?

I reached Loma Linda Drive. Journey's church looked as exaggerated and gaudy in the day as it had at night. The rows of windows, as precisely arranged as facets on a rhinestone, reflected the glare of the California sun against the craggy backdrop of the San Gabriel Mountains.

From my angle as I drove onto the lower parking lot, the mountain peaks towered majestically above the pyramid and obelisk of the extravagant church, the grandeur of the Almighty presiding over the bombastic pretensions of man.

Cars and minivans crowded the upper parking lot. School buses marked with JOURNEY FOR JESUS circled up the driveway and stopped alongside a wide concrete path leading to the church complex. Dozens of children filed out. They linked hands and followed women in frumpy dresses up the path.

For a Monday morning, this campus was a busy place, full of cheery Christians coming to celebrate their brand of love for Jesus. And here I was among them, a vampire detective investigating murder.

I panned the grounds and saw no unusual auras. I masked my eyes with contacts and sunglasses and walked across the parking lot for the church complex. I felt the weight of my pistol and holster against the small of my back.

The glass buildings and asphalt reflected the heat. The morning sun was still climbing, so the day would only get hotter. Sunblock kept my skin from bursting into flames, but the bright light and heat burdened me like a potbellied stove strapped to my back.

Unlike the other visit, when security guards chased away Coyote and me, those who noticed me today acknowledged my presence with friendly smiles. I didn't see any guards, but I did spot black plastic globes tucked among the shrubs. We were all being watched—for our safety, I'm sure.

The concrete path split three ways over a lush grassy incline. The paths left and right led to the wings of the complex. The glass and chrome buildings reflected the blue sky and green lawn in wavy, distorted patterns. The center path curved between tidy flower beds toward the wide steps of the main entrance.

I pushed open a billiard table–size glass door and entered a carpeted vestibule large enough for a game of basketball. An air-conditioned breeze fluttered against me, and I paused for a moment to refresh myself.

On the far wall, announcements in LED lights scrolled across a message board. To my right, a map indicated YOU

MARIO ACEVEDO

ARE HERE with an arrow. I knew where I was; I didn't know where Lara Phillips was.

I opened the magazine I'd brought from Lara's home and read the calender. "Jumping for Jesus" exercise class was taught in the Samson Room, which the map indicated was in the adjoining north wing to my left.

I followed the hall where it curved around the main chapel. Doors wide as garage bays opened onto the sanctuary, which was the size of a soccer stadium. Maintenance workers vacuuming between the pews were projected to heroic size on the JumboTron behind the altar.

Another hundred feet and two left turns later, I passed through a connecting hall and entered the north wing. This building lacked the regal opulence of the main chapel. Plush maroon carpet gave way to beige linoleum. The ridiculously tall doors and walls shrank to human proportions. Commercial fluorescent tubing replaced the gigantic smoked-glass lighting fixtures.

At the end of the hall I found the Samson Room, deserted and quiet. I peeked through the open door and saw a typical exercise studio—stereo at the front, floor-to-ceiling mirrors, a rack with multicolored hand weights, and stacks of platforms for step aerobics. A poster on the back mirror had the face of a cartoon Jesus with a headband (instead of a crown of thorns). The caption under the smiling Savior was: WWJD? WHAT WOULD JESUS DO? EXERCISE, SWEAT, PUT AWAY HIS STEPS AND WEIGHTS.

I heard the clatter of metal lockers behind me. I turned around. A placard on the wall indicated the entrance to the women's shower and changing room. Female voices came from around the corner of the entrance.

I could romp inside. I was curious to see what shape these devout Christian women kept themselves in. Wouldn't want the Lord to get a hernia snatching them heavenward during the Rapture, after all.

Two women came out of the changing room, carrying

gym bags and smelling clean as wet soap. They walked side by side and chatted into their cell phones.

Was one of them Lara? I asked if they knew where I could find her.

The brunette pulled the cell phone from her ear. "The instructor?"

"I guess." How many Lara Phillips were here?

She shrugged. "Dunno." She elbowed her friend. "Lara. The instructor. Where is she?"

Her blonde companion stopped in midsentence and looked at me. "Try the terrazzo." She motioned out the door and cocked her thumb to the right. The two of them resumed their cell phone conversations and walked around me.

I went out the door and followed the walkway to the back side of the main chapel building. The heat from the mirrored glass turned the space into a convection oven. The sun's rays bore upon me from every direction.

Rectangles of roses and boxwood shrubs broke up the monotony of the perfect lawn. Sycamore trees surrounded an oblong shape of terrazzo that spilled from the back entrance of the building like a tongue. Patio chairs and tables were spread about the terrazzo. An older teenage boy in an apron tended a juice cart under a large umbrella.

A petite brunette busied herself at the closest table. She moved within the circular shadow cast by the table's umbrella. She wore a long, pastel green sundress with spaghetti straps over a yellow T-shirt. Glossy shoulder-length hair spilled from under a ball cap. She peeled clementines and arranged the sections on a plate next to cookies. A metal pitcher on the table sweated droplets. Red punch and ice filled two glass tumblers. A writing pad, spreadsheets, pens, and a Palm Pilot sat beside the tumblers.

I stepped close, the table remaining between us. The brow of her ball cap was embroidered with *Eternally Fit for the Lord*. Her scent was of moist hair, lilac shampoo, and "Ocean Breeze" sunblock.

"Excuse me," I said.

The woman looked up, startled. Square mirrored sunglasses reflected the glass and greenery.

She had Roxy's dimples and chin but her nose was shorter and her lips narrower and more full. Maybe she wasn't Roxy's sister.

I said, "I'm looking for Lara Phillips."

CHAPTER
28

"**Y**ES? MAY I HELP YOU?"

What I knew about Lara was a big question mark. I introduced myself and advanced with a calm face, my hands open and the palms facing her. "If you are Lara Phillips, I wanted to ask you a few questions."

"About what?"

"I'm a private investigator. Katz Meow hired me to find out what happened to your sister."

Even with her face darkened in shadow, I could see her blanch. She retreated a step and bumped against an adjacent table. The woman's expression became hard, like clay baking in this heat. "What about my sister?"

Then she *was* Lara Phillips.

The kid at the juice cart looked at us, averted his eyes, and pretended to act busy.

I said, "I'm looking into the circumstances of her murder and—"

"Why? She's dead." A rising anger stiffened Lara's voice. She whisked the sunglasses from her face. The color rushed back into her complexion. She squared her shoulders, all five feet of her standing ramrod straight. The motion tightened the dress across her small breasts.

Her blue eyes—Roxy's were brown—stared as if she were about to hypnotize *me*. "I'm asking again, what about my sister?" Her voice was as toxic as lye.

"Like I said, I want to help."

"Help? It's too late for that," Lara replied. "You should've been here while she was still alive."

"Lara?" a deep masculine voice asked from behind. A tall man walked between the row of chairs and tables and circled around me. Sunglasses rode atop the mass of his well-groomed silver hair. The craggy lines of his ruddy face extended to a prominent jaw and a dimpled chin. He wore a loose short-sleeved shirt in a red tartan pattern and khaki trousers.

The question mark hovering above Lara got even bigger. I recognized this man from photos and his television show. He was Reverend Dale Journey.

The two of them exchanged looks that implied more than a casual working relationship. Her eyes cut back to me while his gaze lingered on her.

Journey stepped beside her and faced me, hands gripping the back of a chair. He wore a wedding ring. During his sermons, Journey often mentioned he was a widower and the gold band reminded him of promises kept to his now departed wife and to God.

"Your name, sir?" he asked in a measured soothing tone.

"Gomez," I replied, moving around the table and extending my hand. "Felix Gomez."

Journey and Lara stared at my fingers as if the digits were soiled from wiping my ass. Neither moved other than to raise their faces toward mine.

I could zap them both right now. I reached to remove my sunglasses. Then what? Juice boy watched us. Things could get complicated. I lowered my hand.

Lara whispered, "He asked about Freya."

Journey frowned. "What is your business here?"

"He's a private detective," Lara said. "A friend of Freya's—Roxy Bronze—hired him."

I hadn't said that Katz Meow was a friend of Roxy's.

"Roxy," Journey muttered. He motioned toward Lara. "Mrs. Phillips—Lara—is a friend. If you're asking about her sister, then you are aware of the trauma Lara has gone through. She's had to overcome an ordeal of shame that only compounded the immense tragedy of losing a sibling."

Journey waved his hand, and juice boy turned as if dismissed, hustling toward the chapel.

Lara's eyes misted. One side of her face twitched. She wiped an eye and put her sunglasses back on. "Mr. Gomez, you came here looking for the truth? I'll give it to you. What do you know about my sister? Can you comprehend the disgrace she brought to my family? To *me*? She had everything. She could do anything. I was the family goat compared to big sister."

Lara's face twitched again. Her voice cracked. "She had straight As; I was the C student. She had Olympic scouts sending her flowers; I got ribbons for good attendance in gym class. They handed my sister scholarships to medical school. And still she acted as if the rest of us owed *her*. She had the keys to the universe. What did she do with them?"

Lara clenched her fists. "My sister gave everything up for *pornography* and died a whore."

"Her death left behind a lot of questions," I said.

"I've had it with people picking at Freya's bones." Lara took a half step forward.

Journey pulled her back and gave her shoulder a light squeeze, as if to say: Let it out; you'll be okay.

Lara picked up a napkin and dabbed her eyes. "She's gone. That part is finished. Let my sister rot in peace as Roxy Bronze."

Definitely the most spiteful bon voyage I'd ever heard.

"Roxy, I mean Freya, led a complicated, tragic life," I said.

Journey raised his hand to interrupt. "Complicated. Tragic. And we'd be remiss not to add disreputable. It'd be easy to bury all the bad with Freya, but we can't. We can only ask Him"—Journey pointed to the sky—"for forgiveness and continue with our lives in His grace."

I expected Journey to end that with an amen.

An LAPD police officer and a security guard in a green uniform with gray pocket flaps marched toward us across the terrazzo. Juice boy followed so close he almost tripped over their heels. The cop went straight to Journey and Lara, and the guard came around my side. The kid stood against his juice cart.

I was outflanked. Both the cop and the guard carried pistols and wore sunglasses.

The cop halted beside Journey. He looked at me even though he spoke to the reverend. "Pastor Dale, there a problem?"

Pastor Dale? How familiar. That meant he attended Journey's church.

The guard took a ready stance, left foot forward, and hooked thumb into a strap close to a can of pepper spray. I'd been doused with that before, and it was as painful to a vampire as it was to a human.

With this heat, in my black clothes I felt like a stick of melting licorice. If it could, my *kundalini noir* would pant like a dog to keep cool. This wasn't the time for a fight. I needed answers, not trouble.

I raised my hands like a meek little citizen. "No problem, officer. I was only here to ask questions."

Juice boy gave a smart-ass grin.

Her voice ice cold, Lara said, "Mr. Gomez was leaving."

His arms crossed he-man style, the cop gave me that pissed-off, big-city lawman glare.

I backed away. "Some other time."

"Worship service is Sundays at nine and eleven A.M.," Journey replied, more of a taunt than an invitation. "Wednesdays at seven in the evening. You're welcome anytime then, Mr. Gomez."

The guard pointed to the back entrance of the chapel. I started that way, the guard and the cop stepping close enough to grab me if they wanted to. They stayed with me until I reached the parking lot. I got into my car, not so much humiliated as suspicious.

Lara Phillips, formerly Lara Krieger, threw a good tantrum of self-pity over the life and death of her sister. I had no reason to doubt her sincerity.

But Lara never asked who Katz Meow was, and she told Journey that a friend of Roxy's hired me. I had never said the friend was Katz Meow—Lara made that conclusion on her own. Which meant Lara knew Katz Meow.

Plus Lara said Roxy brought disgrace to her family. What family? There was only Lara and Roxy; their parents were dead, and they had no other siblings. Or did she mean the family name? I caught the emphasis when Lara said, "to *me*."

That stink-o-meter of mine was back at full tilt.

I drove off and found a café that offered a decent selection of shade-grown coffee. In my car, I mixed Peruvian dark roast with type B-negative I'd brought in a plastic bottle. I thumbed through the day's issue of the *Los Angeles Times* to look busy while thinking about what happened at the church.

I didn't need the nose of a retriever to smell the chemistry between Lara and Journey. He wore a ring to advertise his grief as a widower. How long ago had his wife died? Seven, eight years?

I flipped from the front page to the sports section.

How familiar were the reverend and Lara? Why hide the attraction? Perhaps to prevent the gossip that sprouts when a man—especially a minister—dates a woman less than half his age.

Maybe Lara and Journey were figuring an angle on how

to present their relationship. He was widowed, she divorced. Evangelical churches were big on starting over. I didn't see any reason why they couldn't go public about their arrangement and not hide the fact they bumped uglies.

But the love life of these two wasn't my concern except as how it might relate to Roxy's murder.

I turned from sports back to metro.

Lara Phillips taught exercise classes in Reverend Journey's church, a man she might or might not be porking. Dr. Mordecai Niphe sneaked here in the middle of the night. Journey bought the land for his church at a distressed price from Lucky Rosario in a deal facilitated by Councilwoman Petale Venin.

Lucky Rosario hobnobs with Cragnow Vissoom, porn king and former boss of Roxy Bronze. Did Journey ever meet with Cragnow?

There were a lot of slippery threads here but nothing tied to Roxy's murder.

Who would gain the most from her death? Was Roxy killed out of revenge? Or to shut her up? If that was the case, what did she know?

I set the newspaper aside when I caught a name in the obituary. I read the notice, and the surprise made me cough up coffee and blood.

Fred Daniels, Roxy Bronze's punk of an ex-husband, was dead.

CHAPTER
29

I READ THE OBITUARY twice to make sure this was the same Fred Daniels I visited last week. The right age. Resident of Rosemead.

How did I miss his death? What happened to his sorry ass? Car accident? Was he murdered? The obituary wouldn't say. My mistake for not keeping up with local news. Considering all the deaths in L.A., unless it was a celebrity, blink and you'd miss the mention.

The funeral was today at the Eden Memorial Cemetery in Mission Hills. Someone there could tell me when and how Daniels became worm food.

The cemetery occupied the apex of land where the San Diego and Golden State Freeways merged. Hearses and limousines clogged the lanes leading into the cemetery. Never figured on a traffic jam getting into the afterlife.

The parking lot was full, and I left my car down the block. The hot sun bore upon me like an electric iron. Once in the cemetery I paused in the shadow cast by a statue of the Virgin Mary atop a crypt. I removed my sunglasses and contacts. The uncomfortably bright sunlight made me squint as I scanned auras. No orange, only red. A few undulated in grief, most shimmered in boredom, and a couple burned with nervous, distracted thoughts.

I put my contacts and sunglasses back on. I approached a groundskeeper and asked if he knew which of the funerals was Daniels's.

He shrugged. "Dunno."

I asked again in Spanish.

"*Aya,*" he replied. "*Con la chichona.*" Over there. Where you'll find the lady with the big ta-tas.

I thanked him and followed the direction of his finger toward a knot of people dressed in black. They faced a cheap casket covered with imitation wood paneling. I couldn't see if an unusually busty woman was among them. When I got close I heard a balding man in white ministerial vestments— embroidered with sunbursts, dolphins, and marijuana leaves— mention Fred Daniels.

The "minister" babbled in New Age argle-bargle about loss and the deceased moving on to a better place. I stood in the back and scoped out the mourners. Everyone wore the same dutiful somber expression. Mostly women, mid-to-late twenties. Lots of tattoos and piercings. Fellow porn stars, coke heads, or both?

After mumbling his final words, the minister nodded to a pair of men in well-worn suits on opposite sides of the casket. They tripped the lowering device and the casket sank into the grave. Counting me, there were two dozen present and not one sob or moist eye. I surmised the mourners were here to bank karma points so when it was their turn for the big sleep, they wouldn't get a lonely send-off.

A paunchy, bearded man wearing a ball cap and frayed necktie stood at the head of the grave. Mourners filed past. The minister handed out pamphlets and invited everyone to his "sanctuary." No doubt the church of the burning doobie.

From within the small crowd, a short blonde so top heavy she looked like an inverted bowling pin came forward. She took a pamphlet from the minister and shook hands with the other man. She attracted the gaze of every male, as if her enormous chest had the gravitational pull of two Jupiters. The woman walked on tiptoes to keep the sharp heels of her sandals from plunging into the sod. She wore sunglasses big as snorkeling goggles and carried a leather purse on a strap looped over her shoulder.

Though I was sure I had never met the woman, she seemed familiar. I followed her into the cool shade of a maple tree. She raised the sunglasses and unmasked her face.

It was JJ Jizmee, retired porn star, famous for her all-natural size 42J bust. I was fifteen and coming to grips, so to speak, with my sexuality, when a high school buddy loaned me a videotape featuring JJ. Since then, those humongous boobs of hers had hovered over my bedtime fantasies like a pair of zeppelins from the planet Sex.

JJ fanned herself with the pamphlet. Moist strands of brassy hair clung to the sides of her face. She wore a black blazer over a matching skirt that fell to her knee. Her gray blouse was open and showed enough cleavage to swallow a man's head.

Removing my sunglasses, I approached, smiling, which was easy. But it took a Herculean effort to look above her neck. I fixed on her blue-gray eyes and waited for the opportunity to remove my contacts. "I'm Felix Gomez."

She raised an eyebrow, furrowing one half of her forehead. Her expression indicated, go on. Crow's feet wrinkled the corners of her eyes, and an uneven tan showed through her makeup. A softening jawline and neck, as well as a thick middle, completed her matronly appearance.

I offered a business card and told her I was a private detective investigating the death of Roxy Bronze.

JJ clasped the card between long ultramarine-blue fingernails. She read the card and pointed toward the grave. "If you've come to interview Fred Daniels, you're a little late."

"Maybe you can help me, JJ."

Her carmine red lips curved into that same smile she used to give to the camera before helping herself to a stiff cock. "JJ? I haven't been called that in years. So you're a fan?" She dropped my card into her purse and held out her hand. Heavy gold jewelry decorated her thumb, fingers, and wrist. "Pleased to meet you, Mr. Gomez." Her grip was dry and firm.

"Felix, please. JJ, how well did you know Daniels?"

"I prefer my real name. Polly Smythe. I knew him well enough through the Open Hand in Reseda."

"Small world." Its staff was on my list of people to interview. Half of Roxy's insurance money had gone to Barrios Unidos, the other half to Open Hand.

"You've heard of it?" she asked.

"Sure have. Could you tell me about the half a million dollars Open Hand got from Roxy's insurance?"

The question blind-sided her. Polly blinked and worked her brow as her thoughts churned in surprise. "What are you getting at?"

"Someone dies and someone else gets a shitload of money as a result. Pretty strong motive for mischief."

Polly's complexion darkened. Her gaze stabbed me. "I ought to kick you in the balls for saying that. You've got no reason to be suspicious of me or anyone else at Open Hand."

I needed to zap Polly and lead her away for questioning. With my peripheral vision, I noticed several people staring at us. "JJ . . . Polly, I'm here to find out what happened to Roxy, that's all. I know that Open Hand and Barrio Unidos split the settlement. It's in your trust accounts."

Polly's eyebrows slanted outward.

"Don't look surprised, I'm a PI. Tell me you had nothing to do with her death and we'll go from there."

Her complexion lightened. "I had nothing to do with her death. I don't know who killed her, and you want to find out. Then let me help."

"You don't buy how she got killed?"

"There's a lot about Roxy I didn't understand. Think about

it. Olympic hopeful turns surgeon, then winds up doing porn. Psychologically she must have been all over the map."

"That your professional opinion?" I asked.

"Only a casual observation from an acquaintance."

Polly certainly came across as forthright. I'd hold off on the hypnosis.

She fanned herself again with the pamphlet. "Who's your client?"

Normally I wouldn't say, but since Katz was missing, maybe Polly would mention if she knew. "Katz Meow."

Polly folded the pamphlet and shoved it into her purse. "She and Roxy were tight, as friends, I mean. Katz was bi—who the hell isn't these days—but she preferred men for romance. Roxy, on the other hand, was ambivalent about hooking up with anyone."

"You knew them well?"

"Roxy visited the clinic to help out and donate money. Katz, only because she hung around Roxy. Most porn stars I don't see until they've got problems."

"Have you seen Katz lately?" I asked.

"No. Why? Haven't you?"

"Not for a few days."

Polly's chuckle turned into a stinging laugh. "What kind of a bonehead investigator loses his client?"

"I haven't lost her . . ."

"Lost, misplaced, whatever. Hope you find her." Polly lowered the sunglasses over her eyes and started from the tree back toward the grave. She waved for me to tag along. "All right, Mr. Bad Ass PI. You came to ask about Fred Daniels. Let's talk to an expert."

We walked toward the paunchy man with the ball cap.

"You know how Fred died?" I asked Polly.

"An overdose, according to the coroner. Cocaine and that shit Rush Limbaugh was hooked on, OxyContin."

"How do you know?"

"A nurse on our staff has friends working the morgue."

"When did Fred die?"

"Wednesday night. Kaput in the men's room of a dive in El Monte."

That meant Fred died only hours after Coyote and I had seen him. "Who found him?"

"Don't know. Read last Saturday's *Times*. That's where I got the news."

"That's it?" I asked. "He died of a drug overdose. No foul play?"

"Not according to the coroner," Polly answered. "Didn't surprise me. See, Fred's house caught fire . . ."

How could I forget? Coyote started the blaze by pissing flames.

"Fred wasn't much for handling stress," Polly continued. "The least bit of anxiety would have him reaching for booze, pills, or nose blow. He'd been to my clinic several times."

"For what? STDs?"

Polly shook her head. "Drug addiction. It wasn't a problem until he was broke and couldn't afford them. Then he'd get some money and ditch therapy."

"What did Roxy see in *him*?"

"Blame it on timing, I suppose. You know Roxy went through a bad spell. The medical board thing. Fred was there for her. Together they'd start over as the first couple of porn. She thrived in the business while Fred . . ." Polly's voice trailed away. "Offstage he was as randy as a billy goat, but aim a camera at his pecker and it wilted like a noodle. His nickname on the set was Lack-of-Wood Daniels."

The man with the paunch looked glum, uneasy with his role as the recipient of all the forced condolences and feigned sorrow. His face was as weather-beaten as a tree stump. His cap said DANIELS LANDSCAPING and he wore a navy petty officer insignia for a tie tack.

Polly and I halted before him, at the edge of a bubble of stinking whiskey breath. He looked at her face, then her breasts, me, her breasts again, and back to her face.

Polly waited for his eyes to make the round-trip before

introducing him as Henry, Fred Daniels' older brother from Sacramento. She told him my name and business here.

Henry pulled his gaze from Polly's bosom and stared at me. His eyes were glossy with 150 proof. He sneered. "You wanna know about Fred?"

CHAPTER
30

HENRY SAID, "I've been wiping Fred's ass since his birth. He's a goddamn pain even dead. Left me with his burned-out house, debts, this funeral."

"Sorry to hear that," I said.

"Why? It isn't your problem." Henry looked through me. He even ignored Polly and her mountains. Fred's brother seemed content to let his drunken buzz hold the world at a distance.

"I do have a problem," I replied. "Your brother might have had information about Roxy."

Henry brought his gaze to my eyes. "About her murder?"

"Maybe," I replied.

"Meaning you think he killed her?"

"I never said that."

Henry chuffed. "Fred was too big a pussy."

He hadn't had a problem shooting at me. I asked, "Did Fred tell you something?"

The drunkenness ebbed from Henry's demeanor and he frowned as if the return of sobriety annoyed him. "Fred told me a lot of shit."

"He ever mention Cragnow Vissoom?"

Henry adjusted his cap and set it lower on his brow, like a gate locking into place.

I wanted to snatch his beard and zap him into answering. But I couldn't, not here at the funeral, not in front of so many people.

"I'd like to hear what Fred told you," Polly said. "As a favor to me."

Henry looked at her. His frown turned up at the corners as he fell under the spell of her breasts.

"Fred was always bumming money," Henry said, losing himself in her cleavage, "and when he got around to paying me back, he bragged that he scored big from Cragnow."

"Scored?" I asked. "You mean drugs?" I was certain Cragnow didn't nurse his high with anything but booze, and pedaling drugs wasn't on his résumé.

Henry pulled his eyes from Polly and toward me. "Not drugs, money. Like he had something on Cragnow."

"Something what?"

Henry waved calloused hands to signal ignorance. "I never asked because I didn't want to know."

Maybe Fred's "something" was knowledge of Roxy's murder and other crimes.

Katz Meow had hired me and now she was missing. Coyote and I went to see Rebecca Dwelling and found her ass-end-up in a Dumpster. We talked to Fred and hours later, he was takeout for the morgue. Someone was making sure that a visit with me was a death sentence.

"Maybe Fred didn't die of an accidental overdose," I said, hoping to spur Henry into revealing more.

His eyes narrowed, and I got the impression of a clam closing tight. "I quit worrying about Fred a long time ago."

"Then you won't mind if I look through his house?"

"I do mind."

"Might be a help to me," Polly said.

Henry glanced at her face, started to look away, then fixed on her bosom.

Henry closed his eyes. "I can't. Going through Fred's things is family business." Henry faced me. He brought a hand up to shield his face, not from the sun but from her breasts. "If I find anything suspicious, I'll give it to the cops." His sneer returned. "Get it from them."

The minister interrupted. "I need my speaking honorarium. You got cash?"

Henry gave me the shoulder. Even if he had nothing more to say, I resented the brush-off. I'd decide when the conversation was over.

Polly tugged at my sleeve. "There'll be another time, Felix."

She was right. I'd drop by Fred's house later and poke around. If Henry objected, I'd make him squirm under hypnosis.

Polly led me to the pavement and we turned toward the parking area. Her heels ticked a rapid beat across the asphalt.

"Think Fred's death and Roxy's have something in common?" asked Polly.

"I don't know. Anyway, thanks for getting Fred to talk."

"Don't thank me, thank the girls." Polly laid a hand across her breasts.

"Let's talk about Cragnow Vissoom," I said. "What are your dealings with him?"

"None. He came on the porn scene after I left, thank goodness."

"What's your impression of him?"

"A complete dick-head. From what I've heard. We may have been at the same parties or banquets, but I've never said as much as boo to him."

"Let me toss out another name. Lucius Rosario."

"You mean Lucky?" she asked. "There's a bottom-feeder

for you. He bankrolls Cragnow's productions and as dividends, snacks on the stray pussy."

"What about Mordecai Niphe?"

"The doctor? He was the one who got Roxy's medical license pulled after she snitched on him. Grapevine says he's helped Lucky Rosario over the years."

"In what way?" I asked.

"Mostly real estate."

"Councilwoman Petale Venin?"

"Ever wonder," Polly replied, "What would happen if you mated a shark with a bulldozer?"

"She's that subtle? What's her relationship with Cragnow?"

"As far as I know, none other than the usual influence peddling," Polly said. "This is L.A. The land is paved with crooked politics and shady deals."

I let the next name slip out casually. "The Reverend Dale Journey."

Polly halted. Her lips bunched into a snarl. "That son of a bitch. Journey's done his best to shut off what tiny drops of funding Open Hand gets from the government. Meanwhile that pious bastard swims in tubs of money provided for his 'faith-based initiatives.' Seems he can't tutor school kids or feed the elderly without a new Mercedes every year."

"Would Journey have anything to do with Cragnow?"

"You're kidding? Of course not. That'd be like Larry Flynt and Billy Graham meeting for coffee and donuts. Why do you ask?"

"Because Cragnow and Journey both had the same real estate broker, Rosario."

Polly repeated the name. "Interesting. For Journey to have contact with Cragnow, even through a go-between like Rosario, would be political suicide."

I studied Polly. "You know Roxy had a sister?"

"Where?"

"Here in L.A."

Polly kept silent for a moment. "Wow. She never mentioned a sister." Polly started walking again. "And I don't remember meeting any of Roxy's relatives at the memorial service."

Polly stopped beside a white Infiniti sedan and pulled a remote and keys from her purse. "I've got to get back to the office." She clicked the remote, and the sedan's lights flashed. She reached back into her purse and produced a business card. "In case any more questions come up, call or email."

I took the card and put it in my shirt pocket. "Thanks." I needed to verify what Polly told me, and for that I had to be alone with her. "I'm parked down the way. Could you give a lift?"

"Sure."

We sat in the sweltering interior of the Infiniti, I in the front passenger's side and Polly behind the wheel. While she fit the keys into the ignition, I removed my sunglasses and contacts.

"Polly?"

She turned the air conditioner up full blast and looked at me.

I plucked the sunglasses off her nose. Her hands jerked up and her gaze locked on mine.

Those blue-gray eyes dilated into black circles. Her aura shone like a red lamp. It'd be a treat to fang her and play around—easy enough, considering the tinted windows and the sunshade on the dash gave some privacy—but not now. Business first.

I kneaded her hands and asked my questions. Polly was an easy read. She didn't kill Roxy. She didn't know who did. Everything she told me was the truth. And she knew nothing of vampires.

I put on my contacts and sunglasses. I returned Polly's sunglasses to the bridge of her nose and commanded her to awaken. She rolled her head in a confused, *where am I* motion.

"Anything the matter?" I asked.

She touched her temple. "Must be the heat. And the strain."

"Of what?"

"I feel like a lout for saying it. Managing Open Hand. Fred was the second of my former clients that I buried this month."

"Really?"

"There's no connection," Polly said. "The other client died of HIV-related pneumonia. Open Hand's like a conveyor belt, the same faces and problems coming at you over and over. It's worn me out. I could use a change. Any ideas?"

"Change of what?" I asked.

She sighed. "Everything."

"What are you looking for?"

"A different kind of man, for starters." Polly folded the sunshade and tossed it onto the backseat. She put the Infiniti into drive. "Felix, when I find him, I'll let you know."

CHAPTER
31

THE CONVERSATION WITH POLLY made me want to go quiz Rosario, Cragnow, and Journey. Plus corner Niphe and question him until I got tired of listening. And there was someone I hadn't yet introduced myself to: Councilwoman Petale Venin. I moved her to the top of my list so I could learn what levers she pulled in this conspiracy.

I drove into downtown Los Angeles, parked, and made my way to city hall. In L.A., everything, even the government buildings, led double lives for the camera, and this art deco structure had once served as the home of the *Daily Planet* in the *Superman* TV show. For the longest time, it was the tallest building in the city by ordinance, but it has since been dwarfed by the surrounding banks and corporate offices, the real seats of power.

I climbed the steps into the lobby. Velvet ropes funneled traffic to a security checkpoint with an X-ray machine and a metal detector. How could I get past with my pistol? A notice on an easel pointed left toward a counter and said that everyone had to show a badge or sign in.

A man in a business suit stepped around me, barking, "Excuse me," and glaring, as if I was slowing him down from getting his asshole-of-the-year award. He halted at the counter and signed in with the attending cop, an LAPD officer. The cop selected a badge from the board behind him. The man clipped the badge to his lapel and continued inside, bypassing the security checkpoint.

The cop went back to glancing at a book. When I approached, the cop closed the book, *Selling Your Screenplay,* and flipped it upside down to hide the title.

Deep wrinkles mapped years on his tanned face. No doubt he was tired of being a career police officer.

He pointed to a clipboard. "Show me an ID and sign in." Next he pushed a sheet of paper name tags toward me. "Write your name on one of these, then go through security."

I had to show my ID? I didn't want to leave a trail, and I couldn't go through the metal detector. I would hypnotize the cop and get one of those special badges. But he stood on the opposite side of the counter, and with so many people around, zapping him might be a challenge.

I pointed to the cop's book. "That's a tough racket."

"You a screenwriter?"

"I've been optioned. Nothing's made it to film yet, but it pays my bills."

The cop's eyes glistened with envy. He shook his head. "Man, I've been at it for years and getting nowhere. How do you do it?"

I leaned close. "There are tricks."

"Tricks?" He put his weight on the counter and gave an eager grin.

Perfect. I tapped his book to distract him and removed my contacts. "These kind of tricks."

He looked up. His aura flashed. His posture relaxed and his mouth dropped open.

"Give me a badge." I couldn't risk reaching over and grabbing one myself.

The cop fumbled with the board. He gave me one with numbers written in big red print.

I fastened the badge to my collar and told the cop. "Stare at your book for ten seconds, then wake up."

I put my contacts in and walked away. The cop on the other side of the checkpoint acknowledged me with a nod. I gave a smart wave of thanks. Keep up the good work. The bad guys will never sneak past you.

At the end of the hall, a placard listed the council members by room number. Venin was in 497. I took the elevator to the fourth floor.

Men and women in power suits filed into the elevator when I got off. The doors closed behind me and I was alone on the floor.

Venin's office was at the end of the hall, behind a wide wooden door with a frosted glass window bearing her name and title. This investigation was moving at turtle speed. Time to sprint. I removed my contacts again and decided to bust into Venin's office, my vampire eyes blazing. I was going to hypnotize everybody if I had to. If other vampires were inside, well that's why I had my talons and pistol.

Voices mumbled from inside the room. I put my ear close to the glass pane. The voices quieted. They sensed my presence. Did they expect me, or someone else?

I tensed my legs and grasped the doorknob.

Get ready. Vampire attack.

I pushed the door open and sprang inside.

A dozen voices yelled, "Surprise."

Twelve humans stared at me. They crowded inside Venin's office and held garlands and a banner that read: HAPPY BIRTHDAY.

Their eyes popped open in terror. Waves of panic lashed through their auras. When they twitched to move, I zapped each one in turn, like I was plinking tin cans off a fence.

I nudged the door shut with my foot. I had to work fast, as

this hypnosis wouldn't hold them long. I went down the line and ordered, "Close your eyes and go to sleep." Their arms dropped and they teetered in place.

Colored balloons floated in the room. A cake sat on a round conference table. The cake frosting said *Happy Birthday Cecil.*

I stopped in front of the oldest-looking human, a woman in her thirties. I stared into her eyes to strengthen the hypnosis.

"Who's Cecil?" I asked.

"An intern."

"Where's Venin?"

"In Sacramento."

"When will she return?"

"Late this evening," the woman answered.

A balloon bounced against my face and I slapped it away. I could rifle through the office but I needed to interrogate Venin. Other than learn she wasn't here, this visit gave me bupkus.

I told the woman to sleep. After the group woke up, they'd be confused for sure. Maybe word of that confusion would reach Venin, and if she knew anything about vampires, then I would've made her suspect something. So actually, I did worse than bupkus.

I returned to my car and found a parking ticket stuck under the wiper. The meter had run out.

I stared back at the city hall building. Venin had given me the slip without even trying. And here I thought of myself as a professional.

I balled up the parking ticket and flung it into the trash. My superpowers sure did wonders today.

Hoping to salvage the afternoon, I swung by Katz Meow's town house. It looked more deserted than the first time I visited. With every passing day I was certain I'd never see her alive again.

At 5 P.M. Veronica called. "We still on?"

Her voice lightened my gray mood and made all the good parts of me tingle. "It's the only reason I got out of bed."

"Where are you?" she asked.

"On the Golden State Freeway. About a half hour from your place."

"Great. I'll wait out front. See you then." She hung up, and the screen on my cell phone blinked. My date with Veronica would make up for the frustration of what turned out to be a wasted afternoon.

I finished a coffee frappé mixed with the rest of the blood I'd brought and gobbled Skittles to hide any trace of vampire breath.

I rounded the corner onto Veronica's street. She stepped from the breezeway of her apartment building. After my time with the über-voluptuous JJ Jizmee, Veronica looked downright anorexic. But only for a second. She had plenty of natural padding in all the right places.

Veronica wore sunglasses and her usual capris, in white, that brought out the caramel tan of her shapely legs. She wore a light blue sleeveless blouse. Veronica exercised, and she liked to show off the results.

I slowed and honked the horn. I lowered the window on the passenger's side and called out, "Can Veronica come out and play?"

She slung a canvas musette over one shoulder and bounded down the front steps with the eagerness of a girl let out from school. Veronica paused by the Chrysler and peeked over her sunglasses. "Nice wheels."

"Don't be impressed. It's a rental."

She got in and set the musette on her lap. She pointed south. "That way."

"What's there?"

"The beach."

"And your plan?"

"Visit my mother's."

Oh great. Why not let all the air out of my tires and feed me saltpeter?

Veronica leaned over the center console, kissed my

cheek, and pinched my side. "She's not home. I gotta feed her cats."

Veronica gave directions to Venice, and we arrived at a modest cottage on Dell Avenue. I maneuvered the big 500M into a narrow space between the cottage and the newly built yuppie monstrosity next door.

We squeezed out of the car. A late afternoon breeze whisked through the neighborhood, rustling trees and palms and bringing the heavy scent of ocean air. I put on a black hoodie for the growing chill. Veronica pulled a windbreaker out of her musette and zipped up.

She unlocked the front door and we entered the cottage. The living room was filled with a lifetime's accumulation of bric-a-brac collected from every souvenir shop between here and Mount Rushmore. Veronica filled pet dishes—commemorating a visit to Flagstaff, Arizona—with cat food and water, and we left for the beach.

"There's something I don't understand about Roxy," I said. "I keep hearing that her involvement in Project Eleven is what got her killed. She got the media attention, but stopping Project Eleven was your baby. Why has no one come after you?"

The breeze played with Veronica's hair. She snagged loose strands behind her ears. "Never occurred to me."

"Never?"

"Let me tell you why," she replied. "If you're a community activist, then you'd better be rattling cages on behalf of your constituents. You make enemies. But that's not a bad thing. It builds respect. Street cred."

"And these 'enemies' never threatened you?"

"Not a physical attack," Veronica said. "There's a lot of bluster and bullshit. Plenty of mind games and backroom maneuvering. But I never felt someone wanted to kill me."

"Then what made Roxy different?"

"She knew where to get the real dirt on some very powerful people."

"And that's why you think she was killed?"

"It's a guess."

We crossed a bridge over a shallow canal. A pelican on the bridge railing flexed its wings and took off.

"Did it bother you what Roxy was up to?" I asked.

"Felix, politics is a dirty business. When our opponents made her character an issue, then their character was fair game in return."

We stopped at Pacific Avenue and waited for a gap in traffic.

"So you approve of what Roxy did?"

"Hell yes," Veronica replied. "It's because of her that we made the city ditch Project Eleven."

"Even if that meant Roxy being murdered?"

"So it's my fault she's dead?"

We trotted across the street.

"Of course not," I answered. "In her digging through the *dirt,* did Roxy ever learn anything dangerous?"

"Explain 'dangerous,' " Veronica said.

"Something worth risking murder to keep quiet."

"I don't know. Roxy discovered plenty and aired it all. If she had found something *dangerous,* she never told me about it."

We reached the boardwalk and walked past the pier.

Veronica hooked her arm into mine. "Felix, I appreciate you confiding in me, but I didn't watch the clock today waiting for *this* conversation."

"Me either."

The sun settled into the gray haze above the ocean. The day's remaining vendors along the boardwalk sat bundled in jackets behind card tables piled with candles, tarot cards, and homemade trinkets. All of the crazies were gone except for one die-hard who sat on a plastic crate and bellowed, "I need money. I gotta buy some pot."

Veronica stopped at the window of a pizza stand and asked if I wanted some.

I did, but only if drenched in blood. Otherwise, it'd be like eating paste on newsprint. "No thanks."

I rested my arm on the counter. The sudden, pungent odor of garlic stabbed my nostrils like tear gas. I yanked my arm from the counter in a bee-sting dance. I scrambled for a napkin to brush dirt-colored grains of garlic powder from my sleeve.

"Are you okay?" Veronica asked.

Carefully, I balled the napkin and dropped it into the trash. "This is going to sound weird, but I'm allergic to garlic. Hives. My face swells up. I get gas like nobody's business."

"That would kill the evening." She took a slice of cheese and mushroom. Yellow grease dripped from the stained paper plate. "Not the same without garlic though."

"I'll make it up to you."

Veronica turned the pointy end of the slice toward her mouth. "I'm holding you to that." Her lips parted and presented teeth as iridescent as opals. Her mouth opened wide, and it should've been me instead of that pizza sliding onto her tongue.

Veronica finished the pizza and chewed a tablet of Nicorette gum. We continued past the beach shops for a block and turned around.

I pulled her close. I was going to nibble her ear when I noticed the silver pendant earring. I kissed the back of her neck instead and it smelled delicious. Those good parts of mine tingled even more.

After returning to the cottage, I sat in a leather cigar chair and watched Veronica mix cranberry juice and vodka to make Cape Codders. She filled glasses stenciled: SANDS HOTEL AND CASINO.

She walked barefoot, and her candy red toenails begged me to admire her feet. From there I worked my eyes up the curves of her calves, past the swell of her hips, her trim waist, a nicely formed back and an even nicer chest, the firm muscles of her arms and shoulders, and ending my appraisal where it should—on the smooth skin of her tempting throat. I wanted everything Veronica's body could offer.

She turned to stand against the kitchen counter with her back to me and sliced limes.

I removed my contacts.

Veronica's aura glowed like the filament of an electric heater. The fringes of her aura rippled with sexual excitement. Veronica had very naughty plans.

In my years as a vampire, this was the first time I had romanced a human female. I've bedded quite a few, of course, and used my vampire powers to shuck their panties and inhibitions. Veronica was different. I wanted this to be normal, as normal as it could get when one of us was an undead bloodsucker.

Could such a relationship be possible? How had the situation developed between Coyote and Heather? Would this be the same?

I rose from the chair, debating whether to tell her the truth. My *kundalini noir* turned upon itself in indecision.

Once I—as the Japanese say—opened my kimono, then what? Suppose Veronica rejected me as a lover and saw me as a monster? At that point there was no chance of her serving as a chalice; I'd have to convert her into a vampire or kill her.

Veronica garnished the Cape Codders with lime wedges and clasped the glasses with napkins.

I couldn't decide what to do so I kept my head down as she came close. She hummed a merengue. Veronica bent over to set the glasses on tile coasters on the coffee table.

Her scent was a banquet of sumptuous aromas: the spicy tang of pheromones; the saltiness of perspiration; and the lacing of the perfumes in her shampoo, soap, and deodorant. The heat from her body was like a warm loaf of honey bread waiting to be devoured.

"You're quiet," Veronica said.

I couldn't reveal myself as a vampire. Not yet. Not now.

The kimono stayed closed. For her sake, I'd pretend to be a mortal.

I grasped her wrists and pulled her upright.

Veronica's eyes swiveled to meet mine.

My hypnotic hold was less a stare than a caress. Even so, she wouldn't remember my vampire nature.

The irises of her brown eyes dilated slowly like two dark flowers blossoming. Her aura notched brighter instead of the usual fiery surge.

She leaned into me, and we kissed. I asked her to remove her jewelry and she dropped the silver pieces on the coffee table.

I nuzzled her throat. My fangs hunted for the choicest spot to feed.

Her warm blood jetted over my tongue and I guzzled it with delight. My palate was overcome with layered tastes: pheromones; iron; copper; the traces of vegetables, grains, and spices; and nicotine from her gum. I lapped the puncture wounds to share my narcotic enzymes.

My head swooned in delirious pleasure. I pulled away to pace my feeding.

Veronica rubbed her neck against my chin. "More," she whispered. Her aura sizzled with lust.

I fed again and she fumbled with my belt buckle. Soon we were naked and engaged in a furious bout of jungle love on the cigar chair. We stopped once to slurp the Cape Codders and went back at it with renewed vigor.

By 1 A.M. she was spent and I close to it. We lay naked on the carpet of the living room floor. The cigar chair rested on its back, and the coffee table was upside down with one leg broken.

A beach towel covered Veronica's sleeping from. Her aura radiated a soft sheen of contentment. I traced my hand over her side.

I wanted Veronica more than ever—and not just for sex.

But I was a vampire. I wasn't supposed to have these feelings.

CHAPTER 32

VERONICA AND I were in my Chrysler, stuck in morning traffic. She sipped coffee from a paper cup and nibbled on an apricot muffin.

"After last night," she said, "I figured you'd be famished. Can't believe you don't want at least a hot cup of java."

Only if it's got blood. "I'll manage."

She relaxed contentedly against her seat. "This was a repeat of the first time you stayed with me."

"I was hoping it would be better."

She chuckled. "It was. But I mean the fading in and out. I didn't drink *that* much, did I?"

"If you were a camel, no."

She bopped my cheek with a big muffin crumb. "If that was true, I should have a hangover worse than this traffic."

"I don't know what kind of hangovers you get. We barely know each other."

She hit me with another crumb. "Liar. You know me well enough to play me like a piano."

"That's a compliment, considering I've never had lessons."

Veronica swigged coffee to hide a smile. "Maybe not, but you've done your homework somewhere."

She tugged at the scarf around her neck. "What's with you and these hickies? We're not in high school."

"You complaining?"

"But the scarf makes it obvious what I'm hiding."

"You complaining?"

Veronica took my hand. Her fingers stroked my wrist. "Of course not. If I complain about anything, it's that we haven't spent enough time together."

True.

And now we were about to be apart again. This worried me. Suppose someone threatened Veronica and I wasn't around to protect her? I had to warn her in case of trouble.

"Yesterday we talked about why no one has come after you," I said.

Veronica raised one eyebrow. "Why are you bringing that up?"

"Because you might be in danger. Three of the people I've gone to see in this investigation are either missing or dead."

Veronica's eyebrow flattened, and she pulled her hand from me. "And you've waited until now to tell me? Who were these people?"

"I don't want to say too much. Trust me on this."

"And you told me this, why? What am I supposed to do?"

"Stay alert. At the first sign of anything suspicious, *any-thing,* call me. Protect yourself. Lock your doors. If you're caught in the open, hide. You own a gun?"

"Yeah, I got an arsenal under my bed." She drilled me with the sarcasm. "Of course not. Do the police know this?"

"They do. The problem is I'm certain that rogue cops are in on it. If you call 911, chances could be that the wrong boys in blue show up."

Veronica looked out her window. "Felix, two minutes ago I was on a cloud. How am I supposed to feel now? What am I supposed to do?"

I hadn't thought about this.

Veronica turned in her seat and gave a stare hot as a branding iron. "Answer me. What am I supposed to do?"

"You could stay with me."

"I have a life," she replied. "I have a job. Why don't *you* stay with me?" She put a sarcastic zing in the question.

She knew I had to work on the case. "What would you prefer? That I not tell you? Roxy is dead. And people close to her are turning up dead. I don't want you to be among them."

"So you're telling me, that after you drop me off, it'll be up to me to keep my ass out of the grave?"

"I just want you to be careful."

"And that's why you asked if I had a gun? To be careful?"

We stopped in front of her apartment.

"Veronica, I don't want anything to happen to you."

"That makes two of us." Veronica pulled the door handle.

"I want to see you again," I said. "To continue what we started last night."

Veronica blinked those gorgeous brown eyes. I couldn't read anything in them except anger.

She said finally, "Felix, there's so much about you I don't understand. And now I'm at risk for what reason?"

"I don't . . ."

She put a finger in front of my mouth to shush me. "When you find out, then maybe we'll see what can happen."

Veronica scooted across the leather seat and closed the door.

The sun was too bright and cheery for the mood that settled on me. I needed storm clouds and cold rain. If I wanted this chilly heartache, I would've found a woman in Seattle.

But I was in sunny Los Angeles, and my investigation waited.

CHAPTER
33

AT NOON I HAD an appointment with Andrew Tonic, Roxy's lawyer. I had time before the meeting, so I drove to Rosemead and inspected what was left of Fred Daniels's home.

Piles of furniture, interior accessories, and clothing littered the front grass. Black smudges ringed the windows and doors. Most of the roof had caved in.

For all his guff about protecting "family business," Henry wasn't around to defend his brother's house from thieves or my snooping. As I poked through the discarded belongings, I discovered why. Everything was scorched, stained, and reeked of smoke. A blackened filing cabinet rested across a sofa. I tried one drawer and it opened, dumping a soggy mush of charred paper.

The house wasn't in much better condition. The interior looked like it had been decorated by a suicide bomber. If anything important survived the fire, I'd never find it.

My watch said it was time to go if I wanted to make my appointment with Tonic. I drove to Trixie's Bistro on Wilshire Boulevard, east of a palisade of marble and glass high-rises.

I had much hope in this meeting with Andrew Tonic. Did he know who murdered Roxy? I doubted that. But Tonic knew something useful about the players in this drama. Useful in what way? Could be that these players—including Cragnow Vissoom, Lucky Rosario, Mordecai Niphe, and Petale Venin—had private agendas they didn't want known? And if the right individual—meaning me—knew these agendas, then the conspiracy behind Roxy's murder would unravel.

And still nothing new about the real reason I was in Los Angeles: to unmask vampire–human collusion.

I paused beside a newspaper vending machine on the opposite corner from Trixie's. The bistro was set back from the sidewalk to allow generous seating under the front awning. A white fence bounded the al fresco area. Customers entered between two trellises thick with roses.

Sliding my sunglasses down my nose, I read auras. Specifically, I searched for a vampire's orange blur. There weren't any. None of the red human auras betrayed a threat. When humans schemed violence, no matter how well they cemented a poker face, their auras advertised their emotionals like movie posters.

It was six minutes past noon. I folded my sunglasses into a shirt pocket, put in my contacts, and cut across the intersection.

The maître d', an anorexic brunette sporting a crispy tan she must have gotten in a rotisserie, welcomed me. I said I had a reservation with Andrew Tonic. She traced a finger across her seating chart, waved to a server, and asked that I follow him. We snaked around crowded tables and were engulfed by the din of conversations and rattling dishes.

The server stopped beside a table on the left alongside the

white fence. A balding man in a dark tailored suit put down his cocktail glass and stood to greet me.

I recognized Andrew Tonic from photos on the Internet. Tonic at an award's banquet. Tonic in tennis whites from a country club newsletter. A young and hairy Tonic graduating from the Columbia School of Law.

He had an egg-shaped head, wide at the top and tapering to a dimpled chin. A series of horizontal wrinkles creased his brow, as if the weight of his legal career had caused his skull to sag. Strands of thinning hair covered his smooth pate. I gave him points for this. In L.A., the land of make-believe and cosmetic anything, Tonic chose to forego the vanity of a rug or hair plugs.

Tonic motioned to the chair opposite his. The server pulled it out for me, and I thanked him. Tonic and I sat.

"How's the vodka and tonic?" I asked, knowing how particular Tonic was about the ingredients he used to season his liver.

He smacked his lips dramatically. "Every sip is like Christmas." An alcoholic haze dulled the shine of his gray eyes. He was on seconds, maybe thirds. Tonic rested his elbows on the table. He wore a thick wedding band and gold cuff links.

I scanned the menu. Why did I agree to meet for lunch if I couldn't drench my food with blood? Should I try raw beef? I set the menu aside. "Andrew, I hope you are as eager to talk today as you sounded last week."

"Even more so."

"I'm curious about your motives. What do you have to gain by sharing information with me?"

"Felix, like any lawyer, the skin around my ego is this thick." Tonic pinched a thumb and index finger. "I don't like what happened to Freya Krieger and how that made *me* look. It's one thing to lose a case, quite another to watch my client get tied to a rack and pulled apart."

"Why didn't you appeal?"

Tonic rubbed the stem of his cocktail glass and stared at his drink. "Freya gave up. The process broke her. Spiritually and financially." He cupped the glass and sipped. "I've got to give her credit, though. After resurrecting herself as Roxy Bronze, she walked into my office and handed me a check to square the outstanding balance of my fees."

"And now she's dead."

Tonic nodded and took a sip.

"You can't undo that," I said. "And you didn't answer my question. Why are you talking to me?"

"Vicarious petty revenge." Tonic set the glass down.

"Against whom?" I asked.

"For starters, Dr. Mordecai Niphe."

"You believe he was involved with her murder?"

Tonic looked up and opened his hands, as if pleading to the heavens. "Please, God, what I wouldn't give to see Niphe do the perp walk while singing 'Folsom Prison Blues.' " Tonic folded his hands and turned his eyes back to me. "But the answer is no."

"What do you have against him?" I asked.

"Plenty. He's the hatchet man for the California chapter of the AMA. Niphe has a take-no-prisoners reputation for protecting his fellow members against the state board."

"Isn't that your specialty?" I asked. "Defending doctors before the board?"

"Yes. But in Roxy's case, it was the unusual situation of Niphe siding with the board to attack her. After the board issued its judgment, exonerating Niphe of course, and dumping on Freya, Niphe made sure the AMA publicity machine painted me as her overreaching and inept counsel. The implicit message, Don't screw with Dr. Mordecai Niphe."

The waiter stopped by. Tonic ordered a grilled salmon spinach salad. I asked for a steak so rare it mooed. Tonic picked at the basket of bread, tore loose a piece of ciabatta crust, and buttered it.

I asked, "What do you know about the Reverend Dale Journey?"

Tonic brought the bread to his mouth and paused. "What's he got to do with Freya or Niphe?"

"I'm getting to that. How about if I tell you that Niphe might have been a silent investor for Journey."

Tonic put the bread down. "If Niphe's portfolio has anything to do with Journey's church, it's in deep doo-doo. Journey's ministry is in debt up to here." Tonic slashed his fingers across his chin.

"How do you know?"

"Back nine conversation on the golf course between lawyers. Journey's fending off foreclosure."

"How can Journey go broke? He must have tithes delivered to him by the truckload. Plus the federal government sends him blank checks."

Tonic gave a lawyer's barracuda smile. "Greed disguised as mismanagement. The gross comingling of funds and the stink of embezzlement. Fleets of luxury cars. A corporate jet. Junkets to five-star accommodations. Seems the only thing the good reverend can't afford is an honest accountant."

"What do you make of *this*?" I asked. "I followed Niphe when he detoured in the middle of the night to Journey's church."

"Why would he go there?"

"I was hoping you could fill in the blanks. Later I visit Journey at his church. Guess who he's got on the payroll as an aerobics instructor?"

Tonic motioned with his hands for me to tell him.

"Roxy's little sister," I said.

Tonic reacted like an experienced legal brawler. His expression remained stonelike. Then one corner of his mouth twitched upward. "I didn't know Roxy—Freya—had a sister. What's her name?"

"Lara Phillips."

"Phillips?"

"Married name," I said. "She's divorced."

"Any indications she might be more than an instructor?"

"You mean, are she and Journey screwing? Like minks, I'm sure."

Tonic laughed. "If he can keep it up, then hurray for the randy old bastard. Is there the possibility of hanky-panky between them that led to the breakup of her marriage?"

"Haven't checked into that," I said.

"Was this something Roxy discovered?" Tonic asked with glee.

"I have no idea," I answered. "Suppose Lara and Journey were hiding the salami while she was married, so what?"

Tonic chewed the bread and washed it down with a swallow of his drink. "It would mean a collapse of faith in Journey as a pastor. His evangelical flock might forgive him for robbing them blind, but they won't take it kindly if he's playing loosey-goosey with his dick. He'd lose his church. Everything."

"Then keeping the affair a secret might be worth murder," I replied.

"It might. Why are Dr. Mordecai Niphe, the Reverend Dale Journey, and Roxy's sister, Lara Phillips, sneaking around?" Tonic's hands pulled apart, as if stretching an imaginary length of string. "What ties them together? Roxy's murder?"

"It gets more complicated when you add Lucky Rosario, Cragnow Vissoom, and Councilwoman Petale Venin."

"Venin?" Tonic repeated. "Damn Felix, you're cutting a wide swath. And you expect to bring them all down?"

"Depends on what I find."

"I hope you find a lot." Tonic looked around and snapped his fingers to get the waiter's attention. "As soon as I get another drink, I'll toast your future success."

A ruby red glow sparkled on my silverware. I glanced and saw a red dot the size of a pea flicker on my left shoulder.

The red dot of an aiming laser.

CHAPTER
34

THE DOT HOVERED on my shoulder.
   I bolted from my chair and darted to the right.
   A bullet ripped through the tablecloth and sent the bread basket flying. A second bullet drilled Tonic through the middle of his necktie. He gasped and fell face first into his vodka and tonic. The cocktail glass tipped over and rolled off the table to shatter against the floor.
   Sitting at a table along the fence, I had been in a perfect spot for a drive-by and I hadn't noticed. I stayed crouched, out of the line of fire.
   For the next few seconds it was as if God had turned off the volume and everyone in the restaurant pantomimed their reactions in slow motion.
   A tight-faced, middle-aged woman at the next table no-ticed blood flecked on the sleeve of her white silk blouse. She turned her blond head to frown at me, looked back at her

sleeve, and glared at Tonic's slumped form. Blood dripped from a red stain on the tablecloth.

The woman's eyebrows inched up, crinkling her forehead. Her fingers clutched the air and she let out a scream.

That wail was the signal for everything to jerk into fast-forward and at maximum volume.

People shrieked, sprang from their chairs, and crashed into one another. Food splattered on the floor. Feet and shins pummeled my sides and knocked me off balance. A pair of dainty feet in Manolo Blahniks scrambled across my hands and scraped my knuckles.

A metallic lump glittered under my table. The lump was the size of a fingertip and looked like a deformed mushroom. The thick stem was serrated with flat grooves—like the kind engraved by the lands in a gun barrel.

A bullet. It lay under the gash it had ripped through the table.

I picked up the slug, felt it burn, and flung it away.

A silver bullet.

Meant for me.

I grasped a napkin and reached again for the bullet. It could provide clues about the shooter. A black oxford kicked the slug under a dozen feet stampeding for the exits.

The scream of sirens echoed down the boulevard.

Forget the bullet. I had to get out of here before the police arrived. If Paxton was responsible for the shooting, then his goons in uniform could be coming to get another crack at me.

Tonic's arm swung lifelessly beside his chair. Wasn't much I could do now except feel sorry for the dead bastard.

I melted into the panicked mass crowding the front exit, both to hide my departure and mask myself in case another shooter waited. I kept in the middle of a group walking briskly on Wilshire to the end of the block.

Patrol cars barricaded the intersection. Cops ran out with guns drawn and surrounded the bistro.

The group I was with crossed the street, gabbing excitedly on cell phones.

"It was a shooting. My God, I thought we were in Compton."

"Sally. I'm okay. No biggie, I was almost done with lunch anyway. I got out without paying. Tell my two o'clock I can see him earlier."

I had to get back to my car. I left the group by ducking through a gap in a tall hedge and found myself facing a private patio behind an executive office complex. Men and women in business clothes lunched at tables and stopped in midchew to stare. I waved and ran off.

Nimble as a fox, I sprinted around shrubs and leapt over fences. I reached the street where I had left my Chrysler. I should've felt safe. Instead my fingertips tingled.

Up ahead one block, a white limousine turned the corner and came at me.

Fingers and ears buzzed. My *kundalini noir* bunched and writhed.

A dark blue Escalade followed the limousine. Tinted windows prevented mc from seeing the interior. Both vehicles approached as silently and forebodingly as assassins' shadows.

Behind me, a second Escalade closed the trap from the opposite direction. Polished wheels reflected the sun like rotating scythes. The two Escalades halted, their boxy shapes as menacing as battle tanks.

Whoever was in the limousine and Escalades knew I was coming this way. Was I followed? Who tracked me? Vampires? They could be anywhere, and my aura wouldn't escape their eyes. The trees and tall buildings crowded around me with claustrophobic intensity.

Was the one who shot at me and killed Tonic in one of the vehicles? If so, why not open fire?

The limousine veered across the street to stop along the sidewalk close beside me. The driver's outside mirror almost touched my leg.

The driver's window lowered. Rachel, the receptionist from Cragnow's porn business, smiled from the driver's seat of the limousine. A vampire's red glare beamed from her eyes. She showed off a pair of shiny new fangs.

The rear door lock clicked. "Get in."

CHAPTER
35

THE REAR WINDOW of the Escalade on the left lowered like a gun port on a man-of-war. An orange aura shimmered inside.

"I'd rather not," I replied as I considered Rachel's invitation. "I had other plans."

The rear window of the Escalade on the right lowered, revealing another orange aura.

"You don't have much choice," Rachel said.

"Where are we going?"

"To an interview."

"I have a cell phone," I said. "We could do a conference call. Save you the trouble of driving."

"Felix," Rachel said, "you're not going to get any warning shots."

The snouts of gun barrels slid from the darkness of the open windows.

"Rachel, you'd better think this through. If they shoot, you're in the crossfire."

Something sharp pressed into my crotch. Rachel pushed one of her talons against my scrotum.

"This wouldn't be fatal, but I'm sure you don't want me to play marbles with your balls."

With only the thickness of my clothes between her talon and my jewels, I couldn't move fast enough to avoid singing contralto forever.

"Rachel, keep this up and we won't be friends."

I waved at the Escalades and entered the rear of the limousine. The interior was a plush cocoon of black leather and dark glass. I settled into a wide leather seat, the only passenger in all this room.

Rachel looked through the partition between the driver's and rear compartments. "Get comfy and enjoy the ride." A window of dark glass scrolled upward, isolating me in the back. The door locks snapped, and we glided forward.

An interview with whom? Or was this a trap? If so, why not end it here? They—whoever they were—showed no reluctance at opening fire upon a restaurant.

Rachel drove south. The two Escalades trailed close. I removed my contacts and tried the doors, windows, and sunroof. Everything was locked tight. I didn't like being caged like a dog going to the vet. If I was along for the ride, might as well be under my terms.

I scooted to the front of the passenger compartment, grasped an overhead strap, and kicked the partition window. The glass shattered and fell apart.

Rachel gave a very unvampirelike, girly scream.

I dove through the partition and landed beside Rachel. Her orange aura looked like a ball of burning gasoline. Her fangs and talons extended to maximum length.

She lunged for me. I parried her arms, grabbed a handful of hair, and pressed her open mouth against the steering wheel. She hissed and chomped but I was too strong. The limo whipped back and forth across the lane. Cars scooted out of our way. Their horns honked in disbelief and anger.

I used Rachel's head to steer and straightened our path. "How many vampires have you killed?"

"None," she mumbled, the steering wheel pushing into her mouth like a horse bit.

"Same as me. But I've killed a lot of humans. You want to be my first vampire?"

Her aura dimmed to a pale, weak orange. "No."

"You going to behave yourself?"

"Yes."

I let go of her hair. She spit bits of plastic. Bite marks crimped the steering wheel.

The limousine slowed and glided toward a parked car. Rachel grasped the wheel, jerked the limousine back into the lane, and accelerated.

A cell phone clipped to the dashboard began chiming.

"It's probably your posse." I took the phone and flipped it open. "Hello?"

A gruff voice said, "Who the hell is this?"

I handed the phone to Rachel. "They want to speak to the vampire in charge. I think that's you."

Rachel held the phone to her ear. A firecracker string of expletives made her wince.

"It's under control," she said, sounding like a mewling kitten. "We'll get there."

More expletives. Rachel closed the phone. "You got me in trouble."

We stopped at a red light.

"So what happens? Detention?" I brushed pieces of safety glass off my seat. "Where are we going?"

"I told you. An interview."

"You can either cut the bullshit or go back to eating the steering wheel."

Rachel kept her gaze straight ahead.

"Well?" I asked.

"To see Councilwoman Venin."

The one individual I hadn't yet seen. So far Venin had

been in the margins of my investigation, and now she summoned me with a gesture worthy of a czarist monarch.

The light turned green, and we rolled forward.

"What does she want?"

"To talk."

"She's a vampire, right?"

Rachel shook her head.

"Human?"

"That. And more."

Rachel's vague reply pissed me off. "What's that mean?"

"That's all I know about her," Rachel added.

I reached over and tapped the bite marks on the steering wheel.

Rachel scowled. "Cut me some slack, okay?"

"Maybe. Who's in the Escalades?" I asked. "Vampires?"

"They're to make sure you meet Councilwoman Venin."

"Is one of them the shooter who tried to nail me at the restaurant?"

"Kacy. He's in the Escalade behind us."

"You say that like I'm supposed to know him."

Rachel replied, "You met in Hollywood. He drove a Jaguar."

That Kacy. I left him broken and bloody on the hood of his expensive car. "He carries a grudge, I bet."

"A big one," Rachel said.

"Then why not do me in now?"

"Because Venin wants to talk to you. She said if you survived the shooting, then you are a vampire worth keeping."

"Keeping for what?"

"You'll have to ask her."

I could commandeer the limousine, but how far would I get? Councilwoman Petale Venin wanted to talk, and I suppose this was as good a time as any.

We merged onto the San Diego Freeway and took the exit into Westwood. Rachel drove a few blocks and turned down a narrow side street into an alley shaded by tall mulberry trees.

The alley led into an open parking bay on the back side of a four-story complex. Rachel parked the limo in a space between two support columns. The Escalades blocked us in. Rachel touched a button, and the doors unlocked. A couple of passengers dismounted from one Escalade, their footfalls deliberate. Ominous.

My door jerked open.

Kacy scowled at me, his aura bright as the lamp of an oncoming train. Scars from my beating pitted his face.

Kacy wore a black leather tactical jumpsuit. He towered over the door, powerful and big, like a Mack truck. An M16 rifle in a combat sling hung from his shoulder. His right hand clasped the pistol grip and kept the muzzle of the rifle aimed at my chest. The weapon was outfitted with a silencer, scope, and aiming laser—the extra doodads needed by a modern assassin.

Kacy grasped my collar and dragged me out of the limousine.

"I don't know what kind of luck you've got, asshole," he said, "but I'm betting it ends soon. I've got enough silver bullets for every organ in your miserable body."

His finger twitched on the trigger and the red thread of the aiming laser vibrated between my eyebrows. "I sneeze and your brains are pudding."

A second armed guard, with a complexion the hue of roasted beef, stood next to Kacy. This guard carried an Uzi.

"If this *cabrón* screws up with Venin," the guard said, his Chicano accent coming on too forced, "I get dibs."

The guard might be *raza,* but that didn't mean I wouldn't kill him to escape.

Kacy relaxed his finger and the laser disappeared. I blinked to get the spots out of my eyes. The Chicano guard plucked the sunglasses out of my shirt pocket. "Put these on, *mocoso.*" Snot face. "We'll tell you when to take them off."

Kacy jabbed with the M16 toward a door. "That way."

Venin had a compelling motive to knock off Roxy—revenge for torpedoing Project Eleven. My two vampire escorts meant the councilwoman wasn't shy about applying muscle or spilling blood, especially if Venin was, as Rachel said, more than human. What was that? How close was I to the nexus of vampire–human collusion? Would Cragnow be here?

Deputy Police Chief Julius Paxton waited inside. He gave a bear trap smile. "Look what floated up the sewer."

"Kacy doesn't smell that bad," I said.

Paxton's hand shot at me with lightning speed. His fist smashed into my gut.

The blow stunned my *kundalini noir*. Electric bolts of pain shot through my limbs. The guards grabbed my arms and wrenched my shoulders back.

Paxton's fangs extended from under his upper lip like two ivory stalactites. He clenched and unclenched his right fist. His arm drew back. I saw the second blow coming like a boulder crashing down the mountain but I was helpless to move out of the way.

His fist hit the same spot as before. My insides were torn apart by an explosion of pain. I doubled over.

The guards let go and I dropped to the floor. Paxton kicked my ribs. Blinded with agony, I curled into a ball and lay on my side.

Paxton dug his shoe into my throat and levered my chin up with his heel. He rubbed the sole of his shoe against my Adam's apple.

"I've got the ass with you, smart guy." His voice sounded like words dragged over sandpaper. "Twice you've escaped. First in Pacoima. Today at Trixie's. So that's two times you made me look bad. I can't kill you now because the councilwoman wants an audience. But the third time will be a charm."

Paxton withdrew his shoe. He nodded to the guards, who pulled me upright. I leaned against the wall and waited for the nausea to pass.

My sunglasses sat askew on my nose and the Chicano guard adjusted them. "Tough luck, *ese*."

An air conditioner hummed and a gust of cool air brushed against me. It took a moment to get the strength to say something. "Paxton, so we'll see each other around?"

His fangs retracted. "I wouldn't count on it, shit for brains."

My two escorts took me to an elevator and up to the third floor. We stopped before a door in the middle of the hall. The Chicano guard reached over my shoulder and knocked.

"Enter," answered a woman's voice, sounding brisk and authoritative.

The guard opened the door. Kacy pushed me into a haze of menthol cigarette smoke.

Petale Venin stood behind a desk of polished cherry. She looked exactly like the photos I'd seen of her. A woman in her midforties. Blue, searching irises. Tiny creases around her eyes.

Those eyes. She had a lazy eye. I couldn't decide which one to look at. The left stared at me and the right was a bit off center. Or was it the right eye that stared at me?

A thin, prominent nose was centered between the fleshy cushions of her well-fed face. Skin the color of a manila envelope toasted by the sun. Rouged cheeks. A perfectly normal human, except for the eyes.

Venin toyed with a set of eyeglasses in her manicured hands. She wore a long-sleeved silk blouse. A pleated brown skirt covered her substantial hips. Still a perfectly normal human except for those eyes.

She motioned in a maternal manner to come close. "Felix, you may take off your sunglasses."

I did.

The shock turned my guts into liquid.

A red aura surrounded Petale Venin, a vermillion corona placid as still waters. My naked eyes bore into hers and nothing happened.

Venin was immune to vampire hypnosis. She was definitely more than human.

CHAPTER
36

I CLUTCHED THE BACK of the chair to steady myself.

How was it possible that Councilwoman Venin could resist vampire hypnosis? My *kundalini noir* sputtered and jerked in dismayed confusion.

Kacy retreated, closing the door. The Chicano guard stood behind me, submachine gun at the ready, orange aura shining, his face as impassive as an Aztec statue.

I sat, squeezing the arms of the chair to still my trembling fingers.

Petale Venin was human. Or did she merely have the red aura of a human?

I had only met two other creatures who could resist vampire hypnosis—a delightful forest sprite and a lying, cheating extraterrestrial. The sprite had a green aura, and the alien, yellow.

So was Venin human? Or a mutant hybrid between natural and supernatural? Or something else completely?

"Felix, welcome." Venin sat and put her eyeglasses on. Both pupils latched onto me, walleyed behind the thick lenses. Her wavy black hair was so stiff it looked chiseled. Silver and henna highlights marbled the dark glossy locks. "Thank you for agreeing to visit me."

"What did you mean, 'agreeing'? I wasn't given much choice."

"You could've run," she said. "Of course, then you'd be dead and I'd be talking to myself right now."

I cleared my throat, stalling for time as I took stock of my situation. Venin wanted something; otherwise, her goons would have pumped me full of silver bullets long ago.

Other than an ashtray, I saw no personal effects of Venin: no nameplate or computer on the desk; no plaques or photos on the wall; even the trash was empty. This wasn't her office, rather a place she came to for "special" business. There was a door to her right, which opened to the hall, or to another room? Did another surprise wait in there?

So here we were—Venin, her crooked eyes, an armed vampire guard, and myself. My Colt automatic and holster remained clipped to the back of my trousers. Why hadn't they searched me? Either they didn't have to—bad news for me—or they were complacent—bad news for them.

"I understand you visited my office yesterday." Her voice had a peppy California accent.

"How do you know?"

"Call it woman's intuition." She gave a motherly grin. "Felix, I understand your confusion. Let me answer the questions you might have. Yes, I am human. And yes, I know you are a vampire."

She admitted knowing the big secret? My grip tightened on the chair. Could she read my aura as well?

"There have been some misunderstandings since you've come to L.A. and I want that you and I"—she paddled her hands back and forth between us—"come to an agreement."

"What misunderstandings?"

"The attempts on your"—she made quote marks with her fingers—"*life.* What happened in Pacoima and today at the bistro."

"Those were misunderstandings? You *weren't* trying to kill me?"

"No. Those were Paxton's ideas."

"Was he acting on orders? From you? Or Cragnow Vissoom?"

Venin smiled, the way a snake might if it had lips . . . and a lazy eye. "Cragnow's afraid of you."

He had good reason. "Then he's the one who ordered the hits on me?"

"Please don't hold anything against him if I say yes. We've moved on since then." She opened a drawer and pulled out a packet of Newports.

"So plan A was me dead. Plan B is this meeting."

"Plan A? Plan B?" Venin looked puzzled. After a moment she gave a tinny laugh. "I get it. Yes, plan B. Here you are. Plan B." She lit a cigarette with a cheap plastic lighter and stared cross-eyed at the flame.

"How did you and Cragnow Vissoom get together?"

"Ah that," she drawled, exhaling smoke. Her painted fingernails clicked on the desktop. "He wanted help with zoning variances concerning his porn business. My staff and I were meeting with him in my council office when he took off his sunglasses and gave us *that* look."

"The vampire stare?"

Venin nodded. Cigarette smoke surrounded her head. "Everyone else in the room sat fish-mouthed and stupid-looking. But nothing happened to me. Cragnow gave another stare. He showed his big teeth and claws. It would have been a great Halloween gag . . . except that it was May."

This is how she recalled her introduction to an undead killer? As a joke? "And Cragnow's reaction?"

"He acted more confused that I was."

With those eyes of yours, no shit.

"Afterward, I realized I should have screamed and wet my panties—that is what women are expected to do when they meet a vampire." Venin took a long drag on the Newport. "At the time I was thinking this guy knows how hard it is to schedule a meeting with me and here he was doing a bad impression of Bela Lugosi."

In those situations, a vampire would've attacked. "I'm surprised he let you live."

"Cragnow needed a zoning variance. I couldn't do that dead." Venin crushed the cigarette into the ashtray. "He demonstrated the trance: mesmerizing my staff was no trick when they answered any question, no matter how personal." Venin paused and smiled. "I learned who on my staff cheated on their spouses, who embezzled money, and who leaked stories to my opponents and the press. At that point I grasped the significance of Cragnow's gift."

Venin paused again. "Imagine, Mr. Gomez, searching all your life for an edge, a leg up on the competition. And one day, that supreme advantage walks in your door."

"You're talking about the hypnosis?" I asked.

"What else? If I teamed with Cragnow, no one could keep secrets from us."

"Team with Cragnow? Why would he do that?"

"Because I told him he had this potential, and all *he* wanted was a zoning variance to make nudie pics. What a waste of an opportunity. That also made me realize how small my own ambitions were, especially when he revealed what he was."

"A vampire," I replied. "And that didn't scare you?"

"He had come to my office asking for a shortcut through the red tape. So he wasn't all-powerful."

"And you haven't wondered why his hypnosis doesn't affect you?"

"Neither does Jenny Craig, and you don't hear me whining about that." Venin readied another cigarette, as if the room didn't stink enough.

"You're the only human I've met who can resist hypnosis," I said.

"Apparently."

"Why? How?" My *kundalini noir* knotted and thrashed. "You're among vampires. They drink blood."

"How my constituents gain sustenance isn't my concern." Venin spoke despite having a cigarette in her mouth. One eye followed me, the other bounced along with the cigarette tip. "This is L.A., the home of fad diets."

"Constituents?"

She lit the Newport and dropped the lighter into a drawer. "Cragnow told me about your 'undead' society and that he was the leader. Mr. Gomez, open your eyes."

I couldn't decide which of her eyes to look at.

"One moment I'm Petale Venin, more councilwoman, the next moment I have access to super hypnosis and a secret army of vampires."

Here it was, the target of my investigation—vampire–human collusion.

"With this knowledge," Venin said, "my ambitions grew and grew as we crossed one threshold after another."

"Threshold?"

"Some thresholds involved eliminating those who stood in my way."

"You mean murder?"

"You're a vampire. What do you care about murder?"

"I care about one. Roxy Bronze."

Venin grimaced. "Her again." An ember from the cigarette dropped onto her blouse. Her right eye tracked the falling ash.

"Her name bothers you?" I asked.

"Not as much as it used to."

"Why?"

Venin brushed the ash off her blouse. "Because she's dead."

"How much do you know about her murder?"

"Only what was in the media."

Like I would believe that. "Do you know who killed her?" I didn't expect Venin to jump up and yell, "Me, me," but I had to ask.

"If I did," she replied, "I'd name a street after them."

"Them?" I asked.

"Them. Him. Her. Whoever."

"Considering this arrangement you have with Cragnow, why so much trouble with Roxy? Why didn't you use hypnosis or sic vampires on her?"

"As you know, there are limits to those powers and when you can use them."

"So you tried something?"

Venin stabbed the cigarette butt into the ashtray. "I didn't bring you here to discuss Roxy. I have an offer for you." Her mouth curved into a smile. Both eyes stared in my direction. "Join me."

Join her? This was no public radio membership drive. "Does Cragnow know about this? He *is* trying to kill me."

"Don't concern yourself with him. Cragnow has no say in this matter." Venin's smile cooled.

"I'm sure he'll object and—"

Venin interrupted, her voice chilling several degrees. "Cragnow has no say in this matter."

"Meaning what?"

"You misunderstand the relationship between Cragnow and myself."

"What's to misunderstand? As the vampire, he—"

Again she interrupted, her tone ice cold. "Cragnow Vissoom will do as he's told."

Told? Cragnow was the head of the L.A. *nidus*. Petale Venin—a human—was his boss? She commanded the undead in Southern California? The vampire–human collusion was worse than what the Araneum feared.

"How can you be in charge?" I asked.

"Because I understand Cragnow. I know what he wants. I know how he can get there."

"You've lost me."

"This arrangement he and I have is not about petty zoning variances. It's about laying the foundation for a new tomorrow."

"What kind of new tomorrow?" I recalled Lucky Rosario paraphrasing Cragnow . . . *lifting humanity to a new partnership with the unseen realm . . . the next* step *in social evolution.*

"That doesn't concern you, Mr. Gomez. Not yet."

"Then when?"

"I'll tell you."

"Why aren't you a vampire?" I asked. "Wouldn't you want to take advantage of supernatural powers?"

"Because I know everything, Mr. Gomez. I own many chalice parlors, including the Majestic Lanes."

That admission knocked the breath out of me. Venin mentioned this to flaunt how familiar she was with the secret vampire underworld.

My talons and fangs grew. My *kundalini noir* coiled upon itself, tensing to strike. I forced myself to keep still and not lunge to decapitate her. At the first instant of an attack, the guard behind me would stitch my back with silver bullets.

Venin nodded, enjoying my discomfort. "I know your strengths and weaknesses. The hypnosis, levitation . . . strengths. Your appetite for blood . . . weakness. Your vulnerability to sunlight. Another weakness. And your biggest weakness of all, the fear of being discovered and exterminated by humans."

She didn't mention auras or our transmutation into wolves. So maybe she didn't know everything.

"I join your team and then what?"

"You'll be given a special mission. For some reason, this arrangement between Cragnow and myself is a big taboo. Word of our collaboration got out, and vampire spies were sent to question Cragnow."

Did she mean the agents from the Araneum? "What happened to these spies?"

"Two I witnessed getting roasted by the morning sun. A

marvelous spectacle." Venin wrinkled her nose and smiled, as if sniffing a freshly baked cinnamon roll.

"What do you want me to do?"

"Infiltrate the Araneum."

I might as well shove dynamite up my ass. "Why me?"

"Because Cragnow suspects you may be one of their vampire spies."

I faked a chuckle. "That's ridiculous."

"You'd become a double agent, working for me. So what is your answer? Join me or not?"

"This is a serious decision. I'd have to think about it."

Venin's lips scrunched together, as if she had sucked on a tart lemon. "Think about it? That's a polite way of saying no. My offer is withdrawn." One eye cut to the guard, the other stared at me. Her aura surrounded her like a steady red flame. "It's been a displeasure to know you, Mr. Gomez."

CHAPTER
37

VENIN DIDN'T CHANGE SHAPE, but in the moments that I'd been here she had transformed from a plump matron to one of the most threatening creatures I'd ever seen. I wouldn't have been more surprised if she had grown mandibles and a stinger tail.

The guard rousted me from the chair and pushed me toward the door. I knew better than to resist and get ventilated by silver bullets. A last glance at Venin showed a tiny, smug smile curving her mouth and the mismatched focus of those eyes.

My death was as certain as the coming night.

Except the guard made two mistakes.

One. He still wore his sunglasses, which prevented him from reading my aura.

Two. I had my pistol.

The guard clasped my left shoulder and pressed the muzzle of his Uzi against the small of my back.

My *kundalini noir* writhed and twisted on itself in anticipation.

Strike. Destroy. Kill.

My talons and fangs jutted out.

I whirled to my right and knocked the submachine gun away from me. The gun fired a burst that tore into the door. I popped the guard with an upper cut, hitting his chin hard enough to daze him.

I drew my pistol and thumbed the safety.

I kicked the guard in the crotch, and he doubled toward me. I pressed the muzzle against his forehead and fired once. Vampire blood sprayed into the air and turned into red dust.

The guard fell and landed on his back. Smoke plumed from the hole in his forehead. I aimed for the center of his chest and fired again.

The bullet punched a hole in his shirt. His aura dimmed and was gone, like the flame of a snuffed candle. His body would last until sunlight cremated it into ash.

Now for Venin. With my pistol raised and my talons ready, I panned the room. She was gone, having fled through the door beside her desk.

The elevator pinged. The reports from my pistol summoned attention like an alarm. The doors clicked open and fast, heavy footfalls rushed toward me.

I had learned enough and there was no reason to risk more danger by staying around. Which way out?

The hall? I'd run right into those coming to get me.

The door? I didn't know what waited on the other side.

Then up.

I leaped and clawed through the acoustical tile. The ceiling hung from a concrete slab that separated the floors. The concrete was too thick to break, so I scrambled between the tile ceiling and the concrete, levitating so that I moved as lightly as a beetle. The galvanized ducting of the building's air-conditioning glittered before me.

The ducting was wide enough for me to shimmy through and escape. I tore open the galvanized steel wall.

Cool air tousled my hair. The breeze came from the left, the direction of the air conditioner that should sit on top of the building. I slithered into the ducting and crawled upwind.

Even though I was levitating, to move I had to brace my elbows, knees, and feet against the metal sides and push. The galvanized steel buckled and sent groans echoing down the ducts.

Muted voices called for me. Someone fired a gun and bullets thwacked the ducting, sounding like nails pounded into a can.

I crawled through piles of greasy dust and mouse nests. The little critters leapt before me, as surprised as I would be if a rhino charged through my home.

I climbed the final vertical shaft. Ahead, the fan from the air conditioner roared and spewed an icy blast. I drew close, the squirrel cage fan spinning like a gigantic mincer.

I reached behind me and ripped loose a long strip of the galvanized steel. Carefully, I fed the strip into the fan, backing away and letting go when the blades snagged the steel.

The steel strip wound around the fan cage, slapping the sides, squealing, slowing with a creak, and then stopping. The electric motor driving the fan moaned and began to smoke.

I reached through the fan and tore the drive belt. The electric motor immediately churned free, but no matter, the squirrel cage fan wouldn't move. I grasped the central shaft and levered the fan off its bearings.

Bracing my feet against the ducting, I pushed the fan aside to make room to crawl through. My free hand touched a filter pad silted with the residue of Los Angeles smog.

Christ, we breathed this air?

I straight-armed the filter pad and pushed through a louvered vent cover, folding the metal.

I crawled onto the roof, the asphalt and gravel still warm from the day's sun. I coughed to clear the crap inhaled from inside the ducting. My mouth tasted like I'd been chewing the canister bag of a vacuum cleaner. I couldn't smell anything through my clogged nose.

I sloughed the powdery grime from my clothes. The indigo bowl of the evening sky faded to cobalt blue over the western horizon. All around me, the horizon was lit up from the glow of suburban lights.

The building sat in a small complex along a busy throughfare that ran north and south. My best escape was through a nearby stand of eucalyptus trees and then to find a way of crossing the many miles back to Coyote's.

I dashed across the roof and jumped for the eucalyptus trees. I swung through the twisted branches Tarzan style, weaving through the trees until I was out of sight from the building.

Once I put enough distance between Venin's goons and myself, I dropped to the ground and dashed into the street. I sprinted behind a delivery truck and jumped on the rear bumper. Clinging to the rear door, I rode along for several blocks.

A Buick sedan crowded behind us, the driver a balding man too absorbed with his cell phone to notice me.

We slowed for a traffic light and I dismounted, heading for the parking lot of a Longs Drug. A sprinkler irrigated the grass on the narrow strip between the sidewalk and a row of hedges flanking the parking lot. I stopped to rinse my face and hands. Without makeup, my skin had a translucent pallor. I rinsed my mouth and spat, thankful to finally get rid of the awful taste of air-conditioner duct.

Tall lamps illuminating the parking lot cast shadows on my side of the hedge. Humans in their red auras sauntered to and from the cars and the store. I had dropped my sunglasses and, tapping my pockets, discovered that I had lost my contacts as well.

With my makeup all but gone, in these filthy clothes, and with my eyes unmasked—my *tapetum lucidum* resplendent with an unholy shine—there was no way I could mingle with the humans. A flatulent skunk would be less noticeable.

Still, I had to get away as fast as possible. Venin's undead thugs would cruise the streets, on the watch for my telltale orange aura.

CHAPTER
38

A KIA SEDAN SAT in the middle of the parking lot.
A middle-aged woman in a burgundy dress and blazer
took brisk steps toward the little car. A short ponytail dangled over the back of her collar. She passed through the circle of light under the lamp, and the glare painted sparkling
highlights on her face and blond head. She chatted into a
cell phone, a plastic shopping bag hanging from one arm,
and keys jangling from her free hand.

She approached the Kia from the right. My path to her
would be from the left, her blind side. I could easily traverse
the parking lot and she wouldn't notice me until I was on
her. I crept away from the hedge, wary that Venin's vampires were on the prowl. I walked toward the woman, resist-
ing the urge to break into a run.

The Kia's lights flickered as the woman reached for the
driver's door. She snapped her phone closed.

I said, "Nice car."

The woman turned around, startled. Her aura blazed from surprise.

I gave her a smile and an intense vampire stare.

Her aura lit up brighter, like I had reached into her and turned up the psychic rheostat.

"Relax," I said. "You'll be fine." I walked her to the passenger's side and buckled her in tight.

The drive to Coyote's would take an hour. My gaze wasn't enough to hold this woman in hypnosis. I'd have to fang this blonde to keep her unconscious for a while.

I drove to the side of the store, where I halted in the shadows. I pulled her close, loosened the blazer, and unbuttoned the top of her blouse.

This woman, whoever she was, I guessed to be in her early forties. A dainty, pretty face. Thin, bony frame. Her skirt, hitched above her knees, revealed narrow calves tapering to skinny ankles. She wore a gold wedding set.

I reached over her and released the seat back until her torso lay at a low angle. Caressing her hair, I tilted her head to expose a sumptuous throat.

Pints of savory blood awaited me. My fangs extended and pressed against my lower lip. I lowered my mouth to her neck and gently but firmly pushed my fangs through her skin.

The blood gushed into my mouth, velvety warm and delicious. Minutes ago I wormed my way though filthy air-conditioning ducts and now I enjoyed this human ambrosia.

I only wanted to knock this woman out, but the richness of her blood comforted me like hot soup would a man rescued from an avalanche. My mouth lingered on her neck and I enjoyed the exquisite bouquet of tastes: tangy Thai peppers, onions, wine—chardonnay, I'm sure—lemons; sesame oil; the metallic grate of ibuprofen; and then—garlic.

I barely got the driver's door open before I heaved.

The blood vomit splashed on the asphalt. I wiped my mouth and regretted that bile had replaced the rich taste of her blood. This woman must have popped garlic cloves like they were salted peanuts. My own stink kept me from smelling it on her.

Certain that Venin's guards covered the avenues along the north, since that was the way we had come into Brentwood, I went south to Highway 1 and took the long, long way back to Interstate 10.

At the tiny burg of Belvedere adjacent to Boyle Heights, I parked in front of a busy Asian market with plenty of female customers. I walked the blonde into the driver's seat. She moved dully, only barely obeying my voice.

To make it up to her, I counted two hundred dollars in twenties and tucked the cash into one cup of her padded brassiere. I fixed up her blouse and hair, and locked the door.

When she came to, this woman would have one hell of a time trying to figure out how she got here, and of course, the discovery of the money would deepen the mystery. Then again, this was Los Angeles, so maybe it had happened to her before.

I wound my way through the neighborhood. Dogs barking behind fences marked my trail. Near the freeway, a couple of homeless men tended a small fire and heated a can of stew. I stayed within the gloom under the overpass until I found the ravine leading to Coyote's. Weeds and scrawny shrubs grew along the chain-link fence. I ducked through the gap under the fence and made my way along the muddy creek to Coyote's home.

After what happened today, I remained cautious and stopped for a moment to observe his house. Yellow light peeked from around the edges of a curtain drawn over the kitchen window. I heard the strumming of guitars and the bleating of an accordion set to the strains of a Mexican *corrido*. I was glad not to find anything suspicious. I needed a rest from being hunted.

When I stepped on the porch, Coyote called out, "Felix? That you?" The door opened. He held a mop, and his trousers were rolled to midshin.

"Shit, dude, where you been? No place good, I can tell. *Apestas.*" You stink. He waved a hand before his nose.

I followed him inside. The kitchen table and chairs were jumbled together in one corner. Muddy, soapy water puddled on the tattered linoleum floor.

"I found it," I said. "The vampire–human connection."

"Where?" Coyote turned the radio down.

I recounted the attack with the silver bullets, Tonic's murder, the ride with Rachel, and my meeting with Petale Venin. When I described Venin's eyes and her resistance to hypnosis, Coyote let go of the mop, and it splashed in the water.

"*¿Ojos chuecos?*" Crooked eyes?

I repeated the description.

Coyote's aura glistened with streaks of worry. "*Vato,* this is bad." He picked up the mop and jammed it into a bucket. "I've seen one of these *ojos chuecos* before."

"When?"

"The Inquisition."

"The Spanish Inquisition?"

"No, the Malibu Inquisition. *Chingao*"—dammit—"*vato,* what kind of question is that? Of course the Spanish Inquisition."

"Was this crooked eyes human?" I asked.

"Yes, and like your councilwoman, he was not affected by vampire hypnosis."

"Why?"

"Don't know. You ever hypnotized an *ojos chuecos?*" Coyote made one eye circle right and the other left. "Or somebody with one eye? I never have." Coyote jutted his chin, shut one eye, and squinted through the other to imitate Popeye. "Maybe you need two eyes to get the full effect." He opened both eyes wide and cupped his hands over them, as if he were looking through binoculars. "You know, stereoscopic vision."

"Could it be a supernatural power? Something Venin has in common with the inquisitor? Maybe she's a descendant?"

"Felix, you're supposed to bring me answers, not more questions." Coyote dragged the kitchen table onto a bump of dry floor. He placed a washbasin on the table and took a stockpot from the stove to fill the basin with warm water. He slapped a bar of soap and a towel on the table. *"Andale."* Here.

I took off my shirt and lathered my hands. "What happened with this inquisitor?"

"It was a bad time, *ese*. This crooked eyes was sent by King Charles to hunt for Jews and heretics among the Conquistadores. He was obsessed with finding the red-eyed demons." Coyote lifted his face to me. His eyes glowed crimson as warning lamps.

"Why didn't you attack him?"

"For the same reason you didn't attack Venin," replied Coyote.

"I couldn't. She was protected by vampires."

"The same as the Inquisitor."

"You said he was after red-eyed demons, meaning vampires."

Coyote nodded.

"Then why would vampires protect him?" I asked.

"Where better to hide than among your enemies? Vampires worked for the inquisitor."

"As vampires?"

"Símon. Back then there was no dividing line between the natural and the fantastic. You didn't need scientific proof to believe in devils and *el cucui"*—the bogeyman. "The inquisitor used the powers of these vampires. Remember, the church justified the use of torture and murder to promote the mercy of Christ. Then why not enlist undead bloodsuckers to root out the unbelievers?"

"How many vampires? One? Two? A dozen?"

"I didn't stick around to count. These vampires were the worst. They would perform any act of sadism in the name of the Holy Church."

I asked, "Why would any vampire compromise himself by openly serving a human master?"

"It doesn't start out that way. As humans grow stronger in numbers and knowledge, we vampires have to shrink farther into the shadows to hide. We think an arrangement with humans gives us the chance to use terror and flaunt supernatural powers. But we forget humans are the most cunning and treacherous of predators. Only when it is too late do we realize we're on the wrong end of the leash."

"But we are vampires."

"Our powers are only half of what humans fear about us. The other half is fear of the unknown. We get too close, too familiar, and humans learn our strengths and weaknesses."

Strengths and weaknesses. "Petale Venin used those exact words. So how can she control vampires?"

"By giving vampires what they think they want—the illusion of freedom and control among humans. *Vato,* it's not enough that she can resist hypnosis. Venin recognizes our powers and sees us not as monsters but as tools."

"Cragnow talked about the next step in human evolution," I said. "He saw this partnership with Venin as a means to create a society with humans and the undead."

"The trap is Venin builds her authority until she's more valuable than any vampire. Either follow her orders or the group turns on you. It's like before, *ese.*"

"During the Inquisition?"

"The same. That didn't end well. All the vampires in the king's service . . ." Coyote pretended to gather dust from the table and shift it through his fingers.

"Then it's only a matter of time before Venin sells out the *nidus.*"

Coyote's gaze wandered for a moment and settled on me. "What should we do, *mi jefe?*"

"We've got plenty of questions. Let's go get answers."

CHAPTER
39

C'MON, *VATO*," COYOTE YELLED. His head
thrust through the open window of his truck. "Push
faster. This time it will start for sure."

I gave his Ford pickup a push up the dip in front of his
house. "What happened to the money I lent you? You promised me you'd only spend it on the truck."

"I did. I found this real *chingon* accessory. Gives my ride
a classy touch."

His truck sputtered and coughed. The tailgate pulled
away from me. Success.

Just as his front tires crested the dip, black smoke belched
from the exhaust pipe. The truck slowed, stopped, and rolled
backward.

"Get out of the way," Coyote shouted and waved his arm
for emphasis, as if the ton and a half of rust rumbling at me
wasn't enough to get my attention.

I stepped away and let the truck coast to the bottom of the dip and continue up the other side for twenty feet then slide back to the bottom. I wish I had my big new Chrysler rental, but that remained where I had left it, close to Trixie's Bistro.

Coyote circled his finger and whistled. *"Otra vez."* Again.

"How about I drive and you push?"

"Chale. It takes magic to start this baby."

"Your magic doesn't seem to be working well."

"That's 'cuz you don't believe."

On the third effort, his miserable excuse for transportation chuffed along the street. I ran after it and scrambled into the passenger's seat.

"Looky here." Coyote raised his right leg to show me an oversize chrome pedal in the shape of a foot. "This is what I bought. Classy, no?"

"Not as classy as a starter."

"Vato, you know what your problem is? You have no sense of barrio style."

Cragnow Vissoom lived along the ridge of the Santa Monica Mountains. On the way there we would pass where my rental car was parked, but when we got there, the Chrysler was gone. Stolen? Or towed away by the police or renegade vampires. Regardless, it meant going to Cragnow's in this humiliating wreck.

Coyote asked, "Did you see Veronica?"

"I spent Monday night with her."

"How's that going?"

"Not sure." I told Coyote about my warning to Veronica and her reaction. "But no matter what, I won't let anything happen to her."

"What about the other *vieja*? The one you met at Daniel's funeral." Coyote mimed with his hands, as if he held two large cantaloupes.

"You mean Polly Smythe? She can take care of herself. Why, you want to meet her? By the way . . ." I pulled Coyote's hands farther apart.

His eyebrows danced upward. "That big? Then yeah, maybe soon, *ese.*"

"One thing nags me," I said. "What does Lara Phillips have to do with any of this? There's a lot of shady business between her boyfriend the reverend and the others in this case. Why would she be involved with a man so close to those who wanted Roxy out of the way?"

"Maybe Lara's trying to find answers of her own?"

"I didn't get that impression," I replied. "In fact, the opposite. She's hiding something."

We drove to Beverly Hills and started the ascent up Coldwater Canyon Drive. Some homes were brightly lit and cheery, others ensconced in gloom. We passed acres of stately mansions with manicured hedges and postcard-perfect king palms. Mercedes coupes and sedans along the curbs meant that the fancy wheels—Bentleys, Lamborghinis, and Royces—occupied the garages.

The higher we climbed, the smaller the homes became and the closer they crowded the road. Lawns shrank to narrow strips and disappeared altogether. Near the top of the ridge, Coldwater Canyon merged with Mulholland Drive. At the corner of the next turn, a dirt road led between two rustic stone columns that formed the mouth of a tunnel through the dense overgrowth.

"That's it," I told Coyote. "But don't slow down."

Coldwater Canyon Drive angled away from Mulholland and down to the San Fernando Valley. We stayed on Mulholland until we found a house with a FOR SALE sign. A month's worth of newspapers littered the front stoop. We pulled into the narrow driveway, parked, and sneaked through the underbrush toward Cragnow's estate.

Coyote and I found a clearing in the scrub, waited, and listened. There was no breeze to rustle the leaves and mask movement. Little red auras darted in and out of the thatched cover. A raccoon crawled along the branches of a gnarled oak. Mice skittered in the grass. An owl hooted. A snake pushed through the dry leaves on the ground.

A Land Rover came up Franklin Canyon Drive and turned east on Mulholland. Three red auras advertised the human occupants. The Land Rover drove by and left.

Moving as carefully as the little animals of the night, Coyote and I made our way through the dry thicket and rocky ground. I was on the alert for a supernatural presence, but I shouldn't overlook human methods: video cameras, sensor beams, and trip wires. I didn't see any, but again, we were still a quarter mile from his place.

We eased through a cut in the spine of the ridge and continued in an easterly direction until we came across the driveway onto Cragnow's property. We were farther north than expected. The gravel road curved to the left. Through the tunnel of trees I could see the backs of the stone columns marking the entrance. To the right, light splashed onto the driveway and outlined the trees and brush.

Coyote squatted beside me, touched my shoulder, and pointed to a big oak. He whispered. *"Aya."* Over there. His *tapetum lucidum* glinted red.

I followed the line of his outstretched finger and noticed, on the branch, a video camera aimed toward the entrance. We were behind the camera and out of view. I scanned the other trees and along the ground, looking for the rectangular outline of a camera or the curve of a cable. *Nada.*

Only one camera. No guards. Either Cragnow thought he was safe in his mountain enclave or this was a trap. Or maybe Cragnow wasn't here.

I moved along the shoulder of the driveway toward the house. I was used to sneaking up on humans, but the cover of darkness wouldn't hide me from another vampire. If anything, my orange aura would appear even brighter against the inky night.

The driveway opened into a parking area. I counted four vehicles, a pewter gray Hummer, a black Porsche Cayenne SUV, and two black cars—a BMW coupe and a Mercedes sedan. The BMW was identical to the car Dr. Niphe drove, and the Porsche Cayenne looked a lot like Lucky Rosario's.

Coyote hissed excitedly and motioned to the entrance. He

scrambled into the brush. The beams from headlights swung across the brush and driveway. I followed Coyote's example and ducked behind a shrub.

I kept low to hide my aura. Tires rumbled nearby. When the vehicle moved past, I lifted my head.

A white stretch limo circled by the other cars. Its tail-lights flashed, and the limo halted. A couple of doors clicked open. Women chirped like sparrows. Their shoes clattered across wooden planking. Four, five girls, maybe six. If Cragnow wasn't here, he was missing one hell of a party.

Another set of footfalls moved over the wooden boards in solid, deliberate steps.

I had to sneak closer. Coyote glanced at me and I pantomimed to ask if he'd seen anything. He shook his head and waved me forward.

I picked my way through the dry brush. Branches scratched my shirt and trouser legs. I dropped to a crouch and peered through an opening in the shrubs.

Floodlights illuminated Cragnow's house, turning the structure into a collage of vivid colors and shadow. A wooden deck separated the house from the parking area. The floor plan of the split-level house seemed built upon overlapping circles. Picture windows on the curving walls peeked over hedges trimmed low to not spoil the view. A round cupola with a coolie hat tile roof sat atop the tallest part of the house.

To my left, the lawn sloped toward a vista of Beverly Hills and West Los Angeles, a constellation of lights receding toward the distant illuminated haze above Marina Del Rey.

Coyote disappeared into the chaparral behind me.

I crept around until I observed the south side of the house. Two stories of tall windows and another deck overlooked the vista. Light from inside the house washed over the deck. I crawled around a row of barrel cactus marking the perimeter of the lawn.

Framed within the picture windows, Mordecai Niphe and Lucky Rosario sat on plush wing chairs facing the middle of the room. They both smiled and looked relaxed.

A reedy young woman in a silvery halter top with matching microskirt and stiletto heels strutted before them. A braid of brunette hair trailed down her naked back. She swapped highball glasses with Niphe, taking his empty and giving him a full one.

Niphe pulled the woman onto his lap and undid the knot holding up her top. She rolled her head back and let him nuzzle her neck.

Rosario said something. The woman laughed and pulled herself free from Niphe. The halter top fell to the floor. She walked to the right, out of my view. Niphe picked up the halter top, balled it up, sniffed it, and tossed it out of sight.

Their auras glowed a pleasant red. Everyone here expected a good time.

Niphe and Rosario stood. Cragnow appeared, an old-fashioned in one hand. His aura simmered orange. Small tendrils waved along the penumbra, indicating concern. The sleeves of his white shirt were folded to his elbows. His gray hair was combed back, which emphasized his prominent forehead.

As I studied Cragnow, my talons extended and my *kundalini noir* flexed. I should crash this party and settle the score.

Yet something was wrong. Cragnow had to know I could come after him.

So where were his guards? As clever as I thought I was, this infiltration seemed too easy.

Cragnow faced Niphe and Rosario. They nodded and laughed. What was the joke? Me?

A vampire—his aura gave away his supernatural identity—who looked like a running back entered the scene. He had an African-American complexion and wore a black dinner jacket over black dress trousers. The vampire stood beside Cragnow and whispered into his ear. Cragnow's aura blazed. He turned around and looked right at me through the window.

CHAPTER
40

IME TO SCRAM AND FIND COYOTE.
The smell hit me.

Meaty. Musky.

Wolf.

I crawled from between the cactus and retreated deep into the dry brush. The branches and dead leaves crunched beneath me. Where was that wolf? My talons and fangs extended.

A growl came from the left. Another from the right. And another from the parking lot. Not wolf but wolves. Here were Cragnow's bodyguards, vampires transformed into wolves.

I drew my pistol—grateful that I carried silver bullets—and executed a time-honored military maneuver. I turned and ran.

A wolf lunged from the brush, its aura an orange comet

and the eyes twin embers burning with malevolence. The long jaws snapped, the ferocious teeth flashing like a saw.

I jerked my gun toward it when another wolf tackled me from behind. I fell into a mass of bramble, the thorns raking my face and neck.

The wolf's jaws locked on my left shoe, the teeth tearing into my foot. I kicked the wolf's snout and fought to roll over on my back to get a shot with my pistol.

The first wolf clawed through the bramble and snapped at me in a whirlwind of teeth, fur, and blazing eyes.

I let fly two shots. The wolves backed off enough for me to get up and run limping out of the brush and into the parking lot.

One wolf followed me. The other circled around. No more wild shots. I couldn't afford to waste ammunition.

When I reached the gravel lot, the wolf behind me surged forward, snarling. The second wolf lunged from my right side. His jaws clamped on my pistol hand, my wrist feeling like it had been smashed between bricks. I punched the wolf with my left fist.

The wolf wrenched its head, wrestling to knock me off balance. The other wolf snatched my belt and pulled the other way.

An orange blur streaked from the woods and crashed into the wolf clutching my hand. The wolf let go and spun about, its jaws snapping at empty air.

The blur settled into the shape of a coyote, its jaws a flailing set of teeth.

The wolf hunched its shoulders, the hair on its neck bristling. It lunged forward.

The coyote was in front of the wolf one instant, then beside it the next. The coyote clamped onto the wolf's throat. The two of them snagged forelimbs and rolled into a ball of fur and orange auras.

The other wolf tugged at my waist and nearly pitched me over. I leveled my pistol and squeezed one shot.

The bullet grazed the wolf's flank. It let go, backed off a couple of steps, then reared on its hind legs to spring for my face.

I fired once into its torso.

The wolf stopped, its front paws waving through the air. The fury in its eyes was replaced by a dimming sadness. Its aura tightened around the furry body.

I held the pistol in a two-hand grip. My next shot thumped low in the wolf's sternum, right where the *kundalini noir* should be.

The wolf's limbs twisted and elongated. Fur disappeared into smooth white skin. The snout retreated into a grotesque face, as wolf transformed into dying vampire. I recognized the ragged sandy hair on his big head. Kacy. The vampire who tried to run me over with a Jaguar convertible and later missed again when he shot at me in Trixie's Bistro.

Kacy stood naked, his unfocused eyes staring into oblivion. Smoke curled from the holes my bullets had punched into him. His mouth opened and a gasp escaped. His orange aura shrank around him, becoming a weak glow frail as a tiny candle flame. The glow flickered out. Kacy the vampire was no more.

He was a newly converted vampire, so instead of dissolving into dust, his corpse remained whole—until sunlight hit it. His body toppled backward, leaving the stench of his burning undead flesh lingering in the air.

What about Coyote?

He stood beside the fallen corpse of the other wolf, now writhing as it transformed into a vampire. Coyote panted and acted worn out. Shiny mats of blood spotted his disheveled fur. Coyote glanced from the man to me, giving a look that said, *Where you been?*

Heavy steps stormed over the wooden deck of Cragnow's house, accompanied by the metallic click of weapons being readied.

Time to go.

I ran limping across the parking area, Coyote loping by

my side. We headed for the entrance onto Cragnow's property, into the dark tunnel formed by the overlapping branches of the trees.

There had been three wolves. We killed two. Where was the other one?

I glanced over my shoulder back toward Cragnow's house. Red auras surrounded the men carrying guns. Good. They were human and so couldn't see our auras. That made our escape easier.

A growl turned my attention to the front.

A wolf guarded the mouth into the tunnel. Its orange aura roiled like fire. The two eyes glowed bright as heated iron.

Good show, but this wolf hadn't been paying attention to current events. So far the score was: our side, two; wolves, zero. And I still had bullets in my pistol.

I fired once.

The wolf yelped and jumped.

I fired again.

The wolf's front legs folded, and the animal collapsed, hindquarters and rump sticking into the air. The orange aura vanished, as if blown out.

Coyote and I ran through the tunnel past the dead wolf as it turned into the trim shape of a female vampire. Tattoos encircled the arms. It was Rachel, the human receptionist from Gomorrah Video who later, as a vampire, drove the limo that shuttled me to Petale Venin. I had warned her.

Men jogged through the parking area. Red laser pointers crisscrossed the ground like feelers.

Coyote crashed through the brush ahead of me, and I lost him. I headed west in the scrub parallel to Mulholland Drive. The dense woods and terrain swallowed the noise coming from Cragnow's estate.

Coyote and I had knocked off the primary guard force, the wolves. Smart tactic for Cragnow, if it would've worked. I had expected vampire lookouts and technical surveillance, not furry undead killers.

I loaded a fresh magazine into my pistol.

An orange glow outlined the scrub branches. I raised my pistol.

"Don't shoot, *vato*," whispered Coyote.

He stepped though a gap in the scrub, a skinny old-man frame—naked, save for the tennis shoes on his feet. He carried his clothes wadded under one arm.

"You can get dressed," I said.

"Later, *ese*. The night air feels good." He continued for his truck, the muscles of his scrawny ass cheeks flexing and relaxing as he strode along. Blood trickled from the scratches on his neck and shoulders.

"You okay?" I asked. I massaged the bite on my wrist, feeling the torn flesh mend itself. "You're bleeding."

Coyote wiped the blood from his skin. *"A la Madre.* It's mine. Next time, *vato,* I'll let you handle all the *chingasos."*

We did the usual drill with his beater Ford. I pushed it out into the street and pushed again to start the rusted jalopy. I was getting too much practice at this.

Coyote drove the long way back to Boyle Heights, taking Mulholland to Beverly Glen Boulevard, Sunset, then the 405 and finally the Santa Monica Freeway.

At every intersection and turn I expected the police to ambush us. After all, Cragnow only need jerk the chain of his buddy, Deputy Police Chief Julius Paxton. I kept my pistol handy. I didn't want to kill any human cops if they were doing their jobs and had no idea of this vampire insurrection. But my fellow undead were fair game.

So far, no cops. No one chasing us. No helicopters. "This is too easy," I said.

Coyote's forehead wrinkled and the ends of his mustache quivered. "You crazy? We barely escaped."

"Cragnow expected only me, so three wolves would've been enough, even with my gun," I said. "He underestimated me, or rather, us. Next time, he won't."

CHAPTER
41

WE ARRIVED AT COYOTE'S HOUSE, passing delivery trucks bringing newspapers and fresh bread to convenience stores and markets.

Coyote let his truck roll to the bottom of the dip and turned his heap around so it faced the right way when it was time to leave.

A cerulean band of sky appeared above the mountains of the Angeles National Forest. Dawn approached, and my *kundalini noir* coiled in fear of the morning light.

No suspicious auras lurked in the neighborhood. No cops. The neighborhood was as quiet and serene as a crypt.

On the way into his house, Coyote gathered a handful of sticks. He broke them into pieces the length of a pencil. Coyote paced the perimeter of his yard and worked a stick into the ground every few paces.

"What's that for?" I asked.

"My alarm system. Anybody or anything crosses those sticks"—Coyote snapped his fingers—"I'm awake."

"Where did you learn this?"

"Un guajiro Tarahumara." A shaman from the Tarahumara Indians.

"Does it work?"

"Like magic."

"Like the same magic that starts your truck?" Hope not. With Coyote's "high-tech" security system protecting us, I headed downstairs to rest and escape the morning's rays.

Water dripped from the ceiling where it leaked from the wet kitchen floor. I lay in the coffin and counted the drips splashing against the lid until I fell asleep.

By midafternoon we were up. I inspected the circle of sticks, looking for evidence of tampering or unusual footprints. "Nothing happened."

"Are you surprised, *ese?* Nothing bad can happen to us inside the circle. It worked."

"Just because you put in those sticks and nothing happened," I said, "is like saying a drink of whiskey is good medicine to prevent snakebites."

"It's not?"

"We're going to need more than superstitions to protect us."

"Vato, listen to yourself. A vampire who doesn't believe in superstitions? It's a cosmic contradiction."

Coyote made coffee and stirred blood into a pot of posole. I cleaned up and shaved.

"Let's go have a talk with Dr. Niphe." I sat at the table and sprinkled Cholula hot sauce over a bowl of the posole. "What was he doing up there partying with Cragnow and those hookers? On a school night, no less." I pulled a tortilla from the stack kept warm under a towel.

Coyote tore a piece of tortilla and scooped it into his bowl. "Do we surprise him?"

"Of course we surprise him. This time we'll come in through the roof and pull him out of surgery if we have to."

We finished our meal. I gathered a few of my things into my overnight bag, in case we got delayed. Roxy's file and my laptop remained downstairs, next to the coffin. I topped off my pistol magazines.

Coyote climbed into his truck. I set the overnight bag on the sidewalk. I braced my shoulder against the tailgate of the truck and pushed.

The truck moved up the hill, gaining speed as I advanced from a trot to a run. The truck lurched when the engine caught. I let go. Coyote waved his arm for me to jump aboard.

I turned to fetch my bag. The truck was about to crest the slope when the engine coughed. Sparks shot from the undercarriage.

An explosion ripped open the engine compartment and shook the ground. The fenders flew apart, and the hood went spinning. An enormous fireball welled inside the cab, shattered the windows, and ballooned upward. The hot blast slapped my face.

Coyote.

I screamed his name.

The flaming carcass of the pickup rolled backward down the dip, right toward me. A chorus of car alarms wailed throughout the neighborhood.

I wanted to reach into the cab and snatch Coyote free. But the inferno warned me off. No one could've survived, not even a vampire. Helpless, I stepped back and raised my arm to shield my face from the heat.

The truck jumped the curb and smashed through the chain-link fence. The truck rumbled straight for Coyote's home and crashed through the porch to settle inside his kitchen like a gigantic Molotov cocktail.

A second explosion sent jets of flame cascading out the door and windows. The roof hopped a few inches, fire erupting past the joists, and broke into pieces. The rear end of the truck tipped up as the floor gave way and the house collapsed onto itself.

I stumbled dumbstruck toward the flaming ruins, unwilling to comprehend what I'd witnessed. I wanted to believe that at any second Coyote would reappear, either jumping from the flames like a rodeo clown or simply popping into plain sight as if he'd always been there.

Coyote's magic warning sticks lay trampled under tire marks. His truck had been outside the circle when the bomb was planted. That's why we didn't get a warning.

People streamed from the local houses, approaching cautiously, their faces slack with horror and disbelief. They pointed at me, muttering to one another, "Who is that? Did he kill the *viejo* in the house? Why did he do it?"

The fire ate Coyote's house and the timbers cracked as if the flames had teeth. The roof settled into the burning hole of the basement, the furnacelike heat incinerating everything.

Police sirens blared in the distance.

I didn't need any cops. One of them might have planted the bomb. I had to leave. Now.

I shouldered my overnight bag and retreated into the weeds of the ravine. I hustled through the ravine and into the shade under the overpass

A column of smoke fouled the air to the west. Fire trucks and more police cars zoomed past.

I rested against the concrete pillar of the overpass, dismayed and shocked. I couldn't believe it.

Coyote was dead.

I replayed the horrific ordeal. The sparks shooting from the front. The blast tearing the truck apart. The terrible fire consuming the cab.

Who ordered the hit? Cragnow, I'm sure. With Petale Venin's blessing.

Shock gave way to anger, and my *kundalini noir* tightened.

Who had planted the bomb? The police, some of Paxton's? Or Cragnow's vampire guards?

And why? To kill Coyote and me? Or just me?

The blackest of my thoughts returned. Coyote. Gone. Roasted into ash. The hopelessness of the situation crushed me. My legs folded and I sank against the pillar.

A crow sat on a chain-link fence close to the overpass. The crow squawked and flew into the shadow of the overpass to land on the dirt. The crow stared at me with its glossy marble-like eyes. It squawked again. A shiny metallic capsule clung to its right leg. A message from the Araneum.

A wave of resentment tore at my insides. New orders from my anonymous bosses? What good was their grand omniscience if they let Coyote die?

I snatched a pebble from the ground. "I've had enough of this, you stupid bird." I flung the pebble at the crow.

The pebble bounced off its skull. The bird staggered and fell on its butt. The crow shook its head, extended one wing to lever itself up, and stood. The crow advanced and squawked angrily.

It stopped by my feet and raised the leg with the capsule. I reached for the leg, and the crow hopped back.

"I'm not in the mood for games," I said.

The crow strutted into the darker shadows under the overpass. I pushed myself up and followed.

The crow stopped and raised its legs again.

I knelt to unfasten the capsule.

The crow's beak snapped on my finger.

I pulled away, clasping the injured digit. "You little shit, what was that about?"

The crow tilted its head and squawked. It raised the leg with the capsule.

"Okay, so we're even. But watch yourself. Bite me again and I'll introduce you to a knife and fork."

The crow shrugged its wings, unimpressed by my threat.

I unclipped the capsule. It looked identical to the one I'd seen back in Denver, a pinky-size tube of filigreed platinum and yellow gold. Rubies rimmed the cap.

Opening the capsule, I let the odor of rancid meat escape, a reminder of the source, a swatch of vampire skin.

I tapped the capsule and a thin curled leaf of vampire parchment slid free. I flattened the parchment into a buff-colored translucent square, curious about the instructions sent by the Araneum.

The parchment was bare. I held it up and studied the surface for evidence of writing. Did the ink fade? Had they used an invisible formula? What was the secret?

The crow squawked to get my attention. It picked a short stick from the ground and dragged one end through the dirt, making squiggles. The crow stopped and gazed at me.

"What are you getting at?"

The bird rolled its head, the gesture saying, "Figure it out, stupid," and dragged the stick through the dirt again.

"You're writing something?"

The crow kept working the stick.

"You want me to write something?"

The crow spat the stick.

"What?"

The crow walked back and forth in front of me, leaving claw tracks in the dust.

"A report?"

The crow didn't answer.

The parchment was too flimsy to write on without support. I slipped a notepad out of my overnight back. I placed the parchment on the notepad, clicked my ballpoint, and wondered what to write. Couldn't be much; the parchment was smaller than the palm of my hand and too thin to write on both sides.

What could I say?

I started with the most important.

Coyote dead. Assassinated. The Araneum surely knew who he was.

Cragnow Vissoom betrayed great secret. Takes orders from Councilwoman Petale Venin, human immune to hypnosis. Cragnow and Venin plan coalition of undead and humans, start of new empire.

Far-fetched? Not really, since it was true.

What was I to do?

I finished my message. *Will continue with direct action. Vissoom and Venin to die with undead accomplices.*

Your servant, Felix Gomez.

My writing started with neat block letters and deteriorated into a scrawl bunched up along the bottom of the parchment. I rolled the parchment into the capsule and screwed the cap tight.

The crow hopped close. I fit the capsule to one leg. The crow stepped away. Rather than fly off, it stared at me. Its gaze was pensive, melancholy. What did it know? Was this note to be the last testament from me?

The crow turned about and sprang into the air, its black wings a blurry rush of feathers. The crow sailed into the bright sunlight and disappeared.

A new emotion rose inside me and crowded aside the dark shock of Coyote's death. Something more than anger.

Revenge.

I had my own orders. Direct action. Kill Cragnow and Venin.

How?

I had lost my partner. Roxy's files and most of my possessions were burned up. I gazed at the urban sprawl beyond the sanctuary of the overpass. Which was the way forward?

I had the clothes I wore and what was inside my overnight bag: a few toiletries, a notepad, two loaded magazines of silver bullets, plus the stash of eight thousand dollars.

So I had money, a gun, and ammuntion. That was a start.

My cell phone hummed in my pocket. I withdrew the phone and flipped it open. I didn't recognize the number, a local area code.

"Hello? Hello?" The man's voice sounded familiar.

"Yes," I replied.

"Felix? It's Lucky Rosario."

CHAPTER
42

I COULD'VE TURNED INTO ICE. Rosario calling now?

"I want out, Felix."

"Out from what?"

"Everything. My business with Cragnow. That whole mess."

"Gimme a second." I had to reorient my thoughts from losing Coyote and back to the investigation. "You seemed happy with the arrangement. The money. The girls."

"The hell with that. We're talking about murder."

Damn right, this was about murder. "What do you mean? Whose murder?" I wanted him to say Roxy's.

"Rebecca Dwelling and Fred Daniels."

Big surprise.

"You're saying Cragnow was behind the murder of Rebecca and Fred?" I wanted Rosario to spell it out in bold capital letters.

"Yes."

"Cragnow admitted it?" I asked.

"Admit? Hell, he bragged about ordering the killings. And there's another murder. Katz Meow."

I had expected that news but still, hearing it stung. "What makes you sure Katz was murdered? Last I checked, she was still missing."

"Not anymore. She's in the morgue. With a bullet hole."

A bullet hole. Same as Roxy. "Who killed her?" I asked.

"Don't know."

"What do you want me to do?"

"Give me cover."

"If you mean protection, go to the police. Cut a deal with them."

Rosario's voice lowered to a desperate whisper. "You know I can't. Julius Paxton is in Cragnow's back pocket. I squeal to the cops, and you'll find me on a table next to Katz."

"And you think I can help?"

"Felix, I'll tell you everything I know. Enough to bury them all for good."

The alarm in my *kundalini noir* tripped. Cragnow or Paxton could be using Rosario to track my cell phone.

"Rosario," I said, "I'll call you back at your number. But double-cross me, and I will hurt you."

"Hold on, Felix—" he blurted as I palmed my cell phone and turned it off.

If Rosario's information was any good, it could be my break to get at Cragnow and Venin.

First, get as much distance as possible from here, in case my call had been monitored.

I hiked under the overpass until I came across a path that led into East Los Angeles. I couldn't imagine finishing this investigation chasing after Cragnow in a city bus. I needed wheels. Something fast and cheap.

A Yamaha V-Max motorcycle sat on the lawn of a house. In the world of crotch rockets, the V-Max was king testosterone. A FOR SALE sign asked $4,800 OBO.

Dents, scratches, faded paint, and blued chrome exhaust told me this bike had been ridden awhile. Gray duct tape covered the edges of the seat. The tires had plenty of tread. The wheels and disk brakes looked true.

I sat on the V-Max and worked the foot and hand controls. Other than needing a wash, the bike was in fair shape, considering the high mileage on the odometer.

I could zap the owner and rip him off, but while I might be a lecherous, bloodsucking killer, I was no thief. Besides, bad karma had plagued me enough in this case; I didn't need any more.

I walked up to the house behind the Yamaha and rang the doorbell. A man appeared at the screen door and stepped out. He was a slender Chicano about my height in his late twenties, with the smudge of a soul patch, tattoos, and wearing denim cargo shorts and a wife beater.

We rapped about the bike. He kept calling me *cuñado*. Brother-in-law.

I asked, "How's it run?"

"*Cuñado,* it's got more *huevos* than two of you."

Good enough. We haggled over the price and settled on $3,800.

"*Cuñado,* aren't you going to give it a ride first?"

"If it doesn't have *huevos,*" I said, "I'll come back for yours."

I gave him cash. He handed a pair of stiff leather gloves and an envelope with the title, registration, and keys. He added a beanie helmet in dark matte gray with two bloodshot eyes glued to the front.

"Better wear it, *cuñado.* State law."

I cruised the neighborhood to get a feel for the machine. After a few minutes I couldn't resist and goosed the throttle. The V-Max shot forward like it wanted to fly. This bike had plenty of *huevos.* I smiled.

I stopped at a 7-Eleven to gas up and buy a street map. Rosario wanted to talk. I studied the map, looking for someplace public yet open enough for me to check that Rosario arrived alone. There were plenty of neighborhood parks close to here. Too small. How about Elysian Park north of Dodger Stadium? Maybe.

Beyond that, the much larger Griffith Park with its woodsy, hilly trails. Good enough.

My *kundalini noir* grumbled. Last I had to eat was the posole and blood. A *carnicería* would have cow's blood, but considering the trauma of the day, I wanted something more nourishing and comforting—fresh human.

A red Ducati sport bike glided to the curb in front of the 7-Eleven and stopped next to my V-Max. The rider swung a booted leg off the Ducati. A red leather riding suit with black mesh trim hugged feminine curves. She flipped up the front of her helmet. The cheek pads scrunched her features, but I recognized the eyes. She was the yuppie in the Ferrari that night Coyote and I were chased from Dale Journey's church.

The woman looked at my Yamaha. She gave a dismissive shake of her head, as if to say, *what a P.O.S.*

I was hungry, and this woman had shown up. What timing. I took off my sunglasses and contacts. *Guess what, lady? It's snack time.*

I asked about her bike, we made eye contact, and wham, she was mine.

I led her by the hand around back, where we hid between the crib for recycling cardboard and the Dumpster.

I removed her helmet and unzipped the jacket. Her perspiration and perfume wafted in a mouthwatering aroma. Her neck was more delicious than I remembered. I took my time, no sense being a pig.

My *kundalini noir* satisfied, I put the helmet back on her head, zipped the jacket, and left her slumped against the wall behind the Dumpster.

I rode to Griffith Park. I passed the golf course, then the Greek Theatre, and stopped near the bird sanctuary. Steep, wooded hills hemmed the narrow grassy patches along the road. I could easily move about hidden from view. Rosario would meet me here.

I left Griffith Park and stopped at a pay phone. So what if Cragnow or Paxton listened in? I had a plan.

Rosario answered on the second ring.

"Time to talk." He'd better recognize my voice. "Jot this down." I gave him directions into the park from the south side, entering through Vermont Canyon Road. "Be there at three-thirty."

The phone rustled, as if Rosario was shifting it on his shoulder. I imagined his fat neck sagging against his collar. "Yeah. I got it."

"And Rosario, you want me to help you, right?"

He kept quiet. His reply was heavy. "I'm not playing games with you, Felix."

"Good. I don't think Roxy Bronze or Katz Meow need the company."

CHAPTER
43

I DROVE BACK TO Griffith Park and left my motorcycle close by, where I could get at it in a hurry. I knelt
behind a shrub along the west side of the field and observed
the road winding toward the bird sanctuary.

I gave myself a half hour to reconnoiter the area. Taking
off my sunglasses, I read the auras of the park visitors. No
orange vampire auras. All red, nothing suspicious.

At twenty after, a black Porsche Cayenne drove up Vermont Canyon Road, paused in front of the bird sanctuary,
and U-turned to park in the lot south of the open field. Rosario got out. He was alone. His white dress shirt reflected the
sunlight with a metallic sheen. He carried a folded newspaper under one arm. Looking about, he dabbed his hairline
with a kerchief. Dark circles the size of volleyballs marked
the sweat stains under his armpits. He undid his necktie and
tossed it into his Porsche before shutting the door. The alarm
beeped.

What was with the newspaper? Is that where he carried his .45 automatic?

Rosario made his way around the other cars parked in the lot. A woman pushed a stroller. An elderly couple checked a tourist book.

Rosario halted in the middle of the small clearing, turned his gaze to the left and right, rolled up his sleeves, and stood on the grass with his back to the woods.

His aura bubbled with anxiety. Tendrils of fright snaked and withdrew. His fear was unfocused. He fished the kerchief from his breast pocket and mopped sweat from his face and neck.

I studied the area again. I looked for auras shimmering with aggression. Nothing. Nobody was interested in Rosario but me.

I replaced my sunglasses, palmed my little .380 pistol, and approached Rosario from his left.

He turned his big head and looked at me. Sweat trickled into his eyes, and he squinted at my pistol.

I motioned to the newspaper. "If that's your piece, I hope you put it together right this time."

"It'll shoot straighter than that popgun you got." Rosario wiped his neck again. "It's goddamn hot. Can't we do this in the shade?"

"No. I like the view."

"Where do we start?" he asked.

"At the beginning. What brings you here?"

"To save my ass from prison. White-collar crime is one thing, murder something else. Katz. Rebecca. That scumbag Fred Daniels."

And Roxy Bronze. "When did Cragnow tell you about these murders? How? Over the phone? At your office? His place?" How forthcoming was Rosario going to be? Would he admit to visiting Cragnow's home?

"Last night. At his house up in Coldwater Canyon."

Okay, Rosario was being straight.

He said, "I was at a cocktail party at Cragnow's place."

"A party with whom?"

"Mordecai Niphe and I were there to discuss business with Cragnow. We were passing the time with his girls when . . ." Rosario wadded the kerchief and dabbed his cheek. "We got trouble. First it was big, ferocious dogs barking. They sounded huge, like wolves. Then some shooting began."

I knew about the wolves and the shooting. "Back up. What business do you and Mordecai Niphe have?"

"We go back a few years. Don't you want to hear about the shooting? I might have gotten killed."

"We'll get to that. Does this business have to do with Reverend Dale Journey? Would Councilwoman Petale Venin figure into any of this?"

Rosario's eyes widened like he wanted to spill everything he knew through them. "You have no idea."

CHAPTER
44

"T HEN TELL ME," I SAID.

Rosario cleared his throat. "Felix, have you ever been poor?"

"I know what it's like not to have a bed of my own. But I never saw that as an excuse to break the law or cheat people out of their money."

Rosario shook his head. "Then you weren't poor enough. You didn't see that the world doesn't give a damn when your old man is crushed under the heels of the wealthy. What did my dad get for his years of honest, hard work? Pink slips. Debt. The day we got kicked out of our house, my father dropped to his knees and cried."

"So life screwed your old man."

"You don't understand. Seeing my dad broken like that scarred me to the bone. I promised myself to learn how the game was rigged. Find an angle, work it, and get rich."

"And your angle?"

"Petale Venin," Rosario said.

Petale Venin. The name made me shrink into myself. My *kundalini noir* coiled, wary, suspicious, even a little afraid. I had barely escaped my one meeting with her and the next day a bomb killed Coyote and destroyed his home.

Sweat ran from Rosario's hairline and soaked his collar. I felt the heat as well.

Rosario said, "I had a little real estate business. One afternoon I showed a client some property up in Altadena. That client was Dale Journey, at the time some pissant preacher from Long Beach. He told me God wanted him to build something extraordinary. Better than what's his name down in Garden Grove and the Crystal Cathedral. Journey said the view from Loma Linda Drive in Altadena was perfect. Problem was, there was a neighborhood of some two hundred homes already there. What to do?"

Rosario tapped his temple. "That's when I turned to Councilwoman Venin for help. I'd heard she was eager to make her mark as a visionary friend to big money interests."

"How long ago was this?" I asked.

"Eleven years."

That jibed with the newspaper clippings in Roxy's file, now all burned to ash.

"Clearing Loma Linda Drive was going to be tricky." Rosario knit his brow to express the earnestness of the task. "Never mind the expense of giving those folks fair market value."

"Or doing the right thing," I said. "Maybe what your father would've done."

Rosario shook his head. "The last advice I got from him was screw the world before it screws you. The trick to Loma Linda was, how would Journey get that land? As a man of God and servant of the people, he couldn't very well shove all those families aside. So Venin and I brainstormed this idea for a development trust. We'd lobby the city to use eminent domain and condemn the homes in favor of a new commercial development."

"Who was in that trust?"

"The usual. Lawyers. Doctors. Friends of politicians. The trust was going to build a mall to rival the Galleria down in Glendale, at least that's what the public record says. After all, what is the value of an established neighborhood compared to the projected tax revenue from new business? You flash those dollars and the city administration drops its pants and starts stroking. Families? What families?"

I remembered the story. "Councilwoman Venin couldn't do that. I can imagine tons of ethical violations. Crimes, in other words."

"First rule of politics. It ain't a crime 'til you get caught. Who was going to rat her out? Me? Journey?"

"But the mall was never built," I said. "The development trust went bankrupt. Everyone lost a bundle."

"You kidding? Here's another rule. Never use your own money. The state of California paid for the demolition, using a grant for community development. Both our senators made sure the feds kicked in funds to 'maintain economic stability.' Even without laying one brick, we pocketed a nice profit."

"And the bankruptcy?"

"You ever hear of Hollywood accounting? We hired the same legal firm who does the numbers for a major studio. Ever ask, how can a film cost a hundred million, rake in half a billion, yet those waiting for net profit never see a dime? Those shysters did the same hocus-pocus on our P and L, emphasis on the *L*."

"So the land sat vacant," I said.

Rosario nodded. "Like a big goddamn scar on the hill. Journey comes in and swings a nice deal. It was the Christian thing to do. Everyone profits, except for the families who lost their neighborhood and the taxpayers who footed the bill."

"Interesting civics lesson." Nothing Rosario said contradicted anything I'd learned. Fact was, he shed light into a lot of dark cracks. But he hadn't yet mentioned anything about Roxy's death or the vampire–human collusion.

"Where was Cragnow Vissoom during all this?"

Rosario wiped the sweat collecting on his eyebrows. "Don't know. About four years ago he showed up on my radar screen. He was still a bit player in the skin trade but intended to move up, real estate-wise. Then Cragnow hit it big, pulling in the cash like he owned a casino. Thanks to Roxy."

"And Reverend Journey?" I asked.

"What do you mean?"

"Journey gets the land and then what?"

"He built his church on the hill."

"When does Mordecai Niphe show up?"

Rosario rubbed the sweat from his face with the kerchief. He smiled. "Where do you think the money for Journey's church came from?"

There it was. Niphe, the moneybags behind Journey and his ministry. I thought back to the photo of Rosario, Niphe, and Journey standing together. Rosario and Niphe shoulder to shoulder like army buddies, Journey off to one side, his hesitant smile saying, I'm only here because of the money.

"You had mentioned that party last night at Cragnow's. What did you talk about?"

"Journey's in financial trouble. Niphe wanted to discuss leveraging some of Cragnow's holdings to buy Journey's notes. I need to emphasize, notes that Niphe has an interest in."

The reverend going broke reflected what Andrew Tonic had shared. Journey goes down the tubes and he takes Niphe's money with him.

Rosario said, "Niphe insisted that we act fast before word of Journey's trouble got around. We put together a nice package, reconfigure the loans, and everyone makes out."

"And if Journey's trouble was made public?"

"The attention would make the property value sink like a rock. Add the scandal of anyone following the money trail and making the connection from Cragnow to Journey."

"What else did you discuss?" I asked.

"Cragnow talked about using the church as a base for his plans."

"What plans?"

"That weird crap about lifting humanity to a new partnership with the undead realm. Cragnow might as well be speaking in tongues."

Wow, vampire–human collusion disguised as an evangelical ministry. Could Cragnow and Venin have pulled that off?

"Now we get to the murder part," Rosario said. "Those dogs started barking and Cragnow's men went ape shit. They pulled guns—serious firepower, shotguns and M16s—and hustled outside."

"What did you see?"

"Cragnow wouldn't let us look. He kept us inside and commenced with his ranting. He was already well sauced, so he yelled like there was a fire in his asshole. He blamed us for the trouble."

"Us, who?" I asked.

"Everybody. Me. Niphe. The girls. His guards. Cragnow said he'd do anything to protect himself. That's when he admitted to killing Rebecca Dwelling and Fred Daniels. To shut them up."

"And Katz?"

"That's what bothered him the most," Rosario replied. "Katz was his property. Who had done her in? The same people who knocked off Roxy Bronze?"

"Cragnow worried about who had killed Katz?"

"And you don't know?"

I shook my head.

"Before Niphe and I left, Cragnow let us in on some news," Rosario said. "He had another way to corner Journey into cooperating with us."

"Which was?"

Rosario paused and gave a grin. "You won't believe this. Journey's girlfriend was coming to see Cragnow. Some broad by the name of Lara Phillips."

That stunned me. "Journey's girlfriend? Are you sure?"

Rosario chuckled. "I couldn't make up something like that."

"Why would she see Cragnow?"

"Apparently she wants him to back off Journey."

"How is she going to do that?"

"Probably by sucking Cragnow's dick, for starters." Rosario laughed. The sweat dribbled over the rolls of his neck. "Of course Cragnow has no intention of easing up on Journey. In fact, he'll use Lara to humiliate the preacher. Take his money and his woman. What a naïve bitch."

Naïve didn't describe Lara. I saw her as guarded. Volatile, even. Lara had cruel words for Roxy and her life in porn. Lara had to have known Cragnow's part in Roxy's past.

"Do you know Lara?" I asked.

"Never met her."

How could Lara hope to reason with Cragnow? He was a vampire. She had no chance. Maybe she went with Journey's blessing to work a deal. Cragnow couldn't resist the irony of Roxy Bronze's sister kneeling before him.

But I couldn't see Lara doing that. Nothing about this made sense.

Rosario blotted his forehead with the kerchief. "Isn't this some twisted shit?"

CHAPTER
45

ROSARIO HAD TOLD ME PLENTY. But I needed more.

"When was Lara going—" I heard a noise, like the rattle of thunder. The reverberations grew louder and deeper, then turned into the baritone rumbles of two big-bore motorcycles roaring up Vermont Canyon Road.

I didn't need a sixth sense to know this sounded like trouble.

The two motorcycles—custom Harleys—turned up the twisting road, moving fast. Sun glinted off the chrome. One rider was lean, the other heavyset and bearded. Neither wore sunglasses or goggles to hide their fierce gazes.

I whipped off my sunglasses. Orange auras burned around them. Vampires.

I kept my face averted to hide my eyes from Rosario. I pushed him toward his car. "Hurry. Don't hesitate to shoot. And put your sunglasses on."

"My sunglasses?"

"Trust me." One zap and these vampires would snag Rosario's corpulent ass.

Rosario grasped his .45 and let the newspaper fall away. He scrambled for his Porsche, like a fat horse accelerating into a gallop.

The motorcycle riders separated. They reached into the leather panniers and each pulled out an over-and-under sawed-off shotgun. If their goal was to get the drop on me, these loud bikes were a poor choice. A deaf man could have heard them approaching.

Unless.

My fingers buzzed another warning.

I glanced over my shoulder. Orange auras lurked in the underbrush of the hillside.

The motorcycles were a diversion. This was a trap, and Rosario was the bait.

I thumbed the safety on my pistol, whirled around, and popped four rounds into the shrubs.

A screech like that of a wounded beast echoed above the roar of the motorcycles. One aura behind a bush flattened to the ground and dimmed.

The skinny rider rolled past and panned me with his gun, the muzzle looking like a metal figure eight.

My nerves were raw and I sensed everything at super vampire speed. Fire blossomed out of the top barrel of the shotgun. A swarm of pellets whooshed out, the wadding peeling back. The silver pellets bounced against one another as they sailed toward me.

I dodged the volley and centered the sights of my pistol on the vampire.

His denim vest wrinkled where the three slugs tore into him. He tumbled backward off the motorcycle. The Harley T-boned a parked Lexus. The vampire landed on the asphalt, squirmed, and quit moving. Smoke curled from around his sides. The alarm in the Lexus shrieked.

I reloaded my Colt automatic.

Rosario rushed for the driver's door of his Porsche. The hairy-faced rider swerved around the rear of the Porsche and leveled his shotgun.

Rosario dropped and crawled around the front bumper. The shotgun blast shattered the windows of the Cayenne.

A bullet whizzed past my nose. Another stabbed the ground by my shoes.

I dove to the right onto the grass.

More bullets hunted me.

My shooters were three vampires advancing down the hill. They carried Uzis. I fired a wild shot and they ducked for cover.

I sprang to my feet. More bullets peppered the dirt around me.

The three vampires crouched low to the grass, two males flanking a brunette. My arm panned right to left, my index finger squeezing the trigger with mechanical precision.

The first vampire took a shot in the forehead. His head snapped back and he collapsed.

The next vampire caught one in the sternum, as if the slug couldn't help but go between her boobs. She tumbled forward and the Uzi dropped from her hands.

My sights hovered over the face of the last vampire, a wily-looking bastard with the expression of a starving ferret. His gun jerked rhythmically, the spent casings whirling in the air.

A searing pain hacked my side and I sank to my knees.

My aim drifted off target and I centered the sights again. My bullet cleaved the shooter's nose. Blood sprayed across his cheeks like the pulp of a smashed tomato. He clutched his face and fell, howling in agony.

I struggled to get up. A silver bullet wormed inside of me, the poisonous metal burning flesh like a hot poker.

Rosario knelt by the front of his Porsche. He saw that I was wounded and scrambled toward me. Great, let's bunch up and make it easier for this vampire bastard. I waved that Rosario stay back.

Hairy-face gunned his bike forward and angled the muzzle of his shotgun at Rosario. The raging glow of the vampire's aura froze like a muscle tensing.

I tired to shout a warning but the words came out as a groan. My reactions were sluggish from the pain. By the time I brought my pistol up to fire it was too late.

The vampire's shotgun barked once. Blood spurted from Rosario's back. His arms splayed forward and he fell prone on the ground.

I fired at Hairy-face. He had no problem ducking at vampire speed.

Hairy-face looked at me. His gaze focused on my wound, and he smiled. Long fangs spanned the gap between his mustache and beard. His red eyes glared a message. *Go ahead and waste your ammunition.*

With a jerk of his arm the shotgun broke open and ejected the two empty shells. He snatched fresh shells from a vest pocket and reloaded.

A pistol shot rang out. Hairy-face's aura lit up from the shock of sudden pain. He grabbed his side and jerked his head to the right at Rosario.

Rosario pushed off the grass. His aura burned with defiance. Blood ran from his shirtsleeves and over both of his wrists and hands. He tore the sunglasses from his face. His hand left bloody streaks on his cheeks. He kept his .45 trained on Hairy-face and fired. The big slug ripped the vampire's shoulder.

My turn. I shot again and hit Hairy-face in the center of his chest.

He dropped his shotgun and doubled over. The part in his hair pointed to a bald spot that drew my aim like the bull's-eye of a target.

My bullet punched through his skull. Blood geysered out. The red spew turned into rust-colored flakes. Hairy-face slumped against his handlebars, and the Harley toppled over.

Rosario staggered and fell. He wheezed and clawed at the grass. His aura began to lose its glow.

I cupped my hand over the wound in my side. Blood and smoke oozed past my fingers. I struggled to get upright, the bullet in me heavy as a sack of foul toxin. Once on my feet, I moved in a painful shuffle to stand over Rosario.

He rolled onto his back and stared at the sky. I stood over him to block the sun, but of course, there was no shadow. His eyes wouldn't focus. He held up his .45. "Told you I put it together right."

"So you did." He was a breath away from dying, so I couldn't do anything except say, "I'm sorry, Rosario."

"What for?" His arm dropped and the pistol clattered against the ground. "At least I won't die broke like my old man."

Police sirens closed upon us. I glanced to the road, and when I looked back at Rosario, his aura was gone. Blood snaked through the grass around him.

Shattered windows and bullet holes decorated the cars in the parking lot. Spent shell casings littered the grass and asphalt. Rosario lay dead. The corpses of the vampires smoldered as the sun ate their flesh. What a mess.

The slide of my pistol was locked back, signaling that the gun was empty. I inserted my last magazine and released the catch. The slide snapped forward.

The police sirens echoed louder. I had to hurry.

CHAPTER
46

HUMANS POPPED UP like prairie dogs. Red auras ballooned around them. They gaped at the carnage and at me.

I unfolded my sunglasses and put them on, to hide my eyes. I walked stiffly toward my motorcycle and, despite the agony, moved faster as the sirens approached.

My Yamaha waited between two mock orange shrubs. I bent over and plucked my overnight bag from under the leaves.

I lay across my bike and levered one leg over the seat until I could sit upright. I slipped the bag's straps over my shoulders and inserted the ignition key. I left my helmet clipped to the rear of the seat.

The Yamaha started right away. When I clicked the foot shifter into first, pain jolted through my leg and up my side.

One, two, three police cars swerved into the parking lot.

I released the clutch handle, rolled the throttle grip, and

the Yamaha jumped forward. I steered out of the grass and toward the pavement.

Cops sprang from their cars. I zigzagged around them. Another police car swerved in front of me and blocked my way.

I fishtailed off the pavement and back on the grass. I shot between the shrubs along the base of the hill. Spiny leaves and branches smacked my arms and face. My body was a blur of reflexive motion that obeyed one simple command. *Get away.*

I punished the V-Max, relying little on my riding finesse and more on the brute force of the Yamaha's engine to bash through the vegetation. Every bump jolted me with excruciating pain. Branches pummeled the motorcycle and me, tearing my clothes and ripping off both mirrors.

The rising hill boxed me against the north side of the Greek Theatre. I steered for the stairs and railings to my left and bounced down the steps to land in front of the box office.

I crashed through a wire fence and raced in front of the theater. A maintenance worker piled bags next to an open gate at the far end of the concrete walkway.

I opened the throttle. The worker dove clear as I flashed through the gate and got back on the road.

A police car zoomed past. I left the park and entered the neighborhood of northern Hollywood. I ran stop signs and turned randomly from street to street.

I slowed and looked over my shoulders. No one followed. I paused under a cottonwood tree shading the curb. I picked leaves and twigs from my body. Now that I had stopped and the commotion of my escape lifted from my mind, the pain from the silver bullet crashed into me like a runaway railroad car. A wisp of smoke curled from the tear in my shirt. I clenched my fists and closed my eyes for a moment. I imagined the silver wad of metal frying my insides like meat on a skillet.

Blood seeped down my side and soaked my shirt and

trousers. The rivulets crusted over and broke into clots of dust.

As huge as Los Angeles was, I found myself only blocks from the spot of Roxy's murder. How ironic if I were to die here.

But I wouldn't die. Not soon.

Where to go? Where to get help? Coyote was dead.

Veronica?

I could hide at her place. She would dig the bullet out of me. I had managed to have sex with her in wild acrobatic positions and still kept my undead identity secret. Guiding her hands and a knife through hypnosis would be tricky, but what other option did I have?

My watch said 4:14 P.M. She'd be at work. I slipped the cell phone from my pocket and called.

"About time," she said, her voice hovering between eagerness and displeasure. "Where have you been?"

"Bad trouble," I replied.

Veronica stayed quiet. Her breath rushed against the phone. "I didn't want to hear that. What kind of trouble? With the police?"

"With everybody."

"You . . . you don't sound well," she said.

"I'm not. I'm hurt pretty bad."

"You need me to take you to the hospital?" The phone shifted and I was sure she sat taller and more alert.

"No. I just need a place to rest and recuperate. Until tomorrow."

"My place?" She whispered, her tone guarded, as if she's hoping that I'd say no.

"If you could."

"Where are you?" she asked.

"Doesn't matter. Let's meet at your place."

"I'm way over in Riverside. Probably can't get there until seven."

Three hours from now. Could I stand the pain? "I'll wait."

"Should I get anything? I've got bandages and stuff in the bathroom, but would you need something else?"

"Don't worry about it," I said.

"You call to tell me you're hurt bad and you say not to worry?" Her voice cracked. "Oh Felix."

"It's not that bad." *It's much worse.* "Buy cheese and wine. We'll have a party."

"I gotta go. Seven then," she said and hung up.

The worst was over. All I had to do was survive the next few hours, rest overnight, and go after Cragnow tomorrow.

When I lifted my left leg to set my shoe on the foot peg, a volcano of agony surged up my torso. The pain funneled up my neck and flooded my head. My eyes dimmed. Through sheer force of will, I shoved the fountain of anguish back down.

I rolled the Yamaha from the curb and rode south toward Veronica's apartment.

At every traffic light I thought I'd pass out. I lied to myself to keep going. *Hang on for another hour. I'll stop and rest in fifteen minutes. Just one more block.*

I reached the street where Veronica lived. I pulled into the driveway and maneuvered the Yamaha against the back cinder block wall close to the Dumpster and recycling barrels. My plan was to break into her apartment and rest inside. Hopefully she'd forgive me.

I peeled myself off the motorcycle. The afternoon sun reflected from the back windows of the buildings and baked me. The heat drained my weakening body. I could barely stand. The breezeway seemed an impossible distance.

I'd wait for Veronica out here. I crawled into the shade between the Dumpster and the cinder block wall. The area reeked of decaying food.

Each minute seemed like an hour. The sun's rays angled lower, and the coolness of evening gathered into the darkening shadows.

CHAPTER
47

VERONICA'S BROWN NISSAN turned into the driveway. My *kundalini noir* rustled expectantly. The driver's silhouette, with a mane of long hair, was Veronica's. The Nissan halted inches from the Dumpster and my motorcycle propped against the wall.

I adjusted my sunglasses. I didn't want her to see my eyes until I was ready to hypnotize her.

The driver's door opened and nudged against the Yamaha's handlebar grip. Veronica rose from the Nissan, hitched her purse on one shoulder, and gave my motorcycle a quizzical once-over.

"Veronica," I said.

She turned toward me and bent down. She pulled her sunglasses up and hooked them into her hair. Her expression of puzzlement deepened.

I retrieved my overnight bag, grasped the side of the Dumpster, and dragged myself from the wall.

Veronica gripped my free hand. Helping me stand, she caressed my face and shoulders. "What happened to you? Looks like you wrestled a bear."

"I could've handled a bear." I pressed my hand over the wound.

She tugged at my wrist. "What are you hiding?"

I didn't have the strength to wrench my wrist free.

Veronica touched my shirt around the wound. "Did you get shot? Stabbed?" She leaned close, sniffed, and pulled away in horror. She let go of my wrist. "Is that smoke?"

"Help me inside," I said. "I'll explain."

Her arm clasped my shoulders and I staggered beside her. She led me to the breezeway.

"You got shot, didn't you? Felix, we have to call an ambulance."

"Not yet," I told her. "Take me inside first and help me get fixed up."

"I don't appreciate this," she said. Her voice lost its caring tone and sounded frightened. "Gunshots are supposed to be reported to the police."

"You a doctor?"

"So what? Unless the cops—"

"They didn't do it."

We entered the breezeway. Only another forty feet to the stairs. I looked up to the landing on the second floor. It would be an ordeal, like climbing to the top of a mountain.

"Then who shot you?"

Veronica would have to haul me up the stairs. I could barely stay on my feet, much less work up the energy to fend off her questions.

"Okay," I told her. "I owe you that." I motioned that she bring her face close to mine.

Veronica fixed her eyes on the lenses of my sunglasses. I rallied the strength needed to hypnotize her and dropped the sunglasses from my face.

CHAPTER
48

VERONICA'S EYES DILATED to the size of dimes. Her aura blossomed into a silky crimson.

I clasped her neck and brought her closer, so we stood nose to nose. I wasn't sure of the strength of my flagging powers and concentrated on giving her the maximum dose of hypnotism.

Her aura grew a fuzzy penumbra that vibrated like the cilia of a microscopic creature. It wasn't much of a hold upon her psyche. But enough.

"Help me up the stairs," I said.

Veronica pulled my right arm across her shoulder and trudged upward with the grace of an ox pulling a stubborn plow.

Near the top of the landing, the bullet shifted and an agonizing jolt sawed through me. My legs buckled and I collapsed against the stairs. I dropped my bag. Lying still, I wet my lips and waited for the pain to ease.

Veronica stared at me, her face impassive and dull.

I pointed to her door. "Pull me inside."

Veronica moved as if her thoughts swam through molasses. She pulled the keys from her purse and opened her apartment door.

Blood trickled from my torn shirt and splattered on the steps, each drop turning into a poof of dust. My aura trembled as would a burner flame set on low.

I raised my arm. "Take me inside."

I expected her to lift me to my feet. Instead she grabbed my wrist and yanked my supine body up the stairs.

The pain strangled my howl. My head and feet hammered against the steps as she tugged me onto the landing. She backed into her apartment, dragging me in like a rug.

When my feet cleared the threshold I begged her to stop. "Let go. Get my bag then come back and close and lock the door."

Veronica did as I told her.

I didn't like being in the front room. What if at sunrise I was still here? I crawled to the home office, where I knew I would be safe. Veronica followed me, her aura flowing about her like a cloak.

I lay on the floor and motioned her to kneel beside me. I refreshed the hypnosis.

Time for the real pain. "Go wash your hands. Bring towels, bandages, disinfectant, and your sharpest knives."

I unbuttoned my shirt and removed it and my undershirt. I lay bare-chested on my right side, the wound a jagged mouth drooling blood. Smoke drifted from the lipless opening.

Veronica returned with two terry cloth bath towels, a spool of white adhesive tape, a bottle of hydrogen peroxide, a fistful of kitchen knives, and a sanitary napkin. She sat and arrayed the items on the floor between us.

I inspected the napkin. The label said it was for heavy-flow days.

I pushed aside the butcher knives—too big—and selected a paring knife with a four-inch blade. I ran my thumb along the edge, and the blade cut like a fresh razor. A drop of blood seeped from my thumb.

"Push the towels along my back," I said.

She unfolded both towels and shoved them between my right side and the floor to catch my blood.

I handed Veronica the knife.

"Here," I said, pointing into the wound. "Feel in there for a bullet and cut it out." I'd risk an infection. That bullet would kill me before any germ could.

Veronica's gaze fixed mechanically upon the wound.

I wound my undershirt into a roll that I inserted into my mouth.

She extended the fingers of her left hand and inserted them into the hole.

The agony was like getting split open. I clamped hard on the undershirt, and if I could've wept, the wooden planks of the floor would have been soaked with tears.

Veronica's fingers wiggled inside, touching organs and rib bone. Her eyes gazed at nothing. In this trance, and oblivious to the torture wracking my poor undead body, she continued to probe.

My *kundalini noir* stiffened into near rigor mortis.

Veronica angled the knife and slid it into my side.

Her movements escalated the pain. I doubt I could've been in more agony had she ripped the flesh from my bones.

Her hands withdrew, stained with my blood. Pinched between her left thumb and index finger was the smoking clump of silver.

My *kundalini noir* relaxed. I spit out the undershirt and gasped. "Good job. Now clean the wound."

She uncapped the bottle and splashed hydrogen peroxide over the ripped flesh. The hole bubbled. I squeezed the towel until the pain eased.

"Now cover the wound."

Veronica tore open the sanitary napkin's package and centered the napkin over the hole. She unrolled lengths of tape and secured the napkin against my side.

The gobs of blood on my skin crumbled into tiny flakes. I could wash the towels and clean the floor with a whisk broom. Evidence from vampires was easy to dispose of.

Now to recuperate.

I told her to pull the curtains tight and close the door. Then I said, "Veronica, come lie next to me."

She crawled around me, my blood peeling from her hands. She unfolded her body parallel to mine.

"Loosen your blouse."

Veronica's fingers glided down the buttons of her blouse to her pants, revealing a lilac-colored bra. I only needed the top buttons unfastened, but the view refreshed me.

I rolled onto my belly and pulled myself against her. Her scalp smelled of that familiar apricot shampoo and her ever delicious perspiration.

Fatigue dulled the excitement. I wanted only to feed and rest. The points of my fangs dragged along her throat. I eased into position and bit.

CHAPTER
49

MY SNORING WOKE ME. I lay with my head resting on Veronica's belly. Her aura glowed tranquil and calm.

My muscles ached and my joints creaked as I sat up. My head felt numb. I smacked my lips. Her blood left a pleasing aftertaste.

My wound?

I peeled away the bandage. A mustache of dried blood clung to a scar that looked like a thumbprint pressed into my flesh. I traced my finger over the depression.

No pain, but I was still tired as hell.

Sunlight illumnated the curtains. I checked my watch. Time, 4:47 P.M. We had slept all day.

Moving stiffly, I stood and shuffled into the bathroom. I'm sure my face was a frightful mask. I got my bag, washed up, and applied makeup.

I put in my contacts and returned to Veronica. Her aura

remained smooth. I carried Veronica to her bed. With a towel soaked in warm water, I cleaned the dried blood on her neck. My fang wounds had had all night and day to heal, and even I couldn't find them. I buttoned her blouse.

Veronica would question the gaps in her memory. One moment we were outside, the next, she's in her bedroom and it's afternoon the next day. I didn't know what I could tell her. Relationships with women were difficult enough; try factoring in being undead.

I waited in her kitchen.

The door to Veronica's bedroom creaked. She entered the kitchen, a robe cinched tight over her clothes. Her hair hung in moplike strands. She clutched the lapels of her robe together. She blinked at me. "Last I remember you were . . . shot."

I patted my side. "Much better today."

"But how?" Her gaze swung around the room, as if searching for something to explain her confusion. Her eyes fixed back on me.

This was the problem when feeding from a "friend." Fang a stranger and you could leave them anywhere and let them figure it out. But someone you're close to?

"Last I remember, I was walking you to the stairs . . ." Veronica's head turned to the bedroom. "And I woke up in there."

"Nothing happened." Nothing sexual, anyway. I stepped toward her.

Veronica raised her free hand. "Stop. Something did happen. What?"

The question burned me like another silver bullet. I had no answer. I had been stupid for thinking I could keep fooling Veronica.

What could I say? Tell her the truth, and then what? I faced this dilemna the first time I was here and now I had to resolve it. If I revealed myself as a vampire I could either convert Veronica into one of the undead or offer her the chance to be a chalice. If she refused, I had to kill her.

But there was another way.

I could leave.

"I'm sorry, Veronica." I raised my hand to my eyes.

She tightened her grip on the lapel of her robe. "What are you doing?"

I removed my contacts and zapped Veronica. Her aura blushed with a crimson luminescence.

I had many powers as a supernatural. What I couldn't do was love Veronica as a man loves a woman. A great sadness poured into me, and I felt the curse of being a vampire.

I carried Veronica back to her bed. She would awaken with the same questions about the missing time. Only I wouldn't be here to answer them. I collected my belongings and left.

I had no heart and no soul. Then why did leaving Veronica hurt so much?

I rode my motorcycle to Sunset Boulevard. What if something happened to Veronica? Cragnow, Venin, and Paxton were still out there looking for me. If anything bad happened to Veronica, I had myself to blame.

I stopped in an Internet café and checked my email. No news from my Internet hacker.

I thought about another woman in my undead life. Lara Phillips. Why would she meet with Cragnow? She should hate him for trying to ruin Journey.

I wrote names on a scrap of paper and drew circles around them. Cragnow, Venin, and Paxton in the circle of the *nidus*. Venin, Niphe, and Journey in the circle of the church. Katz, Roxy, and Cragnow in the porn circle. Lara and Roxy in the sister circle. Katz and Roxy in the dead circle.

A circle around Cragnow, Journey, and Lara. Circle labeled what?

I ordered coffee that I didn't drink. I kept thinking about circles when my email Web site refreshed itself. A message waited from my hacker. The email contained two columns, one listing Katz Meow's cell phone calls, and the other Roxy Bronze's. On each column the last call was from the same number.

I didn't know when Katz had been murdered, but the call came in at 3:41 P.M. on the day she went missing.

The call to Roxy's number came at 1:02 A.M., about the time of her death.

Who had called? I pulled the cell phone from my pocket and dialed the number.

The voice on the message recording belonged to Lara Phillips.

CHAPTER
50

I STARED AT THE NUMBER on my cell phone and compared it to the numbers listed in the email.

I compared the numbers again. And again. The last calls to Katz and Roxy before they were killed had come from Lara Phillips.

Was each call a warning? Or a setup?

I looked back to the circles I had drawn around the names. What was the relationship between Lara and Katz? Lara knew Katz, but did Katz know Lara? Had she known Lara was Roxy's sister? If yes, wouldn't Katz have mentioned that to me?

Katz couldn't tell me. She was dead. But Lara could.

I deleted the email, logged off, and went into the night.

I took a detour on my way to Lara's house. I cruised by Veronica's apartment. The light shone through her front windows.

I slowed the motorcycle and throttled back to coast quietly down the street.

I caught a whiff of something familiar. Meaty. Spicy. Rancid. Rat chorizo.

Coyote?

I shut the engine and rolled to a halt. The odor was faint, almost as if I imagined the smell.

"Vato."

The moaning whisper made my *kundalini noir* tingle with joy.

"Coyote? Where are you?" I looked left and right, at the parked cars, the shrubs, the apartment doorways, even along the rooftops.

"Around, *ese.*"

"You're alive?" I laughed, dizzy with giddiness. I took out my contacts and saw nothing supernatural. Was I hallucinating?

"I'm as alive as you." His voice came like the breeze.

Coyote was here. I felt he was close enough to embrace, but how could I touch a phantom? This was beyond the ordinary undead paranormal; this was real magic. "How did you survive the explosion?"

"I got my ways."

"So you escaped?" I tried to find the source of his voice.

"No, *hermano.* I'm in the process of *reconstituting* myself."

Using magic? "What's that mean?"

"It means, *ese,* that you're wasting time with these questions. You need to go. *A la volada.*" Flying. "Get Cragnow. Get Venin. I'll watch over your *mujer.*"

I didn't want to tell him that Veronica was far from being my woman anymore. "Is she safe?"

"Very safe. Don't you worry."

"What do you mean?"

"More *pinchi* questions. Don't you have somewhere to go?"

"One more. Will I see you again?"

"If you don't screw up, *Símon. Ya vete.*" Scram.

CHAPTER
51

PEOPLE AND VAMPIRES were going to die to-night. I had seven rounds in my little Colt automatic as backup to my fangs and talons.

Coyote was back. Sort of. And he watched over Veronica. I'd rather have him by my side, but at least I didn't have to worry about her.

Coyote alive. It sounded great. I opened the throttle and zoomed along the freeway.

I rode to Verdugo City. In Spanish, *verdugo* meant assassin. Lara Phillips lived in the city of the assassin.

I slowed to enter her neighborhood. My fingers and ears tingled from my sixth sense.

Slow down, Felix. Don't stumble into another trap.

I paused at the corner to observe her house. Lara hurried down the steps from her front door and climbed into Niphe's BMW coupe. She carried a canvas bag. Her aura bristled with agitation, as if she expected—or contemplated—trouble.

A red aura and an orange aura waited in the BMW. Niphe drove, and the vampire rode up front.

Why was Lara Phillips riding in Niphe's car? Where were they going? To see Cragnow? Or someone else? Councilwoman Venin?

Did the vampire notice the state of her aura? Or was he wearing contacts?

The BMW pulled away. I followed, keeping a discreet distance.

Niphe drove like a demon. To keep track of him all I had to do was follow the fastest set of taillights busting through traffic.

The BMW left the Ventura Freeway and got on Coldwater Canyon. They headed for Cragnow's estate. Getting in would be difficult, unless I attacked in a form they didn't expect.

I turned off Mulholland and ditched the Yamaha behind a clump of Joshua trees. I found a soft patch of dirt between short desert palms and removed my clothes, folding them into a neat pile that I tucked into the chaparral.

I set my hands and knees into the dirt and summoned the transformation.

Energy like fire burned through my nerves and flesh. My bones twisted and reformed. The marrow boiled with agony. Fur pushed through my skin with needlelike pain. My head felt squeezed in a vise that forced my jaws away from my skull. My fingers retracted into my hand, and my hands and feet turned into stunted, clawed paws.

I lay on my side, panting. The pain of the transformation receded into a fading ache. I flexed my legs and stretched, cognizant of new strengths and powers.

I lifted my snout. The night air filled my nose with a thousand new scents: wild blossoms; waxy leaves; insects; the droppings of birds and mammals. My ears detected tiny creatures scrambling under leaves and across the sand.

I stood on my paws. A glance across the scrub revealed nothing hostile.

I chose a path through the darkest of the shadows in the chaparral and trotted toward Cragnow's home. Branches and spines raked my sides and my fur absorbed the noise. I ducked under the twisted branches of an oak and traveled through the darkest void in the gloom.

A car started and its door slammed. The engine growled and gravel pinged against metal.

I galloped through the weeds and rocks.

I reached the edge of the shrub. Twin red lights flashed at the entrance to Cragnow's estate. The lights dimmed, the car made a right turn at Mulholland, and vanished past the trees. The burning fart smell of the engine hung in the air. Two cars remained on the flat field of gravel. Niphe's car was gone. Who had left, and why in such a hurry?

I stepped away from the chaparral and onto the gravel field. Lights illuminated the inside of Cragnow's home. I moved carefully, ready to jump aside in case a human fire weapon barked at me.

Nothing.

Moving close to the entrance I smelled the sharp odor belched by a fire weapon. Then I smelled blood—human and vampire.

An orange aura appeared from behind a jasmine bush. The aura moved low, as if the vampire crawled on all fours. A musky odor drifted to me. He was also in the form of a wolf.

His eyes glared. He growled, his lips wrinkling to expose long teeth.

I growled back and advanced across the wooden path above a shallow stream of water.

He limped close. I smelled almonds. Blood glistened on his haunches. Pain showed through his aura. He was wounded and what else?

I crept toward him. We snarled. The hair on our necks bristled. Our ears folded back, and our fangs extended to combat length.

We circled to the right. Our bodies trembled in excitement.

He lunged, but his attack was clumsy. I knocked aside his snout with my left shoulder. His jaws snapped along my ear while I twisted my neck to seize his throat.

My teeth sank into fur and I pushed hard to drive my fangs deeper. He tried to pull away and I pushed again, harder still.

I used my paws to trip his front legs. He fell on his side and scrambled to regain his footing. I kept my jaws fastened on his neck.

My teeth worked through the fur and found his windpipe. I bit hard. Blood spurt onto my tongue.

It tasted wrong. I let go and stepped back. I hacked to get rid of the taste in my mouth.

The wolf's legs and head trembled. His wounds and my attack weren't enough to cause this.

His aura flickered.

He wasn't going anywhere soon, and if he died, so what? I stepped around him and proceeded into Cragnow's home. No one seemed to hear the noise of the fight. Why?

I followed the scent of spilled blood. I padded across the downy soft ground of a corridor until it opened into a large human cave.

Niphe lay on the ground, facedown, his feet toward me. No aura flickered around him. A glass rested in the middle of a wet spot on the ground. The spot smelled of almonds. What was this?

Someone rustled farther back in the home.

A vampire and Niphe had brought Lara here. Niphe was dead and the vampire was close to it. Who remained? Lara? Cragnow? What about the shooter?

I advanced cautiously, peeking around the corners of the cave.

Cragnow sat in a chair with his back to a large window filled with night stars. His aura pulsed in agony. Blood wept from two holes in his chest. His broken eyeglasses rested by his feet.

His eyes rolled toward me, and a wave of hatred surged through his aura. He struggled to get up. But he couldn't. His wounds weren't fatal to a vampire, but for now they immobilized him with pain.

I sat on my haunches and ignored his suffering. I listened and sniffed. We were alone.

Good. I needed to question him.

I closed my eyes and began the transformation back into a vampire. Agony wracked me as bones twisted and stretched again. My skin burned where fur withdrew into flesh. Pain engulfed my head as my skull grew round and teeth retracted into the shrinking jaws.

Thoughts collided like spilled marbles. The smells in my nose became pale and the sounds in my ears muted.

I pushed off the carpet, my chest heaving, pain dissolving into memory. I stood naked before Cragnow.

"Greetings," I said. "Hope I'm dressed for the occasion."

His eyes brimmed with malice. "You denied it before, but you're from the Araneum, aren't you?"

"Guilty. But it seems someone else has done the heavy lifting for me. Who?"

"That bitch Lara poisoned us with cyanide. She mixed it with Amaretto to disguise the smell." An empty highball glass sat on an end table beside him.

Cyanide? That's what the wolf's blood had tasted of. I wiped spit from my mouth. Amaretto would mask the almond scent of the poison.

Cragnow coughed. Blood pumped out the holes in his chest. "Then she shot me."

Poisoned and shot? Not enough to kill a vampire like Cragnow but enough to keep him uncomfortable for a long time.

"Why did Lara do this?"

"To kill me. She wants to stop us from taking over Journey's church. And revenge. Lara blamed me for leading Roxy into the life."

"Which you did."

Cragnow gave his head a weak shake. "You couldn't lead Roxy anywhere. She did as she pleased."

"And you let Lara walk in and do this to you?"

"Who would've suspected that little mouse? She offered to work for me if I backed off Journey and came tonight to give me a preview. Imagine that. What a coup. Little sister steps into big sister's high heels and bends over for me. The reverend's girlfriend." Cragnow pressed one hand over his chest to keep the blood from leaking. "But I was careless and didn't read her aura. It was my mistake for underestimating the treachery of humans."

"Where did Lara go?"

"To kill Petale Venin."

"And you've warned Venin?" I asked.

"Why should I? My other mistake was getting involved with Venin. Let them finish each other off."

"Why was Venin a mistake?"

"Because once she understood the potential of my new society, she pulled the other vampires under her control. She knew what to tell them. Who to trust. Who to destroy. What to do next. To get what I wanted, I found myself following her orders as well."

"This was the new society you planned? As flunkie to a human? What made it worth compromising the great secret and defying the Araneum?" I grabbed a nearby chair and broke it apart. I held a leg and raked my talons over one end to sharpen a point.

"What are you doing?"

"You know why I'm here." I fashioned the leg into a dreaded wooden stake. "Where is Petale Venin?"

"Her office in Westwood."

"At this time of night?" I asked.

"She likes to keep busy."

Cragnow stared at the stake. His aura crackled with fear. "Listen to me, Felix. Imagine, no more makeup. No more contacts. No more hiding. No more living in fear at being discovered and hunted. Maybe the Araneum has it wrong."

"That we can't trust the humans? Look around you. This was one human, acting alone."

He clutched the armrest and tried to stand. His aura glowed with frustration and he relented, sinking back into the chair. "There has to be another way. Maybe we can teach them. Don't you see?"

"I see that you've murdered humans and vampires. You tried to get me. Forgive my cynicism."

Pain creased through his aura. He closed his eyes for a moment and gulped. "Tell me that a human yearning no longer burns inside you. We are damned to wander this earth forever, always with a hunger that blood alone can't satisfy."

I let the stake dangle in my hand. I knew that yearning. I knew that hunger. As a vampire I could exist for a thousand human lifetimes and never have what I wanted. Veronica. Maybe there could be another way.

"Think about it, Felix. You and I, we can start this over. We can take Journey's church and put vampires in control. That new society can begin with us."

"You or the Araneum?" I readied the stake. "Not much of a choice. The Araneum has never tried to kill me."

I seized Cragnow's shoulder and held him firm against the chair. His aura lit with panic. He tried to resist, and I thumped his skull with the stake.

I plunged the stake into his sternum, cracking bone. A fountain of blood gushed past my hand.

Cragnow clutched the stake. Blood gurgled from his mouth. His jaw tightened and he fought to speak these words. "Before she left, Lara asked where she could find you." Blood stained his fangs. "After she knocks off Venin, you're next."

"Thanks for the heads-up." I pounded the stake with the heel of my hand until fabric ripped from the back of the chair.

Cragnow's hands fell to his sides and his body clung to the stake pinning him to the chair. His aura withdrew into a faint glow and faded away.

Cragnow's skin withered into a cracked shell. Ancient vampires didn't need sunlight to disintegrate after being staked. His head sagged into his shoulders and his flesh broke apart in chunks that tumbled from his skeleton as the long centuries of being undead caught up with him.

CHAPTER
52

LARA HAD GONE TO KILL Petale Venin. And add that Lara had me on her to-do list, which grew shorter by the hour.

I stood in Cragnow's den, his body now just a pile of dust. I had to get to my clothes and motorcycle. I didn't relish the anguish of transforming back to a wolf and then again to the form of a vampire. That would be four times tonight of making the supernatural switcheroo, and each time was as painful as exfoliating with a bench grinder. But I couldn't risk running naked through the chaparral and bramble with my "stuff" hanging out.

I got on my hands and knees, took a deep breath, and summoned the transformation. Back as a wolf, I returned at a gallop to where I had left my clothes.

Minutes later I was on my Yamaha, zooming south to Westwood. I roared between rows of cars on the roads and risked getting clipped by a mirror or someone jumping a lane.

I arrived at Venin's office complex. A white limousine and dark sedans were parked out front. Niphe's BMW sat in a handicapped parking spot at the end of the block.

I left my motorcycle in the alley. I walked close to the building, put my hands and feet against the wall, and climbed like a gecko to the third floor.

I crept along a narrow ledge to a darkened room. With a talon I scratched a circle the diameter of a melon on the window. I tapped the glass and caught the piece. I inserted my arm through the hole and groped for the window latch. I slipped into the room packed with boxes of files and palmed my pistol.

There was only one door out. Heavy breathing and a steady thumping came from the other side. No light shone under the door. Two guesses what kind of civic debate was going on in there.

I eased the door open.

A man in a suit, with his pants and boxers around his shins, faced a desk. A pair of high heels and stockinged ankles rocked on his shoulders. His naked buttocks pounded rhythmically against a woman lying on the desk. Their red auras rebounded from each other like two balloons slapping.

I tapped his arm. He jerked around. I zapped him, then her. I didn't have time for mischief so I left them in flagrante delicto.

I drew my pistol and walked toward Venin's office.

A figure with an orange aura staggered from her door. The vampire steadied himself against the wall and retched. His bile smelled of almonds. Lara had been here.

The vampire saw me. His aura radiated confusion and pain. He raised a Glock pistol and aimed at me.

I dropped him with two shots.

I crept close to Venin's door and listened for anything

suspicious. Someone gasped inside, as if struggling to breathe.

With my pistol at the ready, I entered the office.

Venin convulsed in her chair. Blood from a bullet hole stained her blouse. Her spectacles rested askew on her nose. Her eyes circled in opposite directions. Bottles of vodka, Amaretto, and seltzer sat on her desk.

So where was Lara?

An alarm sounded. The overhead sprinklers clicked and water dribbled out. What had happened to the water pressure?

Venin gave a weak gasp and fell silent. Her aura dimmed and went out. The feared matriarch of the vampire–human collusion was dead.

Smoke poured from the air conditioner vents. This place was about to burst into flames. In another minute I'd be a briquet.

Smoke filled the hallway and curled toward me. My eyes stung. I had to get out now.

The last time I was here, Venin had escaped out the door on the other side of the room. I didn't have time to be cautious. I ran for the door, put one shoulder forward, and knocked the door off its hinges. I kept running across the empty room and dove for the window.

The glass shattered and I sailed for a willow tree. I grasped the branches to stop my fall and levitated to the ground.

Smoke and sparks circled the buildings. Red flames licked from the windows. Fire alarms screamed. People bolted from the exits like frightened rabbits.

I found my motorcycle where I had left it. I raced up the block and passed the spot where Niphe's car had been.

Lara had gotten away.

CHAPTER
53

I DROVE TO CULVER CITY and stopped in a sports bar. I needed time—and a drink—to plan my next moves.

All the televisions except one were tuned to baseball. That one television showed the burning office complex. A newsman appeared on the screen, positioning himself in front of fire trucks and the burning building. He had the pronounced jawline and thick, groomed hair that advertised him as a personality you could trust. He clutched a microphone and cupped his other hand over an ear. He nodded excitedly at the camera.

I could barely hear the newsman over the patrons roaring in delight at a rerun of the day's game highlights.

"Arson . . . sabotaged the suppression system . . . fire burning out of control." The newsman turned his body, pointed to the building to emphasize the obvious, and faced the camera again.

The newsman continued. "Gunfire . . . a government official not yet been accounted for."

I could account for her.

The waitress dropped off a Manhattan I'd ordered.

Venin, Cragnow, Niphe . . . all dead. Who was left for Lara to kill?

Julius Paxton.

And me.

CHAPTER
54

WITH VENIN AND CRAGNOW dead I doubted Paxton would stay put for long. He lived in Granada Hills, on the northwest side of the San Fernando Valley. I'd start looking for him there.

At one o'clock in the morning, Paxton's neighborhood looked as saccharine as a Thomas Kinkade painting. I rounded the corner at low speed to mute the rumble of my V-Max. A Lincoln Navigator pulled out from Paxton's driveway and jerked to a stop in the middle of the street. The Lincoln's big front tires twisted and ground against the asphalt. Orange and red auras told me that a vampire drove and a human occupied the front passenger's seat.

The orange aura belonged to Paxton. The red, a chalice for sure.

The Lincoln accelerated away from me and took the corner at such speed it seemed about ready to tip over. I hung back one block and followed.

At the next corner, during a left turn that brought the Lincoln broadside to me, Paxton's aura flared with alarm. The Lincoln picked up speed and zoomed through a stop sign.

He must have seen me through his side window. I gunned the engine, and the Yamaha leapt forward like a hungry cheetah.

Paxton raced past traffic lights, oblivious of the cars swerving and braking to avoid him. He shot onto the access ramp for I-405 heading south.

Paxton's aura gave him away like an orange signal marker. He drove fast, the big Lincoln muscling through traffic like it owned the interstate.

We traveled east and south. Where was Paxton going? Palm Springs? Orange County? San Diego? Didn't think so. How about Mexico? That I'd bet on.

He would cross the border and disappear. Except he wouldn't get to Mexico. I'd stop him.

We passed the interchange of the San Diego and Long Beach freeways. Paxton accelerated to a hundred plus.

I opened the throttle to intercept speed, and the rumble of the Yamaha's four cylinders turned into a scream. The wind became an icy hand slapping my face. My clothes whipped against my limbs.

I brought the V-Max directly behind Paxton and closed the gap to within ten feet.

His brake lights illuminated in a panic stop, and the rear end of the Lincoln came at me like an enormous metal boxing glove. I let go of the handlebars and tucked my head against my chin.

The front tire of the Yamaha crashed against the rear bumper. The motorcycle flipped forward, catapulting me helmet-first through the rear window.

Glass exploded around me. I flew into the Lincoln like a spinning cannonball, lost for a moment in a maelstrom of confusion, motion, and pain. Color and light swirled around me. I slammed into a hard surface and fell sideways on something soft and yielding. A seat.

A woman screamed. The Lincoln jerked to the left and right. I fumbled for leverage, grasped a door handle, and sat upright. Boxes and stacks of suitcase crowded around me.

The Lincoln swerved across the lanes. Paxton's aura flamed with surprise and fear. A young woman, with hair and a face like a Barbie doll, beat at his arms and shrieked.

"He's inside, Julius. Shoot him. Shoot him."

I climbed into the middle seat, grabbed the chalice by her long tresses, and pulled her face toward mine. "Shut up." I gave her a glare that could knock out a squad of firemen.

Her aura puffed out and shrank to a muted glow. She sat paralyzed with hypnosis.

I pulled my Colt pistol and jabbed it against the nape of Paxton's neck. "Slow down."

The speedometer dropped below one hundred, then ninety, eighty, and held steady at seventy. A green highway sign announced the next exit as Avalon Boulevard.

"Get off the freeway here." I removed my helmet. "Go north."

"Where are we going?"

"To have a chat. I need to complete a report to the Araneum, and since you're the only one in your merry band who's still walking and talking, well, I guess you're it."

The tendrils of his aura writhed like snakes caught in a trap. Paxton didn't question what I had said about him being the only one remaining from his "merry band."

"We can work a deal."

"Paxton, you got nothing I want except information."

The Lincoln circled down the off ramp to Avalon Boulevard. I directed him into a parking lot. Raccoons scattered in front of us, their auras crimson jewels rolling across the asphalt.

"Stop here," I ordered.

We halted in the middle of the lot.

"I'll tell you everything," Paxton said. "Then let me walk. No one has to know."

The Araneum already considered him more ash. "Afraid not. It would cost me my reputation."

"I got money. I got a harem of chalices."

"And I got you by the balls." I screwed the muzzle of the pistol deeper into his skin. "Who put the bomb in Coyote's truck?"

Paxton's aura brightened like a lamp.

I jabbed the pistol against his neck. "Who?"

"My vampire cops. On Venin's orders."

I gritted my teeth in rage. I pistol-whipped Paxton's head. "Who was in charge of the investigation into Roxy's murder?"

"What's that got to do with this?"

"Answer the question."

"I was," Paxton replied.

"Cragnow didn't kill Roxy. Venin didn't. And you wouldn't wipe your nose unless they told you, so you didn't kill her either. Then who did?"

"I don't know," Paxton answered.

"Then why the cover-up?"

"Because we didn't want to know. Roxy was dead, and whoever murdered her did us all a big favor."

The chalice rolled her head and regained consciousness. She blinked, looked at me, and let out a scream that could echo to the San Gabriel Mountains and back.

I didn't see Paxton throw the punch but I did see plenty of stars. Pain clotted my thinking. I lifted myself from the seat.

Paxton jumped from the Lincoln.

I broke the side window and shot at him.

Paxton stumbled. He regained his footing and limped toward the road.

I jerked the door open, stunned and smarting from Paxton's sucker punch. The chalice lunged for me and grabbed my hair. I slapped her away and tried to zap her. She kept her eyes closed and flailed her arms. I grasped both her wrists with one hand and squeezed. She yelped in pain and opened her eyes. Finally. I left her sitting motionless and got out.

Paxton moved through a cone of headlights bearing across the parking lot. He abruptly turned and limped faster.

The car aimed for him. Paxton's aura burned in panic. The car was a BMW coupe. Lara.

Paxton yelled for help. From whom? The BMW smashed into him and he disappeared under the bumper. An instant later he flopped from behind the coupe and lay still.

The car raced past me and skidded to a stop a hundred feet away. It backed up and swung the headlights upon me. I could barely make out Lara's aura in the dazzle of the head-lights.

I brought my pistol up and sighted down its stubby length. My silver bullets splattered against the windshield and grille. The car swerved around the Lincoln and circled back to the road.

I ran after Lara and got as close as fifty feet. Holding my pistol before me, I squeezed the trigger until the magazine was empty. My bullets plunked against the BMW's trunk lid. I shoved the pistol into its holster and sprinted faster.

The BMW pulled away, bounced over the sidewalk, and careened onto the road.

I angled my path to catch Lara. I leapt as hard as I could and windmilled my arms and legs to keep the momentum.

Slamming across the trunk, I stabbed my talons into the metal to hang on. Lara swerved across the road. Four bright headlights were on me. A large truck blared its horn. The BMW fishtailed to the left. My talons slipped loose and I was flung aside.

The grille of a semi smashed into me, and I was sent fly-ing like a soccer ball. I crashed into a field and rolled into a ditch.

I lay for a moment, flat on my back and blind with agony. Points of starlight bled through the inkiness above me. I wiggled my fingers and toes. The worst of the pain came from my left leg. I propped myself on my elbows and examined the wound.

Blood soaked my trousers from the knee to the cuff. A white splinter of bone poked midway from my shin. I patted the leg and felt a compound fracture of my fibula.

A man in a plaid shirt appeared on the edge of the ditch. "You alive?"

I let the pain ebb before answering. "Not quite."

A siren approached and a car stopped. Flashing blue and red lights flicked across the grass above me. The man went away, and seconds later, a deputy sheriff in a khaki uniform loped into the ditch and knelt in the weeds beside me.

"Hold on," he said. "An ambulance is on the way."

He noticed my eyes. "What the?"

I balled his shirt collar into my hands and yanked him closer. I mustered the strength for a good stare and zapped him.

"Help me up," I said.

He pulled me upright. My leg felt like it was getting broken again. I supported myself against the deputy, took his baton and my belt, and fashioned a splint against my leg.

Once the pain cleared from my head, we hobbled out of the ditch to his patrol car. Torn, muddy clothes hung from my limbs.

The semi truck was down the road, its emergency lights flashing. I had no idea where that murderous bitch Lara had gone. Besides, I was in no condition to hunt her down. I felt like, well, like that semi truck had drop-kicked my hairy vampire ass into a ditch.

I needed to recuperate. Someplace with lots of human blood for the asking. A chalice parlor. The Majestic Lanes.

CHAPTER
55

I LEVERED MYSELF behind the steering wheel and carefully rested the splinted leg to keep from jarring the fracture.

I looked over the parking lot where I had last seen Paxton. He was gone, for good, I hoped, as was his chalice and the Lincoln. I knew getting flattened by the BMW wouldn't finish him. But it would be a while before Paxton did the mattress tango with his chalice.

I drove into Los Angeles, halted outside the Majestic Lanes, and hobbled out of the deputy's cruiser, leaving the motor running and the lights flashing.

Inside the darkened bowling alley, a lobby card read: SORRY! LANES CLOSED! BUT TRY OUR EGGS! COFFEE SHOP OPEN 24 HRS!

Crockery rattled from the opposite end of the building. Who would eat at this dump at 2 A.M. . . . other than the undead?

I found the maintenance door leading to the secret passage for the basement. At first I tried to ease my broken leg down each step of the stairway. No matter what I did it hurt like hell, so I held on to the banister and staggered to the bottom of the stairs as best I could, the wooden splint clanging against the metal steps.

I knocked on the door of the chalice parlor. The little window in the door slid open. I recognized the red vampire eyes of the bouncer from my previous visit. He let me through.

I shuffled in, dragging my broken leg. The bouncer's aura brightened with alarm.

"A little help, please," I said.

He stood behind me and lifted me by my armpits. With one foot he pushed a chair away from a table and sat me down. He knelt and removed the splint. He extended a talon, which he used to slice away the lower part of my left trouser leg.

The bouncer grimaced at the sight of my swollen leg. "Hope you kicked the other guy's ass."

"I might have dented his fender." Except for the bouncer and me, the parlor looked deserted. "What gives? Last time, this place was a goddamn circus. I've seen more life on an autopsy table."

"It's the news about Cragnow."

"What about him?"

The bouncer's aura telegraphed his skepticism with my question. *Like you don't know?* "Don't bullshit me. You're the enforcer from the Araneum."

"Take a look at me. I'm not enforcing anything."

"Maybe not now." The bouncer stood and unfolded a tablecloth from a stack on another table. He tore a long strip and knelt again by my left leg. "Hold steady now. This might hurt." He grasped my knee and ankle.

As he pulled my leg and reset the fracture, it felt like a thousand scorpions were stinging me at once from the inside. My vision dimmed and a rush of noise echoed within my skull. When my eyes focused again and my brain quieted, the bouncer was standing before me, admiring my bandaged leg.

The pain now seemed like only a hundred scorpions were at work. I moved the leg, and it hurt less.

"Why are you helping me?"

"I got a business to run. I don't care which vampire is in charge of the *nidus,* they're all the same to me. The sooner this nonsense stops, the sooner I can go back to making my payroll."

I whisked dust from my shirt. Clumps of dirt and grass fell out of my hair. I had to wash up and change clothes. But first I had to eat and rest. "What's on the menu?"

"Not much. Let me see what I can scrounge."

The bouncer went through a door behind the bar and returned with a steaming plate of Transylvanian lasagna—no garlic, extra ricotta cheese, and drenched with whole human blood. He uncorked a bottle of shiraz. "On the house."

I thanked him and forked helpings into my mouth and cooled the portions with gulps of wine. The pain in my leg now felt like only a dozen scorpions.

A barefoot female chalice in a robe refilled my glass.

"You dessert?" I asked.

She dropped her robe over an empty chair. "I like to think of myself as the main course." She pushed my plate aside, climbed on the table, and lay naked with her nipples and toes pointing to the ceiling. I scooped her head under one arm and curled the other around her waist.

I sank my fangs into her neck. Her aura rose to a low boil. I took my time feeding. She ran her hands over her breasts, across her flat belly, and cupped her vagina, rubbing her fingers in slow circles. She moaned and shuddered in orgasm while I feasted.

Her blood warmed me, and the kinks and knots in my body melted away. I awoke slumped across the table with the chalice curled around my head like a big hairless cat.

I pulled free and rubbed my eyes. My joints and back creaked like they belonged to an old man. I reached for my left leg and touched the bandage. The flesh was still tender. I put weight on the leg. The ache was tolerable.

The bouncer sat at the bar and sipped coffee. "You okay?"

I stamped my left foot. The soreness would last for a day or two. "Fit enough to kick ass, with either leg. You got extra clothes and a place to wash up?"

"The dressing room's got cosmetics and a sink. There are plenty of clothes lying around. Take what fits."

The parlor was empty except for the bouncer, the chalice, and me.

"What time is it?" I asked.

"Three o'clock."

"A.M. or P.M.?"

"P.M."

"Where are your customers?"

"Hiding and waiting," answered the bouncer.

"For what?" I lifted the robe from the chair and covered the chalice.

"To see what you'll do next."

"For that I need wheels."

The bouncer reached into his trouser pocket and tossed a set of keys to me. "Take mine."

A Mitsubishi logo decorated the key fob.

He poured a cup of coffee and topped it off with a long splash of blood from a second carafe. "Where you off to?"

"You know Lara Phillips?"

He pushed the cup across the bar counter in my direction. "Nope."

"Then you won't miss her."

CHAPTER
56

I HAD SCRUBBED myself clean, picked through the clothes littering the dressing room of the chalice parlor, and changed into jeans and a T-shirt that read: TAKE BACK THE STREETS. STOP THE VIOLENCE.

The bouncer owned the only Mitsubishi in the parking lot, a Spyder convertible. Since I was out of ammo, I dumped my pistol into the trunk. I folded the convertible's top down and sped north to Lara's home in Verdugo City.

She had a good head start, but there'd be clues where to find her. The sooner I got to her home, the warmer the trail would be.

I crossed over the concrete viaduct leading to Verdugo City. I halted in front of Lara's home. The same car with the EXPERT MAIDS logo was parked along the sidewalk.

I scanned for auras. I didn't want Lara to ambush me. The way clear, I put my sunglasses on and let myself in through the front door.

The only noise was a rustling from down the hall. I found the blond maid in a back room, stacking clothes on a small couch beside a desk. Two matching suitcases lay open on the floor. She didn't see me approach from behind.

A cork board hung on the wall next to the desk. Across the top of the board was a row of photos. The first two were glamour portraits of Roxy and Katz. Next were pictures from the Internet of Cragnow, Venin, and Paxton. The one of Rosario had been crossed out, probably to indicate she hadn't killed him. The last two were stills from a security camera. From the background I could tell these were taken at Journey's church. These photos were of Mordecai Niphe and me.

How far back had this murder spree been planned? Months? Years? Or did Lara only recently snap?

The maid glanced over her shoulder. Her complexion turned as pale as her white blouse. She whirled about in surprise, stumbled against the couch, and fell onto the cushions.

"Take it easy," I said. "I'm only here to find Lara."

The maid took quick breaths. Her breathing slowed, and the color returned to her face. The fright in her eyes gave way to grief. "Lara's in trouble, isn't she?" With those sad, round eyes and broad, sullen face the maid looked like a forlorn cow.

I nodded. "Where is she?"

"Not here." The maid shrank into the couch. Big tears shined in her eyes. She pulled a tissue from an apron pocket to blow her nose and blot her eyes. "Promise you won't hurt her."

My promise was that I'd terminate the murderous shrew. The petite brunette Gospel aerobics instructor was a rampaging killing machine that a half dozen others had underestimated. Alive, she remained as dangerous as a grenade with the pin pulled. "Why would I hurt her?"

"I just know. Lara's been doing crazy things lately. Like walking around the house and talking to herself. Praying for hours. Today she tells me to pack everything. Then she takes off in a banged-up car I've never seen before."

Niphe's BMW.

The maid picked at the tissue. "Lara's always been kind to me. If she's done anything wrong, she must have a good reason."

"That's what I'm trying to find out. Where did she go?"

"I won't tell you."

My questions meant the maid could implicate me in Lara's death when the police arrived, which they would. Despite the trouble I had interrogating the maid from last time, I had no recourse but to zap her, ask questions, and erase the memory of my visit.

The maid watched with glossy bovine eyes as I removed my sunglasses. Her aura lit up and she sat frozen in my hypnotic grasp.

Cupping her chin, I stroked her head and asked her name. Using her name might make her more receptive to my questions.

The maid stammered under hypnosis as she had before. Every passing moment put Lara farther away from me. The wall clock marked the fleeting seconds with the resolve of a hammer striking an anvil. I fought the impulse to slap the maid into answering.

At last she said, "Amy."

I caressed her face and kept my tone velvety soft. "Amy, let me help Lara." *Help me kill the homicidal bitch.* "Tell me where she went."

The maid smiled beatifically, naïve to my lie. "With Reverend Journey. At his home in Silver Lake."

"Amy, you have an address?"

She motioned to the desk.

I found an empty postmarked envelope addressed to Dale Journey. The return address belonged to the late Councilwoman Petale Venin.

"Good girl." I kissed Amy on the cheek, closed her eyes, and ordered her to sleep. She wouldn't remember anything.

I went out and left in the convertible.

South of Griffith Park, I took the Hyperion exit and climbed the twisting streets of Silver Lake. Journey's house occupied an extravagant double lot with a millionaire's view of the lake below.

The style of his home was traditional California Mediterranean: white stucco, red Spanish tile, and art deco flourishes. Turrets adorned the front of the house, one at each corner, and a larger one in the center with the entrance.

Niphe's BMW sat in the driveway to the right of the lawn. Long scratches and dents marred the smooth lines of the black coupe. The mangled front end drooped like a mutilated snout.

I slowed and looked for auras.

Nothing moved. Not even a cat or songbird.

I drove up the block and parked. I kept my sunglasses off, certain that if trouble started, I couldn't waste even an instant to bring every vampire power to bear.

I cut across the neighbors' lawns to the side of Journey's home, hid myself in the shadow of a dense fir tree, and walked up the wall. I levitated to step quietly over the tiled roof.

A rectangular swimming pool divided the backyard between a patio and a lush lawn. A tall brick fence surrounded the yard. I leaned over the edge of the roof Buster Keaton–style and checked the back wall of the house. A sunroom with beveled glass windows faced the patio. Though this place was big enough to be an orphanage, I had yet to see anybody.

I floated off the roof, opened a French door to the sunroom, and sneaked in. Voices murmured from deep inside the house.

I crossed from the sunroom into a den and then the kitchen. The voices grew louder. One, a woman's—Lara's. The other—tired, grim—was Journey's.

I stepped onto the plush carpet of a formal dining room, the lights off and deep in shadow. Through an arched doorway, I saw Lara standing in the front salon with her back to me. Her aura shined with conviction and energy. The strap of a handbag hung off the left shoulder of a long casual dress. She looked like any other suburban mom out for errands—while her victims crumbled to dust.

Journey seemed poured into a leather armchair, torso folded forward, face downcast over arms and legs limp as wet clay. Tiny bubbles of fear and despair rippled through his aura.

"I can't believe you did this," he kept saying, his voice weakening with each repetition.

Lara sank to her knees before him and clasped his hands. "You told me they were going to take your church away. You said they were out to ruin you. Cragnow. Niphe. Venin. Paxton. So I had to stop them."

"But not like this. Don't you realize what you've done? You've dragged me off the cliff with you."

Not just off a cliff but down a deep hole.

"There's no cliff, my darling. We can run. We have your money. We have time."

Better take his car, then. What's left of Niphe's Beemer wouldn't get you to the freeway. I stayed in the shadows of the dining room. Stalking them like a wolf, I halted and waited beside an end table.

"There is no time." He let go of her hands and curled his fingers into fists. A wave of fresh determination pulsed through his aura. "There's only one way to save myself."

Lara set her hands on his knees and sat back on her heels. "What's that, my darling?"

Journey pushed her hands away and stood. "I have to turn you in."

Tendrils of distress flailed through her aura. "You can't. Not if you love me." The words seeped from her throat in soft whispers. "Not after all I've done for you."

"Lara, this is about murder. I have to tell the police. I'd be an accomplice if I didn't. Then there would be two of us in jail."

Lara stared at the carpet. "Jail?" The tendrils of her aura shrank and turned flaccid. "But I did it for you."

"Please, Lara, face reality. You think we can run away from this? Where could we hide? For how long? Turn yourself in, and I promise you the best legal help and psychiatric care. At the very worst, you can plead insanity."

She levered upright. The tendrils stiffened from her aura like quills. "Insanity. Now I'm crazy? Just because I won't let you snitch on me?"

Rage boiled through her aura. "You're no different from anyone else. You only want to betray me, to humiliate me."

The gunshot startled me.

Journey fell into the chair, a shiny, dark stain spreading across the front of his shirt.

His gaze searched the room, as if groping for respite from his pain. His eyes found me and begged for help.

Lara faced me. Her right arm extended to point a small revolver at me.

At this distance, I couldn't hypnotize her. With my nerves primed like this, I wouldn't have a problem dodging her bullets. I could reveal myself as a vampire but better to keep her talking and get her to tell me things I had to know.

Her aura flared with alarm. She fired. I ducked right. She fired again. I ducked left.

Lara stopped shooting. The pistol shook in her trembling hand. Her aura crackled with fear.

Journey clutched for Lara, his bloody fingers curling into a red claw. "Lara."

"Shut up, lover." Lara steadied her aim upon me. "What do you want, Felix Gomez?"

"To tell you I know who murdered Roxy Bronze." I pointed my finger at her.

A new emotion tinted her aura . . . admiration. "How do you know?"

"Roxy's cell phone records. Your number was the last one. It arrived at one-oh-two in the morning, right about when she had been killed. Kind of a strange time to call and say hello. How did it feel to shoot your sister?"

Lara hesitated. Her fingers adjusted their grip on the revolver. She smiled. "It felt good."

"Why did you do it?"

"Please, Lara." Journey wheezed, blood frothing on his lips and over the hole in his shirt.

"You hush now," she said. "Die quietly."

Cold witch.

"I told you why," Lara said.

"When?"

"The first time we met at the church. Freya, my big famous sister, throwing her talents away while I stumbled behind her. For that she had to die. To erase the shame of being the sister of Roxy Bronze."

"What right did you have to kill her?"

"What right did she have to humiliate me again and again?" Lara's grip tensed on the pistol. "Ask yourself, mister private *dick,* how is it you pieced together what happened through the phone logs and the cops didn't?"

"Ask them. Did you think you'd get away with her murder?"

"Not at first. After I killed her I expected the worst, but nothing happened." Lara's mouth curled with disgust. "I was amazed how those imbecile cops tripped over one another to not solve the case. The police lied about everything. That's when I realized others wanted her out of the way."

"What about Katz Meow?" I asked. "Your number was also the last on her cell phone record."

"She was my sister's best friend in the porn business. But Katz didn't know who I was. She never saw it coming, the stupid whore. It felt good to shoot her, too."

Journey's hands trembled with the palsy of a man at the brink of death. "Please, Lara darling. Call for help."

"I told you to shut up," she replied, not looking at him. Tendrils circled her head as if she were Medusa.

I asked, "And Cragnow?"

"When I told him I was Roxy's sister and wanted to work for him, he drooled at the possibilities. Turned out he was as stupid as everyone else. I've done this city a favor by killing the whole lot of you scum."

"What happens now? This ends the tidy arrangement you had with your boyfriend the pastor. His stealing from the church. You committing murder." I stepped toward Lara.

Her eyes widened. "You're one of them."

"One of the good guys, you mean?"

"No. You're like Cragnow and his guard. I gave them enough cyanide to poison a team of horses, and even then I had to shoot them. It's those eyes. You, Paxton, and the others are . . . different."

I smiled and showed her my fangs.

Her aura exploded with shock. She whispered, "You're a monster."

"I prefer vampire."

She fired.

The bullet flew through the space where I had been.

By the time we locked eyes I was close enough to grab her wrists. Her blue eyes dilated into black circles.

Her expression softened. Her arms relaxed, and the revolver fell to the carpet.

Journey's corpse slumped in the armchair. His head lolled to the side, mouth open, foam clumped on his lips like pink toothpaste. His legs relaxed into parentheses. The bloody stain on his shirt gathered along his waist, his aura gone. Too late for the EMTs.

I could kill Lara by fanging, but her blood was too polluted with the wretched evil of her slaughter. She would die another way.

I placed my left hand behind her neck and the other gripped her jaw. Her eyes gazed at mine with innocent warmth.

Compared to the agony I could inflict, what I was about to do should be considered a gift of mercy.

One quick twist to the left. Her upper spine snapped with

the sound of a broomstick breaking. The atlas and axis vertebrae tore from the base of her skull and severed the medulla oblongata.

Her aura vanished like a light switched off and just as quickly, her soul went to the great beyond. All motor functions instantly ceased. Lara didn't even twitch. Her lifeless body sagged against my palms.

How had this changed anything? Roxy Bronze was still dead.

I didn't worry about leaving clues. The Araneum would order the vampires remaining with the police to scrub this crime scene of any undead evidence.

After the ordeal I'd been through, I needed to end this case with a warning to my fellow vampires. Cross the Araneum, cross *me,* and you will be punished. Your death will be a cleansing. And what better medium for cleansing than water?

I hoisted Lara by the wrists and draped her over one shoulder.

I tossed her into the pool outside. Lara floated with her face to the sky, buoyed by the trapped air puffing inside her dress. Lara bobbed in the water, her expression serene, as if enjoying one final warm kiss from the sun. The air escaped her dress with a wet sigh and her shoulders tipped to one side. She rolled to float facedown. Her brown hair surrounded her head like a wispy, weedy crown.

I'd come to Los Angeles to investigate and undo vampire–human collusion. And that collusion, for all its planning and supernatural resources, was ravaged by the twisted vengeance of one female.

The most dangerous kind.

A human.

CHAPTER
57

I PARKED MY NEWEST rental sedan in the lot just inside the gate of the Oakwood Memorial Park.

An older model Ford pickup truck turned off Valley Circle Boulevard, rattled through the gate, and rolled to a stop beside my car. Coyote sat behind the steering wheel, and he nodded at me.

Three days ago, he had appeared in the backseat of my locked rental—barefoot, asleep, and wearing blackened rags. He looked like he had been shot out of a cannon and landed in a cinder pile. Seeing him again had filled me with the joy of a man finding his lost brother.

I am a vampire. I'm supposed to have shed my human persona and left behind the aches—and smiles—of the mortal world. But that hadn't happened. Not yet. Not completely.

Coyote didn't say much, only that he was hungry. I bought him red chile beef burritos and a six-pack of Löwenbräu. I asked what oblivion was like. In between chomping on the burritos and guzzling one beer after another—raining crumbs and lager on the upholstery—he said it was as boring as a Baptist wedding reception.

Coyote sucked dry a bag of A-positive, and when I turned around to hand him a napkin, he was gone.

Since then, I have driven by Veronica's apartment once. Being close eased the longing, but soon the moment passed and I felt creepy spying on her. I drove off and tried to forget the pain of losing her.

The engine of Coyote's old Ford wheezed like it was dying of tuberculosis. The driver's door creaked open. A couple of screws dropped to the asphalt.

Coyote stepped out, looking freshly bathed and his sunblock neatly applied. His hair was combed back and threaded with silver strands. He wore an embroidered shirt with pearl snaps. His creased jeans fit snug over the tops of yellow cowboy boots.

"*Órale,* Felix," he said. "Good morning."

"*Buenos días.*" I had so many questions, but all I could do was point to Coyote's well-pressed clothes. "This a new look?"

"Sometimes a change of clothes is more than a change of clothes, *raza.*" He smoothed the front of his shirt. "I've had these a while."

"Where? I thought everything was burned up."

He gave one of his Coyote grins, meaning, *vato,* I'm the trickster, and I won't give away any of my secrets.

A white Infiniti turned off the street and parked close to us. Polly Smythe, the infamous JJ Jizmee, got out. A rose-colored scarf covering her neck marked her as a chalice.

Polly waved at me. "Felix, I didn't know you were Coyote's friend."

"We go back."

Coyote offered his hand to her. They clasped fingers and pecked each other on the cheek.

Polly carried a ribbed, knit sweater over one arm. The sweater was the same color and style as the one back in

Coyote's destroyed home. "This is way too small," she said. "It won't even cover one boob."

"Well then, *mi corazón,* we'll have to try something else. Wouldn't want you and your girls to catch cold."

Polly told me back at Fred Daniels's funeral that she wished for a change. I couldn't think of a bigger change than becoming a chalice and dating Coyote.

Polly now belonged to the undead world—it was an irrevocable act. Coyote in turn acted as if he belonged to her—another irrevocable act.

The three of us walked on the narrow road curving through the grass and rows of grave markers. I brought a supermarket bouquet of flowers.

We found a marker decorated with a small brass urn. A sprig of carnations, baby's breath, and roses—the faded blossoms crisp as old paper—drooped from the mouth of the urn.

The marker read:

FREYA KRIEGER A.K.A. ROXY BRONZE
A LOVING SPIRIT WHO SOARS ABOVE US STILL

Under that were the dates of her birth and death. Roxy lived to be thirty-four.

Visiting graves was always anticlimactic. Even when I was human, there was never a rush of emotion. It was just a plot of turf with a plaque to announce the physical passing. What really mattered about anyone was as ephemeral as the wind. The grave was a place to express our tributes, though more honest and sincere words were rendered over drinks in a bar.

I thought about the girl with the bright smile who had welcomed me while others shunned the poor brown kid from Pacoima. I thought about losing Veronica, and the ghosts of my childhood. *Thank you. And vaya con Dios.*

I pushed the bouquet alongside the other flowers in the urn.

"Roxy loved the Valley," Polly said.

From here, you couldn't see much of the Valley. The grass sloped toward the boulevard. A wall of trees—willows and elms—and a chain-link privacy fence overgrown with honeysuckle blocked the view. The rising terrain, the Santa Susana Mountains and Knolls to the north and west, and the Santa Monica Mountains to the south made it clear that we stood on the rim of a gigantic trough extending to the east—the San Fernando Valley.

We headed back to our cars. Coyote and Polly whispered and giggled. I trailed behind.

I stood by Coyote's truck, waiting for him to ask for a final push start.

Polly opened the driver's door to her Infiniti. "Coyote and I are going for coffee or whatever."

The polite tone in her voice implied I was invited, but the "whatever" meant she wanted me to say no. They had plans beside coffee.

"Thanks but no," I said.

Coyote climbed into the passenger's side.

I asked, "You're not taking your truck?"

"*Chale*. The damn thing probably won't start. I'll get it later." Coyote closed his door and rolled the window down. "*Vato,* can't say it was fun . . ."—he broke into laughter—"but it was loco." His face lit up with more joy than I'd ever seen on any of the undead. "*Ay te watcho.*" See you later.

His window raised, and the Infiniti backed up. I waved good-bye.

This assignment was over, thank God. I had nothing left to do but get home, at my leisure. Emphasis on *leisure* to clear my head of Veronica.

A crow cawed and broke my thoughts.

The black bird paced across the roof of my rental car. A metal tube gleamed on one leg.

Flip the page to check out
the next declassified installment
from Mario Acevedo,

THE UNDEAD KAMA SUTRA

Coming in March 2008

CARMEN PULLED ME into the alley. A vampire scent trailed her, an aroma of damp moss and dried roses.

She stopped and faced me. Triangles of a neon-green bikini top barely covered her breasts. Gold and coral earrings dangled alongside her neck. She raised her sunglasses and revealed the reflective red disks of her *tapetum lucidum*. Her smile parted and showed the tips of her fangs. "Felix, it's a good thing we came to your rescue."

Like I needed rescuing from that fatso inside. I smiled back. "What are you doing here?"

She spread her arms. "Isn't it obvious?"

I took in all that taut, sienna-colored skin. Her tan looked perfect, too perfect even for an expert undead application of makeup. I sniffed and detected no trace of cosmetics. This tan was real? Impossible.

"I give. What's your secret?"

Carmen poked me in the stomach. "Geez, Felix, aren't you first going to ask me how I've been? Whadda ya think?" She put an arm out for me to inspect.

I dragged my finger across her wrist, still amazed at how authentic her tan looked. "This can't be real."

"As real as these." Carmen shimmied and her breasts wobbled.

Anyone else, and I would've been all over them. But Carmen's sexual manner was as subtle as a bear trap and she had the reputation of wringing even male vampires dry.

But a vampire with a tan? Pigs flying. Cats doing geometry. Dogs playing poker. All those would've amazed me less. "And you're not even wearing sun block?"

Carmen shook her head. "Nothing between me and the sun but this beautiful bronzed skin. And what brings you to Key West?"

"I heard you're working on *The Undead Kama Sutra*."

The ends of her smile pointed to the dimples in her cheeks. "You naughty boy."

A bar stool crashed through the window of the saloon and landed on the street.

My hands curled into claws and my talons grew. "We better go inside and help your friend."

Carmen laughed. "Jolie can handle a battalion of Marines. Public brawling is her hobby."

Shouts and the smashing of wooden furniture boomed out the broken window.

"Sounds like Jolie's having lots of fun." I started for the door, hoping that she'd left some of Mr. Fish Fear Me for me to thump around the floor.

Carmen grasped my wrist and led me out of the alley toward the two choppers. "Don't spoil it for her."

The thin, almost-nothing strap of Carmen's bikini bisected a sleek, muscular back. Her ponytail pointed to a trim waist. Denim shorts rode low on her hips. Her toned legs glistened like copper in the electric light of the salon marquee.

Carmen looked over her shoulder. "You checkin' me out?"

Maybe I should risk getting wrung dry. I put on my best smirk.

She winked. "Thanks. Otherwise there's no point in dressing like this."

"Where we headed?"

Carmen unclipped the keys hooked to a belt loop on her shorts. "You asked about *The Undead Kama Sutra* and how I got my tan. It's time to show you." She grasped the handlebars of the green chopper, arced her leg over the frame, and settled onto the seat.

I asked, "Did you get my messages?"

"I did."

"Why didn't you reply?"

Carmen inserted the ignition key. "You asked what gives? I wanted you to come and find out. Show me how bad you want to know." She cocked her thumb to the pinion seat of the motorcycle. "Climb on. We're going to the dock."

"I can drive. You ride on the back."

Carmen shook her head. "Like hell. It's my bike. You can either walk or ride bitch."

"I'll follow in my car."

Carmen started the engine. She shouted above the roar from the exhaust pipes. "Quit being such a macho *caga palo*." Take the stick out of your ass. "Forget your goddamn car. It's not going anywhere. Just get on."

You couldn't argue with Carmen. I swung a leg over the rear seat. Carmen reached with her left hand and groped for my arm. She pulled it around her waist. My right arm reached around so that I clasped both arms around her very trim and firm middle. For a vampire she was surprisingly warm, or was that my imagination?

I had barely planted my feet on the rear pegs when the

chopper jumped from the curb. The front wheel tucked to the left, Carmen barely straightened it before we flipped to the side. We swerved past a yellow Porsche Carrera, missing the rear fender by millimeters.

We skimmed close to a row of parked cars. I had to jerk my shoulders aside to avoid getting slapped by the mirrors.

"There's no rule that says you can't drive down the middle of the road," I shouted.

"You want to obey the rules," she shouted back, "then stay away from me. Shut up and enjoy the scenery."

Carmen took Duvall Street and merged into traffic. We approached the harbor and parked alongside a steel-pipe barricade.

I got off the bike first, thankful that we'd made it without being flung against the asphalt. Carmen took a tightly wrapped paper bag out of one of the leather panniers. The quart-sized bag bore a crude inked stamp: *Yerbas de Botánica Oshún. Miami, Florida.*

Herbs of Oshún Apothecary. My mother and aunts used to shop in Mexican *botánicas* for folk remedies, some which worked and others were merely superstitions—and a waste of money. "Is what's in that bag have anything to do with your tan?" Maybe some of the superstitious recipes did work.

Carmen squeezed the bag and crinkled the paper wrapping. "I didn't buy this to make bread."

Typical Carmen answer. "Who's Oshún?"

"She's an *orisha*, a Santeria goddess."

"Santeria? So this is about voodoo? You're going to stick pins in a doll of me?"

"I don't need pins or Santeria. I can kick your ass on my own."

I stepped out of her reach, just in case she wanted to prove something. "How did you get involved with Santeria?"

"I'm Cuban." Carmen crouched to fit a lock on her front

THE UNDEAD KAMA SUTRA 339

brake disk. "It's part of my heritage. The African slaves brought their beliefs to the Caribbean. You don't know much about Santeria, do you?"

"I know some. There's that song *Babalu*, by Ricky Ricardo. That's about Santeria, right?"

"He was Desi Arnaz when he recorded it," Carmen said. "And yes, the song is about Santeria."

"So who is Oshún?"

"The queen of beauty and sensuality. We call upon her magic."

"For what?"

"To make us better lovers, of course."

"How come Desi Arnaz didn't write a song about her?"

"I don't know, Felix. If Desi was alive you could ask him."

Dozens of sailboats and yachts were moored to the pier and their lights twinkled festively over the water. Carmen walked down the ramp to a thirty-foot Bayliner cruiser and hailed someone onboard.

I removed my sunglasses.

A man stepped out of the cabin. A red aura surrounded him. Human.

Carmen stepped off the dock and into the cockpit of the boat. She and the man clasped hands, and he kissed her on the cheek. Her orange aura glistened with affection. Vampires only show that kind of attraction to *chalices*, humans who willingly offer themselves, and their blood, to their vampire masters.

Carmen waved me aboard and I joined her in the cockpit. She introduced me to Thorne, a ropey-muscled man in his mid-twenties. The word strapping came to mind; someone who could satisfy her sexual appetite. Was he her research partner for *The Undead Kama Sutra*? A bandana covered his neck, advertising his status as a chalice to those in the undead family. He didn't say much and smiled politely.

Carmen carried the botanica bag and stooped to enter the boat's cabin. She came out empty-handed and ordered that we shove off.

Moving athletically on his sturdy hairy legs, Thorne cast loose from the moorings. Her hungry gaze followed him.

Thorne took the helm. He flipped switches across the instrument panel. The navigation lights flicked on. The engine coughed to life. Above the cabin, the radar antenna on the mast began to spin. He adjusted the volume of the radio so the squawks of harbor traffic faded into the background. The Bayliner cruised slowly away from the dock.

A woman's shriek—sounding like a cross between a drunken sorority girl and a hyena on fire—echoed from the pier. An orange glow streaked toward us. Jolie.

She bounded from the edge of the pier toward us. Our boat was a good hundred feet way. Jolie sailed through the air and pumped her arms to keep the momentum. She used vampire levitation to land softly beside Carmen and me.

Jolie raised both her arms in a triumphant salute. "Ta-da."

"Yeah, great," Carmen chided. "Where's your motorcycle?"

Jolie's aura dimmed. "Shit. I knew I forgot something."

"How was the fight?" I asked.

"Totally awesome. One of those assholes got the drop on me and nailed me good." She pointed to her shiner on the right eye. "I'll bet it's a beaut."

"Looks . . . wonderful," I said. "Hurt?"

"Stupid question." Jolie touched the swollen tissue around her eye. "Course it hurts. Too bad it'll heal by the time we get home."

"Which is where?" I turned to Carmen.

She loosened the braid of her ponytail. She closed her eyes in a blissful trance as she raked her fingers to untangle the tresses. Leaning against the railing of the gunwale,

Carmen silhouetted herself against the lights of Key West. Her hair shimmered like a lacy halo. "Houghton Island. It's in the Snipe Keys northeast of here."

Once in open water, Thorne opened the throttle and the Bayliner rocked on its wake. Jolie yanked off her boots and socks and scrambled barefoot to the prow, where she sat on the foredeck and sang—more or less—tunes from the '80s. Thorne played with the GPS on the instrument panel and adjusted our course. In the far darkness, red, green, and white lights marked the other boats floating by.

I took a seat on the fantail. "Aren't the Snipe Keys government islands?" I asked.

Carmen's aura sparkled with assurance. "That's what makes our resort so exclusive."

"A resort? How did you manage that?"

Carmen gave a dimpled smile. "We have chalices in high places."

"We?"

"There's a bunch of investors, a few select vampires and chalices. It was my idea . . . and Antoine's. You'll meet him."

"A few select vampires and chalices? High rollers, I'll bet. Fun and games on a private island. Must be paradise."

Carmen's aura prickled with worry. "It was. That's why I'm glad you came here."

"Sounds like someone's found a turd floating in the punch bowl, and I'm supposed to fish it out." Trouble followed me everywhere.

"Lovely visual, Felix. Yeah, I could use your help."

"Doesn't sound like research for *The Undead Kama Sutra.*"

"It's not." Carmen paused for a beat and then explained in a monotone. "A chalice has been missing for two days."

A missing chalice? I already had plenty to keep me busy, thanks to Gilbert Odin and the Araneum. But Carmen as an experienced vampire wouldn't have asked for help unless she needed it.

"You got a name?"

"Marissa Albert. She arrived at the Key West airport and disappeared. Too bad you didn't have a chance to meet her, you might have had a lot in common."

"How so?"

"She's a private investigator."

"Was Marissa here on a case?"

Carmen looked flustered. "She didn't mention it. She called last week and asked for a reservation to the resort. It was kinda sudden, but not too unusual."

"And you know her from where?"

"We met when I was traveling through Minneapolis." Carmen smiled at the memory. "She's a wonderful chalice. It'll be a shame if anything happened to her."

"Why would you suspect that? Maybe she ran into a friend and changed plans."

Carmen lost the smile. "She wasn't the type to not let me know. I wouldn't describe Marissa as flighty."

A missing chalice and an alien threat? Was there a connection? I wanted to share what the Araneum had offered but they had ordered that I keep the information secret.

A series of black humps appeared on the horizon. Thorne pointed the Bayliner toward the largest one.

"Houghton Island," he said.

As we approached, the island and its crown of trees looked like spiked teeth jutting from the water. The word paradise hardly came to mind—it looked like my ass was about to get bit.